IMAGINARY FRIEND

DOUGLAS WHALEY

This book is dedicated to Barbara Shipek, a wonderful friend, far from imaginary, who has been taking care of me for decades.

This is a work of fiction and none of the characters are based on real people, living or dead. Any resemblance, including the names used, is purely coincidental, and the author apologizes for any confusion caused thereby.

CHAPTER 1

POPCORN

Fourteen minutes before the explosion, Franklin Whitestone was contemplating a sin: eating a box of popcorn. Even a small box would push him close to the number of carbohydrates that Dr. Atkins, still giving diet advice from the grave, allowed him for the day, but he was close to making that choice anyway. The Atkins diet no longer enjoyed its prestige of yesteryear, and was even belittled in current dietary circles, but it was the only weight-loss plan that had ever worked for Franklin. He had dropped 22 pounds in two months! And while he was still overweight at 210, his six foot frame was looking better each day. In his youth his natural good looks had taken him far, but these days any glance in the mirror revealed that, at 44, he'd been infected by a severe case of middle age.

Franklin had been sitting in Ohio Stadium, and as the second quarter of the football game began, the word "popcorn" popped into his brain. He'd pooh-poohed the thought immediately—totally beneath consideration. He was not about to go on a carb-binge and throw himself out of the hallowed state of ketosis.

But just as the Ohio State Buckeyes scored and he was celebrating by high-fiving the spectators around him, the word "popcorn" reappeared as if it were an instant message on some internal computer screen, and it continued to pound his consciousness for the remaining five minutes of the half. Popcorn. Popcorn. Popcorn. The game had started at 3:30 p.m., and by now his stomach was rumbling softly, demanding attention.

As the ref's whistle blew and the players lumbered off the field, he turned to Kelly Keyfold, the love of his life, and casually informed her, "I'm going to get a soft drink. Want anything?"

She smiled. "Big hot pretzel, please. And, Frankie, don't forget the mustard."

He nodded, rose, and began the laborious task of getting past the knees and feet of the ten people between him and the aisle. But as he "excused-me"d through them, Franklin knew to a certainty that it wasn't just a drink and pretzel he was fetching. Oh no—there was more! Wise or not, diet or not, sin or not, he was going to buy a box of popcorn, even though (if he considered the matter logically) he really didn't want it.

Franklin had read once that we do not so much *plan* things as explain them *after* we have already done them. He had certainly not *chosen* to have the forbidden box of popcorn, but on some very deep level he had settled definitely on doing it, and now he was a mere servant, a robot, executing an imperial command. There was some comfort in thinking about it this way, even though it was an explanation that resulted in shirking responsibility for his own decisions. He wished that bothered him more than it did.

In an oft-told story, the native of some primitive culture is explaining his religion to an outsider and announces that he believes that the world rests on the back of a giant turtle. When the outsider asks what the turtle stands on, he is told it is another turtle. The inevitable next question produces the response that "it's turtles all the way down." What Franklin had read about consciousness, behavior, and the workings of the brain seemed to produce something very much like that pyramid of turtles. Beyond the level of working thoughts was another layer of subconsciousness, but it was itself informed by instructions from a layer below that, and so on. Just where decision-making occurred in this stack of turtles he did not know. He did know that the decisions were rarely made at the first tier of conscious thought. Perhaps never.

Taking the ramp down to the first level of the stadium, he temporarily bypassed the concession stand and joined one of the amazingly fast moving lines formed by thousands of other men using the huge trough-filled restrooms all over Ohio Stadium. While doing this, he mentally worked on trying to get the popcorn decision reversed by the inner pile of turtles. Surely, he thought to himself, I can simply overrule this urge and forget the popcorn. Have just a diet drink and get Kelly her pretzel. But as Franklin mouthed this plan, he felt its futility; the turtles demanded popcorn. He tried offering them a hotdog (sans bun, lots of mustard) instead. Nope.

Leaving the men's room, Franklin returned to the concession area and stood at the end of another long line. He made one last desperate internal effort to abort the popcorn purchase. There had to be some way to reverse the boss-turtle's fiat. Franklin was a lawyer, so an appeal of this wrong-headed judgment was surely possible. Perhaps he could take his case up with the Head Turtle, whichever one that might be. Someone responsible had to be in charge down there.

He was still contemplating how to do this—what would appeal to the Head Turtle and thus preserve a happy carb count for the day—when the family in front of him abruptly left the counter, laden with things to eat and drink, chatting happily, and the woman behind the counter looked at Franklin and said, "Next." Without noticeable pause he ordered the drink, the pretzel, and the popcorn.

The bomb was inside the large wooden box near the concession stand on which rested condiments, napkins, plastic utensils, and straws. It was to be triggered by a signal from the remote in Mohannad's hand, and from no more than twenty feet away. Assuming all went right, this inevitably meant that Mohannad himself would die in the blast. He stood there staring at the condiment stand in fascination and horror.

His own death.

Right now.

Mohannad had spent all of last night, September 10th, never closing his eyes in the entire five hours that he lay motionless in his bed, contemplating this very moment, the last moment of all his moments. The finality of it stopped his breathing until he suddenly gasped in a desperate intake of air. Had the men of the first September 11th had these same problems on their own September 10th?

Mohannad began to shake. The tremors started in his lower back, and advanced until they visibly affected his whole upper body.

This uncontrollable trembling was painfully embarrassing, unmanning him completely in his own eyes. After all, he had been carefully trained by experts to deal with these very predictable emotions. The highlight of his twenty-three years on this planet had come in the incredible moment seven months ago when he had been chosen by the leaders of *al-Borak* for this vital mission in America. There had been scores of others who had wanted this chance—his chance—and who, when he was selected instead of them, had loudly expressed their envy, mixing in congratulations and subtle doubts that he was in fact the right person for this important task. But at the moment of his choosing (joyous event, praise God!), he himself had had no doubts that he was the ideal choice. Others, he said to himself, would falter, fail, have last minute qualms. Not him.

Mohannad was a warrior, from a family of warrior-ancestors going back centuries, and this great honor would be his and his family's for generations to come. His mother had made a big point of telling him how proud she was that he was to be a martyr to this holy cause. His whole village would share in the glory of his heroic deed. Hereafter his family would be well provided for by the leaders of the movement. This was always done, and was a major incentive for the recruitment and dedication of those, like him, who were willing to make this supreme sacrifice.

But—here—now—in this strange country—it was different, so very different! It was too hard, too much to expect! Strangely, it was not primarily his death that caused his breath to come in such huge gulps. No, his death was a step into a paradise where wondrous things awaited him. This he believed with all his heart. But the deaths of so many others! That did bother him. Was it right, after all, to kill innocents in the name of Allah? To Mohannad, in this stadium, in this bizarre place called Ohio, surrounded by these happy relaxed people, his mission seemed wrong, massively misguided. Yes, he knew they were infidels and that a fatwa had been issued that excused, even demanded, their death. But still . . .

His body, out of control, shook so badly that a tall black man standing near him stared intently at him, and then frowned in sudden concern, as if he would come over and inquire about Mohannad's well being.

I could just throw the remote in the trash and disappear into the crowd, Mohannad thought. Not kill anyone! Not die myself! He looked down at the remote as though it were some dangerous animal held in his hand. Tears coursed down his cheeks. This was a terrible, terrible thing!

But then his training reasserted itself. He pictured his Teacher, and what he would say and think when he heard that Mohannad—the chosen Mohannad, the oh-so-proud Mohannad—had failed in the mission after all! His mother's shame if he faltered! The reaction of all his friends, the members of his village, those he had trained with . . . .

Just as the remote was about to shake itself loose and clatter to the ground, he muttered almost soundlessly, "Allah, be with us all!"

He calmed himself with a supreme act of will, and pressed the *Send* key.

Ohio Stadium was not the only college venue where a bomb went off that afternoon. Another was detonated at the Darrell K Royal-Texas Memorial Stadium in Austin, also at half time.   It was never intended that the bombs would go off simultaneously. The organizers rightly counted on word of the first explosion spreading rapidly throughout the country and then, as the second one detonated, causing stampedes at many of the other college football games in progress throughout the land. This worked amazingly well. Cell phones and, in a surprising large number of cases, scoreboards, stupidly spread news of the first blasts at Columbus and then Austin (both within five minutes of each other), and worked local horrors immediately. The final death toll will never be certain, but best estimates put it at around 425 people, 18 of whom were trampled to death in stadiums containing no bombs of any kind. This latter statistic could of course be gathered accurately once the panicked mob had passed on and the bodies remained behind.

A third bomb, later found in the Ben Hill Griffin Stadium in Gainesville, Florida ("The Swamp"), where Florida had been playing Georgia, had failed to detonate and was discovered two days later by an absolutely dumbfounded janitorial staff.

No one within 30 feet of the blast at Ohio Stadium in any direction survived the explosion. Franklin Whitestone was standing almost 60 feet away from the concession stand when he and the scores of people near him were slammed violently against a nearby wall. His food purchases flew from his hands, never to be seen again. Franklin himself rebounded off other unfortunate people, doubtless adding to their injuries, their many bodies cushioning the impact. He landed painfully on his feet, jarring his back with a loud crack. His legs immediately collapsed under him, and he sat down hard on the concrete floor, beating another jolt into his protesting spine.

Before he could absorb all this, and while his ears were ringing with the thunder of the blast, something large and close collapsed next to him, caroming something (another person?) off his right side and into the blackness. What? What? What? Franklin's mind demanded answers to this madness.

The world around him was a nightmare of darkness, rubble, dust, and chaos. The blast had apparently knocked out his hearing, replacing it first with a loud ringing and then absolute quiet. The sudden silence made the experience surreal. Franklin could see nothing, hear nothing, and smell only an acrid, stingingly pungent aroma that made his eyes water. He coughed spasmodically, finding it hard to stop, finally willing himself to quit breathing until the coughing urge came under control.

But though the dust and darkness kept him from seeing anything, he somehow sensed movement all around. Exactly what was moving he couldn't guess. Debris? Walls collapsing? The poor people he had slammed against in the explosion?

Franklin felt a scream building inside him, but beat it back in favor of a new coughing fit that doubled him in two, his head banging twice off his right knee. Then, as he sat up, a smaller version of the suppressed scream burst from him, and he covered his mouth to try and stop it.

Am I going mad? he thought, terrified of the question. Franklin Whitestone was typically the most unflappable of men, proud master of his ordered world. In one terrible moment all that unexamined certainty was gone, and civilization far off. He had become a spooked animal whimpering in the dark.

Calm yourself and you might save yourself, he commanded. You are *not* an animal!

Franklin clenched his teeth tightly together, as if doing so might make it easier to concentrate and regain control, but he was horrified to find that his jaw refused to stay closed. Instead it bounced up and down wildly, causing his teeth to chatter, chomping on the sides of his tongue painfully as it tried in vain to keep out of the way.

He understood that there must have been a bomb blast or something similar to reduce him to all this, but he was clueless as to whether the danger was past, continuing, or just beginning. Rising to his knees, he carefully patted down his body, trying to determine if he was hurt, bleeding, still clothed. He felt no unexplainable pain, and this manual exploration produced nothing obviously amiss. The explainable agony was to his aching lungs. His every breath pulled in a mouthful of almost solid stinging matter, like inhaling a hundred tiny thorns. He knew instinctively that he was not taking in sufficient breathable air to keep alive. Panic gripped him and the effort to breath deeper triggered another fierce coughing fit. This one felt like his lungs were coming up through his throat in sliced pieces of varying sizes.

Franklin scrambled hurriedly onto his hands and knees, then dipped his head so that his nose was touching the cold, dirty floor. He gulped in the air at this level and it was truly much better, containing significantly less solid junk, yielding the minimum oxygen required to keep going. And yet his deep breaths, nose to floor, were followed by even more violent coughing as dust and other things non-air were inhaled. Franklin immediately yanked his shirt out from under his belt, pulled it up to cover his mouth.

Calm down, calm down, he ordered himself. *Calm down or you're going to die!*

He had heard how people who were meditating willed themselves to think only about the calming effect of breathing. He tried that and was surprised when it helped immediately. He took a breath in very slowly, feeling its balm spread all over his person. He forced himself to pause a second before slowly taking in another breath this time through his mouth. This breath was the first that did not make his lungs convulse in protest.

Something (human?) suddenly fell against his legs, and in revulsion he pulled them free and scurried dog-like away a couple of feet, crawling on all fours, banging his head against something solid (a wall?), birthing a vicious headache immediately. He opened his mouth to yelp, but since he had lowered the shirt in his scramble he again inhaled the noxious, near-solid air—a major assault on his injured lungs. Coughing explosively, Franklin hurriedly dipped his head back to the floor, and concentrated very hard on breathing slowly through the filter of his shirt. One breath.

Another.

Another.

Another.

Am I going to die from breathing this crap? he wondered. How many helpings of this gunk before my lungs cease to function, ruined forever? Did hospitals even do lung transplants? He thought about it. He didn't know.

The business of breathing so completely occupied him that he lost track of time, engrossed in the most basic of human functions, but after awhile it did occur to him that breathing was getting easier. That thought freed him to consider his surroundings with more attention.

Franklin could still see nothing, hear nothing, feel nothing beyond the cold floor under his hands and his throbbing headache, tortured lungs, sprained back. Though he wasn't sure when he'd injured it, his right thigh appeared to be bleeding, and he pressed it with his hand to see if he could staunch the flow. The area was sticky, but not particularly liquid and he quit worrying about it. Franklin knew he was living only at the most basic of levels, but, importantly, he was alive, and he was now sure that many of those around him were not. Somehow that made it even more important that he hang in there, keep breathing, and hope this ordeal would get better.

Then, with some relief, he noticed that his hearing was returning. Desperate shouts from many voices came to his awareness, though they were seemingly far away, pitifully begging for rescue over and over. "*Help me! Help me!*" pleaded a woman's terrified, high-pitched voice. There were horrible screams of agony also (two people, three, more?), one screamer with a piercing voice closer than the others, howling out in terror over and over. Franklin's returning hearing made this cacophony unbearable, and he swivelled his head in the opposite direction, but there were smaller, undulating moans each way he turned.

With a thundering crash something very big gave way off to his right, and the screaming abruptly stopped for a terrible second or two, before resuming with even greater volume. Surely, Franklin thought, this meant that more of the stadium had shifted, fallen, distributing death to new innocents. Panicked, he scurried away on all fours from the direction of the crash, almost immediately colliding with a body on the floor in front of him, falling stupidly on top of it. To his horror, two arms silently grabbed him around the neck, and in revulsion, he pushed them off and jumped in another direction, jostling someone else. His new victim merely gave a yelp of pain and said nothing more, as if insulted but nobly ignoring it. Franklin hurriedly scrambled away, hovering nervously in an area that didn't seem to touch anyone or anything. He began to shake all over, vibrating uncontrollably, his whole body writhing like a snake. In the coming days, his dreams returned him over and over again to this particular moment, waking him up bleating, sweating from every pore.

A man to Franklin's left began yelling "Phyllis" over and over again, growing louder with each repetition, and angrier too, as if this Phyllis were willfully ignoring him, vindictively pouting in the dark.

Then, faintly—at first he wasn't sure—Franklin saw flames through the darkness. *Flames!* Something black and moving kept interfering with his line of sight, but the vision of bright orange flickering came and went. He concentrated. Off to his left there was fire all right. He had no idea how far away it was or if it was moving in his direction.

Just what was needed to make this a complete biblical hell, he thought. Fire.

Later studies of the Ohio Stadium blast showed that it had taken out the ceiling above the bomb and caused the collapse of a large portion of A deck onto the ground floor below where Franklin and others in the halftime crowd were densely packed. Parts of both B and C decks immediately above this part of the stadium had then pancaked down, killing dozens of the open air spectators, who fell with it, some dying instantly and some taking their time about it over the following months, bandaged and drugged in antiseptic hospitals .

Over 100,000 panicked people tried to flee the stadium immediately, trampling each other monstrously as they jammed the exits—civilization gone—nothing more than terrified primates in flight for their lives. The elderly, the weak, the children, and the unlucky went down in droves, tripping others, creating a human-strewn obstacle course where the winners got to live and the losers often did not.

Inanely, a large bell, traditionally rung only at the end of victorious games, pealed loudly for over ten minutes, as if sounding the death knell of the hundreds who died as it rang. There was an investigation into this afterwards, but it was never ascertained who rang the bell or why. Perhaps, some speculated, it was caused by residual vibration from the original insult to the structure. Perversely, the bell survived the whole incident undamaged, but the university stored it somewhere and it was never rung again.

"The bell is ringing!" someone near Franklin shouted, and the terrible human keening around him lessened noticeably as those trapped in this part of the damaged stadium stopped to listen to the peels. They sounded surprisingly close. Was it a signal? Some sort of code in an unpracticed drill?

"Should we go in that direction?" a new voice asked.

"What direction?" someone else demanded. No one replied as they all tried to determine where the ringing originated.

"How many people are here?"

"Count off!" demanded a loud male voice, very much the drill sergeant.

This worked.

"One!" someone promptly yelled. "Two!" said another. "Three!"

Franklin heard himself say "Four!" and the bizarre tally continued. On and on the numbers went, some speakers nearby and others much fainter, then with longer and longer pauses before someone managed to spit out a number, until the last one in the horrible roll call quietly mumbled "Seventy-three!" There was silence then, and when a new number was not forthcoming, they all contemplated the tabulation. Seventy-three who were uninjured enough to participate—and how many more who could not?

Franklin realized that the bell had stopped its racket. How long ago had that happened?

"Is there a fire burning somewhere?" came a woman's voice, surprisingly steady.

They all looked around them. Nothing. Almost pitch black. Franklin could no longer make out any shapes.

"There was fire! I saw it!"

"I did too. Over there!" (As if anyone could see where the speaker was pointing.)

"It went out," said a flat, definitive voice. "I haven't seen it for some time, but it really was burning for awhile."

"Can anyone get through on a cell phone?" someone asked. A number volunteered that they had already made calls and that help would be on the way, but it turned out that no one was certain exactly where in the stadium they were immured. A minor argument broke out over whether they were closest to stadium exit 22 or 24. They had reported both numbers to those they had called (one person had reported that they were at 28, but that couldn't be right). Not knowing the exact location meant that the rescuers, when they came, would have no clear idea where to begin digging, even assuming they had some idea where exits 22 and 24 had once been. Franklin pulled out his own cell phone and looked at it as if he had never seen it before. Amazingly, it had not occurred to him until this moment to try and use it to call for help. He punched the ON button, but there was no signal. He absently returned it to his jacket pocket.

After the stadium geography discussion petered out, there was another pause during which the only sounds were the wretched moans of the most seriously injured.

"Phyllis!" suddenly yelled the man who had been calling that name earlier.

"Shut up!" was the reply, and, to Franklin's surprise, the caller never repeated the plea again. Later Franklin looked carefully at the list of casualties, and could find no Phyllis among them. What did that mean?

"We should pray," someone said, and there was a murmur of agreement. Franklin thought that prayer might be useful in consoling the trapped crowd if they began to despair and were on the verge of panicking, but he thought there were a lot more important things to do first.

"How about the Lord's Prayer?" a woman offered.

"I'm Jewish," a man said in reply, sounding annoyed.

"And I'm an atheist," announced another man. "No prayers please."

"Most of us are Christians, right?" the woman countered. Again there was mumbled agreement, but clearly most people had other matters on their minds.

"I'm wiccan," another woman said in an overly loud voice.

"What the hell is that?" a man asked.

"Let's do the Lord's Prayer," the first woman commanded, and before there could be more discussion, she plunged into the prayer. Others joined her, but Franklin thought it was a pretty pathetic effort. After the prayer ended, there was an awkward silence.

Startlingly, an electric light came on, and everyone jumped at the unexpected brightness. To Franklin's far left was an open door, with a woman silhouetted in the doorway by a light coming from the small room behind her. The clustered mob stared at her, dumb with amazement.

"It's some sort of utility closet," she explained, almost apologetic, gesturing behind her. "I opened the door, and the light switch still works."

"Was it unlocked?" a voice asked.

"It was off its hinges," she replied. "The door sort of fell over when I pulled on it."

"What's in it?"

"Let's see," she said, turning around to look. "All kind of stuff." As she touched things she called off the inventory. "First aid kit, blankets, flashlights, a ladder, other tools."

"Sounds like we've hit the mother lode! Good going!" said a man's voice, incongruously jovial.

"A first aid kit!" said another man. "I'm a doctor, let me have it." He scrambled to the door and went in.

"Pass around those flashlights," someone else suggested.

"Is there any water? I need it now!" a woman asked. It sounded very important to her.

"Is there a fire extinguisher?" came another voice.

"Yes. There's a fire extinguisher right there next to the door," someone else said, pointing.

This was all very comforting to Franklin, and, he could sense, to others too. They could all feel the panic lessening; they were getting organized. Civilization was returning, just as it should, as it always did. Franklin allowed himself to consider that if the building didn't collapse on them they stood an excellent chance of surviving this madness. Very good news. And as he thought this thought, a flashlight was pressed into his hand.

"Look around," was the terse command that accompanied it.

Franklin switched it on and blinked in the surprisingly bright light it provided. At the same time other flashlight beams began to dance in all directions, adding to the sensory overload.

The space he could see was about thirty by fifty feet in area, with the ceiling varying in height from nearly ten feet to too low to stand up straight. The wall closest to him looked like the inside of a scary carnival tunnel ride—concrete with jagged fissures running through it, iron pipes and girders sticking out inappropriately. Water was gurgling from some of the pipes. Might the whole space fill up with water and drown them? Would the water be safe to drink?

Out of the jumble of things half seen, Franklin's light revealed a woman sitting splay legged on the floor in front of him, her dress missing, wearing only panties, and, incongruously, a scarlet Ohio State sweatshirt, with a large string of buckeyes as a necklace around her bloodied neck and face. Disturbed, he quickly flicked the light to the side, passing over a blur of people sitting, standing, some lying very still.

"Look at the walls. Is there any way out?" someone urged.

Franklin pointed his flashlight up, and was startled to see that the ceiling was immediately right above him: a facade of fragmented cement, horrifically cracked, easily touched if he were to raise his hand, mere inches above his head. The ceiling here slanted down to his right, and then up on his left, so he turned the light in that direction and moved quickly into a more open spot. This gave him greater space above his head, and he was able to raise up from the crouching position he'd instinctively assumed on appreciating how low the ceiling was. He couldn't see a far wall in the direction his light now pointed, and there were fewer people there too. He walked slowly past them, bending down to see better, and they turned their heads to look up at him, jaws open, eyes wide, as if he were a being from another planet. These poor people were bathed in blood, and it reflected his light all too well.

11

Where does this open space end? he wondered, cautiously walking, trying to find a wall, any wall, but seeing nothing. A swing of the flashlight beam overhead gave him the reassuring news that there was now plenty of ceiling above him, apparently far out of reaching distance and still slanting up.

When he brought the beam down it came to rest on a human head, eyes open, no body attached.

Instantly, as if a dial had been spun, his heart began to leap around in his chest, feeling much like a small mammal was trapped in there, clawing frantically to get out. The vicious thumping scared Franklin even more than the severed head. He put his hand on his chest and took a couple of deep breaths. Franklin had only recently turned 44—surely too young to have a heart attack. Surely.

Bile rose in his throat. He felt his knees start to buckle once again, and he wrenched the flashlight beam away from the severed head before he could register any macabre details (man or woman, child or adult, its decapitated body nearby?). Involuntarily he backed in the direction he had just come, and as he did so there was a tremendous crash behind him as some new portion of the ceiling gave way in a waterfall of cement, iron beams, and pipes. A hurricane of noxious dust enveloped him once again.

Franklin was hurled to the floor by the concussion, his flashlight bouncing away, leaving him in the same situation he'd been in after the original blast: coughing, prone on the cement floor, enveloped in darkness, miserable with terror, making repetitive grunting sounds, his hands cupping his head protectively, a proto-human. Now his heart seemed weaker, to be failing. No, wait, now it was pounding again.

Then a fierce desire to regain the control he had cultivated all his life yanked him back to personhood, and, making guttural sounds deep in his throat, Franklin forced himself onto his hands and knees, head lowered as before to drink in the purer air close to the floor. As he breathed he tried to clear his mind and concentrate, tried to replace that miserable terror with a calming fatalism.

Probably this is death, he admitted with a strange clarity and resigned certainty. Soon I will be dead, and I must face my death head on, no panicking. With great admiration, Franklin had watched his father, Alexander Whitestone, somehow manage to die with dignity even while surrounded by the technological horrors of a modern hospital. During that ordeal, Franklin had contemplated how best to deal with the final personal moment that all must face, and his father had set the bar high. Die with dignity. Okay, he now told himself, he could do that. His father had always emphasized that Franklin should ask himself what he "stood for." Surely he stood for something other than being a dithering mess. Was this his time? If so, he resolved do it right, even if he himself were the only audience to his exit.

But then he shifted focus. Wait a minute! Don't give up hope so damned quickly. You're still alive! Accept the situation, see what can be done, work to keep going until there's nothing more to do, and only then accept death as the closing chapter of a life that, taken as a whole, gave him pride. After all, a heart attack, an auto accident, something sudden like that, could claim anyone, anytime. Perhaps this *was* his time, but also perhaps it was not. Best to proceed on the theory that a spooked heart, subjected to all this madness, would of course jump around wildly in his chest, and he should assume that it would soon return to a more normal rhythm, as—now that he thought about it—it appeared to be doing.

It helped that the dust settled more quickly this time, probably due to the larger space he had moved into, and—better and better—his hearing proved to be unaffected by this latest blast.

Terribly, the initial screaming which had died down to chorused moaning, resumed with increased volume, as victims both old and new suffered being torn apart while still conscious.

Over this primal wailing Franklin could hear shouted exchanges, as those who were not seriously hurt tried to find each other in the murky miasma. The survivors crisscrossed their flashlight beams in patternless wavings, as they congregated and took stock some distance off from him, and then parted again. Phantasmagoria.

Franklin thought he saw his lost flashlight in the momentary gleam of one of these sudden passing illuminations, and he reached his hand towards where he believed it to be, only to jerk it back violently as he remembered that the terrible head lay in that same direction. The ugly thought of what it would feel like to touch it in the dark dealt him an icy shiver, making his spine contract, his teeth chatter, and the little animal in his chest resume its escape attempt.

I *am* going mad! Isn't *this* what going mad is like? Will I just let go and howl, surrendering sanity? That would be so easy, strangely welcome. Mad!

Unnerved, close to the very edge of what he could handle and what he could not, Franklin scrambled to his feet, terrified by his own panic, and backed speedily away from where he supposed the severed head to be. Almost instantly his foot kicked his own flashlight, which, as he looked around, he now saw on the ground some three feet behind him, its light still on. As if it represented all his departing sanity, he eagerly reached down and grabbed it. He remained there immobile, trembling, lost in this ugly world. Unable to fight, unable to flee, Franklin hugged the flashlight tightly to his

13

chest and rocked back and forth, humming tunelessly as he waged a dicey internal battle to fend off madness.

As the Channel 7 helicopter circled the middle of the football field, a phalanx of angry cops and firemen frantically waved it off, going so far as to use their bodies to block possible landing sites.

"Jesus!" said Harold Wang, star reporter for the Channel and one of the most popular men in central Ohio. "Are they willing to die to keep us from getting this story?"

"I told you this was a waste of time," scolded Alice Vanderbilt, his chief assistant and field director, a tiny little woman with a big voice. "We should have landed in the parking lot on the west side and come in one of the stadium exits there."

"Should I try and scare them off—threaten to land on top of them and make them scatter?" asked the pilot, sounding like that would be a fun thing to do.

"No," shouted back Harold Wang, struggling to be heard. "Just set us down anywhere in the west parking lot and we'll go in from there.

"Good," said Alice, pleased. He was doing it her way.

The copter rose and gracefully arched over the stadium wall toward the nominated destination. The rescue personnel went back to work dealing with the catastrophe that was Ohio Stadium.

"Mom?" Todd Whitestone, age sixteen, said, sticking his head into the living room. Mary Whitestone, a handsome woman in her forties, looked up from her knitting.

Todd held out the cordless phone. "It's Kelly Keyfold."

They looked at each other. After the Whitestone divorce three years ago, Kelly Keyfold had become Franklin's new love, and it was more than odd that she should call Mary Whitestone about anything. They'd never exchanged more than five words in their lives.

"This should be interesting," Mary muttered to her son, taking the phone and holding it up to her ear. "Yes?" she said with a distinct lack of warmth.

"Mary, it's about Franklin. He and I were together at the Buckeye game, and at halftime he went down into the concession area just before the bomb went off."

"BOMB?"

"Haven't you had your tv on? Bombs went off at a couple of college stadiums during games this afternoon. Lots of people are dead, blown up or trampled. It's 9/11 all over again."

"Oh, God!" Mary said.

"What is it?" Todd asked, alarmed.

"Turn on the tv," Mary commanded. "A bomb at Ohio Stadium!" Into the phone she said, "Is Franklin hurt?"

"I don't know. He never came back. The stands collapsed under me, and I was trapped in debris for a few minutes before I could climb out. The concession area was under the stands I was in."

There was a pause as they both thought about this.

"Is Dad okay?" Todd asked, panic in his voice. The tv jumped to life, revealing the Channel 7 news team setting up on the field of Ohio Stadium, smoke and carnage filling the background. When she didn't reply, but just sat there looking blank, he said, "Mom?" louder.

"How about you? Are *you* hurt?" Mary asked Kelly.

"My wrist may be broken. I'm on my way to the hospital now. I thought I'd better call and let you know about Franklin. I'm sick whenever I think what could have happened, but I guessed you'd want to know, even from me."

"Yes, yes," Mary assured her. "Thank you. Please let me know immediately if you hear from him or," she paused slightly, "anything about him."

"I promise."

"And I hope your injuries are minor."

"Thanks for that too. I'll talk to you later." They both hung up.

"Mom!" Todd insisted, his eyes wide as he stared at the tv. "What is going on? Is Dad hurt?"

She looked at him, her face a blank. Then suddenly tears poured down her face and she just sat there, letting them fall, her hands tightly gripping each other.

"It could be bad," she said.

Franklin was sitting on the cold floor next to the woman who had found the utility closet, whose name he had learned was Hannah. Everyone was now calling her this, as if she were an old friend of the entire group. Apparently she had been a major force in organizing things while he had been off on his aborted exploration; she was definitely popular. To his considerable annoyance, Hannah didn't seem a bit concerned about being entombed, possibly forever, in this little pocket under the rubble of the huge

15

stadium, and she was close to being cheerful. Unfazed by the occasional screams that sounded all around, she was quite chatty.

"I wonder if they'll just pick up the game where it left off?" she speculated. No reply. "In a couple of weeks or so," she added.

Football! That made Franklin very angry. Wasn't she aware that with one structural vibration they all could be killed instantly? He was as dedicated a Buckeye fan as any of them, but he somehow doubted he would ever care about the outcome of a game that had probably killed thousands. The stadium held over 100,000 spectators, and, as was the norm for these games in Columbus, it had been completely sold out. There had to be many, many dead, and a much larger number seriously injured.

What about Kelly, who had asked him to bring her back a pretzel with mustard? Was she alive? Buried in the concrete that had collapsed under her? She was his love, and, with the exception of his extraordinary son, Todd, the most important person in his life. Kelly, a law professor at Ohio State, was smart, and fun to be with, and also pretty in a non-Hollywood way: nicely carrying her little too much weight with an air that said she didn't worry much about appearances. He'd tried not to think about her—it was too painful.

He discovered he was crying.

I'll never see her again, Franklin thought, and a tiny sob escaped him as he hung his head and let the tears drop free to the floor. Hannah didn't seem to notice.

If he died now, had his life been worth living? Would the people at his funeral be sincere in the things they'd say about him? He'd begun thinking about that funeral.

Franklin was a highly successful lawyer, a specialist on the details of the Uniform Commercial Code and related statutes (such as the Bankruptcy Code, the Federal Tax Lien Act, etc.), good at negotiations, not bad at litigation. Come to think of it, and being as objective as he could, he was proud of the things he'd accomplished on behalf of his clients. He had skillfully guided them through many complicated legal mazes. And, he told himself carefully, he'd more than earned the considerable amount of money he received as a partner in the downtown Columbus firm of Factor, Marroni, & Ray.

Franklin had certainly known love in his life. Wonderful parents, incredible siblings—altogether a happy family. He had been lucky in finding many good friends, exchanging great affection with them. He had had two major loves in his life: Kelly, and, before her, his first romance with Mary, for whom he still had much affection.

Then there was Todd.

Franklin shook his head with a smile. No one on the planet was like Todd. He . . .

"Wait a minute!" said Hannah, jumping happily to her feet. "We should *sing*!"

Franklin looked at her dumbfounded. Sing? Had she gone mad?

"Sing?" someone else asked amid a couple of similar mumbles.

"How will the rescue workers know we're alive if we don't signal them somehow?" Hannah offered.

"THEY'LL HEAR THE SCREAMS, YOU IDIOT!" roared a different man, angry at Hannah's preposterous suggestion. As he said this, two different agonized souls proved his point with toe-curling wails.

"Maybe," Hannah countered, "but also maybe not. How well would screams travel through concrete?"

"And just how would the rescuers know where a scream had come from?" another woman commented.

"Singing does travel far. They would hear that," volunteered a man from a different part of their communal space. "I'm a professor of music, and I know a lot about how sound carries. Hannah is right. It would allow the rescue team to hone in on us with some precision."

They discussed this, and finally reached agreement that it wouldn't hurt to try. Franklin said nothing during this discussion. He was pretty sure that no matter what they decided, he couldn't sing a note in this crazy environment.

"What shall we try?" someone asked.

Hannah jumped right on that. "The Star Spangled Banner!" she proclaimed. "This was a terrorist attack on the United States!"

"Let's show them they can't win that easily!" agreed another man.

So, with more enthusiasm than Franklin would have thought possible, the gathered survivors began to sing the national anthem, hesitantly for the first couple of bars, and then with strength. It was strangely moving. Almost at once, Franklin felt himself start to tear up, and, to his surprise, he joined in about the time they got to "Oh, say, does that star-spangled banner still wave?"

Fifteen minutes later, one of the lead rescue workers cocked his head. Something was different. He considered what had caught his attention.

"Do you hear anything?" asked Reginald Cosby, the grime-covered fire chief directing rescue procedures near A Deck Section 22, where the explosion had done the most damage.

"Jake," he called to the operator of the mechanical digger, a Spencer Giant Claw that had just begun to clear away the rubble. "Shut down the motor for a bit and let's listen." To the others he waved an arm up and down in a motion meaning "cool it."

Jake complied and the huge machine went quiet.

Instantly a melodic noise was clearly audible, muffled by tons of debris, but recognizable without effort.

"They're singing!" said one of the emergency response team members, awe in his voice.

"The Buckeye Fight Song!" chimed in another, equally amazed.

They cheered, and turned their efforts more accurately toward the buried choir. One of them shouted, "Go Bucks!"

CHAPTER 2

LONDON BRIDGE

The Channel 7 team had worked its way from the parking lot where its helicopter landed, and made it into the stadium, setting up in the middle of the football field. The rescue operation, large yellow machines and scores of personnel, was centered on the lower part of 22AA, right behind the benches for the visiting team, so the Channel 7 camera operator, Casey Bronski, standing on the 50 yard line twenty feet from the sidelines nearest the heavy equipment, had a clear shot over the shoulder of reporter Harold Wang, catching all the frenetic activity going on in the background. Alice Vanderbilt, the field director, was still in Bronski's ear, giving him the same obvious instructions she had been repeating all evening.

"Start out tight on Harold, then pull back," she whispered into her mike, as if Casey had not done this since the cows were young. Bronski thought she sounded more than usually hoarse as he listened to her rasping voice. She was relaying instructions from the director of production back at the studio, but these instructions hadn't changed much since they arrived. No one had thought of anything very original to do at the site of the bomb blast itself, and everyone who could be interviewed for information from the Governor to the President of Ohio State University had been thoroughly debriefed on camera.

The Channel 7 team had been at the stadium for five hours, and Harold Wang was obviously running on empty and nowhere near a gas station. But they were still on the air, as they had been since their arrival, broadcasting live to an attentive audience (and sometimes going national with their coverage—a professional triumph).

It was now ten o'clock at night, but the stadium lights were on, and the surreal scene was brightly illuminated. The football field was crowded with people: rescue workers, government and university officials, police and members of the National Guard, reporters, plus a large number of unexplained individuals, many of whom looked suspiciously like students, though the public was, in theory, banned from the area. Security was struggling valiantly to ascertain who was who in this mass of bodies. Outside the stadium there was a large and still growing crowd of worried people huddled together unhappily, wishing they could get in, praying for their trapped loved ones, co-workers, friends.

19

"Nothing new from the field here, Sally," Harold Wang was saying in response to a question from the anchor team in the studio, "and we're not sure whether the rescue workers can still hear anything from inside the rubble. They've stopped singing." He gestured at the chaos behind him—men, machinery, unmannered piles of stone looking horribly wrong in the middle of the undamaged part of the stadium, everything grey in the glare of the lights. "The workers are still trying hard to free them." Harold was dressed in casual clothes and not his usual on-camera suit. This was his way of showing that during this time of terrible trouble and in spite of the local fame he enjoyed, he was just a regular guy, as worried as the next person about the fate of those buried in the rubble.

"What's happening?" said an unfamiliar voice at Bronski's elbow. He glanced that way and saw a grime-covered rescue worker standing next to him, Coke in hand, obviously on a break. "I have a rescue worker here," Bronski mumbled in his mike. "Interview him," Alice commanded, and Harold Wang, hearing the exchange, jumped to comply, smoothly taking the man by the elbow as Bronski stepped back and centered them in the picture.

"Are you one of the members of the rescue team?" Harold asked.

"Yes, Sir. Jake Richardson, Columbus Fire and Rescue Auxiliary. Eight years." He was a thin, tall man, with bright blue eyes and a prominent Adam's apple. His light grey uniform shirt had a large "CFRA" on both the front and back.

"Tell us about your job, Jake," Wang prompted.

"I run the Giant Claw—we call her 'Suzy May.' For the last two hours, her and I have been dragging out parts of the building, clearing a space to get closer, and right now I'm taking a little break. Pete Shipek took my place for a bit."

Wang nodded. "And do you work full time for the CFRA?" he asked.

"Well, the Auxiliary is sort of like volunteer firemen. Normally Suzy May and I work for Abion Construction and Demolition. We were just brought in for this special wall removal."

"Tell me, Jake. Do you think you are about to break through to the trapped fans?"

"Don't know. Praise Jesus, it could be any minute, but might be hours, or—can't tell—even days. The stadium is very, very thick at its base where we think they're trapped. Another crew is trying to get at them from the other side, but I think we're closer to them here. All we can do is work hard, pray hard, and hope the Good Lord lets us find these poor people before more of this stadium falls down on them."

20

Wang lowered his voice reverently. "Are you a religious man, Jake?"

Richardson nodded with enthusiasm. "Yup. Found God at age seven and am still hangin' onto Him for dear life. I feel Him in my wrists every time I move the claw, so God Hisself is doing the dangerous work. Suzy May and me are just His robots."

"Why 'dangerous'?" asked Wang, probing for the obvious.

Richardson shrugged, and to the annoyance of the TV crew, he wasted air time by taking a long sip of his Coke before replying. "Pull out too much at once and the whole shebang caves in. Pull out too little and you ain't getting nowhere. Touchy, see?"

"It sounds like a lot of responsibility," Wang said, shaking his head in supposed amazement. "You must be glad when someone else is at the controls."

Richardson stuck out his lower lip. "Nope. I done told you. God called me to this work, and I have faith that I can do His bidding. Plus there's one other thing."

"Yes?" Wang prompted.

Richardson winked. "I could play tiddlywinks with that claw. I'm very, very good."

Franklin awoke with a sudden start as his body, propped against the wall, began to topple over and he caught himself with one hand. He had a momentary confusion before remembering that he was immured in this awful place, and immediately his heart jumped into the rhythm of a kettle drum, having been the ping of a triangle mere seconds before. He put his head on his knees, gasping for air, and tried to get control of himself before he had a heart attack or a stroke or began running around screaming wildly. He gyrated unsteadily between terror, depression, and then an overwhelming sense of utter helplessness.

Franklin forced himself to take five very slow breaths, and tried to recall some of the other calming techniques vaguely remembered from his brief flirtation with yoga and meditation. To his relief the slow breathing again worked. He was able to stabilize his emotions enough to be more or less rational. But the breaths had a negative effect of stinging his nostrils with ghastly smells: urine, excrement, and an odor he had begun to recognize as blood.

"How could I possibly have fallen asleep in this hell hole?" he muttered aloud, shaking his head, annoyed. "I could be dying at any moment and I'm sleeping away my last hours?" But sleep, he then decided, was probably an appropriate response to exhaustion—a defense mechanism to keep him from wigging out completely. A product of shock.

"I have to assume I will get out of this," he said to no one in particular. Even if this conclusion were untrue, he'd decided it was bad on many levels to simply give up and accept that this situation would necessarily end in his death. With a forced optimism, he decided he must now devote himself to life. He struggled to his feet. "Life," he insisted. "Life."

People around him were still murky shadows, some moving, some moaning, some ominously still. Yet others were talking more or less normally, as if this were some fun spelunking expedition and they were merely on a break.

But then he noticed something else, something important: the sound of big machinery. Close. He looked at his watch. It was 7:30 a.m. He had slept much of the night away!

And in fact, the redoubtable Jake Richardson was at the controls of the Suzy May when the key moment came just fifteen minutes later. As the cameras captured it all from three different angles, the claw suddenly pulverized a large section of wall, and the stunned people inside their turned wide-eyed, blinking in the morning light.

Franklin Whitestone was standing right next to the tear in the wall the claw had created as it gobbled up a handful of the stadium and flung it off to one side. The tv cameras were perfectly positioned to focus on his startled expression as he peered uncertainly through the new opening, confused, trying to see what had just happened. It would become the starting shot for the famous video that followed.

The claw had exposed an opening just about Franklin's height and no more than five feet in width. Before he could react to his sudden freedom in any way, he instinctively ducked as he was attacked by a just-released iron beam—a girder—anchored in the upper part of the hole away from him, the loose end swinging lethally like a giant snake angrily striking at his head.

What next occurred happened so fast and was accomplished so efficiently that it looked as if it had been carefully rehearsed, instead of being merely the gut reactions of a number of terrified people.

Franklin reached up and grabbed the beam's end, protecting himself and stopping its swing just as it was about to slam into the top of the hole created by the claw. This jammed his body solidly against the wall, and he dug in his feet to keep the beam from further movement. To his surprise he was able to arrest the beam's swing, and he braced himself, keeping a tight hold.

Everyone was yelling. On the field the rescue workers gave cheers and shouts of praise, joy, tears, relief—they had done this incredible thing and made it work out right! Inside the hole the trapped victims screamed at each other to "GET OUT NOW," before the beam moved again and the hole collapsed. The survivors surged forward as one, and Franklin felt certain they would knock him down, unleashing the beam. Instead, starting with Hannah who had been right next to Franklin when the hole opened up, the crowd ducked under the beam, one by one, closely following each other, and flowing smoothly into the sunlight. A later count taken from the tv footage would show 53 people popping through the small opening between Franklin and the other side of the hole, all deftly playing a dangerous game of "London Bridge" as they passed under the beam and his upheld arms holding it in place. It took less than a minute for them all to get by Franklin and fall into the arms of those outside.

The rescue workers held back until the last of the survivors emerged, and then they sprang to Franklin's aid. Four burly men grabbed various parts of the girder, and then yelled at Franklin to let go himself and get out.

He looked at them blankly, nodded, and promptly slumped to the ground without taking a step. Of course he'd meant to do what they ordered, but his head was spinning in the bright sun, and his arms were atremble, stupidly flapping like the wings of a large bird trying vainly to take off. Impatiently, other rescuers scooped him up and yanked him away from the opening, which was now alive with a construction crew shoring up the hole, and emergency teams anxious to get inside to find survivors who were not ambulatory.

A tall woman in a hard hat said to Franklin, "Sir, are you all right?"

He looked up at her. "I'm fine, I'm fine," he replied in a very small voice, and immediately fainted.

He came to minutes later as they were loading him into an ambulance. He sternly insisted he was all right, that he just wanted to go home, but he could not persuade anyone of this. Siren blaring, the ambulance whisked him off to the OSU hospitals' emergency entrance, only a couple of blocks away. There, after a short wait, a doctor pronounced him largely unhurt, though they bandaged some scrapes on his arms and knees, and tightly wrapped a major gash on his left thigh, after which they showed him to a bathroom to wash up. It took almost an hour to escape from the hospital, with the bulk of the time spent either waiting around or filling out forms. He used his cell phone to call Kelly, and she screamed with excitement on first hearing his voice. She promised to call his ex-wife and son and relieve their anxiety, and they both agreed to meet at his home in half an hour.

After thinking hard about the issue, he finally remembered where he'd parked his car prior to the game (was it just yesterday?), and hiked the short distance to it. His automobile was standing almost alone in the huge parking lot. The other vehicles dotting the landscape here and there spoke ominously of owners who were probably not coming to claim their cars any time soon.

At 10:05 a.m., he turned his Honda into the cul de sac where he lived in a condo purchased only four months before. A major surprise awaited him in the form of vehicles of all sizes and shapes filling the streets and blocking his driveway. The largest of these had signs painted on their sides indicating the news organizations they variously represented. Dozens of reporters and technical staff surrounded his home, and they all leaped into excited action as his car crawled to a halt two houses down from his own. The journalistic mob ran toward him like twenty marathoners all sprinting for the finish line at the same time. A hundred questions were lobbed at him in one confused jumble. It was terrifying.

He wasn't in any condition to deal with this new complication. Franklin was almost comatose from lack of sleep and the drain of the ordeal he'd been through. Nonetheless, he had the presence of mind to throw the Honda into reverse and back out of the cul de sac onto Martin Road, where he sped away, pleased to note that none of the fourth estaters could get their vehicles into action quickly enough to follow.

How had they found his home this quickly? It hadn't been much more than two hours since he escaped from that hellhole at the stadium, and except for the hospital personnel, he'd given his name to no one. But the media had somehow tracked him to ground in that very short period of time, and all of them wanted his story for their very own. It occurred to him—surprise!—that he was temporarily famous, and that the fifteen minutes Andy Warhol promised everyone had begun for Franklin Whitestone.

Trembling, Franklin pulled into the parking lot of the grocery chain a mile from his home, and sat there shivering until he calmed down enough to think through his next step.

He called Kelly's cell phone from his own, and she answered on the first ring.

"Where are you, Frankie?" she asked, sounding breathless herself.

"At Kroger's off 161," He replied. "I couldn't get to my house because of news hounds waiting for me there."

"I know," she said. "I tried to go to your house myself, and was forced to back off. They even tried to interview me, though no one seemed to know for certain if I was connected to you or not. They were just hungry to talk to anyone who would talk back. I beat it out of there."

He took a deep breath, hunched up his shoulders, and then, tired to the bone, sagged down into the driver's seat. "Oh, Kelly, now what? I've got to go somewhere—take a bath, get some sleep."

"I've been thinking. Meet me at Joan's right now," she urged, meaning the nearby home of her jogging partner. "I have a key, and the reporters certainly won't think to look there. I'd suggest my place, but it's already been compromised."

"Compromised? You aren't a secret agent, Kelly! What the hell does 'compromised' mean?" This wasn't like her at all.

She paused to consider her answer. "It's to the good actually . . . I think. Even exciting! There's more and I'll tell you the details when you get to Joan's. Will you come?"

He sighed loudly again, but sat up straighter in his car seat. "Run the bath water," he said. "I'll be there in ten minutes."

Their meeting in the driveway of Joan's home was more emotional than either of them had planned. By just the fortune of it all, at Ohio Stadium each had escaped death while those around them were buried in rubble. Neither had known what had happened to the other, and now, here they were, Kelly with her sprained wrist in a splint, Franklin with bandages on various parts of his battered body, but both more or less unhurt.

In the driveway, Franklin only had time to say her name before Kelly grabbed him and held him tightly. She couldn't talk at all, but sobbed and moaned and buried her face in his shoulder, overcome. This triggered a similar reaction in him, and he gagged on the raw emotions that filled his throat with ragged catches of breath. Kelly was so much smaller than he was that she almost disappeared in the folds of his embrace. Worrying that he might smother her, he pulled back so he could see her face.

"It's all right, it's all right," he mumbled, making low shushing sounds. "We're fine, honey, fine."

"We're lucky!" she said, her voice jagged. "Thank God we made it out of there alive. I was so worried about you."

"I was so worried about me too," he confessed with a small laugh. "I was frozen in fear for all those hours I was trapped, trying not to think about everything that was going on. But one thought kept haunting me: my Kelly. Where is she now?"

She sobbed even louder and pressed closer.

This was very unlike her. She was normally all calmness and competence—on top of every situation—something of a control freak. She could be warm and fun to be with (and incredible in bed), but he had never seen her cry. It both touched and disturbed him. All of life seemed upside down.

They'd met almost three years ago at a law school alumni function sponsored by his firm, Factor, Marroni, & Ray, which also hosted the event. She was an Associate Professor of Law at The Ohio State University, in her fourth year of teaching, one of six African-Americans on the faculty. She primarily taught courses in two areas: Contracts and Commercial Law. Franklin was a graduate of the University of Michigan School of Law (a connection that caused him no little trouble, living, as he did, in Columbus), but all members of the firm, even those not connected in any way with OSU, were asked to attend. Howard Ray, the Managing Partner, had introduced them, saying that they both were specialists in the same field and ought to get to know each other.

Franklin had been divorced for three years. His first marriage to the intelligent and charming Mary Balston, a childhood sweetheart, had begun well and finished badly eighteen years later. During that period, for reasons that Franklin had never quite understood, their initial compatibility had faded, and towards the end they were all but strangers living in the same house. In the final year, Franklin and Mary had quarreled more often than they talked, and by then they slept in separate beds. If it weren't for their redoubtable son, Todd, they would probably have divorced long before they actually did. She'd not resumed her maiden name, since her considerable professional reputation as a writer had been made as Mary Whitestone. Nowadays Franklin thought about his marriage as little as possible; the subject was too painful. A part of him much missed the Mary he had married, but not the one he had divorced. In the past year, things had improved dramatically between them, and, to the relief of both, they were becoming friends again.

At that law firm/law school function, and within minutes of their meeting, Franklin and Kelly came together like two magnets, both almost pulsing in the strength of their attraction to one another. Even Managing Partner Howard Ray, not the most empathetic person on the planet, had noticed that they spent most of the evening talking in a very, very friendly fashion. "Watch out for that one," he'd warned Franklin later. "She's hot for you." Franklin, uncharacteristically, blushed.

Fifteen minutes after they met, Kelly invited him to come to the law school the following Monday and speak to her Commercial Law class, to explain to the students what the actual practice of commercial law was like. Franklin accepted with alacrity, and during the weekend he over-prepared his talk as if it were the most important speech of his career, neglecting other matters, lying awake into the night in his bed thinking, trying to get it just right. He said to himself he was doing this to impress the students, knowing it wasn't true.

On Monday at 2:50 p.m. he met her in her office at the law school, ten minutes before the class began. They shook hands in the doorway, and both felt suddenly warmer than the temperature in the room would suggest. Awkwardly she walked him down the hall to the classroom, making small talk, but a minute later she was all business when she stood up in front of the class and introduced him. Franklin's talk to the class and his handling of the students' questions went well, and he surprised himself by getting into the whole experience to the point where he stopped wondering how the professor herself was reacting.

"Here's the thing," he told one student who had asked him for advice on how to keep motivated in school to study law, night after tedious night. "When you're in law school you're in a nice womb-like existence for three years, and it is separate from anything that comes before or follows after. Right now you yearn for the real world and for the start of your professional career, and you want out of here as fast as possible. But you no sooner leave law school and are pitched into that real world, and immediately things happen that make you to want to scurry right back into the academic womb and this time pay much more attention to your lessons.

"Take the course in Evidence. In one of my first trials the judge made a ruling in my favor while admonishing me, 'Mr. Whitestone, I'm going to allow this evidence to come in, but first you must lay a foundation.' I had no idea what 'lay a foundation' meant, so this was a bad moment. I stammered something stupid like, 'Yes, your Honor, I'm going to lay that foundation right down,' and, sweating bullets, I took the witness back through some of preliminary facts. Amazingly, the judge seemed satisfied. If I were to repeat the course in Evidence nowadays, I would hang on every detail, paying particular attention to the meaning of 'lay a foundation.'

"The clients are coming. Your clients. They will expect you to know the law." He paused for effect. "Make sure you do."

"You were wonderful!" Professor Keyfold said, beaming, as they had coffee at the restaurant across the street from the law school, immediately after class. Franklin thought she was the one who was wonderful—smart and funny, with beautiful light brown skin and softly curling black hair that fell to her shoulders. All in all it was a golden day, to be replayed with affection and laughter in the retelling as the months, and then years went by.

At last, still clutching him tightly in her friend's driveway, Kelly's sobbing subsided. She took a deep breath and then looked up at him, a slight smile belying her tear-streaked face. "Okay!" she said, mostly to herself. "I have some very interesting news to tell you," she said.

"All right. What?"

"Let's go into the house. I'll get us something to drink, and explain it all to you."

"I do need food," Franklin replied, suddenly aware of how important this was to him.

When they were seated together on the sofa in Joan's living room, sharing coffee and some doughnuts Kelly had found in her friend's kitchen, Kelly lifted one eyebrow in amusement as she said, "Here's the news. As it happened, we didn't escape the media completely."

"Oh?" he said, sipping the coffee. "Tell me what that means."

She paused to consider her words. "I find it incredible that they got through to me, and in so short a period of time, and that they knew my connection to you, etc. But by eight o'clock this morning a representative from the Jimmy Ball Show left a message on my cell phone, begging me to call him back."

The Jimmy Ball Show was a live call-in talk/news program on CNN, airing twice-a-week at 8 p.m. for one hour, and usually divided into two half hour segments with a different guest for each. After each guest verbally jousted with Jimmy Ball, the genial host, for awhile, they took phone calls from interested viewers. It was very popular.

"Uh oh," he said, seeing where this was going.

"Now listen, Frankie," she urged. "This is exciting! They want you to be on the show tonight!"

"TONIGHT!" he exclaimed. Was she crazy?

"Here's what they offered. A private jet would fly you and guest—moi," she touched a finger to her chest, "to New York, leaving Columbus at four. We would be met by a limo, and taken to dinner at a major restaurant, then spirited off to the studio where you would appear on the second part of the show. Afterwards the jet would fly us back to Columbus, arriving more or less at midnight." She paused while he took it all in. "I told them I would pass it on to you and let them know what you decided."

He pushed fingers through his rumpled hair, frowning. "But I've just spent the night sitting on a dirty floor surrounded by the dead and dying. I need sleep, a bath."

"I called Joan and she said we may have the run of the house. You can bathe now and sleep for hours before we'd need to be at the airport. And it's precisely because you've been through holy hell that they want you on the show. Jimmy Ball's assistant called you a hero, and said that all of America wants to know more about the brave thing you did."

"Oh, come on! It wasn't brave. That girder pivoted toward me and I reached up and grabbed it to protect myself. It was a reflex. While I was trying to figure out what to do next, all those people ran out under the girder. Then the rescue squad took over and I fainted. What is heroic about that?" He frowned. "I've never fainted before in my life! How embarrassing!"

She encased both of his hands in hers. "Frankie, you *were* a hero! Wait until you see the video. You were fantastic!" He detested being called anything other than "Franklin," but somehow found it endearing when Kelly called him "Frankie."

"There's a video?"

"Cameras captured it from a couple of different angles. They all show you leaping into action like Superman. Everyone is talking about it. That's the reason your house is surrounded by media trucks and we have to hide out here."

"But I have nothing to say to Jimmy Ball," he protested.

"Of course you do. You haven't been on some kind of happy picnic for the last 24 hours. You managed to survive a terror attack that killed hundreds, maybe thousands of people."

"Terror attack? Are you certain?"

"Yes. Some terrorist group I have never heard of is on the Internet claiming credit for the bombings. I'll show you their post before we leave for New York."

"The bombings, plural? There was more than one?"

"Two. Each at half time of a football game. The other was in Texas. Plus a lot of people were trampled in the panic that broke out at other stadiums that had no bombs."

"No bombs?"

"The news of bombs going off at half times in college stadiums spread like lightning across the country, and fans panicked most everywhere that a game was still in progress. The television films are sickening. The country's in shock. Everyone is glued to their tvs, hungry for more news."

"How many dead?" he asked.

"No one knows."

"But are planes still flying?"

"I think so. The Jimmy Ball people were sure that a private jet would be allowed to take off from Port Columbus."

He put his head in his hands and rubbed his face.

"Oh, Kelly, I don't think I can, or should. I don't want to relive the horrors I've been through." He looked deep into her eyes. "I saw people blown apart, limbs everywhere, walls suddenly collapsing on those who thought they were survivors, people screaming for hours and hours! That wouldn't make entertaining television."

She shuddered thinking about this, but took his hands again. "Your particular story is one of the few from this horrible weekend with a happy ending. You saved fifty three people when you grabbed that girder. The country needs something to cheer about."

"Hmm," he said, confused. Maybe she was right. That did seem important.

"And telling it all on national tv would be a catharsis for you, the beginning of closure, a chance to put it all into perspective and seal it off so you could get on with life."

That also sounded right. A full minute went by without either of them speaking.

Finally he said, "Do you have a phone number to call?"

Newscaster Harold Wang was very proud of the second interview he conducted with Big Claw operator Jake Richardson because it promptly veered off in a heart wrenching direction that he didn't see coming. Channel 7 showed this interview five times on September 12th. In it Wang caught up with Richardson shortly after the survivors emerged from the hole that the Claw had dug, and the machinery worker was asked how he felt now.

"It was the most awesome moment of my life!" Richardson said, clapping his hands together. "Jesus be praised that it had such a happy ending! Jesus be praised!"

"Of course," Wang commented, "not everyone got out of there alive."

"I know, and I'm very sorry for the ones which didn't make it, but they're in heaven now, and that's where we all want to end up."

"You told me when last we talked that you were a real talent at the controls of that big machine, and now you've proven it. You're a hero too, Jake! What do you say to that?"

Instead of replying, Richardson bowed his head and didn't speak for a moment. When he looked up his eyes glistened with tears.

"I ain't always led a life I'm proud of," he said. "My wife left me last year, and she won't even let me see my little girl, my darling Charity, excepting twice with a social worker watching every move." The tears started down his cheeks, but he just looked right into the camera and let them fall. "If I done good now, like you say, Mr. Wang, maybe she'll forgive me. And if she can't take me back, at least please, please let me see my girl. Please, Heather! I'm a hero now. I've changed."

It was all Wang could do to keep from smiling—this was the perfect cap on the whole stadium disaster story. He could feel the emmy in his hands already.

"Dad's going to be on tv," Todd told his mother. "He called."

"Your Dad is already on tv," Mary Whitestone replied. "They keep showing that video of him holding up the girder, and I suspect that everyone in the United States who has a tv is getting tired of it."

Todd beamed. "No, I mean he's going to be on a program, live. The Jimmy Ball Show."

Mary looked up from the computer where she was sitting, writing her monthly travel column for Jaunt Magazine. "Really? That is news. When?"

"Tonight. 8 o'clock.

"Tonight! That can't be right. He was still trapped in the stadium this morning and now he's made it all the way to, what, New York?"

"New York," confirmed her son, nodding. "Long day for old Dad."

31

"Beyond belief," she replied, nonetheless somehow believing it. "Set the DVR so we can record it."

"I plan to watch it live," Todd replied.

"We both will," his mother said, "but let's make sure we have a permanent record. Someday you can show your grandchildren what a truly great hero their great-grandfather was."

Sitting in Le Blue Royale, a very posh Manhattan restaurant, about to order one of the finest meals of his life, Franklin Whitestone found to his surprise that he had little appetite.

"What's wrong with you, Frankie?" Kelly asked, menu held in her good hand. "You're sweating like a long distance runner and I don't like your color."

"I'm scared," he confessed.

"Scared of what? The hard part is over."

"The dangerous part is over, but going on the Jimmy Ball Show in front of the entire country is very scary. Look, my hands are trembling." He held them out for her inspection. There was indeed a perceptible tremor to them.

"Frankie, please, calm yourself. For God's sake, you've argued a case before the United States Supreme Court! Is this scarier than that?"

"That case centered on the issue of the exact moment a check is considered paid for purposes of Regulation CC. I was nervous, yes, but it wasn't a heart-pounding experience like this."

"You'll feel better when you eat something," she predicted.

"If I eat something that will only mean fatter butterflies in my stomach."

Just then the waiter, a thin man in his forties with an accent Franklin could not place, arrived at their table. Smiling affably he welcomed them to the restaurant and proceeded to explain in breathless detail the specials the chef had prepared for them (and, Franklin surmised, for a hundred or so other people as well).

"You order for me," Franklin told Kelly. "I can't think. Make it something light."

"We'll both have the first special you mentioned," Kelly told the waiter. "Make sure the salad dressing is on the side." The waiter nodded and hurried off, to be replaced almost instantly by the sommelier.

"Good evening, Sir and Madam," said the handsomely dressed, corpulent man, bowing slightly. "Will you be having wine with your dinners tonight?" He handed large wine menus to each of them.

"Yes," Kelly replied. "Suggest something moderately expensive—someone else is paying the bill of fare."

"No wine for me," Franklin hurriedly corrected her. "I mustn't be drunk on the air."

"Oh, Frankie," she replied with a little wave of her hand. "One glass won't make you drunk—moreover it's likely to have the very beneficial effect of calming you down. Besides, we're going to need a whole bottle; I'm planning on having a couple of glasses. I don't often get wine of this quality."

Miserable, his mind elsewhere, Franklin said nothing. Let her make herself happy, he thought. At least one of them would be.

Kelly and the sommelier had an extended discussion before agreeing on the appropriate choice. The man appeared much taken with Kelly and delightedly answered all her questions, even explaining details of his job when she asked.

"I consider that choosing the right wine for a meal is more than a pleasant occupation," he told her, "it is an ethical duty."

"Very high standards indeed," she replied.

"Madam is most kind," he said. "I will return in a moment."

True to his word he was almost instantly back at their table, sommelier knife twisting effortlessly through the cork, the wine poured into their glasses, and the bottle placed in an ice bucket on a small table next to them. That done, he bowed again and disappeared.

Kelly studied Franklin with concern. "Frankie," she said. And when he didn't look up, lost in his thoughts, she turned on her classroom voice and commanded, "Frankie, look at me!"

He did, worry clouding his face. She picked up her wine glass and with a gesture indicated he should do the same. "Time for a toast to my hero, Franklin Whitestone, the man who saved 53 people from death."

"I didn't save 53 people from death," he protested, reaching for his glass all the same. "What I did was to keep the door open so they could run out."

"Don't spoil my toast, Frankie," she scolded. "Bask a little in your wonderful accomplishment. Who would have thought that when we went to the football game yesterday that it would end with this incredible night in New York City? So," she raised her wine glass, "to my hero and my love."

He smiled wanly, and then with a slight shrug, he clinked his glass against hers, and had a drink.

"Oh, my," he said in surprise. "That is good!"

"Very, very good," she agreed.

He took another small sip, rolled it around in his mouth as he'd been taught, and then swallowed. "Incredible," he told her. "Easily the best wine I've ever tasted!"

"And I'll bet the food will be equally as stupendous if you can just relax enough to enjoy it," she said.

He nodded slightly. "You're right. I'll try." He took another small sip.

Shortly, a small army of waiters and their helpers brought dish after dish to them, and Franklin realized with pleasure that he was hungry after all. By this time the wine had begun to do the task assigned, and Franklin relaxed enough to enjoy eating. The meal was every bit the triumph of the gourmet art they'd expected, and, given all he'd been through, Franklin decided to give the Atkins diet the night off.

Finding just the topic to banish thoughts of the coming tv show, Kelly launched into something that she'd been avoiding for a week.

"Okay," she said, with a small sigh. "I guess it's time to tell you. My parents want to come up and spend Thanksgiving with me in Columbus. My brother and sister and their families too."

Franklin brightened. "Great news!" he said with enthusiasm. Kelly's parents lived in Birmingham, Alabama, and he had never met them, though he'd spoken with them a couple of times on the phone when he happened to be there when they'd called. The last occasion was Kelly's birthday four months ago. "I'm so looking forward to finally meeting them. We've been together for over two years, and it's embarrassing that I've never even seen your family."

Kelly gave him a small smile with no humor in it. "Well, as it happens, there's a reason for that, and that's why I've postponed telling you that they're demanding to come for a visit."

"Demanding?"

"Yes. The truth is that I've repeatedly discouraged them, and they've finally rebelled and insisted. I gave in."

He regarded her with concern, the Jimmy Ball Show forgotten. "Better tell me all," he counseled.

"You're right, of course. Okay, here goes.

"I've had good romantic relationships with some fine black men, but the two great passionate loves of my life were both whites. It just happened that way. The first occurred when I was in law school, and I sat

34

next to Clayton Kneller during my first year classes—we were seated alphabetically. He was a good looking guy with wavy blond hair, lots of personality, smart and dedicated to improving the world—I was hooked from day one. After dating for three years—dating, hell, we were living together for the last two years of law school. Oh sure, we both had separate places where we lived, but we were mostly at my place day in and day out. He had a roommate, but the guy mostly had the place to himself."

"Something bad must have happened," Franklin commented. "What was it?"

"My birthday party in May of that third year. I turned 25, and my parents insisted on throwing a party for me in Birmingham, so I bravely took Clayton home with me. I'd told them he was very important to me, and they weren't happy about him being white, but they appeared to accept it at first. The day before we left for Birmingham—we'd just finished final exams and graduation was scheduled in two weeks—Clayton proposed to me, and I accepted. This was no surprise. I knew it was going to happen. We'd talked about getting married for almost a year. We both had jobs waiting for us in Chicago: him with Legal Aid, me with a downtown firm. Everything seemed to be coming together beautifully.

"We arrived in Birmingham, and my parents and sibling were friendly when they met Clayton—what else could they do? He was one of the most charming human beings on the planet. But trouble arose almost immediately: my mother had assigned us to different bedrooms. I put my foot down about that, telling her that Clayton and I were on the verge of getting married, and this led to a scene involving my father, which ended with tears and shouting (Clayton wasn't there, thank God), but in the end, I won. We shared the same bed.

"Over dinner that evening, when we were all at the table, Clayton and I announced our engagement, and Daddy, who had had a couple of drinks, went nuts. He started yelling at Clayton about his motives in marrying outside his race—saying Clayton was just attracted by the exoticness of it all, and didn't really love me, and Clayton, furious, yelled back. He said that Daddy was a racist, which was true, of course, but it infuriated Daddy even more. He called Clayton a 'son of a bitch.' Clayton went red in the face, thinking, probably correctly, that this was meant as an insult to his mother. By this time we were all on our feet trying to calm them down, keep them apart, mouthing soothing things. My mother was crying, and I probably said one or two things that didn't help the situation—I was plenty mad at Daddy. After that everything happened so fast. Clayton called Daddy a 'bigot.' Daddy grabbed a fire poker and

35

swung it at Clayton, who jumped back, fell across a coffee table, and broke his arm."

There was silence at the table for a bit, as they both considered this.

"Then what?" Franklin finally asked.

She shrugged. "We never recovered from that. Clayton went to the airport straight from the hospital, and I didn't even realize he'd left until after he was gone. By the time I returned to law school, he had moved all of his things back to his apartment, and he told me coldly that it was over between us. I pleaded with him not to let my family's attitude affect us, but he wanted nothing to do with them, and, by extension, me, and he wouldn't discuss the subject. We were both living in the City of Chicago for two years thereafter, until I moved on to my first teaching job, but we almost never saw each other during that whole period."

Her eyes were swimming with tears. "Oh, Frankie, I loved him so much; it just broke my heart! I was sure I'd never love anyone again. I kept all my subsequent dating on a pretty superficial level—all with black men, by the way. I thought I was through with passionate romance. And then I met you, and passion returned, doubled in strength.

"Now," she concluded, "you can see why my family coming for Thanksgiving has me staring at the ceiling at night. I hope Daddy will be better behaved this time—he has hinted as much, without actually apologizing for the last catastrophe—but . . . well, you are white, and you are sleeping with his little girl. You might be risking a broken arm or worse. It scares me."

"Hey," Franklin said, reaching out to touch her cheek gently. "Don't worry about it. We'll get through this. I'm a big boy, and good at finessing difficult situations."

"And it doesn't bother you—walking into this minefield?"

He shrugged. "I long ago gave up worrying about discrimination in so far as it affects me personally, and by that I mean all forms of discrimination. I don't care about race, or gender, or whether people are short, tall, fat, foreign, gay—except that I loathe seeing these things used to harm good people. As for me, I stick with 'content of character' as a measuring stick for the worth of those I meet."

"And you never had any thoughts—good or bad—about getting involved with a black woman?"

He leered at her, the wine doing its job. "I did notice the woman part. Truth to tell, I've never before been so attracted to anyone as I am to you. But that bewitchment has nothing to do with your skin." He raised an eyebrow. "Now, your breasts . . ."

Kelly looked around, embarrassed. He'd said "breasts" far too loudly. "Franklin!" she warned.

He took another sip from his goblet. "Anyway, about your family. Now that I'm properly briefed, I'm sure we can figure out a way to navigate your 'minefield' without major explosions. And if we can't, that will be their problem, not ours." He smiled. "But I do have something important to ask you, based on what you've just said."

"Ask away."

He looked deep into her eyes, a smile on his face. "Do you really think we have a 'passionate romance'?"

She took her time in replying, lowering her head, her eyebrows raised challengingly, a sly smile on her own face. "Yes, I do . . . lover." She purred these words in a certain way she had that always sent him into sexual overdrive. "Both of us are passionate people. Right?" She rolled the "r" in "right." It drove Franklin crazy. He almost knocked over the table as he started to stand, but stopped himself because Kelly, seeing his reaction, held up a hand like a traffic cop.

"Later," she said in an urgent whisper.

He hesitated, considering his options, and then sighed. "Later," he agreed while privately wondering whether it would be too late to explore the passion issue when they got home tonight. Probably, he decided. She had a ten o'clock class in the morning, and he had a meeting at his office at nine. Hmm. Maybe they could get in some serious cuddling on the private jet flying home (they would be the only passengers on board, after all). Or, he thought, suddenly excited by the idea, maybe we could have a stab at joining the mile high club. He felt a mile high at the prospect.

Franklin didn't notice when one of the waiters refilled his wine glass. He took a sip before realizing the goblet had been topped off. "News," he said, holding the glass up so she could see. "Apparently I'm having two glasses of wine tonight."

"Perfectly fine," she told him. "Stop at two, and those drinks will put you in just the right mood to sail through your encounter with Jimmy Ball."

"When you're right, you're right," he said, tucking into the main course.

The limousine deposited them in front of the television studio at 7 p.m., where they were escorted into the building by a Mr. Malone (they never got his first name), who was all smiles and welcomes. Franklin

37

could detect a definite internal buzz from the wine, but—he assured himself—he was not in any danger of being drunk. Malone had informed him that he would be the guest for the second part of the evening, so he had an hour and a half to allow the buzz to wear off. Malone turned Kelly over to a page, who escorted her to a seat from which she would view the show, while he himself walked Franklin down to Makeup.

"I don't think I've ever been made-up before," Franklin told the matronly woman, introduced merely as Judith, who was lathering him with something as he sat in her chair.

"You have very smooth skin," she informed him. "It will take makeup beautifully, and no one will notice that you have any on. How old are you?"

'Forty-four," he replied.

"Well, you're fortunate. You have the skin of a twenty-five year old. Her hands flew around his head with strange implements. "Hold still."

After ten minutes she paused and looked at her work, nodding in satisfaction. But as she leaned in close to inspect some nagging detail, she suddenly sniffed.

"Is that wine on your breath?" she asked in a matter of fact way, not being accusatory.

Franklin looked sheepish. "Yes, a little courage before face—the—nation time."

She reached into a drawer and handed him a small vial. "Here," she said. "Right before you go on, gargle with this and no one will notice."

He slipped it in his suit pocket. "Many thanks, Judith," he told her. "I wouldn't want Jimmy Ball to think I'm a wino."

"Jimmy Ball talks so much that the wind keeps him from smelling anything within a ten foot radius." She removed the large paper napkin from around Franklin's neck, and indicated he should get up.

"Well, thanks anyway," he said as he did so.

She smiled. "Break a leg," she said, which proved prescient.

Malone next ushered Franklin into what he called the "Green Room," which was in fact painted green, and told him that he should wait here until it was time to take him to the studio. He pointed out an adjacent restroom and a refrigerator filled with soft drinks and bottled water, and gave Franklin a remote control for a large television mounted on a wall.

"You may or may not want to watch the show," he said. "Guests vary as to whether that is a good idea or not. No one will think less of you if you choose to watch one of our competitors while you wait." Franklin fingered the remote absently. "Now where is Hubie?" Malone worried, looking at his very expensive watch.

"Hubie?" Franklin inquired. Then, before Malone could answer, he jumped to the right conclusion. "Hubie Lulland?"

"Yes," Malone replied with a nod of his head. "He's tonight's first guest. His latest comedy, 'Wife Trouble,' opened on Friday, and he's here to plug it. I just hope he's sober."

Sober? Franklin thought about it, and remembered Lulland's large red drinker's nose. The Jimmy Ball Show must have had problems with the comic in the past.

"I'm sure it will be fine," Malone said, apparently trying to reassure himself.

And just then the Green Room door opened, and Hubie Lulland himself, all 300 pounds, waddled into the room. He threw his arms around a squirming Malone and hugged him tightly.

"Donald, baby," he boomed. "Were you taking bets on whether I'd make it or not?"

Malone freed himself with as much dignity as he could muster.

"Not at all. You are ever the professional, Mr. Lulland," Malone lied. "I'm pleased to see that you're already made up."

Lulland put his huge overcoat on a hanger by the door, and then took off his suit coat which he hung next to it. Great sweat marks bathed the area of his shirt under his armpits. The shirt was a bright yellow, and in that color the sweat bands looked vaguely obscene. "Yup," he replied to Malone. "I stopped in for a little love fest with Judith before hurrying over here to see you." He turned and smiled at Franklin. "Fifth time on this show," he said with a wink. "You?"

Barely believing that a famous person like Hubie Lulland was treating him so casually, Franklin grinned back stupidly, his nerves once again trying to escape the confines of his skin. "My first," he said in reply.

"First time, eh?" Lulland said, far too loudly.

"My first time on nationwide tv, in fact."

"Mr. Lulland," Malone interrupted, "I will come for you in about ten minutes and escort you to the studio," and he slipped out the door of the Green Room before Lulland could respond, shutting it behind him.

"Your first time, eh?" Lulland repeated. "Nervous?"

"Oh yes. Very."

"To be expected. What brought you to the attention of the Jimmy Ball Show?"

Franklin paused, unsure how to answer. "I was in an explosion at a football stadium and I ended up on tv," he explained, gesturing palm up as if to say it was no big deal.

Lulland looked at him carefully. "Wait a minute. You're the guy who held onto that thing and let all the people run under it!"

"Okay. Yes."

"Well, hell, I certainly want to shake your hand, dude," Lulland said, grabbing it and pumping vigorously. "Goddamn it, man, you were awesome!"

That made Franklin feel even worse. "I wish people would stop saying that. I didn't do much of anything—it all happened so fast. Now I'm jumpy as a dog in a thunderstorm."

"Here," Lulland said, walking over to his overcoat, reaching into the pocket, and pulling out a silver flask. "Have a drink of this and calm yourself down." He unscrewed the cap and had a swallow, and then held it out to Franklin.

"Oh, no," the latter said, waiving it away. "Best not to."

"Friend, this is how I get through everything, and I mean everything. Look," he said, returning the flask to the overcoat pocket, "it's in here. Help yourself if you change your mind. Very good scotch, a malt produced by Balvenie especially for a few customers, of which I'm one. Private label. Best alcohol you've ever tasted."

Thinking of the wine from dinner, Franklin doubted that, but smiled and replied, "Thanks anyway."

"Well, you shouldn't underestimate the curative powers of good whiskey. Just one sip and you'll feel like a tiger. Eat Jimmy Ball and those callers right up. Let me tell you about the first time I was stupid enough to go on this show." And he launched into a long story about being a guest here right after getting a messy and very public divorce. It involved his ex-wife phoning him on the air and accusing him of bestiality.

"Almost ruined my career, and I wasn't even guilty! I loved that basset hound, you understand, but not in the way she insinuated. Bitch was just trying to take me down."

"Time to go, Mr. Lulland," Malone said as he popped into the room. He took Lulland's suit jacket down from the rack and helped him into it.

Lulland shook Franklin's hand once more as he left. "You're a hell of man, kid," he said. "A hell of a man!"

Alone in the Green Room, Franklin couldn't sit, couldn't think. His hands were trembling again, and he stuck them into his pockets trying to stop that. How in the world was he going to get through this?

Without thinking about it, Franklin found himself with the silver flask in his hand, and hurriedly took a small sip.

It burned his throat all the way into his stomach, but it tasted every bit as good as Lulland had promised. Franklin was not much of a drinker, and he hadn't had scotch in years, but, as promised, this beverage vied with the evening's wine for the best alcohol in his life. He allowed himself a small amount more.

He put the flask back in Lullhand's overcoat pocket and sat down in a large comfortable leather chair just as the Jimmy Ball Show came on the tv. Strangely, Franklin did feel much calmer, and this happened almost immediately. After all, he asked himself, how hard could this really be? All he had to do was explain what he'd been through in the past day, take a few calls, accept congratulations, and get the hell out of here. Then the plane flight home with Kelly! Anticipating that made him smile.

He did notice the buzz was back.

CHAPTER 3

IMAGINARY FRIEND

Jake Richardson propped his feet up on the small table in front of his recliner, and put a bag of microwaved popcorn on the floor beside him. He was a tall man, and the room he called his living room was small and crowded with both furniture and debris. He had to move two pizza boxes and a huge bowl filled with something from last week just to find a spot for the popcorn. Jake balanced a beer on the arm of his chair as he settled down to watch the Jimmy Ball Show.

He knew he shouldn't be drinking beer at all, especially now that he was a hero and was in the process of reforming old bad habits, but there was a six pack in the frig, and he couldn't bring himself to throw it away. I'll quit drinking at midnight tonight, he thought. Just now I need to relax. Been a bitch of a day. I wonder if they'll mention me on the Jimmy Ball Show? Maybe run that interview with the chink. Maybe Heather would call—oh, wait, his cell phone wasn't working since he stopped paying the bills, when was it, last month? The month before?

He took a healthy slug of the beer as the Jimmy Ball Show came on, and was annoyed to learn that Franklin Whitestone wouldn't appear until the second half of the program. First he'd have to endure a half hour of that dickhead Hubie Lulland. Crap. That man hadn't made a decent movie since "*Udder Nonsense.*"

Jake took another healthy slug of the beer. It was 8:00 pm. If he was going to quit drinking at midnight he still had five unopened beers to get through, but he was sure he'd be able to handle that.

"So, Hubie," Jimmy Ball said, too loudly, his bald head catching a glare from the lights in spite of Judith's careful work to prevent this, "is your new movie going to be as bad as the last one?" He took a sip of the glass of water on the desk before him and then wiped his large walrus mustache with the back of his hand.

"Worse!" Hubie exclaimed, guffawing, not unaware of what his agent and those who had worked so hard on this movie would think about this candid evaluation. "But it features lots of belching and fart jokes, so it'll be a big hit with the teenagers. That's all that matters, Jimmy!"

"On that note, we'll take a break," the host said into the camera. "When we return we will have a major hero as our guest." He turned back to

Lulland and extended his hand. "And. Hubie, we'll see you back here when your next stinker opens!"

"About time," Mary Whitestone said. "I couldn't take another minute of that troglodyte." She turned to Todd. "Tell me the worst, have you ever seen one of his movies?"

Todd's face screwed up with disgust. "Oh, Mom," he said, "really now! About the only movies I go to are independent films, mostly foreign ones. The last mainstream movie I saw was 'Brokeback Mountain,' unless you count documentaries such as 'An Inconvenient Truth.'"

"You saw 'Brokeback Mountain?'" she asked. He was sixteen, worldly wise for his age, and in no way (alas) restrained by convention. She'd been afraid to ask about his sexual orientation. He'd never been on a date as far as she knew, and she'd thought about the issue.

"Of course. A beautiful film. And if I were gay I'd watch it over and over again. It is a milestone in the history of movies."

She relaxed from a tension she had not known she felt. "But you're *not* gay?" she ventured.

"I might explore around some day, but no. Heterosexual. You?"

"Yes, me too."

Just then the Jimmy Ball Show returned from its commercial interlude.

"We're back," Jimmy Ball announced as if it were necessary to explain his sudden reappearance onscreen. His voice then dropped an octave and his normally twinkling blue eyes narrowed with concern.

"As you know," he intoned, "yesterday was the worst nightmare for this great country has endured since the horrors of 9/11, 2001. The news is still coming in from both horrific explosions, and this news organization will have a two hour special exploring the latest developments following this program.

"But first we have a bright spot as an anodyne for your pain."

"'Anodyne,'" Todd murmured, impressed.

"Football fans died on two college campuses, and people were hurt at a number of schools where no bombs at all went off. The awful extent of the casualties is still being tallied, but hundreds, perhaps thousands died, and many more were injured. Our prayers are that more survivors will be found in the rubble of the two stadia."

"'Stadia!'" Todd marveled.

"But this morning 68 people were pulled from the cave-in at Ohio Stadium in Columbus. Amazingly, 54 of them got out under their own power when rescue teams and construction workers, after digging all night, knocked down a wall early this morning. What happened then has been replayed over and over today, but even if you have seen it multiple times, it's worth watching once more.

"Roll it, Marty" he commanded.

Standing backstage, Franklin watched mesmerized as a monitor near him displayed the now famous footage. He'd not seen it until this moment, and the drama of the collapsing wall, he himself suddenly exposed, blinking in the sunlight, unbelievably dirty, turning startled as the beam circled with deadly accuracy towards his head, grabbing on and holding it, posed like a hero in an action movie while what seemed like an endless stream of people ran under his arms—it all floored him. Had it really happened like that? To him? No wonder they'd flown him to New York to be on this show!

When the video ended (with a shot of Franklin letting go as workers surrounded him, and he went down in their midst), there was even applause from the television crew in the studio (there was no live audience present), and Franklin was startled as the clapping backstage began all around him. Jimmy Ball was telling his audience that Franklin Whitestone, the "courageous man who stood his ground like Atlas" was his next guest. Malone, standing behind Franklin, gave him a slight push, and he walked unsteadily into the bright lights of the studio set, shook hands with Jimmy Ball, who motioned him to a plush chair on the other side of Ball's desk, and sat down.

"What a day for you!" Ball exclaimed, clapping his hands lightly twice.

"You have no idea," Franklin said, feeling very good about himself and his place in the universe. Why in hell had he been nervous? This was the highlight of his life and it felt incredible.

"You're right, I don't. May I call you 'Frank'?" he asked.

"'Franklin,' please."

"Of course. Franklin, that was an amazing video we just watched. What goes through your mind as you see it?"

"Actually, Jimmy, it was my first time to watch it. I'm still in shock about the whole thing."

"Where were you when the bomb went off?" Ball asked.

So Franklin related, the best he could remember, everything that happened from the time he went for popcorn until the workers took the girder from his grasp and dragged him away from the opening.

"It's hard to tell from the video," Franklin added, "but the last thing that occurred immediately after the workers got to me was that I collapsed and passed out."

He meant this to be self-effacing, but Ball simply said, "Who wouldn't? How hurt were you?"

"I got banged around in the explosion and the terrors that followed, but really all I suffered were some cuts—one large gash on my thigh that is causing me some pain and makes me limp a little—and some bruises that are already bright purple. But I'm okay—very, very lucky."

Jimmy Ball shook his head and ran a hand over his bald pate. "Incredible story, my man, incredible! All America is proud of you! You married? Have children?"

"Divorced," he said. "I have one son, Todd, a teenager—probably watching now." Franklin waived his hand vaguely at the camera.

"And what do you do for a living?"

"I'm a partner in the Columbus law firm of Factor, Marroni, & Ray, specializing in commercial law. In fact, I have to get back to Columbus and go to work in the morning."

"After all you've been through, you mean you aren't going to take some time off? If it were me, buddy, I'd go to Mexico and sun myself on the beach for about a month."

"Sounds good, but I have a major trial coming up. Mexico will have to wait."

"You're a fantastic person, Franklin Whitestone," Ball said. "Now we'll see what America has to say to you. Let's go to the phones." He paused to listen to the voice in his ear. "The first caller is Ralph in Chicago. You there, Ralph?"

"Yes, Jimmy," said a disembodied male voice filling the studio, seeming to Franklin to come to from all sides at once. "I just want to thank your guest for the incredible courage he showed on that video! What an inspiration to us all!"

Franklin smiled happily. A golden glow infused his inner being. So this is what it meant to be on top of the world! "Thanks," he said, the humble hero.

"If you get to Chicago, my man," Ralph continued, "you look me up! I'll take you out on the town and treat you like royalty!"

"That'd be great," Franklin mumbled, at a loss for something better. Was there to be no substance to these calls? This guy hadn't even asked a question. Piece of cake.

The next two callers were similar. Ginny from Atlanta wanted to know if Franklin had seen his son since he'd been rescued (no he hadn't), and Manny from San Antonio asked how Franklin had gotten on this show so quickly.

"I'll take that one," Jimmy Ball said with a chuckle. "My crack staff zeroed right in on this important story and plucked the hero at the heart of it right out of Columbus to bring him here to talk to you! At my show, we work very hard to stay on top of the biggest stories of the day. Thanks for calling, Manny. Next is Doris from Salt Lake City. Hello, Doris!"

And then the world changed forever for Franklin.

"Mr. Whitestone," Doris began, "when you were hanging on to that girder for dear life, were you praying to God that you would have the strength to hold it long enough for all those poor people to escape?"

Franklin shook his head. "Oh, no," he said, almost jovially. "I certainly wasn't *praying*. God was the *problem*, not the solution."

"What do you mean?" Doris asked, puzzled.

"The bombs went off *because* of a belief in God! Same as 9/11. In both cases religious nuts killed people simply because they thought their God commanded them to do so."

There was a shocked silence in the studio; it lasted for a couple of beats.

"But God saved all those people that ran out under your arms!" Doris exclaimed, clearly upset. "And He saved your life too."

"At the same time that he was allowing the deaths of thousands in other stadiums? I don't think so. It never ceases to amaze me," Franklin said, as if leading a slow student, "that God gets credit when things go right, but is never to blame when things go horribly wrong, even where, as with these explosions, religion is clearly the motivating force."

"*GOD DIDN'T CAUSE THE EXPLOSIONS!!!*" Doris yelled, her voice overwhelming the studio mikes.

"Oh? From what I hear there is a website making that very claim. *'The infidels are dead—praise be to Allah!'*"

"I . . . I . . . I," Doris sputtered, unable to talk.

"Wow!" Jimmy Ball said. "My director tells me that the phone lines just jammed up solid!"

"I THOUGHT, I THOUGHT YOU WERE . . . A HERO! BUT YOU ARE GOING TO GO TO HELL!!!" Doris screamed.

"We are running out of time," Ball said, deep concern on his face, cutting her off, "but let *me* ask you some questions, Franklin. You are an atheist, right?"

"I suppose. I don't give myself labels for not engaging in the supernatural. But I do believe in finding out what's true and what's not. I have to keep reminding myself that there are intelligent people who—incredibly—think that some magical being is watching our every move, counting the sparrows as they drop, when there is not the slightest bit of evidence this is true." He waved a hand airily. "Actually, you know, the evidence completely goes the other way. In all of recorded history there is not one verifiable incident of supernatural intervention in the affairs of human beings. Not one. Now, Doris, if you were an almighty god, don't you think you'd clear up your existence in some obvious way? Leave the issue beyond doubt so that everyone would salute and get with the program?"

Jimmy Ball's eyes got wider than his audience had ever seen.

"You don't believe in any form of divine guidance!?" he asked.

Franklin smiled, giving a small shake of his head. "Let me put it like this, Jimmy. When I was a child I had an imaginary friend who was with me everywhere I went, helping me out, very real to me. I loved him with all my heart. But as I got older I didn't need that crutch anymore, and one day he just wasn't there—nor did I miss him. As an adult I'd be embarrassed if I still needed an imaginary friend to help me run my life."

More dead air while that statement floated around the room for a few seconds. Then Jimmy Ball found his voice.

"Well, we clearly have material there for a very different show, and we may have to invite you back, Franklin, to talk about this . . . controversial topic at length. But now it is past time to wrap up." He turned and looked into the camera. "Thank you all for watching, and tune in next time when my guest will be Heisman trophy candidate Randolph Jones." He paused, then added, "Good night." He usually tacked on, "and God bless," but he somehow omitted it this particular evening, an oversight for which he profusely apologized after he saw his mountain of mail on this very point. He was never quite forgiven for the misstep, which caused him grief until the day he died twelve years later.

Kelly had watched the show from a private viewing area near the director's booth. Mr. Malone had gotten her a bottled water, and asked her to avoid making any noises that would carry to the set (but she had nonetheless joined in the staff's applause when the video ended).

At the start of Franklin's segment she'd been so proud, and then was very impressed with how he handled the interview and the first couple of questions. He wasn't nervous at all in spite of his earlier worries. Then came that call from the woman in Salt Lake City.

Now Kelly sat very still in her seat.

"Incredibly brave! Stupendous! I couldn't be more proud of

Dad!"Todd rejoiced, dancing around the television, both fists in the air.

Mary, firmly seated in her favorite leather chair, the cat, Elliot, on her lap, was more sanguine. She used the remote to turn off the tv. "Your father has a lot of characteristics, but stupidity is not usually one of them," she told him.

Todd paused in his dance, one foot still raised. "What do you mean? He was great!"

"It couldn't have been dumber. I wonder if he was on drugs. That Kelly woman has been bad for him. This is just the latest example."

"Mom, what was dumb about Dad's courageous stand on behalf of non-belief? He refused to be bullied by that religious nut. She deserved to be put in her place."

"He dragged his atheism into a conversation where it was irrelevant, and I'm afraid he'll pay dearly for it."

Todd leaned in close to her. "Mom, you're an atheist yourself. You both brought me up not believing all those religious delusions! Don't be a hypocrite."

"Yes," she conceded, rising and dumping Elliot on the floor, "I'm an atheist, but his remarks were so over the top that they offended even me."

"Offended you? Are you ashamed of being a nonbeliever?" He followed her into the kitchen.

"No, but I am circumspect about the occasions on which I bring it up. I certainly wouldn't do so gratuitously on national television."

He thought about that for a second. "Okay, when would you think it 'circumspect'?"

"When about to embark on a serious romantic relationship, or when asked by a friend to be a godmother to some child, or when explaining to my own son how the world works. But, make no doubt, atheists are controversial, only a tiny percentage of the population. It's the only minority left where discrimination is encouraged. So, Todd, you have to be careful. You can't stick your head into a beehive without instantly regretting it."

Todd looked unconvinced. "Well, Dad is *my* hero. He's not afraid of the consequences of telling the truth."

"Then he's a fool. Holy hell—and I do mean that in the religious sense—is about to break loose."

"DAMN HIM, DAMN HIM, DAMN HIM!!!" Jake Richardson screamed, pounding rhythmically on the wall with each "damn." "I saved the fucker and he's BETRAYED me!!!" He pushed off from the wall violently, careening into a standing lamp, which went down with a thud, the bulb breaking with a spectacular spray of glass. He turned back and kicked the lamp into the side of the tv, spreading small shards everywhere. Sometime during the show itself he had jumped to his feet. Popcorn from the bowl on his lap was flung like confetti to the four corners of the room. He'd knocked over his beer too.

Jake stopped in the middle of the floor, his lip curled, fists at his side, his face pointed up toward the ceiling. "He betrayed the Lord!" he moaned. "The Lord our God! How could he *do* that? Fuck, fuck, fuck!" It was a strange sort of incantation.

"That asshole must be brought to the truth," he said, taking a deep breath, his fists relaxing. "Yes, yes! He too is one of God's children, and he has strayed from the flock. It's my duty as a Christian to bring him back." He nodded his head up and down with vigorous determination.

"I saved him once. I will save him again."

When the director signaled that the camera was no longer live, Jimmy Ball just sat there looking quizzically at Franklin.

"Oh, you are in such trouble, my friend," he said, sadly shaking his head.

"I thought I was a hero," Franklin commented, still in the moment, still pleased with himself.

"That's over. You'll be picking tar and feathers out of your hair for months. We have a saying about guests on this show who do what you just did: big mouth, big mistake, big trouble."

"Nonsense," Franklin replied with a smile. "I believe what I believe, and I don't hesitate to say so. She asked, I answered."

"How does a foot taste that far back in your throat?" Ball asked as he came to his feet.

"You're being too dramatic," Franklin countered, unclipping his microphone and leaving it on the desk, rising himself. "But I'm very pleased you had me on the show." He extended his hand. "Thank you for everything."

As they shook hands, Ball said, "Oh, believe me, the pleasure is mine, all mine. There's no such thing in show business as bad publicity, and the show we just finished is going down in tv history! So thank you a hundred times over."

"Glad to help," Franklin said, turning to leave until Ball touched his arm.

"And I was serious about what I said on the air. If you want to come back on the show, say in a week or two, I'll give you the whole hour and you

49

may say whatever you like. The ratings would go through the roof!"

Kelly was waiting for Franklin as he emerged from the men's room where he had scrubbed off his makeup. She looked crestfallen, leaning against the wall, arms folded, head down. Franklin had had a few minutes to think, and he was beginning to see that his flip answers about religion were probably not going to go over so well. He smiled as he walked up to her.

"Hi, Sweetie," he said, reaching out a hand to touch her.

She turned and headed for the front door of the building. "Let's get out of here," she said.

He followed her to the curb where the limousine was waiting to take them back to the airport. She climbed in without a word, so he joined her silently, worried now. The limo driver pulled into the New York traffic.

Finally he ventured, "Upset with me?"

She didn't answer at first, and the long silence was awkward, making Franklin tense up. This was worse than he thought.

Finally she spoke.

"You ruined the best evening of my life. You just *ruined* it."

Now he paused. Then he said, low, "I'm very sorry. That would've been the last thing I intended."

He heard her sniffle, and looked at her face carefully. Was she crying?

"Oh, Franklin!" she said (not "Frankie," he noticed). "Do you have any idea what you've done?"

"Done? To whom?"

"To the people who watched the show. To me. To your family. Hell, to *my* family. Can you imagine how my parents are going to react to you now?"

He hesitated.

"I guess not. Tell me what you mean."

She turned toward him for the first time, and there were tears in her lovely eyes. It broke his heart. "Religion is *important* to the world. Don't you know that? It comforts people, helps them get through the bad spots of life, makes it easier to bear all kinds of burdens. Taking that away is cruel. I didn't know you could be so callous."

He took a deep breath before replying. "Callous? For saying what I believe? Well, ask yourself this one: if what I said is right, and there is no God, you're deluding yourself. Isn't that worth knowing?"

"No," she replied, very sure of this. "First of all, you're not right. There clearly *is* a God, and you have just offended Him greatly. Worry about

50

that tonight when you put your head on your pillow."

He rolled his eyes, as disappointed in her as she was in him. "Not you too," he moaned. "You can't believe that pap!"

"Pap! How *dare* you say that to me?" she snapped, teeth bared.

"But I didn't know you believed in God!" he pressed. "You never said much about the topic, and you knew I was an atheist! Why didn't you speak up?"

"I didn't think it was worth fighting about. You could believe what you wanted and I could believe the opposite. It wasn't like we were planning on having children, or anything, so that it was important to clear it up."

"How religious are you?"

"I was raised a Baptist, and I went to church every Sunday all the time I was growing up. I *loved* going to church. It was one of my favorite things. Granted, I haven't gone very often as an adult, but I feel *guilty* about that. It's something I always mean to change . . . to become better at tending to my faith. I've been busy, so I stupidly neglected it. Well, no more. Next Sunday I'll be back in the pews."

Exasperated, he ran a hand through his hair. "Oh, no. Please, no," he mumbled. He slumped back in his seat. Jimmy Ball was right. What was that about big mouth, big trouble? Now he'd have to think fast or lose this woman he cared so very much about. But on this issue, they were very far apart. He could no more conjure up a belief in God than he could in leprechauns, nor was she likely to forgive him for thinking that church-going was a colossal waste of time. How, he asked himself, could they have had years together without knowing these fundamental things about each other? Had their relationship been that shallow?

Finally, he spoke. "What can I say to make things better?" he asked, really meaning it.

"Don't say anything," she told him, also meaning it. "You've said plenty tonight."

"I do apologize, Kelly. I never meant to hurt you, or cause you distress in any way. I'm very, very sorry."

She was having none of that. "Not now! I just told you to stop talking, but you're making things worse."

"But . . ."

"SHUT UP!" she yelled. The limousine driver snapped his head back to look back at them, frowning. He'd had passengers get into physical brawls in his back seat before, and it made for a bad ride.

Franklin, feeling the sting of her anger, did as she asked.

Without exchanging another word, they reached the airport and climbed on board the private jet. They buckled in, and as soon as the plane

51

took off, she reclined her seat and closed her eyes for the rest of the journey. When they landed in Columbus, Franklin thanked the pilot and the attendant for the way they'd handled the whole trip, but Kelly didn't speak a word. Silently they walked to his car, which was parked in the short term parking lot next to the concourse.

As the car entered the freeway circling the city and they headed north, she finally spoke.

"Take me home and drop me off."

"That's what I'm doing," he said, contrite.

Another short pause, then he asked, "How can I get you to forgive me? Please, Kelly. I'll do anything."

She turned to him. "Convert. Tell me you believe in God."

He paused. "No."

Her lip curled in a sneer he had never seen before. "I thought you were the one who didn't discriminate on any basis. So much for that."

That made him angry. "I do discriminate when it comes to unblinking adherence to superstition."

"You know," she said, having none of that, "on the plane I got to thinking about a biblical verse I heard often as a child: "Be ye not unequally yoked together with unbelievers."

That was a conversation stopper, he thought, and he was right. Nothing more was said even as they parted. When Franklin pulled up to the curb in front of her house, Kelly jumped out as fast as she could and shut the car door firmly, walking away without a backward glance.

By this time Franklin's stomach ached, his head hurt, and the bandaged cut on his thigh throbbed, demanding his immediate attention, though the care—the rest—it needed would have to wait until he got home. His hands were shaking so bad he doubted he could drive.

So, for minutes, he just sat there at the wheel in front of Kelly's house, trying to get hold of himself. Then, to add to his misery, he suddenly realized he was about to break down and cry, and not just ordinary tears, but a waterfall of misery.

No! No! he thought. I *won't* let her see me sitting out here sobbing!

Quickly he put the car into drive and shot off down the street, making strange little "uh uh uh" sounds deep in his throat. As soon as he turned a corner, he pulled over to the curb and let it all out, leaning over so that his head was down on the passenger's seat, sobbing, his mid-section draped painfully over the gear shift.

Franklin was not sure how long he stayed like that, but finally he straightened up, sniffed deeply a few times, put the car in gear, and slowly resumed the trip home. Ten minutes later as he came up to the intersection

52

leading to his street he saw to his horror that the news trucks were still parked all around the front of his house, spilling onto lawns, blocking his neighbors' driveways.

Quickly he accelerated and kept going straight, hoping that he wouldn't be detected. He glanced at the dashboard clock. It was shortly after midnight! Had they been there all this time? Were they nuts? Was it going to be like this from now on?

Even my problems have problems, he thought.

About as unhappy as a man could get, Franklin parked on the street that ran behind his condo development and walked across the yard of the young couple who lived immediately behind his unit. He quietly let himself through the gate into their back yard, then climbed the short fence that circled the condos (which made his injured thigh throb), and then let himself in through his rear patio door. Careful not to turn on a light and thereby attract the attention of the mob outside, he shut himself up in the master bedroom, washed up, and climbed into bed.

He lay there staring at the ceiling for over an hour.

Knowing it was a mistake to keep going over it, he replayed the life-changing day he had just been through. This very morning he'd awakened in a hell hole where he thought he might die any minute, been rescued while at the same time saving others in what looked on tv like a herculean stunt, then was whisked off to New York, treated like a VIP, put on the air, and immediately said all the wrong things. Now his hero status was very much in doubt, and the woman he loved hated him.

Quite a day, he thought, a sour taste in his mouth. Quite a day. Tomorrow had to be better.

But he was wrong.

CHAPTER 4

THE GREAT TURTLE

The shock waves and reactions of what came to be known as "9/11 (II)" were the same combination of surrealism, outrage, sorrow, and anger that had defined the first attack, although, since a lot fewer people died in this new horror, its impact was not as great. All over the United States, Americans told each other that they'd been waiting for the second shoe to drop and so they weren't surprised when it came. But it wasn't that simple. On some level, and in spite of what they said after the fact, people hadn't really been all that sure that another attack was on the cards. There had been a growing hope that increased vigilance, combined with the destruction of many *al-Qaeda* training camps and financial structure, meant that they could sleep easier in their beds. The second attack had nevertheless come and even managed to cause cruel carnage in cities that had suffered no bomb explosions at all, destroying any illusions of normality. The terrorists' message was clear: nowhere in the country were Americans safe.

And, even worse, everyone worried that there was even a third shoe yet to come.

It took awhile, but the authorities eventually figured out how the terrorists had managed to secrete bombs in three different stadiums across the country without any of them being discovered before September 11th.

The bombs were all cleverly wired and concealed inside condiment stands in the concession areas of the stadiums, and all these stands were manufactured and sold by the same entity: Sam's Specialty Foods, Inc., a prosperous California company that had been in existence for thirty-four years. However, five years ago the company had undergone a change of management when a hostile takeover occurred. The new shareholders replaced everyone: the old Board, the upper management, and every single one of the employees, excepting only the five percent of the existing workforce who were already under the control of the new owners. These employees had been previously inserted into the company to learn the business and, once management changed, to keep going without attracting undue attention.

The new stockholders turned out to be a Delaware holding company and its subsidiaries, all of which were owned by a bank in Egypt, which itself was controlled by a business consortium in Pakistan, etc., until the track the authorities were following mysteriously disappeared into Saudi Arabia and was thereafter lost. The internet site of the terrorists claiming credit for the bombings (a group that called itself *al-Borak*—"The Lightning") bragged online about its clever steps in acquiring and then controlling Sam's Specialty Foods, and extolled in detail the names, photos, and farewell messages of the two suicide bombers who had been martyred in the explosions. What had happened to the third terrorist, whose bomb somehow failed to detonate, was never explained, nor was his identity revealed.

The new management at Sam's Specialty Foods had been run the business as always for five years, with one major new innovation. The Sales Director for Sam's had contacted fifteen colleges and universities on major campuses throughout the United States with a proposition. Sam's, it was explained, had developed a new type of condiment stand by the trade name of Sam's Toppings Supreme, and was anxious to market it to stadiums and arenas. To get business started the Sales Director offered to have his company donate $10,000 to the general scholarship funds of each of the universities if Sam's were allowed to install one condiment stand—free of charge—in each stadium for one year. If at the end of that period the university was not interested in purchasing additional stands, the original would be removed, and there would be no further obligations between the parties. A number of universities initially expressed interest, but only three had agreed to a one year trial for Sam's Toppings Supreme: Ohio State, Texas, Florida, big schools with big stadiums.

"Mr. Whitestone's misguided bashing of the overwhelming percentage of the people on this planet who believe in God was not only offensive, but juvenile, ignorant, and an affront to those of us who know the joy of salvation and the love of our Lord Jesus Christ." This was the opening salvo by the Christian Conservative Coalition, delivered Monday morning and broadcast over national tv. The spokesman, the Reverend Joseph David, thundered the response of his organization (a powerhouse on the religious right) from what looked like a pulpit, but was actually a set on a sound stage at the Coalition's headquarters in Oklahoma City, Oklahoma.

"God is at the foundation of all of human civilization. Following His commandments is not the unthinking action of unsophisticated morons, but the natural response to the grace He has shown us by sending His only son to pay for our sins. Civilization was built by the worshipers of God, and particularly was Christianity responsible for the tremendous accomplishments that have taken us from the caves to outer space. The message of love espoused by Jesus Christ, and, indeed, all of the great religions, has produced harmony, charity, and sparked the worldwide emphasis on altruism that is the fastest growing movement we know.

55

"Yes, there are and have been some wars that were fought over religious issues, but a deeper study of these wars shows that religion was only the pretext for the awful conflicts that occurred, and that the underlying causes were particularly secular in all but the rarest of cases. As the apostle Paul tells us in 1 Timothy 6:10, it is the love of money that is at the root of all evil, not the love of God. Mr. Whitestone would have known this if he had ever humbled himself and read God's unerring word to us, the Bible. In it, He commands us to love one's neighbor as one's self, and to do unto others as you would have them do unto you, rightly called the '*Golden*' Rule. Not only is this an example of God's loving guidance, it is something Mr. Whitestone would do well to think about before he attacks that which he obviously doesn't understand.

"Mr. Whitestone conveniently skips over the huge benefits of religion when he makes his cheap attacks. A belief in God is the central comfort most people have in times of trouble, and this comfort is available to the meanest sinner on the planet. God has shepherded billions of people who were trapped in situations of absolute misery and heartache, and He has protected the innocent, cheered the depressed, and dispensed hope to those who would otherwise be hopeless. Would Mr. Whitestone be so heartless to strip this balm from the wounds of the inflicted?

"What kind of world would it be if Mr. Whitestone did have his way and God were banished from our public conscience? Sinners would not be punished, virtue would not be rewarded, and those in trouble would not be comforted. Mankind would be no more than intelligent animals, aware of our mortality but unable to do anything about it—naked and alone in a belligerent universe. The love of a beneficent God saves us from that fate and makes our lives worth living . . .gives them meaning.

"Poor Mr. Whitestone. He must lead a pitiful life—one filled with hatred, devoid of love, oblivious to the wonders of the world. Those of us who know God dread the coming of a far worse fate for him when he dies and learns, too late, that his denial of God merits a terrible penalty on judgment day."

Reverend David paused to take a sip of water before continuing. He was warming to his task. "Mr. Whitestone, being a lawyer, demands that we produce *evidence* of God's existence. Evidence? Is he blind? Once again the word of God Himself speaks to this. In Romans 1:20 Paul says, 'For since the creation of the world God's invisible qualities—His eternal power and divine nature—have been clearly seen, being understood from what has been made, so that men are without excuse.' God is in every detail of everything we see, moment by moment, from the time we are born until we are laid in our grave and then welcomed into His embrace in heaven! Mr. Whitestone should recognize that he has no evidence that God *doesn't* exist, so all he can do is take cheap shots at those who need no evidence for what all intelligent people absolutely know. What we have that he does not, poor man, is *faith*, a faith in God Almighty, the center of our being."

Reverend David had almost finished his peroration. The director switched to Camera 2, and the minister, much practiced in this, effortlessly turned to look deep into the eyes of his video audience. He smiled.

"As you know—all of you who are listening to me now—Jesus Christ is our one true friend. And He is far from imaginary.

"God bless you all."

Like the collision of hot and cold fronts that produce a hurricane, the combination of the events at Ohio Stadium and the Jimmy Ball Show left Franklin Whitestone standing bewildered as he surveyed the wreckage that had become his life, all of this occurring more or less in the same awful day. Trying to sleep that terrible Sunday night was its own version of hell, alternating between a churning brain filled with self-loathing thoughts, and fitful sleep in which he had nightmares that brought him instantly awake, trembling. In one he stumbled through a smoky darkness and came across his own decapitated head. Just before seven in the morning, he abandoned his bed, made himself some coffee, and slowly worked up the courage to face the day.

An hour later, very unhappy, Franklin peered through a slit in his living room window. Reporters as far as the eye could see. Shit!

Bleary of brain, he debated what to do next. Of course, he needed to get to work downtown—he really did have a trial set for next week and a slew of other projects queued up, all demanding his attention. Should he sneak out through the patio again, trespassing on his neighbors' yard (neighbors, alas, he'd never even met them in the few months he had lived in his new condo), fleeing like a refugee from his own house?

Fuck that, he thought. It was time to get it over with and face the press.

Sober reflection in bed last night and again this morning had convinced Franklin that he had made an ass of himself on national tv, and that he was truly in major trouble. Thinking about Kelly caused a sharp pain in his stomach, and he agonized over possible ways to fix his gauche handling of her. Perhaps if he now said the right things to the press she'd be inclined to rethink the ugly ending of last night's snafu.

After brushing his teeth, putting on his coat and tie, making sure he looked his best, Franklin Whitestone, smiled bravely and opened the front door. He stepped out into the media maelstrom. Reporters, who had been lounging casually around, talking to each other, warming themselves against the nippy fall weather with hot beverages, jerked to attention like prairie dogs alerted by a sudden noise, straining to see over each other and the mounds of tv equipment. Then they all began yelling his name and asking questions at once, producing a kind of madness, as though they were frenzied members of a church congregation outdoing each other speaking in tongues.

As a reflex he nearly turned and ran back into the house, slamming the door on the verbal barrage. Instead he steeled himself to the task, and smiled even more brightly for the multitude of cameras, and then walked confidently toward the microphones extended hopefully in his direction. He raised his hands and made a couple of bowing motions with them, meaning that they should all calm down and let him speak. He said, over and over, "Let me talk. Please, folks, let me talk!" After twenty seconds of this, and after some yelling at each other to shush, something like a break in the chaos allowed him to start feeding them substance, at which point they did quiet down.

"I'm certainly not used to attention from the press," Franklin began, "and I have nothing planned to say. The last couple of days have been as shocking to me as to everyone else, and I'm saddened by the many deaths, and angry at those who caused them. I'm not the heroic type, as you can see," he made a gesture up and down his all-too-chunky body, "and anything I did at the stadium was just an instinctive reaction that anyone standing where I was would've done. I'm very grateful that so many of us got out alive."

"Are you grateful to God?" a reporter yelled. That produced a rapt silence as they all hungered for his reply.

What to say?

"I'm grateful to all those who worked so hard to get us out of that nightmare," he said as quickly as the thought occurred to him.

"Including God?" the same reporter demanded.

"My beliefs about religion are personal, and I don't plan to go into them now."

"Unlike last night on national tv?"

This wasn't going well. Now what? Tell them he had had a few drinks and should have watched his mouth? *In vino veritas* would be the inevitable response. He definitely was not willing to disown the views he had expressed last night, and this was true whatever the consequences. It was a difficult journey along a tortuous road to arrive at those views, and he wasn't going to retrace his steps.

"I apologize to anyone I offended by those ill-considered comments," he said at last. "I certainly respect the rights of all people to follow the faith of their choice, and I would hope that you all would extend that same respect to my beliefs."

A female reporter right in the middle of the pack, microphone extended, pinned him to the wall by asking, "Do you respect those religious beliefs themselves?"

"I believe in freedom of religion," he countered.

"That doesn't answer the question. In your personal opinion, are those religious beliefs themselves admirable?

"Some of them," he said, knowing how weak that sounded.

"But not all of them," she concluded. Now he recognized her. Molly Schultz from WMJZ. He had never liked her.

"Please, I must get to work. No more of this." They all began shouting questions, most of which were unintelligible. Franklin tried to advance through their ranks with determination, but they were a solid wall, and he had no chance of penetrating it. He could be here for hours.

Fight or flight?

He attempted the latter first, turning suddenly to go back inside only to discover reporters were now behind him, blocking the door. That made him angry. It was time to choose fight.

In a fury of action that made for wonderful tv on evening news programs all over the country that same night, Franklin began snatching microphones out the hands of the startled reporters and throwing them to the ground as hard as he could, trying to break them, while at the same time screaming at them, "GET OFF MY PROPERTY! GET OFF MY PROPERTY! *I'm a lawyer and you're trespassing! Leave immediately, or I will file suit this afternoon against each one of you personally and against your organizations too!*"

He shoved one cameraman into another and both went down. In the startled confusion that followed, he pushed through them all and headed for the street. When two of their number made as if to follow him, he turned furiously and snarled at them, "Follow me and I'll pummel you!" He later wondered at that when he saw it on tv. "Pummel"? What sort of scary threat is a pummeling?

Nonetheless, it worked. They all stayed put, staring in amazement as he loped off down the street, turned the corner, and fled to his car.

Jake Richardson struggled from bed with only a mild headache, and dragged himself to his job while half asleep. Coffee and fresh air revived him once he was on the worksite and doing familiar things with enormous construction equipment of various tonnages. As he worked he planned his approach to Franklin Whitestone.

Jake was rotten at personal relations and knew it. Under anyone's standards, he'd made a shit pile of his private life. Walled off by lawyers and protective relatives, his ex-wife was not returning his phone calls. Soon he'd have to take action about that—knock on her door and demand his right to see his daughter, and if that didn't work, well . . .

But maybe what had happened at the stadium would soften Heather up. However, the certainty he'd had about this possibility last night vanished with the arrival of the sun.

Jake decided that the best thing would be to have that heart-to-heart talk with Whitestone, and begin introducing him to the wonderful word of Jesus, and the joy it brought to those who believed. At lunch time he went into the office and borrowed a phone book, and laboriously looked up Franklin Whitestone. That paid off big time, as the phone book had listings for both Whitestone's home and work numbers, plus the address of a house in Dublin, a suburb of Columbus on the northwest side. Jake talked Suzy at the front desk into letting him use the office phone, so he called Whitestone's home number. No answer, of course, since Whitestone was surely at work, but Jake left a message at the beep.

"Franklin, this is Jake Richardson. I was the operator of the Big Crane that pulled down the wall yesterday morning and freed you people. I don't think I did nothing much, but still I'd like to talk to you when you get time.

"I just want to rejoice with you in the workings of God that allowed things to end so happily. I know that you are not right now in God's fold, but we can work on that when we meet. Please call me. God bless and keep you!" And then Jake left the number of his cell phone. It wasn't until after he'd hung up that he remembered his phone service had been cut off. Have to catch up on the payments today, he thought, juggling financial priorities in his mind. Whitestone might call this evening. Come to that, Heather might call too.

He spent the rest of the workday planning what he'd say to each of them.

There were also reporters outside his office building Franklin discovered when he started to pull into the building's parking lot, so he quickly accelerated before they could spot him. He later learned that since 5:00 a.m. the newspeople had been camped in front of the entrance to the firm's offices on the 23rd floor, but had been evicted by Security, which forced them out the front door and onto the street.

This problem was more easily solved than the debacle at home. Used mostly by the custodial staff and for deliveries, there was a back entrance to the building, so Franklin slipped in there and hightailed it to the 23rd floor without incident. Four associates were standing immediately inside the firm's main door, talking with the receptionist, and all five of them went silent when he walked in.

"Good morning," he said as cheerfully as he could, and nodded pleasantly as he passed them on his way to his own office down the hall to the right. They mumbled greetings in response, looking embarrassed by his appearance, and Franklin would have bet big money that they were anxious for him to get out of sight so the gossip could commence. His own paralegal, Rhonda Annuncio, looked up expectantly when he came past her office, and even seemed pleased to see him.

"Good! You made it," she said, and they exchanged greetings. She continued, "I was wondering if you were going to come in today, what with all the complicated things in your life." That seemed a politic way to put it, Franklin thought, as he nodded in reply, set his briefcase on his desk, and hung up his coat. Annuncio followed him into his office.

"There is a major development of the Swindon clock problem," she told him. "Mr. Ray sent you three emails about it, and last Friday night he left a phone message too. The buyer of the clock has refused to return it, and Swindon is frantic. Mr. Ray wants you to do something today to get that clock back, and then call Mr. Swindon and make sure he's a happy client."

This was a big problem, but Franklin was pleased to return to the practice of law, safely away from terrorist bombs, Jimmy Ball, God, and reporters.

Arnold Swindon was the CEO of the firm's largest corporate client, but the clock thing was a personal consumer problem of his own. Normally Factor, Marroni, & Ray would not touch a consumer issue, but to keep in the good graces of Arnold Swindon there were no limits to what the firm would do.

The clock in question was an antique grandfather clock, built in 1790, with beautiful workmanship, mahogany finish, and even signed by its famous English creator. The clock, valued at upwards of $13,000, had been in the Swindon family for two generations. The trouble began when it was sent to be cleaned and to have its regulator adjusted by a Pittsburgh firm specializing in clocks. By accident (or, according to some of the speculation, a plot to steal it), the Pittsburgh company sold the clock to a woman in Nashville, and had it shipped there before it realized its mistake and asked that the clock be returned, offering a full refund of the $9,000 purchase price. Ray's emails, printed out and displayed prominently in the center of his desk, revealed that the customer in Nashville, very pleased with the clock and the bargain price she'd paid for it, had said no. She was keeping it. Arnold Swindon was very upset. "Do whatever it takes," he had instructed Paul Factor, the firm's senior partner, "but get that clock back." The case had been promptly handed over to Franklin, the firm's expert on commercial law, and he had been working on it for the past week with two associates, Janet Dubois and Nancy Cohen.

"Get Janet and Wanda in my office right away," Franklin told Rhonda Annuncio adding, "and I want you sit in on this one too." She got on the phone immediately and in five minutes they were all seated in a semi-circle ready to work. None of them said a word about his recent terrifying ordeal or the debacle last night on tv. Apparently they'd all decided that silence, coupled with their usual splendid work ethic, was the way to go. Good, he thought. The faster things reverted to normal the better.

First Franklin reminded them of the facts of the Swindon grandfather clock case, and then he reviewed the major legal principle at issue.

"What we have is a classic entrusting problem," Franklin lectured. "Section 2-403 of the Uniform Commercial Code states that if you entrust your goods to a merchant who deals in goods of that kind, and the merchant then turns around and sells the goods to a buyer in the ordinary course of business, the buyer gets good title to the goods and you can't retrieve them."

"Bummer," Janet Debois commented. "How is that fair?"

"Well," Franklin replied, "our law has a strong policy if favor of protecting buyers in the ordinary course of business. Think about it. That's you and me every time we go into a retail store and make a purchase. We don't want the seller to come chasing down the street after us, saying he has changed his mind and wants the goods back."

"Sort of hard on poor Mr. Swindon," Nancy Cohen observed. "Shouldn't the law care about him too?"

"Yes, and it does. He still has rights against the merchant for mishandling his goods. So Mr. Swindon will be awarded damages—the value of the lost clock—from the Pittsburgh firm that was supposed to clean and return it. However, he can't get the clock itself. As between Swindon and the innocent buyer, the law awards the clock to the buyer. After all, Swindon chose to place his clock with the entity that then mistakenly sold it. Between the two of them, Swindon had the most control over the situation and ought to have the bigger risk."

"Why is it a risk at all?" Debois asked. "Whichever one of them doesn't get the clock at least gets full damages from the merchant."

"Oh," said Franklin, one eyebrow raised. "What if the merchant has no money or declares bankruptcy? Many a company is in hock so completely that there are no funds available to pay damages. If that were the case here, it's the clock or nothing."

"Hmm. Right."

Cohen looked unhappy. "So our client is screwed? Assuming what Swindon cares most about is keeping that clock in the family, he won't like hearing that all he might get is money."

"Not necessarily. There are still some legal arguments that might prevail and allow him to retrieve the clock. All right, you're on. Who sees what these arguments are?"

They all stared at section 2-403 in the statute books on their laps and came up blank. Franklin frowned at them. He drummed this one important precept into their heads: lawyers are not in the business of telling their clients that they can't do things. It is the lawyer's job to show them how—legally—they could come out on top.

"Nobody? All right. There are two things that both have to happen before the buyer prevails. First the firm to whom Swindon entrusted the clock must 'regularly' deal in goods of that kind."

Cohen shrugged. "It cleans clocks. Isn't that enough?"

"Do they routinely *sell* clocks? Antique clocks of great value? If the answer is no, Swindon will win. One of you should look into that." Rhonda Annuncio raised her hand, and Franklin nodded.

"What's the second issue?" Dubois asked.

"Whether the buyer was buying in the ordinary course of business. In part that overlaps with the merchant issue. If the merchant didn't routinely sell antique clocks then the buyer could hardly be buying in the 'ordinary course.' But it's more than that. What if the buyer were in cahoots with the merchant and knew about Swindon's ownership? Then she wouldn't be in good faith, a major requirement for buying in the ordinary course."

"Or," Cohen said, "if when she walked into the store the merchant lowered his voice and told her—pssst, little lady!—come into the back room, great deal going down on a rare clock. That wouldn't likely be held as a sale in the ordinary course. So let *her* cough up the clock and then sue the merchant."

Franklin smiled, pleased. "Now you've got the rhythm of it. Nancy, you look into that aspect and report back."

"And me?" Dubois asked.

"You start pulling up 2-403 cases that are similar to this one and see what the courts have been saying."

"Got it."

Their session over, they all rose to go just as Manny Cardoza, administrative assistant to Howard Ray, Managing Partner, stuck his head in the door.

"Franklin," Cardoza said, "Howard would like to see you. Now, if possible."

Franklin nodded and followed Cardoza back to Ray's office. The door was open, and Ray motioned him to come in, rising at the same time and gesturing toward one of the plush chairs sitting in the corner next to the floor-to-ceiling window with a spectacular view of the Ohio Statehouse across the street. "Have a seat, Franklin," he said, walking over to close the office door as Franklin sat. They were alone. Ray lowered his massively overweight body down in another (and identical) chair next to Franklin's. Ray was a man somewhere in his mid-fifties, much wrinkled, and with a full head of very grey hair. In spite of his hail-fellow-well-met attitude, he was sharp as a knife and smart as any lawyer in the State of Ohio.

"I figured you'd want to talk to me," Franklin said with a small smile.

Ray didn't smile back. "Oh, yes. Much going on with you. Things are hopping."

"Let me have it," Franklin said casually, as if Ray were merely going to shake his finger at him.

Ray wrinkled his brow and sat forward in his chair, speaking confidentially.

"We were all very worried about you on Saturday, scared shitless that you'd died in the attack on the stadium. I called Kelly and she was in the same pickle. She promised to let me know if she heard anything about your fate.

"Then came the news that not only had you been rescued, but that you'd saved a lot of other people, and were to be on the Jimmy Ball Show. That video of your heroics was shown over and over again. At that point we were all proud of you, and very pleased that it would reflect satisfactorily on the firm. Very pleased." He paused. "So, like half the people in the United States, I was watching the Ball show when you self-destructed right before my eyes."

"Just a disagreement with a caller who tried to pigeonhole me."

"Would that were true," Ray countered with a determined shake of his head. "Franklin, you made fun of religious people! How do you think *that* reflects back on the firm?"

"My religious views should have nothing to do with the firm."

Ray made a short raspberry noise. "What planet do you live on? All morning, our phones have been jumping up and down like those in cartoons,

64

and the emails about you threaten to blow our computers through the wall! Have you looked at *your* emails? Listened to *your* phone messages?"

Franklin shook his head. "I haven't had time," he said.

"Oh? Too busy attacking members of the press?" Ray said this with no trace of humor in his voice.

"I DID NOT ATTACK MEMBERS OF THE PRESS!" he said, irate of a sudden.

Ray shook his head again. "Oh, Franklin, Franklin, wake up and smell the fiasco! If I turn on that tv over there," he pointed to the large one in the wall facing his desk, "and select a channel at random, odds are splendid that we can watch a new video of you—one made this very morning—showing what a model citizen you are! One of those cameramen you pushed broke his arm, and you destroyed some very expensive equipment."

"Well," Franklin said, "actually that warms my heart. You should've seen the alligator pit I had to wade through to get to work. And that reminds me: there may be good news on the Swindon clock problem." This wasn't necessarily true, but Franklin was hoping to swing the conversation to a happier topic.

"Fuck the clock," Ray replied, causing a startlingly interesting image in Franklin's mind. "That damned clock is a mosquito compared with the damage you've done to the firm, and, not incidentally, to yourself as a member of that firm."

A moment of silence passed as that threat hung in the air.

"What are you saying?" Franklin asked, his voice low.

Ray shrugged. "I think—hell, all the partners think—that it would be a good time for you to take a few days off, let this thing cool down. Let's call it a vacation. Help you relax some after your terrible travail in the stadium."

"I can't do that, Howard. My desk is piled high with work, and I have the McGill trial next week."

"Forget all that. We'll parcel it out to others. You're a valuable player, Franklin, but not the only lawyer in the firm who can handle these things. We'll muddle through without you."

Embarrassingly, Franklin began to plead. "Why can't I just keep my head low while working here, or at least at home?"

"Because we need to be able to tell our very upset clients that you are not currently handling affairs at Factor, Marroni, & Ray."

Franklin's mouth opened slightly in surprise. "'Not currently handing affairs?" he repeated. "What the hell does that mean?"

Ray looked away, not meeting his gaze. "Just a vacation, that's all."

Franklin thought about all this might lead to. There was suddenly a cold feeling deep in his gut.

"I don't like that solution, Howard," he said. "Can't we try something else? Something that keeps me productive?"

Ray now stared at him steely-eyed, and when he spoke his voice was sharp with authority. "You idiot! The villagers are lighting their torches as we speak, and we damn well don't want them to burn down this building as collateral damage to their immolation of you!"

"Nonsense! No one cares that much! This is a bump in the road, and things will be back to normal overnight."

Ray stood. "I don't want to talk about it anymore," he said. "Those villagers—well, your alligators at least—were trying to muscle their way into the firm's office this morning. We had to have Security escort them out, and, believe me, that wasn't easy. Very determined bunch, the press. Right now they're camped out in front of the building, and anyone from Factor, Marroni & Ray—attorney, secretary, janitor—who walks out is promptly put on tv, talking about you. I won't have that, Franklin. Do what I tell you! Go home, or, better—much better—get out of town, and then we'll see what we'll see."

The anger that had caused him problems all his life, jumped to the forefront, and Franklin was on the edge of uncaging it—yelling, or another pummeling, or something equally bad all around. With an effort he controlled the urge to respond, and simply stormed from Ray's office, not quite running, but not quite walking either.

Stubby Allen was the first to bring the latest news to Todd that morning at school.

"First your Dad bad-mouths God on national tv, and then he goes berserk and starts swinging at local reporters," said Stubby with a smirk. "Should he be running around loose?"

"What are you talking about, Stubby?" Todd asked, worried about the answer.

"It's on all the news channels, dude—probably make the national news tonight too. He's a dangerous man, your Dad."

"Well, that certainly wasn't his reputation before this weekend. I've always found him to be something of a marshmallow. Do you know what happened?"

Stubby flapped his hands meaninglessly. "He decked a couple of news hounds and ruined a lot of equipment. Broke some guy's arm."

"*My Dad*? Franklin Whitestone?"

"Yup."

"Hmm. Sounds improbable, but somehow eerily in line with the events of the past weekend. Thanks, Stubby. I'll look into it."

The two of them were standing in front of their lockers in the high school's basement following third period. Now that he thought about it, Todd realized that many people had been looking at him strangely this morning, but that was not really unusual, so it didn't set off any alarms. Normally the strange looks resulted from Todd's own activities: having a column published in *Newsweek*, getting away with racy double entendres about the faculty over his weekly radio broadcasts on the high school P.A. system, skipping his senior year in favor of an early admission to M.I.T., where he planned to major in one of the developing computer sciences. His goal had been to make a perfect score on his SATs, but in the event he didn't even come close, barely finishing in the top two percent. At only sixteen, Todd was already something of a mythical figure locally, and everyone from teachers to fellow students dealt with him gingerly.

His next period was free, so Todd slipped into the library and fired up his computer. A Google search for "Franklin Whitestone" proved eye-opening. There were 27,000 hits, up 18,000 from the day before. A number of sites offered him the video of this morning's melee with the press, which Todd watched with a grim expression. His worry, however, was mixed with a certain glee. Who knew Dad was such a tiger? Made him proud.

But the parental tiger was in clearly in trouble. What could a son do to help? Obviously, it was time for a major overhaul of Todd's website and the popular blog he updated daily. Todd had a ton of things to say on the topic of a belief in God, things he had so far only hinted at in his cyberspace reflections. Perhaps he could divert attention from Dad for a spell—give him a respite.

He began to plan his moves. An interesting idea occurred to him at once.

Catherine Whitestone, Franklin's mother, lived in a suburb of Columbus called Upper Arlington, in a home that was far too large for one person, but, alas, she was the sole remaining resident of what was once a family of six. Her four children were grown and gone, and her much-loved husband, Alexander, to her considerable annoyance, had died on her just two years before, leaving Catherine to rattle around the big house alone. She was loath to move, having terra-formed this lovely domicile through the decades to suit her every whim, but she was 69 years old now, and she knew, sadly, that it was time to trade down and move to someplace smaller, easier to care for, a place with fewer steps and a washer and dryer on the same floor as the master bedroom.

This Monday morning she sat in front of her tv, remote in hand, having just snapped the picture off when that local news showoff Harold Wang concluded his onsite reporting of the "vicious attack" Franklin Whitestone had made on the innocent members of the media. Catherine, a dangerous woman herself when aroused, was fuming. It was obvious to the veriest dunce that when Franklin lost it and stampeded through the reporters it was because they had baited him beyond endurance. He'd inherited his hair-trigger temper from her, and she knew that in his situation she would have done much the same thing. Being smaller, she might have had to knee a few of them in the gonads (or some similar anatomy for the women), but she too would have bulled her way through, pleased to see any of them go down.

However, Catherine was annoyed that her second oldest had made a fool of himself on national tv. An atheist herself, as was her late husband, Alexander, she had little tolerance for those who really believed in what Franklin had called an "imaginary friend." How could any serious person put such nonsense at the center of life? Hadn't they investigated the history and underpinnings of their faith (which, if done with an open mind, usually resulted in depression at the shallowness and sordidness of it all)? Weren't they interested in what was true and what was not?

These were strongly held beliefs in the Whitestone family, where the familial goal had always been grounded in reality. But it was also understood that such opinions put them in a distinct minority, and it was foolishness to needlessly poke the religious bear. Do that and of course you were going to be mauled, which was what was happening to her son. The things he said on the Jimmy Ball Show were beliefs better confined to a sympathetic gathering, say the Whitestone dining room table at meal time. And what made her even more cross was that Franklin knew this. She and Alexander had drilled it into their children that speaking up on this topic at the wrong moment was verboten. If you sneezed and people said, "God Bless You," you said "thank you" in reply. If a public prayer was offered at some gathering and everyone bowed their heads in communal reverence, you didn't need to bow yours, but you also didn't look disrespectful or disgusted by the assumption that all present were comfortable with obeisance to whichever god was being addressed.

And, as a general rule, the children were taught that if someone had the effrontery to ask what religion you belonged to it was perfectly all right to say "none," and, if they persisted, to explain, respectfully, your personal stance on this mass delusion. However, general rules have exceptions, and she had always emphasized the one that Franklin had demonstrably forgotten last night: if your explanation is likely to get you slugged in the nose, duck the question and avoid having to duck the punch. Now Franklin appeared to be out for the count, and, like any good mother, she was concerned.

While she was mulling this over, the doorbell rang. Catherine peeked through the living room curtains, which had an angled view of the front door, and was very surprised to see Molly Schultz and a camera crew from WMJZ on her doorstep. Catherine smiled, lacing her fingers together, turning them over, cracking her knuckles. This was going to be fun.

The Google search that Todd initiated accurately reflected what was going on everywhere. Franklin's remarks on the Jimmy Ball show were widely disseminated, and even more widely condemned. Moreover, the condemnation came from virtually every religion on the planet. Christian groups varied in their response from mere denunciation of secular humanism to calls for the execution of atheists. Muslims said much the same thing, pointing out that imposing the death penalty for atheism is arguably one of the tenets of the Quran, and that even if it were not, atheism was certainly illegal in most Muslim countries. Jews, as a group, were the most moderate, typically condemning non-belief, but not punishing it either. On the other side, there was a rather vocal positive response from various groups of atheists and freethinkers, lauding Franklin for stating so publicly what they had been saying for centuries. Theirs, however, was a small voice, hard to hear in the global hurricane.

The defenses of God and religion were both traditional ("Where did it all come from if there were no cosmic creator") to original ("Whitestone has to be kidding—he must be God's mouthpiece, sent to test our commitment to His message").

Blogs, chatrooms, emails, pulpits, talk shows, letters to the editor and the like were firestorms of controversy, and each day the volume increased, both in number and in the ferocity of response. Arguments broke out at work, in schools, over the dinner table, at cocktail parties, on dates, in bars, and even in bed, as pillow talk degenerated to pillow fights and worse.

The story grew and grew. Atheism had been around for a long time, of course, but suddenly it was in the gun sights of a lot of very angry people, and anyone framed in the cross hairs was in trouble. Franklin Whitestone had become the poster child for this firestorm, an even unhappier position.

Later that same day, the response from the evangelical wing of the far right was delivered by Pastor Evan Johnson, spiritual head and undisputed leader of the Great Harvest Today mega church located in a Columbus suburb, but seen nationwide by over 400,000 of the faithful every week thanks to the wonder of cable television.

"What I don't understand," said Pastor Johnson on his afternoon tv program, The Gospel Half Hour, "is how anyone can deny the existence of God when the evidence is all around us. Look at all the miracles occurring day after day!"

His guest for this program, Annie Couture, replied, "Oh, I agree, Evan! God is *everywhere*! He talks to me all day long, and He's part of every decision I make!"

"Mine too, and Amen to that" said Billy Keck, Evan Johnson's announcer and co-host. He raised his hands and bowed his head.

"What Franklin Whitestone doesn't appreciate," said Johnson, bringing the focus back to himself, "is how God is at work every day in the lives of those of us who've been blessed by His grace and born again. We couldn't get through a single day without God. I know I sure couldn't."

Keck and Couture nodded their heads enthusiastically. "Amens" and "Praise Gods" emanated from the panel and the audience for a full ten seconds.

Johnson earnestly added, "Can you imagine what the world would be like if there were no God?"

There was an uncharacteristic pause in the show, as they all three thought about this.

"No, Evan," Couture finally said, "I can't imagine that. It's too foreign an idea."

Johnson elaborated. "If I woke up one morning and no longer believed in God, life wouldn't be worth living. I *need* for Him to be there for me. He's my life preserver."

Keck continued this theme. "If I awoke and my faith was gone, I don't know how I could cope. I can't imagine a world without God there to support me, and I don't want to start all over, spiritually naked, with no guarantees, no one to pray to at night to help solve my problems."

"No life after death," Couture commented. They paused again to consider that.

"It gives me the willies. It's too gruesome," Johnson finally said with a shake of his head. "I would rather not have been born than to exist in a world without God." He looked into the camera. "So I have a message for Mr. Franklin Whitestone, who thinks he knows everything." Johnson raised his head as the camera pulled in tight to give the home viewers a close-up of his dark brown eyes. "*You're wrong!*" he declared in a tone brooking no opposition. "And if you were just talking about tomorrow's weather forecast or predicting the score of some sporting event, I wouldn't give you a second thought, and neither should my Brothers and Sisters in Christ."

Now he started to get to the heart of the matter. He stood up and the camera panned back as he began to pace back and forth, his voice starting the sing-song quality that mesmerized his followers and made him the force that he was in the evangelical world.

"NO!" he boomed as he halted long enough to point into the camera. "Franklin Whitestone isn't talking about the weather." He began pacing again with a purposeful strut that made him look strikingly similar to Mick Jagger during an encore at a Rolling Stones concert. "He was talking about God! God—the Lord Almighty. God—the Maker of Heaven and Earth. God—the Divine creator of all things good and holy. And that is something entirely different from a mere weather forecast!" Johnson stopped again, sweating now and breathing hard, ready to deliver his coup de grâce.

"Brothers and sisters, the apostle John tells us in his gospel exactly what kind of man claims that God does not exist. He said, 'You belong to your father, *the devil*, and you want to carry out your father's desire. He was a murderer from the beginning, not holding to the truth, for there is no truth in him. When he lies, he speaks his native language, for he is a liar and the father of lies.'

"And I say to you, Mr. Franklin Whitestone, stop doing the work of Satan! Turn back to the love of God while you still have time! Accept the Lord Jesus Christ as your savior and you shall know the eternal and perfect love of God. Refuse, and you will spend all eternity in Hell!" The camera had been moving in tighter and tighter and finally had framed Johnson's face. He paused for just a moment and then said, "We'll be right back." (And that did seem likely.)

"Jesus!" Franklin Whitestone said, as he cut his thumb and began to bleed all over his kitchen counter. He'd been cutting a lemon peel for his martini when the blade slipped. He grabbed a towel to stem the flow of blood, which worked, but the wound itself hurt like hell. "Goddamn it!" he muttered. While he brought the situation under control, it occurred to Franklin that the leading atheist in the country oughtn't to be using religious expletives.

He'd had this thought in the past, but attention to it was now a more urgent priority. People were going to be judging everything he said very closely. The problem was that these religious references were so ingrained in everyone's vocabulary that they were hard to avoid and replace with other more appropriate phrases. Show Americans, believers or not, some amazing sight, like a train wreck or a total eclipse of the sun, and the words "Oh, my God!" uniformly sprang to their lips.

Franklin had never before in his life fixed a martini at noon—indeed he rarely drank at all, his weekend misadventure in NYC notwithstanding. But today a martini seemed the appropriate response to having his life crash around him like a building imploding

He'd begun to appreciate his precarious situation half an hour ago when he'd again managed to sneak into his home via the neighbors' back yard and his own patio door, and found things were no better. To begin with, the reporters were camped out on his doorstep in even larger numbers than before.

As he came through the patio door, the phone was ringing, and he'd made the mistake of answering it.

"We are watching your house, Numb Nuts," the male caller said in a level, unemotional voice. "Guns are trained on your front door. We're waiting for you, you bastard! If you don't come out, Goddamned sissy that you are, we're gonna set fire to your house!" The caller continued to talk, but Franklin hurriedly hung up, and backed away from the phone, which, demonically, immediately began to ring immediately. He disconnected the receiver from the jack in the wall. Subsequent callers would reach a busy signal.

His answering machine had quit accepting messages after it reached 99, and Franklin only played a few of these. Some were from friends and family (his mother insisted he call her, and Franklin made a note to do that—his mother was not to be trifled with), but most were from strangers. And while there were supportive messages ("Just wanted to say congratulations on pulling the rug out from under all those religious goofs"), most were threats delivered at top volume and describing not only eternal damnation in the next world, but likely events in Franklin's immediate future, such as castration, de-tonguing, stoning, and quite often torture and death by other, very inventive, means. His cell phone was also a delivery system for identical threats, and he'd shut it off after clearing it of messages. How had his cell's number gotten out?

A quick glance at his emails revealed the same treatment there too, and he'd also deleted them unread, his hands beginning to shake. Franklin had no doubt that tomorrow would mark the start of tons of snail mail that it would not be profitable to read.

Slowly, as if he were 90 years old and unsteady on his feet, Franklin had felt along the walls until he arrived at his kitchen. There he'd used the ice dispenser in his refrigerator to fill a large glass, and then bent over a low cabinet from which he extracted bottles of gin and vermouth. He was pleased

72

to find a still-good lemon in the basket of fruit he kept on the kitchen counter. A martini was an occasional pleasure, and he did like to have the ingredients at hand when it came up. Shortly thereafter he'd cut his thumb and immediately strung together three inappropriate religious references: "Jesus," "hurt like hell," and "Goddamn it!" One more problem, this one linguistic, to add to all the others.

Now, he took a sip from the martini. Yes, yes, this might help. He staggered back to the living room and plopped down in his overstuffed easy chair, taking increasingly bigger gulps.

What was going to happen to him? Kelly was pissed, his job appeared to be in toilet, and huge numbers of people were demanding his head on a pole. He remembered his prediction last night that today would be a better day than yesterday, and the thought made him snort in something like amusement.

Happily, the trembling in his hands stopped as the martini did its job.

With a sigh, he mumbled, "Oh, Lord!" and then immediately frowned. He'd done it again—an automatic religious response to a non-religious stimulus.

Well, if he couldn't solve any of his other problems, perhaps he could do something about this minor annoyance. What could he substitute—train himself to say—in situations where some sort of phrase was needed to express surprise, or dismay, or wonder?

He tried to think of famous ejaculations used by others. Shakespeare's characters said things like "odd bodkins" or "egad," but those sounded too stilted. Little Orphan Annie was famous for "leaping lizards," but Franklin was far too macho to imitate that sad child. Charlie Brown's favorite exclamation was "rats!" and Franklin experimented with saying that out loud a couple of times before discarding it. Part of him liked "rats," but another part thought it came across as forced, unoriginal. What I need, he thought, is a euphemism with punch. Something no one else says. Something individual to me, Franklin Whitestone.

Perhaps he could invoke the names of now-discredited gods of old: "By Zeus!" for example, or "Oh, Baal!" Hmm.

Then he remembered the alleged primitive belief that the world rests on the back of a giant turtle (which in turn sits atop a stack of other turtles, etc.). Perhaps there was a solution there.

"Great Turtle!" he exclaimed out loud, and that made him laugh.

As the martini disappeared over the course of the next twenty minutes, Franklin went to the kitchen to fix another. Of course, that probably wasn't wise, but—truth be told—nothing else sounded better. He pictured his cleaning lady coming in tomorrow and finding him snoring atop a mound of empty gin bottles.

"Turtles preserve us," he muttered as he looked around for the remains of the lemon.

CHAPTER FIVE

TODD IS GOD

They had talked about it steadily since Sunday night.

"The man must die," Nan finally said to Dan.

"Yes," Dan replied.

"You get the guns and I'll get the car."

That surprised him. "Now?" He asked her.

"Now."

After the slightest of pauses he nodded.

When he should have been doing other things, Todd Whitestone spent the rest of his Monday high school day working at his computer, and then went home and continued his labors until two o'clock in the morning.

His project was interrupted only by a quick dinner with his mother.

"Here's something interesting. Did you know that your grandmother had a run-in with the media today?" Mary Whitestone asked her son, passing him his plate.

"No," he said. "Grandma Catherine, you mean?"

"Yes. She called here with the news; she's trying to get in touch with your father. WMJZ arrived on her doorstep this afternoon, anxious to interview her about the religious views of her son."

"Uh oh," Todd said. "How bad did it get?"

Mary smiled. "They decided not to run the piece. Apparently she told them to go fuck themselves, and they had trouble paraphrasing that."

They both laughed. That was Catherine Whitestone all right.

Supper over, Todd returned to his room and fired up the computer. He returned to redoing his website *cum* blog so that it now focused on a complete refutation of religious belief, and did so in as convincing a manner as his considerable talents allowed.

Todd arranged it so that any visitor to the site would first be faced with a quote on point, one that he planned would change weekly. From his considerable collection of religious themed quotations, the one Todd selected for the first day was the famous aphorism from "The Ethics of Belief" (1877) by William Kingdon Clifford, an English philosopher/mathematician: "It is wrong always, everywhere, and for anyone, to believe anything upon insufficient evidence." His father had brought this stark assertion to Todd's attention years ago. It would, of course, appeal to a lawyer. And although there had been stern attacks on Clifford's statement as a philosophy, most notably by William James, both father and son believed it stood the test of time.

The second thing Todd's website offered was a selection of "click here" options, the most prominent of which was a link to Todd's blog, now entitled provocatively "TODD IS GOD." He thought that would get the visitor's attention (which in the event proved only too true). After that heading, the entry began:

Since it is obvious to anyone who approaches the question objectively that there is no God, heaven, hell, angels, devils, Valhalla, paradise, or the survival after death of any sort of "soul," it is necessary to ask what should replace these things? Once all this superstition stops running the world, how can we possibly carry on?

The answer is that each of us has to become our *own* God and personally work to make this world as perfect as we can. Under this concept, I, Todd, am God, but so are you, and you, and you. Each of us must jump to the oars in the human lifeboat and row mightily to keep the craft afloat and moving steadily through the waters.

Religion is not, as is often supposed, necessary to teach morality. We don't need some ancient book to tell us that it is wrong to kill, steal, commit adultery, as well as a host of sins not specifically listed in the decalogue: lying, dumping toxic wastes in the woods, failing to return a favor, and _____ (fill in the blank with any conduct that truly pisses you off).

This lecture went on for twelve paragraphs, much of it a rehash of famous arguments against the existence of God (but his were, Todd thought happily, exceedingly well expressed).

The reader was then invited to view a video Todd had prepared this very day (but which he planned to tweak for months thereafter to make it more and more persuasive). The link was entitled "WHERE GOD CAME FROM." Clicking on it to start this visual screed led to the following:

It began with a cartoon showed a tribe of cavemen huddled around a fire. Todd's voice-over intoned, "In the early days, human beings did not understand how nature worked, so when there was some sort of problem, say with the weather," here the cartoon changed to depict the unfortunate cavemen being struck by lightning, "they were understandably terrified, and

76

all they could think was that they must have offended some sort of awesome unseen presence—their version of god."

The video switched to Todd himself talking directly to the camera. "We now know that no god was responsible for the weather disaster. The cavemen were scared by a simple meteorological phenomenon that we now understand well. God wasn't guilty. But their misapprehension of what was going on was nonetheless useful to primitive man: it calmed him down and, by giving power to those who explained the disaster and how to prevent it in the future (worship this god, make animal sacrifices, behave better in the future, do what I tell you), unified the tribe and allowed it move forward."

The picture switched to a new cartoon, this one depicting a man in medieval garb staring at the stars through a telescope. Todd's voice said, "As time went on, gods were used as the answer to all mysteries. How did the heavens work? God created the earth at the center of everything and made the sun and stars revolve around it—pushed by angels according to some religions! Those who questioned this were accused of heresy or witchcraft and treated badly." The cartoon showed the same astronomer tied to a stake, engulfed by flames, screaming in terror.

The camera returned to Todd, who said, "Charles Dickens once commented that 'The earth would still move round the sun, though the whole Catholic Church said No,' and he was right. Angels were not necessary to move celestial bodies. Astronomy is an exact science and we now know to a certainty that the earth is not at the center of the universe. It is instead one of a number of planets revolving around a sun that is only one of 100,000 billion suns in a galaxy we call the Milky Way, which itself is only one of 100,000 billion or so other galaxies. We are on a mere dot in the universe. Think of that! It isn't fiction! I'm not making this up! We know it to be real, folks. We are floating around in all that immensity right now as you hear this. Isn't that wonderful? Scary, too."

The picture now changed to a beautiful view of the planet Earth taken from the moon. "One after another the explanations that God was responsible for this and that—earthquakes, tsunamis, hurricanes, pestilence, famine, or whatever the current terrible problem—turned out to be wrong. As civilization explored and understood more and more, there was less and less for a god to do. Nonetheless people couldn't, wouldn't give up their gods. If something bad happened . . . ," the cartoon showed a drawing of the battle of Gettysburg, "there just had to be some divine reason for allowing it, with the divinity 'working in mysterious ways,' it was said. Abraham Lincoln once speculated that God must have had some deep, unknown reason for permitting the Civil War to wreak its awful destruction." The picture switched to a photo of emaciated prisoners in Auschwitz. "Pope Pius XI, at the rise of the Nazi movement, made a similar comment: 'Kindly God, who has allowed all this happen at present, undoubtedly has his purpose.'"

Todd came back on. "What sort of omnipotent god would allow, much less want, these horrible things to occur? Come on, people! The instigator of these horrors was no god, but man himself, unable to control his worst impulses. God, once again, is innocent."

The picture was now of General Stonewall Jackson.

"That didn't keep the participants in these events from seeing their god everywhere. After one bloody battle in which the South prevailed, the victorious Stonewall Jackson exulted, '[H]e who does not see the hand of God in this is blind, sir, blind!' I somehow doubt that any god would advance the cause of slavery in such a brutal fashion. Jackson was simply wrong."

Todd himself once again took the screen.

"So let's sum up. In all of history no god was necessary to influence events or make the physical world work. People, from the caves right up to the present day, are simply mistaken thinking otherwise, but they have so much invested in the existence of their gods that they definitely don't want to hear what is clearly true. They put their hands over their ears and make la-la-la sounds to drown out the possible explosion of their beliefs. Explain how life was created and evolved to reach the amazing complexity we now see all over this fascinating planet, and very religious people will be outraged at the exclusion of their god from the explanation. They will demand the reinstatement of that god in spite of the complete lack of evidence of His participation in any of it."

The picture changed to a color photo of a remote galaxy, the stars swirling about each other in a spiral of beauty.

"So, if there are no gods, where did it all come from? The answer is that we don't know, though there are some very interesting hypothesizes around: string theory being the most recent tantalizing possibility. But the fact that we haven't yet figured this out doesn't mean that a god is the answer, any more than it meant that god was the answer for why the cavemen were struck by lightning. We'll keep exploring. Eventually we'll discover what is really going on."

The camera returned to Todd. "The late Isaac Asimov, a scientist who dedicated his life to explaining to the public how things worked, was once asked if he believed in UFOs. He surprised everyone by saying yes, but then he explained that the initials should be taken literally: *unidentified* flying objects. The fact that we haven't yet labeled the object doesn't mean it was an alien spacecraft. That is highly unlikely. To Asimov a UFO was nothing more than a phenomenon still under investigation."

A photo of a church congregation deep in prayer filled the screen. "I know how hard it is—how scary it is—to give up a belief in your god, and to see the world for what it truly is. But I urge you to take a deep breath and make that effort—look around you with open eyes. All that you can see—the stars, the flowers, the hardships of life, the joy of your family—these things have perfectly natural explanations. Nothing supernatural is needed. The clothes have no emperor."

Todd appeared one last time. "It is surely a mistake to run society based on a mistaken principle. So in place of a god doing all the work, do it yourself. Ponder what your personal role should be in our complicated civilization. Be your own god—regulate your own world." He smiled his most winning smile. "I'll try to hold up my end too."

The screen went blank.

Franklin had fallen asleep Monday afternoon, the martinis having made him relax way too much, and awoke with a vicious headache just before four o'clock. He downed two aspirins and plopped down heavily in his leather armchair to consider carefully the mess his life had become.

The reporters were still outside. He could hear them, and once in awhile someone pounded on the door, or the bell rang. Incredibly, the patio entrance trick (with its necessity of trespassing on the rear neighbors' yard) seemed to have eluded their notice, but Franklin knew that that little secret couldn't be kept much longer. He might go in or out at the most two more times before the jig would be up and he would be trapped either in or outside his home.

Clearly, it was time to move somewhere else until things calmed down, but where to go? In spite of Howard Ray's suggestion that he leave town, Franklin was stubbornly not yet ready to do that. Kelly's place, of course, was out, and this was an odd and painful thought. Her house had been a second home for him for the last two years. Half his personal stuff—clothing, toiletries, etc.—was still over there. Kelly necessarily must see it constantly, reminding her of him. Would that help or hurt their shaky relationship? He didn't know.

Perhaps Mary would take him in. He thought about that. In spite of their troubled history, they'd become friends once again, weekly talking at length on the telephone, supposedly about Todd's progress through life (they were both a bit afraid of him, truth to tell), but really just for the pleasure they'd regained from conversation with each other. But even if she were willing to have him, would that be smart? The press was not likely to be so easily thrown off the trail, and Franklin could readily imagine the whole

79

hungry hoard showing up tomorrow, like the morning newspaper, on Mary and Todd's doorstep, forcing him to climb out their window or leap from the roof or something equally improbable.

If not there, where?

He rejected the idea of his mother's house for two reasons. Not only would there be the same likelihood that the reporters would quickly track him down, but Franklin could only take limited exposure to the control-freak-in-chief before he'd have to leap from her roof even with no reporter in sight.

His head pounding, Franklin risked taking another aspirin, and then decided to see if he couldn't flush out his system with liquids that were actually good for him. He started with a glass of milk, and although it tasted like paste to his damaged palate, he drank the whole glass with a dedicated determination. A half hour after that he had a big slug of water. There was orange juice in the refrigerator, but the thought of its acidity made his stomach twist like taffy.

Without knowing where he was going, but determined to get out of here, Franklin began packing. How about a hotel? That would be expensive, but he could use the pampering and convenience it provided (room service, a maid, wake up calls, etc.), and, carefully considered, he certainly could afford it for a week (month?) or so. Come to think of it there were a couple of first rate bed and breakfast inns around the city, and it would be cheaper to lodge in one of them for the duration. There was a new one in German Village (called Rise and Shine, he remembered); he might check it out.

How would he pay for it? If he used a credit card that would leave a trail determined trackers might follow, and Franklin didn't want to have to move more than once after he next fled out his patio door. Cash would work, of course, and he could get a steady supply of it from any ATM. That, coupled with registration under an assumed name, should allow him to stay hidden.

His immediate future settled, Franklin called the *Columbus Dispatch* and stopped delivery, instructed the post office to hold his mail, adjusted the thermostat to its lowest functioning level, made sure all the lights were out, picked up his suitcase and laptop, and slipped out the patio door.

He wondered how long it would be it would be safe to come home again. The answer would have surprised him.

Nan and Dan drove their SUV onto the street where Whitestone lived, but the crowd in front of his door caused them to keep right on going to the next corner, where they quickly turned.

"How are we going to get to him now?" Dan asked, pulling over.

80

Silence while they thought about it.

"Nab him going in or out of his office?" Nan suggested.

"Yes," said Dan, taking a map from the glove compartment.

By Tuesday morning, Jake Richardson was having similar problems. Whitestone hadn't returned his phone call, and that really steamed him. Jake had been on his knees for nearly half an hour last night praying for Whitestone's soul, in addition to his usual petitions to God for various causes: the return of his wife and daughter, help with controlling his drinking and his temper, forgiveness for the anger he still felt against his parents, and his own certain knowledge that he was not living his life the way a true Christian should.

Jake's mother had disappeared early one December when he was about to turn nine years old. There was never an explanation. She'd been there that morning when Jake went off to school, and wasn't there when he got home. Instead he found his father rampaging around the place, swearing and banging the walls, his eyes wide with anger, his breath foul with alcohol. Trembling—in such a mood it was a good idea to stay out of Dad's way— Jake scurried past him to the small room he shared with his four year old brother, Eddie, pleased that Dad didn't seem to notice him. As usual, little Eddie, crying in gasping gulps of terror, was hiding in the corner of their bedroom, shielded in part by the bed itself, staying as far from the door as possible. When, whispering, Jake asked what was going on, Eddie just cried the harder, rolling onto his side and curling up into a ball. Even when things were comparatively good, the kid barely spoke, and, Jake thought, his brother was only alive in the physical sense—he'd never had a personality any different than a terrified puppy. Jake pulled Eddie off the floor and onto the bed they shared, and held him tightly, making shushing sounds.

"We don't want Dad to hear us," he warned in a soft voice, knowing from experience that it was futile. Eddie was beyond comforting. The good thing was that Dad was making such a racket that he couldn't hear them, and even if he did pause for breath, the sound of Eddie crying was not unusual or worth investigating.

Jake's mother was never seen again, and, when Jake finally worked up the courage to ask where she had gone, his father smacked him across the face and told him to mind his own fucking business. Following this Jake cried himself to sleep steadily each night for the next five months. The truth was that he still sometimes cried over her loss, most recently just three days ago.

81

Both of his parents had been very, very religious, demanding that Jake memorize verses from the Bible every night, a task made all the harder because Jake had a great deal of trouble reading. There were a lot of incentives to get these recitations right—his father yanked off his belt and flogged Jake hard if the boy made mistakes. Later in life, Jake liked to say that this harsh treatment made him stronger, and perhaps it did.

Jake's mother had always been a kind woman, and Jake would have never accepted the Word of God as completely as he now did if his mother hadn't shown him what being a Christian really meant. The whole family went to church on Sunday and to services of various kinds on one or more weekday evenings, and this continued even after his mother disappeared. The boys never missed Sunday school, and Jake managed to sing a passable tenor in the church choir up through the second year of high school, when his voice changed and ruined everything.

When his father died of a diseased liver, Jake, already a tall kid and able to pass for older than his 15 years, ran away from the foster care home to which he and Eddie had been sent. Jake promptly found a job in construction, and had been at that ever since, not counting the times he'd been fired for missing too much work, or because of his terrible temper, or, in one case that still pissed him off, because he proselytized his fellow workers to the point that they complained in a body to that asshole foreman. There had also been the terrible year he had spent in prison for manslaughter—Jake, drunk, had collided with another car and killed two teenagers.

Jake never knew what had happened to his brother, Eddie. He regretted not putting any effort into finding him. Maybe he would ask around in a week or so when things were less complicated.

After a quick cup of coffee, Jake hurried off to work, and actually had a very productive day. He and the gigantic Suzy May, his one true friend, dug a sewer together. All day Jake thought hard about how to get to Franklin Whitestone, both spiritually and physically. He was going to have to knock on his door, that was clear, but what could he say when they were face to face that would bring this nonbeliever to the healing power of Jesus Christ? He rehearsed some possible biblical verses in his head, but none sounded quite right to him. He decided he'd have to trust God to put the right words in his mouth when the important moment came to witness for Whitestone.

Jake returned home just before six o'clock and had a bowl of soup while he watched the evening news. For the first time he saw Whitestone's battle with the press, and was sickened by the blatant sneering Whitestone once again did at religion, while pretending to be oh, so superior. A fancy lawyer, a know-it-all. Psalm 17:14 sprang to his lips: "O Lord, by your hand save me from such men, from men of this world whose reward is in this life."

It didn't look possible to get to Whitestone simply by knocking on his door. Maybe it would be easier to catch him coming or going to his office, or to a friend's house. Jake wasn't sure what to try first, but he trusted that the Lord would guide him in this, as in all things. He'd pray on it tonight.

The phone started ringing at the home Mary Whitestone shared with her son on Tuesday morning just after ten o'clock. Mary was at the computer writing her next travel column for Jaunt Magazine. Since the headquarters of that periodical was in New York, she almost always worked from home except for the extensive periods each year when she was on the road gathering material for both the column and a new book she was writing on the waterfalls of the world.

"Hello?" she said into the phone.

"Tell your smart-aleck son that he can eat shit and die!" the high-pitched voice on the other end (male, female?) said, and hung up before she could reply.

Stunned, Mary cradled the phone. Now what had Todd done? There had been, alas, a number of very unfavorable reactions to some of his past projects, like the time he wrote a letter to every newspaper in Ohio demanding the impeachment of the President of the United States for what he deemed "outrageous crimes against all decency." Not only had that produced a barrage of overly interesting phone calls and letters, but it had attracted the attention of the Secret Service.

She was tempted to call Todd on his cell and find out what was what going on this time, but land line phone rang almost immediately and answered that question before it was asked.

It was Betty Alice, a good friend from dance class. "Have you seen Todd's website recently?" she asked.

"Uh, no," Mary replied, dread spreading through her bones.

"Oh, Mary, honey, it's bad!"

"What does it say?"

"It is the same sort of rant that your ex-husband let loose with on tv the other night, only there's more of it and even comes with Todd's own personal video proving that there is no God. He goes on to say that *he* is God."

Mary's eyebrows smashed into her hairline. "*Todd* is God?"

"That's what he says. A couple of times."

Mary didn't know how to reply to that one. All she could manage was "I'll make him take it off right away."

Betty Alice continued, "Oh, I'm afraid it's too late for that. It's all over the internet and spreading fast. Todd will be on the news by this evening. The national news."

"Oh, God!"

"Prayers like that probably won't help either. The crazies are going to be after his hide. Now listen! Lock up your house and be careful who you let in!"

Mary thought about that. Finally she said, "Thanks for the heads-up, Betty Alice. I need to do damage control fast. Talk to you later."

As she hung up she decided that she should pull Todd out of school right away and move him to someplace safe. As she went online to look up the number for the main office of the high school, the front door opened and Todd walked in. Surprised—he hadn't been at school very long—she called out his name, and he came to her, smiling hesitantly.

"Hi, Mom. Some trouble at school, so Principal Barnhart thought it would be wise for me to get out of there. He said I should check in with him before coming back. Oh, and he wants you to call him."

"Todd! What happened at school? Are you all right?" She put her arm around his waist.

He shrugged. "Sure. When I got to school some guys were yelling at me in the parking lot, but I didn't catch what it was about. Then my friend Stubby Allen caught up to me as I was entering the building and clapped me on the back, saying I was the bravest dude he ever met. From that I figured out what he was talking about. It was . . ."

"Your website," she said, cutting him off, disengaging her arm to face him squarely.

He looked sheepish. "You read it?" he asked.

She glanced in the direction of the telephone. "There've been calls. No, I haven't read it. You and I are about to look at it together, and then we're going to wipe it clean. You will replace it with cartoon bunnies gamboling amidst flowers or something like that."

His eyebrows turned down sharply. "Mom, I'm not going to erase what I said! I'm proud of it, and—even better— it helps get Dad off the hook!"

"And hangs you up in his place! No, Todd. I won't have it!"

"You haven't even read what I posted! You'll agree with the things I said!"

"I will read it in a few minutes, but assuming it says what everyone says it says, it's history."

He folded his arms. "I don't think so," he said.

She folded hers. "You don't get to vote," she replied.

He unfolded his arms and raised them, palms up, toward the ceiling. "Mom!" he pleaded, "don't do this to me. I'll look like a spineless jerk if I pull the website!"

She took his left forearm in hers and looked earnestly into his eyes. "Now listen carefully," she instructed. "Both your father and I have more or less given you free reign to explore your vast talents, and while it has not always been easy to gulp and support you, we've been very, very proud of almost everything you've done. Note the word 'almost.'

"But you're only sixteen, and at that age even the brightest of us makes mistakes. You have made one now, and it's a dangerous misstep. Some moron using fowl language called a couple of minutes ago and threatened your life. Think how much fun that is for a mother to hear. And he won't be the only one."

Todd looked somber at this. He started to say something but thought better of it.

Mary continued. "I don't think I've ever put my foot down and flatly overruled what you want to do, or at least not since you were seven years old and that incident with the dying skunk, but that moment has come. We're going to look over the controversial content you posted last night, and if I think it's dangerous, get out the gamboling bunnies." She paused and stared into his eyes. "Do you understand me?"

Todd's shoulders fell and he sighed loudly. "I do," he said, clearly unhappy.

"Good. Now tell me what happened at school that so caught Principal Barnhart's attention."

Todd rolled his eyes and made a gesture of exasperation as he said, "Well, these students surrounded me at my locker and started yelling. It was all nonsense about God and hell and threats of boils and warts, and some other crap I don't remember now. Then things got loud and the crowd grew bigger. Some of them were on my side, I guess, because there was a scuffle of some sort off to my left, near the vending machines. I was trying to explain my position calmly when one of the students hit me over the head with a calculus book, and it really hurt! I would have fought back, but— well, she was a girl. In fact, all of the ones who surrounded me to begin with were girls, so what was I to do? Being hit like that made me mad, and I knocked her calculus book to the ground and, gee, I guess, I also sort of . . . *snarled* at them. I'm not proud of that, but I was cornered and I went primitive. It must've scared them, because the girls quit talking and backed away. One of them screamed something like '*MAD DOG!*' and that's when two of the teachers waded into the crowd."

"And they took you to the Principal's office?"

"Yeah, just like a third-grader caught with spit balls or something. Principal Barnhart was actually pretty cool about it all. He told me he had just been reading my website, and that I had flabbergasted him once again, whatever that meant. It's a compliment, right?"

Now his mother sighed. "I know only too well what he meant. Let's go look at it." She led the way down the hall to her office where her computer was up and running, and she motioned him into the chair. "Do it," she said. Todd tapped the keys and then sat back as the colorful Todd Whitestone website sprang to the screen. "There," he said, pride in his voice.

"Get up and let me sit," she told him, and they switched places.

Mary began reading and her eyes got wider and wider.

On the way to Rise and Shine, the bed-and-breakfast that had taken his reservation over the phone (he used "William Blackstone" as a pseudonym, sort of a legal joke as well as a play on his own name), it occurred to Franklin that he'd become far too recognizable in the last couple of days and that he couldn't successfully hide out anywhere for very long if he continued to look like himself. He pondered what to do about that, and ended up at a costume shop on the northwest side of town that he found on Google. It was called "Masquerade," but the elegance of its title was belied by the shabbiness of the store itself, which was located in a seedy strip mall among similar small businesses, all appearing to be in a contest to see which would go under first. He later learned that this gave a false impression of the durability of Masquerade. It had been operating on this same spot for twenty years, and was actually doing quite well.

A bell tinkled loudly as Franklin entered. He was apparently the only customer, and consequently he was waited upon immediately when a giant, very muscular man with a buzz cut stepped out from one of the rows, a clipboard in his hand, and said, "May I help you?"

Thinking that this guy looked like he should be selling barbells and not theatrical accessories, Franklin nodded as the man lumbered up to him, all smiles.

"I have a sort of strange request," Franklin began. "For reasons I don't want to go into, I have to be disguised for the next couple of days when I am out in public, and I figured you could show me how to do that." He smiled sheepishly, as if confessing a major embarrassment.

The giant smiled even more broadly and said, "You don't have to explain the reasons, Mr. Whitestone. I'm up to speed on this one."

Franklin blanched. "You know me?"

The man laughed and gently clapped his shoulder. "Most of the world knows you." Seeing Franklin's face, he added, "Don't worry. You're among friends. I'd be pleased to help you escape from the God Squad, and I promise not to blow the whistle on you when you leave the store."

Much relieved by this, but worried at how recognizable he'd become, Franklin said thanks and asked the man's name.

"Corbin Milk," the clerk replied. "No lie. Real name. Okay—feel free to make jokes, particularly if you can think of some I haven't heard. Try to avoid 'Got milk?' or anything with a cow in it."

Franklin smiled at the big man. "Please help me, Mr. Milk," he said with great sincerity.

"Corbin."

"Franklin then."

"I'm honored to help you, Franklin. Come over here," and he walked Franklin to a shelf two rows over from the front door. He began pulling bottles off the shelf and then turned to shelves behind him and took down four boxes. "This way," he directed, and they went to the back of the store where there was a dressing table, mirrored on three sides. Milk gestured Franklin into a chair at the table. He dragged another chair up beside him and sat down.

"First," Milk began, opening a box, "I suggest a mustache, at least until you can grow one of your own. I have a couple here to choose from, but I'd recommend you look at this one first. You want one big enough that it calls attention away from the other features of your face, but not so large that it seems grotesque. What do you think of this?" He held up a dark brown piece of hair that was a good color match for Franklin's real hair.

"It looks awfully small," Franklin commented.

"That's because it is only half of the whole. See." Mile held up an identical slice of hair. "We paste one half close to the other just under your nose."

Franklin nodded. "I see. How do we make it stick? It would be very embarrassing if it came off at the wrong moment."

Milk agreed. "More than embarrassing. It could get you hurt. Have you been listening to the talk shows today? All about Franklin Whitestone. Really more yelling than talk."

That caused a shiver to run down Franklin's spine. "I haven't seen any tv," he said.

"Actually I was talking about the radio. It's on in the back room. But I did happen see your tv exploits, both the one in New York on Sunday and your encounter with the Columbus news hounds yesterday morning."

"Oh."

"I was floored by everything you did, and pleased that you had the courage to do it. Are you, by any chance, gay?"

That caused Franklin's eyebrows to turn up in surprise. "Uh, no," he said.

"Pity," Milk replied. "That would have made it even better. All right, now let me introduce you to the world of spirit gum, and then we'll talk about cheek fillers." He pulled out one of the bottles.

"Cheek fillers?"

"It alters the face tremendously if you stick these things in your mouth," he held up a small pink spongy object oblong in shape and not much over an inch in size. "You lodge it between your upper gum and your cheek and wedge it in there. It creates a whole new face. Add the mustache, and speak in a lower or higher tone than usual, and no one will know you, not even your mother."

"Oh, you don't know my mother," Franklin said. "She has powers beyond human."

"Hmm. Mine too," Milk observed.

Franklin examined the cheek filler closely, turning it over in his hand. "I assume you put one on each side of the mouth." Milk nodded. "But don't they fall out?"

Shaking his head, Milk said, "You'd be surprised how snugly they fit. Just take it carefully when you're eating or you'll get a nasty surprise. Okay, now let me show you how to apply the spirit gum. First you get it tacky, and then stick on the mustache. You'll also need spirit gum remover." He indicated a different bottle.

"Give me the full treatment," Franklin commanded. "It's important I get this right."

The demonstration didn't take long, and soon Franklin looked in the mirror and saw a complete stranger gazing back at him. This man had Franklin's tall, quasi-pudgy build, but that was about it. The face, with the good-sized mustache and the puffy cheeks, didn't look like anyone in Franklin's family, much less the man himself.

"That's incredible!" Franklin said, turning his head to see various angles in the mirror.

"I suggest you also wear some sort of a cap when you're out in public. And you might also try putting a round pebble in your shoe. That will change your gait.

"A cap?"

"Yes. It'll hide a number of features that might otherwise identify you. Make sure the cap doesn't call attention to itself. You want to be as ordinary as possible."

"What do you recommend?'

"Something similar to 'Go Bucks!' won't cause a second glance in this town."

"Right. That'll be easy; every drug store in town has a rack of them."

As they strolled to the cash register, Milk added, "If your cover gets blown and you need a new look, think about dyeing your hair, or shaving it all off. There are some other possibilities too." Milk punched numbers into the register, took Franklin's credit card, and completed the sale. Franklin was handed a small shopping bag filled with the secrets of the theater. As he signed the credit card receipt, he suddenly thought better of leaving a trail that led to this store, so he asked Milk if they could undo the credit transaction and let him pay cash instead.

"Good idea," Milk said, tapping various computer keys. Franklin gave him the money from his wallet, and the big man made change.

Franklin, a grin on his new face, held out his hand and Milk shook it firmly. "Many thanks," Franklin said, grateful and glad that he had had the foresight to stop here and get someone like Milk to show him all these tricks. The man was amazing.

"My job," Milk commented, but then he reached below the counter and came up with a business card. "One other thing," he said, sounding very serious of a sudden. "If you get into trouble—any kind of trouble—call me and I'll do what I can to help. This isn't a come-on. I mean it." He flipped the card over and wrote on it. "This is my cell phone number and my email address. The store's number is on the front. Use them if and when it all gets too hot for you out there. Particularly call me if you have problems with the makeup, or, as I said, you need a new secret identity, or even if you're on the lamb and need a place to hide. I have some experience handling this sort of thing."

Franklin was touched by the man's concern, and he thanked him again. He slid the card into his wallet.

Who knows? he thought as he climbed back into his car. He might very well need some saving that had nothing to do with his soul.

CHAPTER SIX

FOREST FIRE

The uproar over the statements that Franklin made on the Jimmy Ball Show was a small breeze compared to the leveling winds that now began to bellow across the land

At his mother's direction, Todd had wiped the website clean, and then, as a joke, complied with her suggestion that he replace it with bunnies and flowers. But this was, of course, far too late. The original content had been downloaded over and over again, and then emailed and printed out and shared with friends. It was available on dozens of sites in cyberspace, easily retrievable by the clumsiest Google search. In the coming days, snippets of it were broadcast on tv, and 'read aloud on the radio. Newspapers reprinted parts of it and all three major national news magazines chose it for their cover story, running photos of Todd (pulled from his high school yearbook) and Franklin (from the website of Factor, Marroni, & Ray). *Free Inquiry*, the magazine of the Council for Secular Humanism, put out a special issue, trying to beef up its subscription base while the topic was hot. Chat rooms, talk shows (both radio and tv), preachers in their pulpits, and tipplers in their bars, debated its message, fought terrible verbal battles over it, sometimes coming to blows, all at top volume. For the next week what was called the "imaginary friend" story was unavoidable wherever you went, not just in the United States, but also at all spots on the globe where any form of media reached.

Todd Whitestone had entered the history books, perhaps even eclipsing his notorious dad.

But Franklin Whitestone, like any good father, was scrambling to keep his son from being consumed by this inferno. When he first heard about the damning website on Tuesday late in the morning, he called Mary on her cell phone and yelled at her to get them both out of the house and do it now! "Don't stop to pack! Get in the car and keep going until you are sure no one is after you. Check into a motel and call me at this new number." He gave her the number of the cell phone he'd just purchased and activated.

Mary had been thinking similar thoughts herself, and his call triggered the very reaction he'd demanded. She pulled Todd away from his computer, and, over his protests and questions, hustled him into the minivan in the garage.

90

With more steely resolve in her voice than Todd had ever heard, his mother told him, "Lie down in the back and don't raise your head until I tell you it's okay." Catching her mood, and with a new appreciation of the situation, he did as directed, at which point Mary started the van, opened the garage door, and barreled down the driveway just as a fleet of cars began parking on the street outside their house. People climbing from those cars scattered frantically to get out of her way, swearing and screaming, and some of them began pointing at the van as they scrambled back into their own vehicles.

With her maternal instinct informing every move she made, Mary drove with the concentration of a veteran Formula One race car driver through the streets of Bexley, Ohio, their suburb, turning down little used streets she knew well, cutting though an alley, driving through the parking lot of the Jewish Center, and making it to Interstate 70 with no one else in the race. She headed west towards Dayton, constantly checking her rear view mirror to make certain she'd lost them all, glancing up now and then to spot any aerial surveillance. Nothing. They were forty miles west of Columbus and passing Springfield before she let Todd sit up in the back of the van.

"Awesome job, Mom," he said. "Want me to drive?"

"No," she said, curt, still upset, trying to control herself, proud of the fact that she wasn't yelling at him. "You call your father and tell him where we are. The number's in my purse." She indicated the bag on the passenger's seat next to her. "I could use some advice."

Franklin answered on the first ring. He told Todd to hand the phone to his mother. "Where are you?" he asked.

"Nearing Dayton. Apparently we escaped clean. I'm certain no one is following us."

Franklin felt some of the tension ease from his shoulders and chest. "Very good," he said. "I've been pacing around this place, unable to sit."

"Exactly what place are you in?"

"'Rise and Shine,'" he responded. "The B&B that recently opened in German Village. I'm registered under the name 'William Blackstone,' and wearing a false mustache."

"You're kidding," she said.

"I swear on the Great Turtle it's true. I'm in hiding and you should be too."

"The Great what?"

"Long story. Sorry, that slipped out. I've been practicing."

She looked annoyed. "Franklin, I'm in *trouble* here and I need for you to focus. We could be in serious danger."

91

"I know, I know. All right. I told you to check into a motel, but before you do that, a couple of other things. First, stop and get as much cash as you can from an ATM. When you register at the motel, don't use your real names and don't use any credit cards or even visit an ATM again. I'll figure a way to get you more money."

"Okay," she said.

"What's he saying?" Todd asked from the back of the van.

"Shhh," she replied, and went back to the phone. "Anything else?"

"Yes, you'll both need to be in disguise when you go out in public."

"You're kidding!"

"I'm not. There is a manhunt on for Todd by large numbers of people, some of whom just want to interview him, but others are planning to demonstrate the Christian point of view with a baseball bat. Not a lot of people know what you look like, but a close-up of Todd's face talking directly to the camera for ten minutes is circling the globe, much studied. Every other person you meet is going to say, 'Aren't you Todd Whitestone?'"

"Oh, shit," she said, exasperated. "It's true!"

"So keep him out of sight, even at gas stations or when you check into a motel. I mean *sneak* him in, do you hear me?"

"Yes."

"Now I want you to write down a number and call it as soon as possible, even while driving."

"Hang on." She turned back to Todd and told him to get a pen out of her purse and write down the number she was about to give him.

"I'll just program it into my cell," he said, and she nodded.

Franklin read off the various phone numbers from the business card that Corbin Milk had given him earlier today, and Mary relayed them to Todd. Then Franklin explained how very useful Milk had been in helping him go to ground.

"Just tell him who you are and that I said you should call him immediately."

"Okay. But do you really trust him not to blow the whistle on us all?"

"Oh, yes. He's an oak tree, and I'm not wrong on this. Call me when you're settled in Dayton and we'll plan our next moves."

"One other thing, Franklin," Mary said. "Please call Betty Alice and ask her if she would please go over to the house and pick up the cat and keep him for a few days until I figure out what to do with him."

Franklin agreed to that, and they said goodbye. As directed, Todd called Milk's cell number. He handed the phone to his mother while it was still ringing.

92

"Hello," said the smooth bass voice on the other end.

"This is Mary Whitestone, mother of Todd. We're in sort of a bind, and my ex-husband, Franklin, suggested that I call you. He said you might have some good advice for us."

"Yes, I do," Milk replied.

And they began to talk.

Franklin called his mother shortly after he spoke with Mary, and it was the first time they'd talked since a brief conversation on Sunday afternoon right before he flew to New York for his momentous appearance on the Jimmy Ball Show. He felt guilty about not calling her sooner, but, of course, he'd been legitimately busy. He told her that, knowing it wouldn't mollify her even slightly.

"Franklin, dear," she said, "even in all your running around, surely you could've found time for a quick call to let me know you hadn't been kidnapped or something. I've been beside myself with worry."

"I know, I know. I'm sorry," he replied, feeling like he was ten years old again. These phone conversations dramatically reduced his age mere seconds after they began.

"So you're in hiding?"

"Yes, until this all calms down."

"About ten years from now?"

"Oh, Mom, I don't know. Todd's website increased the craziness by a factor of one hundred."

"Too low," she told him. "No sentient insurance agent would sell either of you a life insurance policy, and that's what scares me, scares me very much. I studied Todd's website carefully. Very original. We should all change our names and move to Brazil."

"I do wish he'd run it by any of the adults in his life before he posted the damn thing."

"And I wish you'd called your mother before you decided to go on national tv and tell a woman in Salt Lake City that she was silly for believing in an imaginary friend."

That went right through him to his core. She'd done it again. "Next time," he promised.

"Just out of curiosity, Franklin, if you could go back and change things, what would you say to her when she asked if you were praying to God while holding that girder?"

He paused slightly before replying, "I would tell her that in that moment, girder in hand, I'd have been glad for help wherever it came from."

"Good answer. Shame you didn't think of it on Sunday. Had you been drinking?"

This is why he didn't call her more often. These conversations sometimes ended with him whimpering in the corner.

"A glass of wine at dinner."

"Only one?"

"Well, the waiter refilled my glass, so I guess it was really two."

"And that was it?"

"Yes," he lied, and changed the subject. "Are the reporters and all still bothering you?"

"No. Things have quieted down since I started throwing pails of cold water on whoever was loitering on my doorstep when I answered the bell."

"I wish I'd thought of that."

"Well," she told him, "I'm too old to punch out the members of the press and lay them flat. I'll leave that to you. I did post a sign warning them that they were trespassers, and that I would deal with them accordingly, so if the worst that happened to them was being doused with ice water, that seemed a mild enough response. Did you know that in younger days I was quite a scrapper? I once hit Urbie Schutz in the face with a brick?"

"WHAT? WHO?"

"I was only eleven. I'd just had braces put on my teeth, and Urbie made fun of me, so I called him a monkey because he had big ears that stuck out like a chimpanzee's. He was furious, so he pushed me down and then kicked me twice. It ruined my dress and, of course, it made me mad."

Franklin squirmed thinking about this. Catherine Whitestone (well, Brown then) was a hurricane when angry. "So you hit him with a brick?" he asked.

Though he couldn't see her, she nodded. "I went home crying and changed my torn dress, then I took a brick from the construction site next door, and waited by the wall near Urbie's home, some blocks away. When he came around the corner, I smacked him with it good. Then I ran away."

"Mother! That was criminal!"

"Oh, I put the brick back before anyone noticed it was gone."

"You can't be *proud* of this!" Franklin insisted.

"No, but I was eleven and I didn't like being powerless. You know me. I get creative when aroused."

"So what happened?"

"Urbie lost two teeth. His father came over to our house that same night, Urbie in tow, and spoke with my father about the incident. I think they were both embarrassed to be complaining that the big lug had been felled by an eleven year old girl. Dad called me in and I gave him my version of events, and then there was a long pause while he thought it through. Eventually he told Mr. Schutz that he would pay for Urbie's dental repairs and they seemed satisfied with that, so they left. Of course, I was punished. Your grandfather made me write Urbie a letter apologizing, and I was confined to the house for two weeks, except for school. I hated that. But— does this sounds strange?—I do think that on some level Dad was actually proud of me."

"You got off pretty easy."

"The confinement didn't mean anything. I just read books and practiced the piano a lot. But the letter burned me up! *Apologize* to that cretin!"

"Did he accept your apology?"

"I don't know. He kept a good distance between us from then on, and we never spoke."

"Smart move."

"Oh, yes. I knew where there were more bricks."

Thos seemed a good place to end the conversation, so Franklin gave her his new cell number, and promised to be better at keeping her informed. Sincerely, and with much concern in her voice, Catherine replied that all this terrified her, and that he and Todd should lay low and watch out for the loonies. He told her that they'd taken steps to stay in hiding for the immediate future, and reiterated the things that Corbin Milk had suggested. She moved on to other topics.

"You also need to get an agent and a lawyer, my boy," she informed him.

"An agent? A lawyer? Why?"

"You'll need someone to control the media for you, give it what they call 'spin,' and advise you what you should be doing to get right with the world."

"Hmm. Maybe. Where would I find such an agent?"

"Try Google. You're in the interesting position of being a very attractive client for someone in public relations. The whole world is watching you. Media specialists will climb over each other to get to you."

"How would I pay such a person?"

"Ask him."

"All right. I'll look into that. But why a lawyer? I'm a lawyer, and a good one."

"Because you're about to be fired, and that will mean, as the very least, threats of a lawsuit. You can't represent yourself in the subsequent imbroglio."

"I'm *not* about to be fired!"

95

"Yes, darling, you are. A mother knows these things, or at least this mother does."

Franklin put one hand up to his eyes and rubbed them. She was almost never wrong when making these sorts of pronouncements. A headache began matriculating.

"One last thing, Franklin. And remember this when you're at your wit's end. If you need me, I can be very, very helpful. I am a clever person, and, for you and my grandson, I'm never short of good advice or a swinging brick. Everyone needs a mother from time to time, and, modesty aside, I am a particularly talented mother to have. Think of me as a resource. Make use of me."

"I know it, Mom. You take care too. I love you."

She said she loved him, and they exchanged goodbyes and hung up.

Franklin stood looking at the phone, thinking about her. A swinging brick!

"Are you comfortable enough?" Nan asked Dan when he'd settled down.

"Yes," Dan said to Nan. As she took up her position, he made the mistake of asking, "You won't fall asleep or anything?"

She just looked at him, and he dropped it.

"Wake me in four hours," he told her, plumping up his pillow.

"Yes," Nan replied. "I will."

"Are we going out to eat?" Todd asked, drying his hair with a big towel from the motel bathroom. "I'm hungry. I haven't had anything to eat except a bowl of cereal this morning, and those gas station potato chips."

Mary sighed and looked at him. With his newly dyed blond hair he did look very different from the Todd she knew so well. She had colored her own hair too—a dark brown—and applied more makeup than she usually wore.

"I wouldn't trust any food this motel would bring us. I suppose we might venture out and see how it goes. What sounds good to you?"

"We passed a Texas Roadhouse two miles back. How about that?"

"I guess. Put on your Ohio State cap."

He did so, commenting, "I'm really not much of a football fan."

"Don't say that," she replied. "It violates a Columbus Municipal Ordinance."

He grinned at her. "We're in Dayton, remember." He struggled into his windbreaker.

"Don't forget your glasses," she told him, putting her own on as she said it.

Mr. Milk had advised them both to start wearing glasses since that disguised the face quite well, particularly if the glasses had dark frames, attracting attention to the glasses themselves. He'd suggested a store in Dayton where they could buy glasses with clear lens in them (they were used on stage by actors with normal vision). Mary and Todd had stopped there and purchased some before checking into the motel. Milk had particularly warned them not to wear sunglasses. "That always suggests you have something to hide—the last thing you want people thinking."

"Are you in surveillance or police work?" Todd had asked.

"Let's just say that I've led an interesting life," Milk replied.

As they climbed into the van, Mary said, "We're also going to have to get a new vehicle. The media knows what this one looks like, and they'll be tracking the license plate too. Your father is working on ways to funnel money to us without leaving a trail—I think Mr. Milk is also helping him with that. Probably we'll rent a car tomorrow."

As they drove to the restaurant, Todd fidgeted in the seat next to her. "Mom," he said with a slight whine to his voice, "I *really* have to get back to the house and pull some things out of there. I need my computer, my books, my guitar, my clothes, my toothbrush, and lots of other things."

"No," she said, her jaw tightening. "You'll live. You know that we can't risk going back, at least now for awhile. They'd be all over us. Don't even think about it. We'll pick up clothes and toiletries as we survive from day to day. Your father was very definite about our staying put in Dayton. We'll also need new identities. I signed the motel register as Nancy Jones. What would you like me to call you?"

Adjusting the ill-fitting glasses on his nose, Todd replied, "How about Clark Kent?"

Jake Richardson combined Bible reading with beer every night as he wandered around his small home, trying to figure out a way to find Franklin Whitestone. So far nothing had worked. Attempted stakeouts at both Whitestone's home and office were failures. Jake had to work during the day, and he could devote only so much time in the evenings and early mornings to his search, and so there were plenty of opportunities for Whitestone to sneak back in to either place unseen. Jake had tried writing Whitestone a letter, but, like his phone calls, that so far had produced zilch. Whitestone was stiff-arming him. God, too, was apparently letting Jake work this out by himself. So far his prayers had gone unanswered (or, it bothered him to think, perhaps the answer was no—but surely that couldn't be right).

On Monday evening he'd phoned Heather, and to his surprise she answered immediately. He begged her to let him see Charity the next day, and, not sounding happy about it, she had finally agreed that a girl should see her father, but only for an hour on Wednesday at five p.m. Jake was excited by this development, and was grateful to her until he made the mistake of asking her if she'd seen him on tv this past weekend..

"Yes," Heather had replied. "You were great. As my mother said, if only you could handle your life as well as you handle that machine you wouldn't be the mess you are today."

That stoked his fire good, and he would have yelled something back, but he stopped himself just in time. He knew that that would scotch the visit with Charity the next day, so he bit his lip. The bitch! Why did he even want to get back together with someone that mean? Maybe tomorrow he ought to just grab Charity and run off somewhere. Start over in a new state.

That was worth thinking about.

When Jake arrived on Wednesday at the house Heather shared with her hateful mother, Heather herself (the sissy) was not there. Instead, the mother, Nadia, a small fat cow who sneered constantly when Jake was around (she'd even been snide to him at the wedding), chaperoned the visit, sitting in the room and watching every move as Jake tried to talk and play with his daughter. His mother-in-law (herself a bitch) was clearly worried that Jake would try to hurt Charity—as if anyone could harm someone as beautiful as his darling child! Charity was only three and looked so much like Heather that it hurt Jake's heart to be near her. What kind of monster did they think he was?

Charity was nice enough to her father, but she seemed to have no idea who Jake was. In turn, he couldn't think of much to do with her, and quickly tired of hearing her chatter about dolls and clothes and some kind of talking sponge. After about half an hour, Jake had had enough, and got out of there, giving his daughter a quick kiss, and, in the spirit of Christian forgiveness, he even said good night to Nadia. The old cow told him that he smelled bad and that if he ever came over again he should bathe first. Then she glared at him as he slammed out the door and, furious, climbed into his truck.

Now, back in his own house, beer at his side, his world a mess, Jake turned on the tv hoping to be able to relax and chill out. Instead, with growing fury, he watched the news stories that for the first time told him about the Whitestone son's outrageous attacks on God! How could they do this? Why would the tv then spread these lies around? Was everyone going crazy? Why did God allow it? Were they all being tested somehow?

The televised bits of the webcast that the boy had created didn't mean much to Jake. What was all that about some math guy in England? And that crap that mixed God up with the Civil War (hadn't that been over for years?) was just garbage. The kid was just trying to use big words to confuse the faithful. That wouldn't work. God wouldn't let it. The whole world believed in religion one way or another. God was still on top.

But, unlike most viewers, Jake didn't blame Todd Whitestone for putting this shit on the web. Todd's father was the asshole who had rammed all this down the kid's throat, probably starting when the kid was a baby. Ruined the boy, perverted his mind. Fathers should set the example that they want their sons to follow. His father sure had.

It happened when Jake was eleven. One day at school one of the guys he played pickup basketball with, Sandy Manx, told him that he'd learned a secret that adults were keeping from their kids. The two of them were sitting on the grass, just off the tennis courts next to the gymnasium, and Sandy was very serious about letting Jake in on what he knew.

"What?" Jake asked, suspicious that anyone would tell him a secret. He had no real friends.

"There ain't no God," Sandy reported in a whisper.

"Nah!" Jake gave Sandy a one-handed shove that meant "stop pulling my leg."

"It's *true*," Sandy said. "I heard my uncle Ralph talking to my stepmom about it. Said it was all just pretending."

"That's bullshit," Jake said with a sneer. "Any fool knows there's a God. It's in the Bible."

"My uncle says that, yah, some people really think there's a God, only they're mistaken, see? Others know there's no God, but pretend there is anyways."

"Why would they pretend?"

"It's like Santa Claus. You gotta be old enough before they let you know what's really going on."

"Crap. My Daddy sure believes in God, and no fooling. He'd slap you silly if he heard you saying there weren't none."

Sandy shrugged. "Then he's one of the ones that is mistaken. Lots of grownups are."

Jake shook his head. He didn't believe it.

Saying there was no God was just nonsense. Not worth thinking about. But over the next couple of weeks, he did think about it. That conversation with Sandy stayed with him, and he kept asking himself if it was in any way possible Sandy was right. Of course, Jake didn't *want* to believe it, damn sure. He had been raised with God. God was right in the center of his world. But . . . but . . .

On one hand, Jake was surrounded by people, both relatives, fellow parishioners, and neighbors, who were true believers, and who weren't hiding no secret about just pretending. His father was one. Mean as the man was, he was still devoted to Jesus, heart and soul.

On the other hand, Jake's father was wrong about so many things that Jake knew he was often a dipshit. Daddy thought that the moonwalk was phony—that the sons of bitches who reported the news was just lying when they said men had gone up there. The only times Jake paid attention in school was when outer space was the subject—Jake was fascinated by the planets, and space travel, and all that. He watched the school movies and television shows about astronauts and their rocket ships whenever he could, and he knew his Daddy was an ignorant asshole when it came to science things. The same with government (which his father called "guvmint"). Unlike what Daddy believed, Jake was pretty sure no one was reading their mail, or tapping the Richardson phone line, and he also believed that if people voted, the votes really *were* counted, so that the man who got the most would be the winner.

Watching people in church was confusing too. Most of them, almost all of them, seemed sincere—hell, *were* sincere. But it wasn't hard to spot a few showoffs who were just pretending. Those who went too far when testifying, or speaking in tongues, or writhing on the floor in so-called ecstasy. Bad actors, some of these idiots. Embarrassing to everybody what saw them.

So, was Sandy right? There weren't really no God, and those who said there were either mistaken or lying? Jake thought about the disappearance of his mother. If there was a God, would He let that happen? Would God let his Daddy beat his kids so much, and in particular, beat on poor little Eddie, who couldn't even defend hisself at all?

One night, when his father'd been drinking and started yelling at Jake over some fuckup or other, Jake having finally had enough, made the mistake of yelling back. As usual, that got him swatted so hard he bounced off the wall, but, different from all the other times this had happened, being swatted just made Jake madder. Seeing red, he picked hisself up and screamed, "FUCK YOU!" at Daddy.

Daddy, who was halfway across the room, turned with a savage growl. *"What you say, boy?"*

100

"Fuck you!" Jake repeated, somewhat softer, looking around for a weapon to defend hisself with.

Daddy advanced, crouched, shoulders forward, death in his eyes. "Bible says 'Honor thy father and thy mother,' don't it? Say 'yes,' boy."

"I don't believe in that God crap no more," Jake said, too mad to think what this would lead to.

"*WHAT!* No son of mine . . . ." Daddy didn't finish this thought, but instead charged—slamming into Jake like a freight train. The two of them went down together, his father on top. Daddy grabbed Jake's head by the hair and started slamming his head up and down on the floor, over and over, till Jake was knocked out cold.

When he came to, he discovered he was tied by clothesline to one of the kitchen chairs, with the clothesline wrapped all around his body, pinning his arms to his side. Jake's head was pounding with pain, and everything was spinning,. He finally realized that his eyes were caked almost completely shut with blood, but a few vigorous blinks cleared things up enough that he could sort of see. His feet were cold. What had happened to his shoes and socks?

Nobody appeared to be around, not Daddy, not Eddie, and Jake couldn't do nothing but sit there until one of them showed up. Finally, feeling small, Jake called out, "Is anybody there?" and jumped when his father stuck his head in from the kitchen.

"Awake, eh?" Daddy said, sounding a lot more sober that he had been earlier when he knocked Jake unconscious. "Got something for you, sonny boy of mine. Be right there." He banged around in the kitchen for a minute more, and then came into the living room where Jake was tied up. Daddy was carrying a large bucket, steaming with boiling hot water. He set it down in front of Jake's chair and then leaned down to look Jake straight in the face.

"So, boy," he said, "you don't believe in God? Ain't that what you said? Don't believe in Jesus Christ, your savior? You know what happens to pieces of shit what say that?"

Jake, eyes wide, slowly shook his head. He was scared and no two ways about it.

"Why, boy, they goes to *hell*! Got to make you believe, don't I? Ain't that right?"

Jake said nothing rather than say the wrong thing. Saying the wrong thing to Daddy was always a big mistake.

Daddy's nose was just inches from Jake's, and Daddy was sweating. Why? Probably the steam coming out of the bucket was making him hot.

"Know what *hell* feels like, Jake?" he asked, his tone friendly as all get out.

Jake shook his head. Please let this be over soon, he thought. Please . . . God?

"LIKE THIS!" And Daddy leaned down, picked up Jake's right leg, and plunged his foot into the boiling water, holding it down with both hands.

Of course, poor Jake had screamed and screamed to the point where the neighbors, pretty much used to the Richardson kids howling, noticed that the noise was different, worse. Some considered calling the police, but, knowing that Richardson was a vengeful man, nary a one of them did.

Finally, Daddy pulled Jake's foot from the bucket and lowered it, red as a lobster, to the floor. The foot felt like it still was in the fiery flames, and taking it from the bucket didn't lessen the pain one bit. Jake continued to scream and twist in the chair until his Daddy clamped his hand over Jake's mouth and told him to shut the hell up. He said he was tired of all that complaining. Knowing he must, Jake bit back his pain and swallowed it whole.

Now Daddy smiled at him. He moved his face close to Jake's again.

"How was hell? Hurt plenty?"

Tears and pain combining, the boy could only nod.

"Here's the bad news," Daddy said. "That bucket was a paradise of comfort compared with what you'll *really* feel in hell, which is, by God, where I swear you'll go if you don't return to the fold right here and now. And hell isn't over when you try and pull your foot out, oh, no! It goes on and on, and then on and on some more, and then on and on, *for all eternity.* You want that, boy?"

Jake shook his head violently from side to side.

Daddy lifted one eyebrow. "Say! You got another foot here! Want it to have a taste of hell too?"

"NO, DADDY, PLEASE NO!"

"I gotta do it if'n you still don't believe in God."

"I BELIEVE, I BELIEVE!"

"You ain't just saying that, are you?"

"No, Daddy!" And he truly meant it deep in his heart of hearts. God, heaven, and, especially, hell, were very real to him now.

Daddy rose to his full height.

"Okay, then. Tell you what, Jakey. I'm gonna set you free. But if you ever give me cause to think you're backsliding, I'll get out that bucket and remind you that backsliding's a bad, bad idea. You hear me?"

"Yes, Daddy. I hear."

Now, decades later, Jake thought about this painful lesson and how it tied in with the Whitestones. Franklin's father should have done something like this when he first discovered his son was listening to the devil's

102

temptations. And then Franklin should have done the same for his son, Todd. It was a father's job. Okay, brutal, sure, but it got their attention and showed them the straight and narrow path.

Now that Whitestone was an adult, it was going to be a lot harder for Jake to get the man's attention and capture his soul for Jesus. A whole lot harder.

That left Jake where he began. He'd hit a dry hole trying to get to Whitestone through the usual means. Was there some new way to do this? Hell, Whitestone probably had friends. Maybe Jake could visit them, appeal to their sense of right and wrong, get them to connect him up with Whitestone. Or maybe the man's relatives would be the way to go. A sister or something.

Wait a minute! Just in the past day or so, Jake had heard on the tv that Whitestone had a mother right here in Columbus. She shouldn't be so hard to find, and Jake guessed (rightly as it turned out) that she would be listed in the phone book, her address too.

Yes. Calling on the mother was a good idea. He'd do that tomorrow.

Catherine Whitestone was also on her son Franklin's mind, particularly her troubling prediction that he was about to be let go from the firm. Could that possibly be true? He had difficulty sleeping Tuesday night as he lay in his bed, thinking though the variables. If the firm wanted to get rid of him, could they do it? What would be their grounds? It couldn't be disagreement with his religious views since that would be employment discrimination based on religion, which was clearly forbidden by law—federal, state, and municipal. What other pretext could they use? The fact that he had become controversial? Surely if he was controversial *because* of his religious views, that would also, at least arguably, trigger the protection of the same civil rights laws. Exactly what did the partnership agreement he'd signed say about powers of termination? He needed to get out his contract and study it.

The problem was that his records were in two inaccessible places: his office downtown and his office at home. When he'd last gone out the door of his condo he'd had time to grab only the basics (underwear, toothbrush, etc.), plus his laptop computer, and it was becoming clear he was going to have to make another trip and bring more things to his temporary abode at the Rise and Shine. He began to compile a mental list of what he needed to retrieve soon if he was to lead any sort of a normal life. There were credit cards, his checkbook, an address book, that really good novel currently sitting on his bed stand sadly abandoned in mid-chapter, the medicine for the arthritis in his shoulder, computer files, cds, dvds, photos, the magazines he subscribed to, and on and on. The list seemed endless. He also needed more clothing (particularly shoes) and the more complicated toiletries. It would fill a couple of suitcases.

Then Franklin thought about the words "temporary abode." Just how temporary was this stay away from his true home going to be?

A week?

A month?

Forever?

That scared him. What if he had to hide out for the rest of his life? Todd too. They'd be like two people stashed away in a self-created witness protection program, always afraid of disclosure, ready to run for it at a moment's notice. And how would Todd go to school? For that matter, how would Franklin earn a living to support them? It was all impossible.

Franklin's mother had said he ought to get an agent to help him get through all this. What would that mean? Assuming he could find one, how could he afford to pay this person? His savings, such as they were, were earmarked for Todd's start at M.I.T. next year. Franklin earned a great deal of money as a partner at a major law firm, and, of course, it had never occurred to him that that source of income would suddenly dry up. Could Mary afford on her own to send Todd to college? What did her writings earn nowadays? Would M.I.T. still want Todd? Would Todd's life ever calm down to the point where he could concentrate on his studies like any normal student?

These musings got worse. If law were truly closed to Franklin as a career, then what? At 44 he was surely too old a dog for a completely new set of tricks. No matter what job he sought, even flipping burgers in some fast food emporium, it could be gone in a flash if Franklin's true identity became known. Religious employers or even those non-religious employers (like his own law firm) who depended on the good will of the public, might drop him like a hot rock. Normally one job leads to another, with references, and an ability to point with pride at one's last post. His new career track would be the very opposite: shame and feeble explanations in a pitiful attempt to move on from his latest shellacking

Maybe he could do legal work with some very liberal group: the ACLU or a civil rights firm. They wouldn't think atheism relevant one way or the other to his job. The problem with that solution was that Franklin's training and interests all centered on commercial law. He wouldn't have a clue what to do in the controversial liberal arenas—even worse, Franklin wasn't that much of a liberal to begin with.

Then there was the danger. Franklin had listened to enough of his phone calls, read enough of his emails, watched enough tv, to appreciate the very real hatred that was directed at him from many sources, many different religious groups. He'd managed to offend them all, and was now an equal opportunity target. For that matter, so was Todd. In fact Todd appeared to be even more despised than his much-reviled father. How nice. A family tradition of infamy.

So, at 4 a.m. on that Wednesday morning, Franklin lay staring at the ceiling. Life swirled around him like a sand storm, stinging on many sides. Bleak, bleak, and bleaker.

He decided to take his mother's advice—almost always the smart thing to do—and hunt up both an employment lawyer and a public relations firm. Let the experts have a run at his problems.

He'd make some calls later in the morning.

On Wednesday morning at 7:30 a.m., Todd was in the bathroom of the motel room, quietly making a phone call. He decided that one last use of his cell phone wouldn't hurt, and he needed to get some important things out of his home right away. The call was to his best friend, Stubby Allen, who lived only two blocks from Todd. At this early hour Stubby would be getting ready for school, and thus free to talk for a minute or two. This proved to be right, for Stubby answered on the first ring.

"Hello, fugitive," he said with a smirk. His caller ID had pegged the familiar number of Todd's cell.

"Stubby, listen. I can't talk long—Mom'll wake up soon. I'm in Dayton and I need for you to get some things for me from my house and then send them to me here, or, better yet, get your brother, Roger, to drive them over."

"What things?" Stubby asked, uninspired.

Todd gave him a brief list: his laptop, school books, acne medicine, some specified articles of clothing (which sounds like half his closet), two notebooks from the top shelf of the bookcase in his room, and the brown folder under his bed which contained two Playboys and a tattered magazine of nude women that he'd found under the high school football field bleachers last July.

Stubby was even more reluctant. "I don't know, Todd. That's a lot of stuff. Need a boxcar to get it all to Dayton."

"No. I figured it out. It'll all fit in the large black trunk in the northwest corner of the basement, and then the trunk will fit in the car—probably the back seat is best."

"But I don't have a key to your house. How would I get in?"

"There's a key under the third stone step leading to the faucet just outside the dining room window. Lift it up, get the key, unlock the door, load up the trunk, and then hop over to Dayton."

"Gee, Todd. I don't think so. It would be hard to get away, and setting it all up . . . ." He trailed off.

"Ah, yes, the logistics. But, Stubby, my friend, but you owe this to me! Need I remind you about the purloined science project last May, and how I saved your ass from sure expulsion?"

"No," said Stubby, sullen, unhappy, "You needn't remind me." He also knew what was about to be dropped onto the bargaining table next.

"Good boy. And then there is your genuine affection for our friendship. We met in fourth grade seven years ago. Blood brothers and all— you remember the ceremony?"

Stubby groaned. "Yes."

"And the pledge, with the exchange of blood and the spitting on the ground?"

"Todd, we were seven, for God's sake!"

"You meant what you said back then! Are you saying you don't mean it now."

Stubby sighed heavily. "There are times when I so hate you," he said, but his voice suggested resignation, not hate.

"Very popular opinion of me this week. But, blood brother, rejoice! I have something to sweeten the pot."

"Oh?"

"As a way of saying thank you for all this trouble, I am giving you the brown folder and its contents—all three magazines!"

Speechless for a few seconds, Stubby finally blurted out, "Wow! Really? Oh, Todd, that's . . . that's . . . ." Todd, of course, knew this would be the tipping point. Both of them had spent much time studying the magazines, jaws dropped. Their favorite was Amandia Orange, Miss September, whose amazing breastworks could only be explained by photo manipulation, devil-may-care surgery, or birth on another planet. Todd commented that if she happened to fall over, the poor woman would have a tough time getting back up. "Yes, but it would be fun to watch," was Stubby's carefully considered reply.

"Will you do it? Sneak in tonight?"

"Not tonight, Todd. I have football practice. We're getting ready for the big game on Friday." Stubby was a backup offensive lineman for the high school team, the Polecats, and he took his responsibilities very seriously.

106

Sports was the center of Stubby's universe. "But tomorrow night, just after it gets dark. That might work."

"You're the Man! I knew you'd come through for me."

"And will you please also help me with the 'Merchant of Venice' paper I have to do for next week."

"Absolutely. The quality of mercy is not strained."

"Huh?"

"Glad to help. We'll have to do it by phone, or email. Get me that laptop and it'll be a cinch."

"All right. Give the name and address of the place where you're hiding. I'll see what I can work out with my brother when he comes home tonight. You've picked a good time. He owes me big."

"Why?"

"Very interesting story that. When I see you I'll tell you about the whole stupid fuckup."

That Wednesday when Catherine Whitestone's doorbell rang at 5:30 p.m., she checked to make sure that the bucket of water was in place next to the door and then looked cautiously through the peephole. Her view was of a tall, skinny man she didn't know, so she left the chain in place as she opened the door and said, "Yes?"

He nodded his head and smiled winningly at her. "Ma'am, my name is Jake Richardson. I'm the guy who operated the Big Crane and pulled down the wall that let your son and all those people out of the stadium where they was trapped. I was on tv and all."

Suspicious, but seeing that he wasn't very fast on his feet, she decided to probe some. "What is the name of the company you work for?"

He looked puzzled by her question. "It's Abion Construction and Demolition. I've worked there for eight years. But we also make up part of the Columbus Fire and Rescue Auxiliary. That's what we were doing at the stadium. You could call 'em and ask."

"And what do you want with me, Mr. Richardson?"

"I'm trying to find your son, Franklin, so I can talk with him. I think it would be worthwhile comparing our stories and just shooting the breeze about that awful day. One of the reporters told me that they wanted to do a story about the two of us with photos and all. I'd like that, but I can't seem to get hold of him. He doesn't answer his phone."

She thought about it a second, and decided he was who he said he was. "Hang on," she instructed, shut the door, took off the chain, and then let him in. "We'll talk in here," she said, as she led the way to the comfortable,

107

no nonsense living room where she spent most of her day. She motioned him into a chair, and he sat carefully, looking around at her piano and the shelf displaying her collection of antique salt and pepper shakers. She offered him something to drink, but he said "No, Ma'am, but thank you much."

"How can I help you?" she asked, eager to get this over with and him out of the house. She had a bridge tournament to organize.

"All I really need is to find a way to talk to Franklin. As I said, he's hard to find—not living at his home, not answering his phone. I sent him a letter too, but I guess it got sorta lost in all the crap going on. Can you help?"

"I can, but why should I? What would you say to him if you got to see him?"

"Well, we'd talk about last Sunday morning first of all. Very exciting to pull down that wall and see him and those other poor people standing there, all confused and scared and happy at the same time. Then that big iron thing started swinging and your son got hold of it and held on until the ones who could still walk escaped. I thought about trying to grab the thing with Suzy May, but decided it was too risky."

"Suzy May?"

He looked sheepish, and gave her an endearing smile. "Sorry, Ma'am. That's what we call the Big Claw I was operating. So, can you help me?"

"Is there anything more you'd like to say to Franklin? There's a lot of confusion in his life just now, as you undoubtedly know, and I suspect this is a bad time for happy reminiscences about the events of last Sunday."

Jake wiped a hand across his face, clearly not sure how much to tell her. He looked carefully into her eyes, and she looked back, unblinking. She seemed like a good person, so he decided to take the next step. "I guess I should tell you too that I have been very deeply troubled, deeply troubled, about things he said. On that tv show."

Catherine nodded. "I thought that was it. What troubled you most?" She put on her most sympathetic face.

"All of it! Calling God an imaginary friend and saying He set off the bombs that killed all those people! That's just wrong, Ma'am, just wrong! It must have wounded your heart—you being his mother—to hear him say those evil, evil things. I know you raised him better than that."

She paused to consider her response. It wouldn't be hard to verbally slice him to ribbons right here in the living room, but was that wise? She had as much chance of changing his views on religion as he did in changing hers, so the exercise, however much fun it might be, would be purposeless wheel-spinning. It also occurred to her that it could be dangerous. Who knew what sort of nut this visitor might turn out to be? Catherine wasn't afraid of him, but it was always a bad idea to poke a bear.

108

"I did do my best to put Franklin on the path to the truth," she told him, and left it at that. She stood and made a gesture that he should stand too. "I'll tell him what you said and if he wants to talk to you, he'll get in touch."

Jake climbed to his feet slowly, bothered that this talk, which had been going so well, was suddenly ending. "I'll give you my address and phone number," he mumbled, and was surprised by how quickly she whipped a notebook and pen from a drawer in the small table next to her chair and handed it to him.

"Do that," she said. "I'll see that it gets to the right place."

In big awkward writing he wrote down the contact information, and then handed the pen and notebook back to her. As she took it, she also took his hand and gave it a firm shake.

"As a mother, I want to thank you for saving my son's life. Your own mother must be very proud of you too." She smiled at him.

Jake blinked twice. His own mother? Would she really be proud of him? It was a new idea. He tried to remember her smile, or anything at all about her, and failed.

Catherine hustled him to the door, opened it, and saw him to the porch. "Thank you for coming, Mr. Richardson. Good night." She patted him gently on the arm, and then closed the door. She put the chain back on and stood with her back against the door for a few seconds, bothered, thinking.

All her instincts told her that Richardson was very bad news, and, unfortunately, he now knew exactly where she lived. Even worse, she was sure they had not seen the last of him.

That was true, but she wouldn't be physically in his presence again until she took the witness stand at his trial.

CHAPTER SEVEN

PHONE CALLS

It took no time at all for Franklin to find a lawyer to represent him in his incipient dispute with the firm. He knew dozens in Columbus, and the leading expert on employment discrimination was an old friend, Carol Lebeau. What made it even better was that she was *persona non grata* at Factor, Marroni, & Ray ever since, some years ago, she'd represented the plaintiff (a legal secretary who had been sexually harassed by a member of the firm's maintenance staff) in a lawsuit that had ended up costing Factor, Marroni, & Ray $900,000. With a strange satisfaction in the act, Franklin gave her a call on Wednesday, shortly after noon, and her secretary put her through almost instantly.

"Hello, Franklin," she began. "To what do I owe this pleasure?"

"I'm being fired."

"You're kidding!"

"All right, maybe not fired—*pre*-fired. I'm plenty worried. It appears that my sudden notoriety has caused the other partners to ask me to keep my distance, at least for a week or so. But, given all that is going on, I can't imagine that things will be much better in that short a time. I need to figure out where I stand. You do know about my recent encounters with the press?"

She gave a small snort. "Everyone who owns a tv knows. Congratulations on your heroics at the stadium. Condolences on everything that's happened since."

"Thanks for both. Will you help me?"

Carol paused only a few seconds. "Tentatively, yes. I need to do the usual checks to make sure there are no conflicts of interest, etc. I work at the rate of $350 an hour. Is that within your budget?"

It seemed high to Franklin, but there was no doubt she was worth it. "Yes," he said, adding no qualifications. If her fee began to exceed his ability to pay, he'd simply terminate her representation, with thanks for all she had done up to that point. If necessary he could handle the case himself, *pro se.*

"What would be the grounds for termination? Do you know?"

"No, and I want to make it clear that there has been no direct threat of being fired as of today. Howard Ray and I had a tumultuous conversation on Monday about all this, and I could feel the way the wind was blowing, but he didn't tell me anything more certain than I should take some time off from work for the immediate future."

She paused to think that over. "Are you sure that you want to bring a lawyer representing you into this matter right now? Might it not be better to wait and see what they decide to do?"

Franklin considered that. "I'm sure they're talking about how to get rid of me as we speak. I want to slow those discussions down as much as possible by making it clear I won't go without a major, all-too-public, dust-up. Employing someone with your sterling reputation may cause them to think twice before they pull the plug."

"Thanks for your kind words, but I'm having trouble believing that Factor, Marroni, & Ray would so casually get rid of a lawyer as valuable as you are."

"As I *was*. You ought to see my hate mail. And, no joke, the firm is getting all sorts of pressure from major clients—clients who pay big bills—to distance themselves from the lightning rod fixed to the top of my head."

"Hmm."

"Carol, I'm living in *hiding*, wearing a disguise that includes a mustache, and without the ability to visit my own home."

"You're kidding!"

"I wish I were. My ex-wife and son are also undercover. You know about Todd's contribution to all this, I assume."

"Oh, yes. Very provocative website he created. Reading it was like watching dynamite explode in slow motion. He'll make one fine lawyer some day."

"If he lives." That was said too glibly, Franklin thought, annoyed with himself. The possibility that Todd would die over this was not funny. "What next?" he asked Carol.

"We need to sign the representation agreement, and I'll want a retainer. We can do all that quickly via FAX or messenger service."

"If you like, I could drop by your office and sign the papers."

"That would be fun. I'd love to see your disguise."

He laughed. "Actually, I'm growing fond of the way I look with a mustache. May have to grow my own."

"We need to act fast on this for the reason you mentioned. After we settle the preliminary details, I'll give Howard Ray a call and let him know that I'm on the case. After our last encounter, that should give them pause. I'll arrange a meeting between the two of us and whichever members of your firm are participating in the decision about your fate. That meeting should also happen as soon as possible. You're free these days?"

That made Franklin laugh.

Finding a public relations agent was almost as easy. Franklin took his mother's advice and did a Google search for the names of possible firms. This produced a formidable list, and—why not? Franklin thought—he decided to start with the biggest and best known: the Martin Turnbill agency, located in Los Angeles. He selected the "Contact Us" option on the firm's website, typed in his email address, and composed the following message:

My name is Franklin Whitestone. As a result of some uninspired remarks on the Jimmy Ball Show last Sunday (and my involvement with the collapse of Ohio Stadium the day before), I am trapped in a public relations nightmare, and need assistance. It was suggested that I contact a public relations agency, and I am doing so with this email. Because of the controversies in my life, I'm not reading my emails at the moment, but I can be reached at the following phone number. Please let me know if you are interested in discussing this.

Then he signed it by typing his name and the number of his new cell, and hit the "Send" key.

He wondered if he'd have to repeat this process with a large number of companies before he found one that would nibble at the bait (surely some, perhaps many, would have religious objections to representing him), but his phone rang thirty-eight minutes later and it was a call from the Martin Turnbill agency.

"Mr. Whitestone," began the smooth, slightly unctuous, male voice on the other end of the line, "this is Jonathan Harker with Martin Turnbill, responding to your email."

"That was fast," Franklin observed, impressed.

"Yes, Sir," Harker agreed. "We like to think of ourselves as both efficient and on top of the difficult situations that sometimes confront our clients." He paused slightly and then went into his pitch. "We are *very* interested in handling your affairs in so far as they relate to public perceptions of you in the media."

"Quick decision, Mr. Harker. Why was it made with such speed? Surely you don't respond with that alacrity to everyone who asks."

Harker was downright jovial as he responded. "Come, Mr. Whitestone, don't be coy! To someone in our profession you're the *mother lode*! There isn't a PR firm in the country that wouldn't grovel at your feet for the chance to represent you. You—and your son too, I might add—are the hottest commodities going! I'm trying not to salivate and short out the phone."

"I hadn't thought of myself as a commodity."

"Sorry. Professional jargon."

"Okay. Let's assume we sign a contract agreeing that you represent me. I need to warn you that my source of income as an attorney is on shaky grounds, given the chaos surrounding me. How in the world would it be worth your while to take me on as a client if I'm a potential financial disaster?"

"Oh, but you're not a potential financial disaster!" Harker replied with a chuckle. "As I talk to you now all sorts of exciting possibilities are cavorting around my mind: the book deal, the tv movie, the speaking engagements, and, most importantly, the talk show appearances, to flog all of the above. It goes on and on. It makes me quite giddy to contemplate!"

There was a word Franklin didn't hear often: giddy.

"And this would pay?"

"Yes, yes, yes, Mr. Whitestone! Probably more than the large six figure numbers I am anticipating. If you handle this right—or, to be blunt, Martin Turnbill handles it for you—you could make millions of dollars in the coming years."

Franklin pulled the phone away from his ear and stared at it. Millions?

He put the phone back to its accustomed spot. "Millions?" he repeated, his voice barely audible. This couldn't be happening. It wasn't real. What kind of world was he living in?

Matching him with the same soft voice, almost purring, Harker said, "It's a whole new ballgame, Mr. Whitestone! Your life was turned upside down last weekend, and that was a tragedy. You have my sympathies. But if you can make the mental adjustment to the reality of your new situation, truly wonderful things can come of it. So far things have been a disaster, am I right?"

"Too right."

Then let Martin Turnbill take charge and we'll show you the good future that comes from the bad past."

"If I even *have* a future. I don't think I'm exaggerating when I tell you that my life is in danger."

"Not to worry. Among much else, we are experts at client security. If you and I come to terms, we'll have our top-flight protection team surrounding you and your family almost immediately. Are you willing to discuss this in more detail and then possibly sign a contract?"

Franklin didn't hesitate. "Yes, I am. Very interested. What's the next step?"

"I'll fly to Columbus tomorrow morning and then take a cab to wherever you are. Give me your address."

So they talked a couple of minutes more, setting up the details of Jonathan Harker's trip. Franklin hung up the phone and found he was in a considerably better mood than he'd been when he'd picked it up.

Now, with the calls to his new lawyer and his new PR firm completed, he finally appeared to be getting some control over this mess. It occurred to him that once again his amazing mother had been the source of this happy change of circumstances. Just to please her, he resolved to phone her this evening with his thanks. That would make her day.

"If we fire Franklin—well, edge him out the door—what will become of him? Don't we have some sort of a moral duty to try and find a place for him to land?" This was one of the questions at the Factor, Marroni, & Ray senior partners meeting late Wednesday afternoon.

"How could we do that?" someone else asked. "Who'd take him? It's like he's radioactive, infecting everyone around him."

"Maybe he could be moved overseas, say to Europe. They're pretty laissez faire about non-religion. Didn't France just elect an atheist President?"

"Fuck, Whitestone!" thundered Paul Factor, the senior named partner. "He brought this on himself, the godless bastard! Wait until the devil snatches him, and he'll get what he deserves for mocking Our Lord!"

That produced a silence. Factor was, well, a major factor in any decision made by the firm, but, lawyers all, they knew they couldn't let religious judgments enter the picture without queering the lawsuit. Even worse, everyone in the room except Factor, who was old and losing it, immediately envisioned being deposed or on the witness stand and asked the dreaded question, "Was there any discussion condemning Mr. Whitestone's religious views?" That would now require a very delicately phrased response.

Howard Ray jumped into the void. "I had quite a talk with him on Monday, and I made it clear that the ice was thawing under his skates. Franklin's no dummy. He'll appreciate that we have no realistic choice but to let him go. Maybe he'll even see reason and depart quietly. After all, arguably he has even more to lose than we do if there is a public battle about whether he's fit to practice law. Let me meet with him again and report back."

There was general agreement that Ray should have a go at making Whitestone compliant, though few had any real hope of that succeeding. Amidst some grousing, the meeting broke up, and Howard Ray walked wearily back to his office. It was only Wednesday and it had already been a bear of a week. As he neared his office door, Manny Cardoza, his administrative assistant, stopped him.

"Carol Lebeau called. She wants to talk to you right away."

Ray frowned. "What the hell could she want this time? Have you taken to hitting on the female associates?"

"Never on Wednesdays, boss."

Ray went to his desk and sat down, Cardoza following him into the office.

"Let me have her number," Ray said with an exasperated sigh. "Might as well give her a call and see what she's got brewing in her cauldron."

Martha Waxman, the youngest of the four children of Alexander and Catherine Whitestone, was the organizer of the family, and she'd taken it upon herself to put together a conference call with two of her other siblings: Jefferson, the eldest, and Abigail, who was two years older than Martha. Franklin, the second born, was not included in the conference call for two reasons: they wanted to talk about what to do to help him without having to censor what they said, and—the clincher—they had idea how to reach him. He wasn't returning phone calls. Their mother probably had his contact information, but finding that out would have required a phone call to her, and none of them volunteered to do that.

The children's names were the second generation of a new family tradition. Their father, Alexander, had been so named because his father was an ardent fan of Alexander Hamilton. When Alexander himself came to name his children, Catherine suggested historical names from the same period, and thus Jefferson, Franklin, Abigail, and Martha. Only one small argument broke out between the parents as to these selections. Alexander Whitestone was not a fan of Thomas Jefferson (Hamilton's most vocal critic), and resisted naming his first born after the man. But Catherine particularly liked the name "Jefferson" as a boy's first name, and, as usual, she'd gotten her way.

The children had certain characteristics in common: they were all intelligent, personable, and possessing a keen sense of humor. Much differentiated them from each other, however. Jefferson had never settled down in life, switching jobs, traveling all over the world, never marrying. Martha called him the "family hippie," and there was some truth to that.

Currently he was in Seattle, supposedly making a living writing freelance columns for magazines and newspapers. They all privately hoped he was not close to, or actually living on, the streets.

Abigail too had never married, but she lived in Columbus with a wonderful woman named Beth Anglin. They had been together for nine years, and it was a source of family annoyance that Abigail had never admitted to her family that she was lesbian. Why would she keep silent about something they all knew anyway? It had certainly been obvious long before she moved in with another woman. Abigail had captained her basketball teams in both high school and college, was a golf pro at one of the largest courses in town, and the two women had named their cats Gertrude and Alice. The Whitestones were one of the most freethinking families around, and it would've made things easier if Abigail were more forthcoming.

Martha herself had married early, during her first year of college, to the handsome, but scatterbrained, Douglas Waxman, an elementary school teacher, and the two of them had promptly produced three grandchildren for Alexander and Catherine. The whole Waxman clan lived in Cincinnati, where Martha worked as special assistant to the mayor. It was generally agreed that Martha, something of a control freak, was in completely in charge of all conferences between the Whitestone siblings. This surprised no one who knew her mother.

Franklin was the most traditional of them all, growing up as a dutiful family member, earning good grades, doing well in college and law school, joining a law firm and making partner in the shortest period of time possible. The most remarkable thing about him was his son, Todd. Martha had first learned that the boy was not cut from the common mold when, at age five, he had solemnly informed her that it was all right for her to have three babies, because the other siblings had only one (that being him), and so the Whitestone line as a whole was getting smaller, and thus not adding to the problem of too many people on the planet Earth.

Jefferson had resisted participating in this conference call ("What could we three possibly do that isn't already being done?" to which Martha replied, "That's the very thing we're going to discuss"), but he had been brought around by Martha's suggestion that he might get a publishable column or two out of the mess. Abigail, all business as usual, agreed right away.

On Wednesday evening, at the appointed hour, Martha talked to the operator and made sure the relevant connections went through, and the three of them were soon on the line together.

"Both Franklin and Todd, along with Mary, have dropped out of sight," Martha began. "The press and who-knows-who-else are searching for them like people trying to find a dropped lit match."

"I'm very worried," Abigail said. "It's no exaggeration to say that this could be dangerous."

"I agree," Martha replied. "Okay. We're clever people. How do we help?"

"They could move to Seattle and live with me," Jefferson offered. "I just bought a house, and I've got plenty of room."

"WHAT?" both sisters said together.

"Yes. It's in the Capitol Hill district. Things have been going sort of well financially, and I'm thinking of getting married."

"WHAT?" both sisters said again.

"It's time. I'm 45 and can't put it off much longer. You should all come out for the wedding and meet Joanne. Wonderful woman. Her father took a liking to me and got me a job as an editor at the Seattle publishing firm he runs."

"Mom will love this!" Martha enthused, wonder in her voice.

"Makes you ask if there isn't a God after all," Abigail mused.

"How about this? The three of us, as his brother and sisters, make some sort of public statement supporting Franklin and Todd," Martha suggested.

Jefferson pooh-poohed that. "To what end? The press would just ask us what our own religious views are, and we'd have to admit that we are godless heathens, and then all three of us would also be looking for places to hide."

Abigail broke in. "Actually, I've started going to church."

Martha almost dropped the phone.

"WHAT?" she and Jefferson said together.

"Don't worry," Abigail soothed. "Beth and I decided to join the local Unitarian Church because a lot of our friends go there. The Unitarians don't preach any particular dogma, and in fact a number of their members are atheists."

"A Whitestone in church!" Jefferson said, wonder in his voice. "Doomsday to follow immediately. Oh, Abby, I have to be there when you tell Mom!"

"*She doesn't have to know!*" said Abigail, sounding every bit as stern as their mother did when making a definitive ruling on some family matter. "And the sibling who tells her will have to answer to me." She paused. "Do you both hear me, siblings?"

117

"Yes," they said together. As children they'd all learned what a mistake it was to get on Abigail's bad side.

"This church is a very calm, soothing environment in a beautiful, tasteful building. The pastor is a lesbian, so it's very welcoming to gay people. Beth and I like that."

There was a stunned silence at how casually Abigail had just come out to them. Another milestone in family history had been achieved.

"This is some phone call," Martha observed, thinking that their mother would be pleased this revelation was now behind them. "But congratulations to you and Beth—I think. Even a very liberal congregation like that must contain some elements who disapprove of what Franklin and Todd have said so publicly."

"I'll keep my ears open, and let you know, but I don't think so. The Unitarians are determinedly non-judgmental. With no god at the center, and no defined agenda being pushed, it hardly seems religious at all. More like a Sunday social group. You two should explore your local versions and see what I mean."

"Do you know the old riddle?" Martha asked, suddenly remembering it. "What do you get if you cross a Jehovah's Witness with a Unitarian?"

"Tell me," Abigail replied, suspicious.

"Someone who goes door to door for no ostensible purpose."

Polite laughter at this, and then Jefferson said, "Actually, I'm not eligible to be a Unitarian. I don't meet the membership requirements."

"Nonsense," Abigail protested. "There are no membership requirements."

"Yes, there are," Jefferson informed her. "You have to swear to respect the beliefs of others, and I can't do that. I think most people's beliefs are despicable."

"Hmm. Not qualifying to join the Unitarians is a new low for you, Jeff," Martha commented.

"Not at all. I am upholding the Catherine Whitestone standard for non-religious purity. Mom would be proud of me. It's Abby who has strayed from the fold and is in danger of becoming a lost lamb."

"Bah," Abigail bleated.

That evening Franklin made up his mind that sometime after midnight he would sneak back to his home and load his car with the items he needed to make his stay in the B&B more comfortable. A couple of suitcases filled with various things should do it, so he compiled a list. His basement contained a number of empty suitcases of various sizes to choose from, and if he didn't dawdle he should be in and out in under twenty minutes.

With this nocturnal trip in mind he took a nap around 6 p.m., waking an hour later, refreshed and ready for his midnight adventure.

Shortly thereafter his mother called.

"Franklin, you need to watch out for a man named Jake Richardson. He's looking for you, and he could be major trouble."

"Who is he?"

"He's a religious nut who also happens to be the worker who was operating the machine that knocked down the wall and freed you Sunday morning."

"Big tall skinny guy?"

"Yes. Dark hair."

"I saw a tv interview with him on Sunday afternoon before I flew to New York. It occurred to me then that I ought to look him up and say 'thank you,' but I've been a little sidetracked."

"Oh, I think you'd be well advised to skip that gesture. He was over at my house just minutes ago explaining to me how you need to have more of God in your life. He was very upset, and I mean *very* upset, with your extemporaneous musings on the Jimmy Ball Show. He's planning on telling you just what you should be saying in the future."

"Did he threaten you?" Franklin sounded worried.

She gave a small laugh. "Oh, no. He somehow got the impression that I was on his side, so we parted buddies."

"How did he get into your house in the first place?"

"Through the front door. I let him in, heard him out, and then, like Bugs Bunny with Elmer Fudd, kissed him on the forehead and sent him on his way. I did promise him I'd pass on his message to you, and with this phone call my duties in the matter are completed. Want his address and phone number? I have that too."

"No thanks. And from now on don't let any strangers in your house!"

"Oh, Franklin, you of all people should appreciate that I can take care of myself. If I'd have wanted to, I could have eaten Mr. Richardson alive. You know that."

"Mom, do I have to yell at you? *Don't let any more strangers in your house!*"

"Not even little ones?"

"MOM!"

"Okay, okay. I promise. Are you done doing stupid things yourself?"

Thinking about his planned midnight foray, Franklin paused only slightly before saying, "Yes, yes. I've had enough to last me the rest of the year."

"Just what any loving mother wants to hear. Well, I have to go now. The national evening news is coming on, and these days I count on it to keep me abreast of what my family is doing. Are Todd and Mary safely hidden and out of trouble?"

"Yes. We all are, Mom. I promise."

"Keep it that way. And if you meet a man who introduces himself as Jake Richardson, run. Religious people are always saying that there's a devil out there waiting to drag us down. In this case they may be right. Good night, honey."

"Wait, Mom. There's something I need to thank you for." And he brought her up to date on the auspicious changes that were in store for Franklin and his family.

Dan and Nan had a quick meal before settling down for the night. It was Nan's turn to take the first shift, so Dan climbed inside his sleeping bag and zipped it shut against the unseasonably cold September air.

"I love you" Dan said to Nan.

"I love you too," Nan said to Dan. But her tone was flat, and he wondered if she meant it.

Mary and Todd were keeping to themselves as much as possible, and one way to do this was to eat a lot of fast food—take out and drive-throughs being their favorite hunting and gathering choices. Wednesday evening they decided on pizza, and placed an order with Donatos for delivery to their motel room.

They'd also agreed that it was smartest for Mary alone to conduct all dealings with the public, so when there was a knock on the motel door twenty minutes after they had phoned in their order, she took a quick peek through the tiny aperture in the door and, seeing the distorted shape of what appeared to be a kid in a red hat, opened up. Todd was safely hidden in the bathroom. Possibly being too cautious, but not wanting the pizza man to see inside the room at all, Mary stepped out of the motel room and closed the door behind her. It really was the pizza boy of course, a skinny kid who looked all of twelve, and she quickly paid and bid him good night. As she was turning to go back in, pizza box in hand, she noticed movement of some kind near the back of her van, which was parked directly in front of their motel room.

Adrenalin immediately began pumping in gallons through her system. Mary paused to stare carefully at the van. She waited a few seconds, but saw nothing more. She debated putting down the pizza box and having a quick walk around the van just to be sure, but decided she was being too jumpy.

Mary turned around, but then discovered to her annoyance that she had locked herself out. Feeling foolish, she knocked on the door, and called out, "Todd! I'm locked out!"

After a moment, he opened the door and looked at her quizzically. "Did you have to yell out 'Todd?' What happened to 'Clark'?"

Carrying the pizza box, she brushed past him and closed the door. "You're right, of course. I'm sorry. I got rattled. Just now I thought I saw somebody lurking around the van."

That got Todd's attention and he looked worriedly at the door. "What did you see?" he asked.

"Probably nothing. There's been entirely too much excitement in the last couple of days, and my nerves are shot."

As she said this there was a loud knock at the door. They both jumped as if tasered, and, eyes wide, they stared at each other, confused.

The knock was repeated.

"*Get in the bathroom!*" Mary hissed.

"Mom!" he protested, unwilling to leave her alone to face whatever was on the other side of that door.

"*Do it!*" she commanded, steel in her voice. With a dubious look on his face, Todd stepped into the bathroom and partially closed the door, peering through the slit this left.

"Who is it?" Mary said through the motel door without opening it.

"Pizza. I gave you the wrong box by mistake."

She stared at the pizza box sitting on a table next to the door, as if waiting for the box to confirm or deny its correctness. Mary considered the situation.

"Ma'am?" said the voice on the other side of the door.

It did *sound* like the pizza boy, so, impulsively, tired of all this drama, she opened the door.

Once again it really *was* the pizza boy, and he dutifully held out a new box. "Sorry," he said. "My bad. This is the right one." Seeing the original box on the table, he deftly switched the two, nodded, and went out the door. Relieved, but wanting to have another quick glance around the parking lot, Mary stepped out after him, this time being careful to take the room key with her.

All seemed quiet except for the noises made by the pizza boy as he climbed into his car and drove off. It was chilly outside, but otherwise a beautiful night. As Mary turned to go back into the motel room, inserting the key in the lock, a car alarm went off from the parking lot to her right. She jumped and banged painfully against the door jamb. The shrill insistent BEEP BEEP BEEP caused doors to open on this side of the motel, and a number of guests peered out.

One of them said, "Sorry, folks. It's mine! Damn thing has been going off for no reason at all recently." The man rushed from his room to the car, and in a few seconds the dreaded beeping stopped, replaced by a welcome silence.

"I can't take much more of this," Mary mumbled to herself. Were they in danger or not? How close were any pursuers? Should they move again? How expensive would that be? Per Franklin's instruction they had taken $500 from an ATM on the other side of Dayton, so they had enough cash to hold them over for the present. He'd promised to figure out a way to wire them more money. Todd opened the motel door and looked at her. "What's going on, Mom? Everything all right?"

She was annoyed that he was visible to passers-by, and he wasn't wearing his ersatz glasses. "Yes, get inside, *Clark*" she replied, accenting the last word for all within earshot to hear, and then followed him into the room, shutting the door firmly behind her. "Let's eat."

They sat at the little table and bit into the lukewarm pizza. Mary had forgotten to order a beverage, and she thought briefly about making a run to the vending area for soft drinks, but decided she had had enough of going outside for awhile, and settled for tap water.

Suddenly there was another knock at the door. Loud.

Pizzas in hand, they exchanged startled glances. Now what?

"Hello?" a voice said from outside.

"Yes?" Mary called, hesitant, both worry and anger mixing in that 'yes.'

"You've left your key in the door," came the answer. "Thought you'd want to know." There followed the sound of someone walking away rapidly.

Her hands trembling, Mary opened the door slowly, peered out and saw no one. She glanced at the key sitting stupidly in the lock, snatched it out, and closed the door once more.

She looked wearily at Todd, who had resumed eating. "It's like a Marx Brothers movie," she observed.

"Yes, isn't this fun?" he replied. "A trip with an experienced travel writer is always one surprise after another."

"Wake up, Dan," Nan said, shaking him. "Time for your shift."

He sat up on one elbow, blinking.

"You take midnight until four a.m., and then it's me again."

Climbing out of his sleeping bag in the back of their van, Dan said, "Right. Any activity?"

"Nothing happening at all," Nan replied.

CHAPTER EIGHT

OUTSIDE THE DOOR

On his last two trips home, Franklin had parked his car on the street behind his condo, sneaked through the gate that led to the back yard of the young couple who lived between that road and the condominium development, climbed the slatted wooden fence that separated their property from his, and sneaked into the patio door at the back of his unit. This had worked well enough—the fence was only slightly taller than waist high—and he assumed that they hadn't noticed his various trespasses across their property. But for this particular midnight foray he wanted to avoid this route entirely, and leave their yard alone. So this time Franklin parked his rental car two blocks from his condo unit on the street facing the front of the development, and crept cautiously up to the side of the first unit, and then walked quickly around back and made his way by this longer route to his patio door, which he unlocked and entered. Apparently no one saw him. Good.

The drapes and blinds were still closed from his last visit, so Franklin saw little risk in turning on a central hallway light, which wouldn't be visible from the outside. This gave him enough illumination that he could walk around the first floor gathering the items on his list and putting them one by one in a pile he made on the living room sofa. When the relevant articles were assembled, he went down into the basement and brought up two large suitcases, into which he then packed his booty.

Ready to leave, Franklin stood irresolutely in the living room next to the front door and considered his options. The safest thing to do would be to elect his usual exit route and take the suitcases out the patio door and then retrace his steps to the car. The problem with this solution was that it meant carrying two rather heavy suitcases a considerably greater distance than if he simply went out the front door, walked to the street, turned right and walked a block to where the car was parked.

What to do?

All his instincts, carefully considered, told him that the neighborhood was free of surreptitious surveillance and that he was alone in his nocturnal wanderings. It had been two days since he was last here, and clearly the media were gone, seeking him elsewhere after deciding that this place was a dry hole. Nor was it likely that anyone who intended him harm would still be staking out his neighborhood, particularly not at this time of the night. Where would they hide? Wouldn't they have better things to do than to keep careful watch over an abandoned abode?

The whole disguise thing was getting old, and Franklin felt sillier every time he painstakingly attached his phony mustache to his upper lip with spirit gum, looking worriedly at his efforts in the mirror. Surely this was overkill. Whatever anxiety he'd caused to people who would wish him harm was likely to have abated over the last 48 hours, at least to the point where the risk of going out the front door—carefully, silently—was a sound gamble.

Oh? he asked himself. A sound gamble even if betting your life?

That gave him pause, and he stood at the front door, suitcases on either side of him, frozen with indecision. A line from Shakespeare (his favorite author, one he had studied with fascination since he was a boy) came to him: "Like a man to double business bound, I stand in pause where I shall first begin, and both neglect."

Clearly it would be smarter to exit out the back, walk the extra distance, and be free of hazard. There *were* people who'd like to see him dead. He wasn't imagining their existence. He'd read the emails and they iced his spine.

I'm being too melodramatic! he thought. I can't live the rest of my life scurrying around like a mouse in a house full of cats. *All* existence involves some degree of risk, and it's merely a matter of gauging the acceptable degree.

Without consciously having come to a decision, as if compelled by the same mysterious internal direction (the Great Turtle?) that on Saturday had sent him to the concession stand to buy popcorn all the while knowing it was a bad idea, Franklin gently opened the front door and peered around.

The night view of the cul de sac in the front of his house, a view that he saw every time he went out the front door, was silent and still, ordinary and uninteresting. There were some vehicles parked in the semicircle roadway outlining the condo units, but that was usually the case, and meant nothing. None of them looked suspicious. They were all empty.

Slowly nodding his head, as if approving of his own choice, Franklin picked up the suitcases and stepped quietly out onto the front stoop. He set the suitcases down, and turned to close the door behind him.

That movement saved his life.

A bullet, making no sound other than a high-pitched ZING, raced past his ear and buried itself in the corner of the door he was reaching to close, hitting with an impact that showered him and the stoop with shards of wood, sending him falling to his knees. Now, with another move that also saved his life, he rolled off the stoop and onto the lawn next to it. He regained his balance on hands and knees (was that another ZING he heard?), and he frantically crawled around the corner, out of sight of the front door, where he leaped to his feet and ran like an Olympic sprinter down the side of the unit, around the back, and dove headfirst into the yard of the young couple who lived behind him, crashing painfully into the swing set, which loudly clanged its contents together.

Franklin scrambled to his feet and, running across the yard, he again scaled the small fence on the side that led to the front of the house. He could, of course, have just stopped and opened the gate, but he had no time for that, and knew he'd lose time fumbling with the latch. Lights were coming on both in this house and the one next to it, and before any serious investigation could expose him, he ran to the street, turned right, and kept on going.

"*HOW COULD YOU HAVE MISSED HIM? HE WAS A BIG STATIONARY TARGET!*" Nan was furious, looking as if, in her anger, she'd smack Dan with the butt of the rifle she'd snatched up when the first shot was fired. She had jerked herself out of the sleeping bag, reaching his side just as he got off the second round.

Sheepish, and at the same time afraid of her, Dan could only mumble, "He was *not* stationary. He *moved* just as I fired and that's why I missed him. Then he sort of dropped out of view on the other side of the porch and ran like a madman. I squeezed off another round, but that was just out of frustration. There was no chance of hitting him once he dove into the yard."

She stared hard at him for a few seconds, saying nothing. He looked away.

Her silence got to him. They had to get out of here, so he said to her, "Whitestone made a racket as he went around the back of the building." She still didn't reply. "Nan, people will be *coming!*"

"Ain't no penalty for shooting you right here," Nan said, clearly considering it.

"*Please*, honey, control yourself! We'll have another chance at him, or a chance at his son, I promise. You need to keep thinking about what we have to do before Friday at 8 p.m. You know you're gonna need me until then. You cain't do this thing alone."

She worked this through. Finally, saying nothing, she put down her rifle and started securing the weapons they'd laid out in the back of the van on arrival. "You drive," she said at last, "and I'll take care of all this." He gave her a tight smile, pleased, and she added with more urgency, "Let's go—and pull out slowly. We can't afford to be stopped and then have to kill some poor cop."

126

Dan did as instructed, climbing into the driver's seat and starting the van after first checking in all directions to make sure they weren't being observed. He waited to turn on the headlights until they were out of the cul de sac and turning onto Martin.

Nan finished her chores in the back, and then climb into the front seat. They drove in silence for two miles before she spoke.

"I really like the idea of giving up on Whitestone and going after the boy."

Dan was relieved to hear her talk about it rationally. The fire was gone from her eyes, which had resumed the dullness they'd had since last Friday.

"Yes," he said, nodding enthusiastically. "The kid next."

They began discussing how they were going to do that.

Ever since Sunday evening late, when Franklin dropped her off at her home, Kelly Keyfold cried. Sunday night had been the worst, filled with sobs that convulsed her body like someone having a seizure, and moans that were not quite shrieks. Sleep had been impossible, and she'd spent the night rolling around in her bed. If she started to doze off, which happened two or three times, she'd put her arm out reflexively to the spot where Franklin normally lay, and finding he was not there would jerk her awake and start a new, terrible flow of tears.

How could this have happened so suddenly when things had been so good for so long? This same question persistently tortured her, and didn't seem to be abating much in the days since that awful moment in New York City when Franklin had labeled her and all other believers "embarrassments" for pretending to be "intelligent" while relying on an "imaginary friend." Those hateful words played out repeatedly in her head.

Her crying hadn't been 24/7, but it had been her default state when she wasn't absolutely engaged in tasks that forbade it. She'd been able to keep herself under control at work. In fact, she felt her most normal in the classroom where the concentration required to stop seventy very bright law students from sensing weakness and going for the jugular, kept her attention admirably fixed on the task at hand.

On the other hand, embarrassingly, she had been caught crying at inappropriate moments, such as taking her trash out to the curb. One of the large plastic bags she was carrying had split open, dumping its messy contents at the edge of Kelly's driveway, and as she half-heartedly began picking up the slimy debris to throw in her trash bin, it all seemed a metaphor for her life, and she suddenly lost it and sobbed.

This behavior attracted the attention of her next door neighbor, Ellen Sanders, a kindly woman in her 40s, who was toting her own trash to the curb. In the three years that Kelly had lived next door, the two women had talked off and on when they met coming and going, and were friendly, without being friends. But now, seeing Kelly weeping over her trash, Ellen rushed to her, put her arm around the kneeling woman, pulled her to her feet, and hugged her close.

Kelly was crying too hard to talk, and Ellen asked no questions. She did quietly offer consoling phrases such as "It's all right," and "Take your time and let it out," and, when Kelly subsided some, led her back into the Sanders house. She sat Kelly on the living room sofa, and then, without being invited to do so, made her a cup of hot chocolate. Kelly hadn't had hot chocolate since she was a little girl, and drinking it absolutely violated her dietary rules, but it tasted wonderful, and as she consumed it she stopped keening and went silent.

Finally, Ellen ventured a question. "Man trouble?" she guessed.

Kelly gave her a wry smile. "I'm dating Franklin Whitestone," she replied.

Ellen's eyebrows shot up. "Oh, my!" she said.

"I don't know what to do. I'm a Baptist and he's . . . he's, " but she couldn't finish the sentence. Ellen, sitting next to her on the sofa, took her hand.

"I'm a Christian, too," Ellen told her. "But it isn't the Christian way to condemn. You and Franklin Whitestone have had a disagreement. Does that mean you've ceased to love him?"

"No," Kelly mumbled after a small hesitation.

"Jesus's message is one of compassion and understanding. You should concentrate on that. You're focusing inward on the hurt you've suffered. But, have you considered that in this situation you might have a higher calling? To help and heal him?"

That gave Kelly pause. It was true. She had been completely self absorbed.

"Hmm," was all she could manage in reply.

Ellen smiled. "I don't mean that you should try and convert him," she assured Kelly. "That would be nice, but probably futile. But you can do a lot just by setting a Christian example of love and caring. Let him come to you and perhaps, as time goes by, he might also find his way to God."

Kelly didn't know how to respond. She found herself saying, "But the Bible says 'be not unequally yoked with nonbelievers."

128

Ellen shrugged. "One has to deal with whatever life sends. Nonbelievers exist, and if you love one, shunning isn't the answer. Have you tried prayer?"

Kelly nodded. She had been praying.

"Try more prayer."

This advice and the tender, unexpected affection that accompanied it, helped Kelly a great deal, and she had since redoubled her dedicated attempts at serious prayer.

But there was a problem with that, as well. Not long into any prayer session she would catch her mind wandering off into forbidden territory. A major reason for this straying was her disturbing reaction to Todd Whitestone's pernicious webcast.

When first she worked her way through it, Kelly had sneered with contempt at the posting's quotations, cutesy cartoons, and puerile logic. But she'd always had a keen intellect and a raging curiosity about the world and its workings, and Todd's lecture began to get to her. What if he (and, by extension, his father) were right?

What if there were no God?

When this thought first occurred to her she'd brushed it off. Like most thinking people she had, in her past, contemplated the possibility that God didn't exist, but her last serious exploration of the issue had stopped at age fifteen when she had talked to her parents about her budding doubts, and was told not to be silly, that God was as certain as the ground they all stood upon, His existence proven beyond question by the wonders of the world. Her mother had pointed out how often He granted them the things they prayed for, and how comforting He was in times of sorrow and trouble. One had only to read the newspaper to see evidence of miracle after miracle as miraculous things happened like babies surviving falls out of fourth story windows, or terminally ill patients returning to perfect health after being written off as hopeless, or the face of Jesus appearing magically on surfaces such as the glare off a large office building window.

This last sort of miracle had always struck her as suspicious. Kelly's next door neighbor as she grew up was Mary Comstock, an other-worldly child, very religious, always talking aloud about seeing God everywhere. One memorable time, Mary had burned some toast and while scrapping off the burnt part with a kitchen knife had suddenly realized that the remaining blackened portions created a silhouette of Jesus's face, complete with halo. With trembling hands, Mary had shown this piece of toast to Kelly, and it *did* look startlingly like Jesus. But on sober reflection, even at age ten Kelly had thought it unlikely that Jesus was manifesting His presence through the malfunction of a toaster.

Having read Todd's heresy over the first time, Kelly had nearly pressed the Delete key and sent it back into cyberspace, not to be thought of again. But, without quite knowing why, she'd left it on the screen when she turned off the monitor. Sitting down at her desk three hours later to check email, she found Todd's webcast patiently waiting for her. Kelly made the mistake of rereading it and this time it bothered her more. Was she so close-minded that she couldn't ask herself basic questions about her beliefs? Was her belief that shallow? Or was she really afraid that religion was some monumental misunderstanding of how life actually worked?

These questions both scared and intrigued Kelly.

If there were no God, she mused, think of all the wasted time and effort that went into supporting this universal delusion. Example after example came to mind: all the holy men and women (ministers, mullahs, rabbis, nuns, the Pope himself) devoting their lives to worshiping a shadow, the billions of people falling to their knees day after day and begging for help that wasn't coming, the hatred that led to war and killings over competing versions of the supposed demands of a nonexistent deity. She was bothered most by one of Todd's concluding thoughts, which she read over and over again: "It is surely an error to run the world according to a mistaken principle."

All this terrified her, and she threw it off as quickly as she could, Todd must be wrong. He was only a sixteen year old kid. Everyone thought he was wrong.

Kelly thought so too.

She really did.

Winded and wheezing, Franklin Whitestone, no jogger, finally stopped running when he reached Sawmill Road, using a circuitous route which he adopted in part because he was rushing blindly through the dark, but also because it was calculated, he hoped, to shake off any pursuer. In what seemed a very short period of time, he discovered that he'd run more than a mile, the first time he'd done that since his sophomore year in college. His heart was jumping around in his chest the same way it had in the stadium disaster, and sweat spewed from every pore in his body. Even though it was a chilly September night and he was wearing only a windbreaker, he was hot. He bent over, hands on his knees, panting like an asthma victim.

And—he was startled to find—he was strangely happy, joyous still to be alive, invigorated. On Saturday, a mere three days ago, he'd been sure he was dying when the bomb went off, and now he'd narrowly missed another form of death as a bullet whizzed by his head and struck inches away from where he was standing. Was he invincible? Franklin felt charmed, able to leap small buildings in a couple of bounds or so. Wasn't there a Winston Churchill quote that went something like "Nothing in life is so exhilarating as to be shot at without result"? He now knew what Winnie meant.

Still, on more sober reflection, he decided he was willing to forego any similar death-defying moments for the rest of a life that he hoped would be both long and dull. Any doubts that he'd had that there really were people out there who not only wanted his death, but would act upon that mania, were gone. He was *not* being paranoid in wearing a false mustache and hiding his whereabouts. He was being prudent.

Thinking these thoughts brought him around to consideration of Corbin Milk's offer of further aid. Milk had already proved very useful in his advice to Franklin and then to Todd and Mary, and it now he needed the big man once again.

But first, how to return to his car? Thinking the issue through suspiciously, not wanting to make another mistake, Franklin decided that it wasn't much of a risk to sneak back. The car was parked more than a block from his condo, and no one knew it was there. But what was he going to do about the two suitcases still sitting on his front stoop? And, try as he might to remember, Franklin couldn't be sure he'd even closed the front door. Hmm. An open-doored house would fill with reporters, curious passers-by, souvenir hunters, and assorted other riffraff.

As he resumed walking, Franklin pulled his cell phone from his pocket and punched Milk's number on the speed dial. Milk answered on the second ring.

"Hello," he said, sleep clogging his voice.

"Corbin, it's Franklin Whitestone. I'm sorry to wake you at this time of the morning, but I've managed to get myself into more trouble—big trouble—and I need to take you up on your kind offer of help."

"Of course," Milk said without hesitation, coming awake. "What time is it?"

Franklin looked at the display on the phone. "1:04 a.m.," he replied.

"Give me a minute—are you in a position to wait that long?"

"Yes. I was shot at—and I'm sure glad *that's* over—and now I'm walking back to my car. I'm in no immediate danger." I *think*, he thought.

"Hang on," Milk said. Thirty seconds went by while Milk accomplished some mysterious task, and then he was back on the phone. "Okay," he said, sounding more alert. "Tell me everything that happened and your current status, and I'll see what I can do."

So Franklin narrated the story of his evening, finishing with his fence dives and the marathon sprint through the streets of northwest Columbus. He then explained about the suitcases and making sure the front door was latched.

After a small pause, Milk commented, "I assume you know how stupid your decision to return home was?"

"Very stupid," Franklin replied, meaning it.

"Just asking. You should've called me before any of this. Modesty aside, I know how to get things done without gratuitous gunplay. Are you hurt?"

"Not from the bullet. All this running around has set my thigh wound bleeding. I don't think it's bad." He felt along his left thigh, which was tightly bandaged under his pants. Now that he had focused on it, the wound hurt more than he'd realized. His pants leg felt sticky, but he didn't think the problem was serious. He slowed deliberately as he walked.

"Well," Milk said, "I can't help with your medical issues, but I will go by your condo as soon as it's daylight and pick up those suitcases. I'll bring them to you at your B&B. Give me that address again."

"Aren't *you* worried about being shot at?"

"No. Why would anyone want to shoot me? No one is going to mistake me for you. We look nothing alike."

Picturing Milk's physical resemblance to Arnold Schwarzenegger, Franklin allowed that it was true. "But," he asked, worried, "is it safe to bring the suitcases to me? You could be followed."

"Ah, no," Milk said with assurance.

"No? Why not?"

"Franklin, I wouldn't do anything to put you in more danger, and, if you like, I can suggest several other stratagems for getting those bags to you. But you can also trust me to do what I say I can do. No one, and I mean *no one*, is going to be able to follow me."

Intrigued, Franklin asked, "Care to explain that?"

"Not now. When I see you."

So they talked a couple of minutes more, making sure that they had their plans straight, and Franklin thanked Milk profusely.

"Corbin, I'm so in your debt—Mary and Todd too. What can we ever do to repay you?"

Milk was ready with the answer to that one. "I want to play myself in the movie they're going to make about all this."

"There's a woman waiting to see you," the receptionist at Abion Construction and Demolition informed Jake Richardson when he came into work on Thursday morning. He blinked at her in surprise.

"See me?" Jake asked, confused. He had never heard of anyone having a visitor here at the office, much less one there for him. What was this all about?

"Over there," the receptionist said, pointing to the chair by the front door.

The waiting visitor proved to be a woman in her thirties, with wispy brown hair. She was tall like Jake himself, but startlingly thinner. He'd never seen her before.

"Yes, Ma'am," he said to her as he walked up. She stood.

"Mr. Richardson?"

"That's right."

"My name is Celia Hawkins." She held out her hand and he shook it awkwardly. "I know it is somewhat forward of me to bother you at work, but I didn't know how else to contact you. My sister Betty was one of the people who was trapped in Ohio Stadium last weekend, and your wonderful talents with the Big Claw saved her. I just wanted to say thanks for restoring her to her family!" At this she teared up, dabbed at her eyes with the back of her hand, and, after the briefest of pauses, impetuously hugged him.

Jake turned bright red instantly. He had no idea what to say in reply, but she saved him by going on herself.

"I saw the interview you did on tv with Harold Wang, and I was very impressed at how cool you were in that stressful situation. You were incredible! Thank you! Thank you, Mr. Richardson!"

"Well, thanks yourself," he said to her, very pleased. "Call me Jake."

Celia glanced at the receptionist, who was carefully listening to every word.

"Could I talk to you outside for a minute?" Celia asked, making a gesture toward the door Jake had just come through.

"Sure," he said, nodding his head and opening the door for her. They stepped outside the office door and onto the sidewalk bordering the company parking lot. It was chilly in the morning sun, but warmer than yesterday. Celia turned to him and put her hand on his arm.

"We thought Betty had died! It was the hardest 24 hours of my life. I cried more or less nonstop, but what I mostly did was pray to God that she would somehow come out of that nightmare alive."

Jake smiled. "I was sure praying myself," he told her.

"I also saw the second interview after the rescue was over, and you were wonderful then too."

"Well, thank you kindly, Ma'am"

She paused, unsure how to phrase her next thought. "Jake, you said on tv that you found Jesus Christ at an early age."

Jake bobbed his head vigorously up and down, agreeing, "Oh, yes, Ma'am. He guides my every move!"

She teared up again. "Me too," she said, looking at him earnestly, searching his eyes.

Instinct taking over, Jake suddenly understood that she was coming on to him! Well . . . *all right!* He been on tv and now he had himself a groupie!

Jake looked at her in a new light. Not a bad looking woman once he eyeballed her closely. Too skinny, and no boobs at all, but what did that matter? Heather had big bazookers, and look how that had turned out.

"Look," he said after a slight pause, "I've got to go to work, but would you like to meet me at the Havana Diner," he pointed to the small eatery across the street, "when I get done? We could have some coffee and talk."

Celia beamed with pleasure, reddening herself. "Oh, yes!" she said with great enthusiasm.

"About 5:15?" She nodded. "We might also get a bite to eat. I'll be sweaty and dusty you understand," Jake added. "I hope that's okay."

"'In the sweat of thy face shalt thou eat bread, till thou return unto the ground,'" she quoted with a smile.

Jake knew that one. It was Genesis 3:19, the first book in the Bible that he'd memorized completely. They awkwardly shook hands and parted.

This encounter had an inevitable ending. Jake and Celia spent the entire night together, barely sleeping at all. Both were devout people, but they appeared to have missed all those homilies against fornication.

When Stubby Allen went to the Whitestone house on Thursday around 5:00 p.m. to retrieve Todd's things, he took along his eight year old sister, Wendy. It was his plan to use her as a lookout while he went inside the Whitestone residence. Stubby's older brother Roger had agreed that he'd drive Stubby and Todd's swag to Dayton later in the evening.

Stubby, Wendy beside him (pleased as always for any attention her brothers gave her), drove Roger's car over to the Todd's, and parked it on the side of the house, in a part of the driveway not visible from the street. He found the key, as directed, under the third stone step leading to the faucet just outside the dining room, and then led Wendy over to the front door. He told her to stay on the porch and keep a careful watch for any strangers coming up the walk.

"What do I do if I see someone?" the little girl asked, not liking this at all.

"Ring the doorbell," he replied, pointing to it. "That will bring me running, and I'll deal with it."

"What's going to happen, Stubby? Please don't leave me out here!"

He put his hand on her shoulder. "Just a precaution, Wendy" he said. "It won't take me more than ten minutes and then we'll go home. Nothing's going to happen. Chill out."

She frowned, but then brightened. "Could we stop at the Dairy Queen when we're done?"

That would take them two blocks out of their way, but Stubby needing for her to be focused on this task, agreed. Plus, Stubby was a growing boy still, and he did like his snacks. Even with this small detour, he and Roger could still get to Dayton and back in under three hours (given Roger's heavy foot on the gas pedal).

After glancing around and making sure that no one was watching, Stubby unlocked the door, told Wendy to keep her eyes open, and slipped inside, shutting the door behind him.

All was quiet in the house, and Stubby looked around cautiously. Where was Elliot the cat? Why wasn't he on the list? Was somebody else feeding Elliot? Stubby resolved to ask Todd about this when he saw him. He liked animals in general, and this cat in particular. Better get moving.

Todd's list had grown in the two conversations they'd had since Stubby had been wheedled and bribed into all this, and it took more like twenty minutes to find the large trunk in the basement, carry it up to Todd's room, and fill it up with the books, medicine, clothes, shoes, notebooks, and other items Todd had said were essential. Also, and more importantly, Stubby made sure to retrieve the brown folder from under Todd's bed, and put it and its precious contents of classy porn up against one of the inside walls of the trunk where he could easily pull it out and stow it under his own bed at home. He didn't want it visible in the car and have the ever-curious Wendy glancing through its contents on the way home.

Stubby dragged the overloaded trunk out of Todd's bedroom, and then started lugging it down the hall to the living room. It was going to be a bear to get this thing out to the car and load it in the trunk. Ah, well, what the hell, he'd sweat his way through it.

As he manhandled the trunk into the living room, banging it loudly against the dining room table as he passed, Stubby looked up in surprise to see Wendy standing inside the front door with a strange man and a strange woman on either side of her.

"They wouldn't let me ring the doorbell, Stubby," Wendy mewed, on the edge of tears.

"Who are you? What do you want?" her brother demanded, angry and suspicious. He jumped when he saw a small gun pressed against the side of his sister's head.

"Oh, you'll get to know us pretty well," Nan told him. "We four are going on a trip tonight to visit your friend Todd. We'll be leaving just as soon as you tell us where he is."

"Are you still in love with Dad?" Todd asked. He and his mother had tired of watching television all day, and their conversations were getting deeper into heretofore unexplored areas.

The question surprised Mary. "Better leave that one alone," she ruled. "Maybe when you're older I'll be willing to talk with you about what happened, but not now."

"Mom," Todd protested, "I'm sixteen, and, as you know, not just an ordinary sixteen year old. Modesty aside, I'm older than my peers."

"All too true," she admitted, "but you're still my son, and the question is far too personal." She changed the subject. "Let me ask you something. That huge post that you put up on your website, the one that got us in such trouble, did you create that all in one day?"

"Oh, no. I'd been writing up my thoughts on religion for some time, with the intention of publishing an article, or perhaps even a book. So I just adapted that text for my 'Todd is God' lecture."

"Another unfortunate choice of words."

"It got their attention."

"Yes, it did."

They both went silent as they considered that.

"Now the graphics presentation with all the quotes and my voice-over I created on Monday," Todd added. "And I was very pleased with how it came out." He saw the look on her face. "I mean," he added, "until it caused all the trouble."

She regarded her eccentric child. He'd been a source of both pride and concern to his parents from the moment when he began to talk. His first words, "Sugar, please," had been a complete sentence.

"One thing I forgot to mention," Todd said, hanging his head slightly. "Stubby Allen is stopping by this evening to bring us a few items from home."

"WHAT?"

He raised both hands in protest, explaining in a rush, "Now don't make too much of this, Mom. It's perfectly safe. They can't trace a cell phone connection unless the conversation goes on for something in excess of three minutes, so I kept it short when Stubby and I talked."

"YOU COULD GET US KILLED!" Mary said.

"NO, NO!" Todd protested. "Stubby and I figured out how to do it. He'll sneak into the house, and have a lookout, and his brother will drive him over with our things. And, Mom, there are things that I need—and I mean NEED DESPERATELY: clothes, and video games, and some projects that I'm working on, and most of all, my computer! I've never been away from my computer for this long in all my life! I'm in *withdrawal*—look, look, my hands are shaking!" He held them out with exaggerated trembles.

"Todd," his mother said, "I'm *furious* with you!" Her mind was racing. Should they leave the motel now and find someplace else to hide? Should she call Franklin?

"I know, I know," Todd soothed, "but, Mom, you have to trust me on this. I'm a very clever person, and I made sure *nothing* could go wrong. Plus, I didn't forget *your* needs. I told Stubby to be certain to bring along your sewing basket and the book of the New York Times crossword puzzles. They were next to your living room chair, right?"

That stopped her. Crocheting and solving crosswords were her favorite pastimes, and she had truly missed them both during their confinement to this small room.

"When will he arrive?" she asked, still not happy, but somewhat mollified.

"Any minute."

She considered it. There was nothing she could do about it now.

"Let's talk about something else," she dictated. Todd was pleased to comply.

"All right," he said, "tell me about your early religious experiences. The things that led you to give up on it all. You were raised a Catholic. What went wrong?"

She thought for a few moments about how to answer this. Then she said, "Well, in the beginning I loved the Catholic Church. I was very impressed by the rituals of Mass, and particularly when the Mass was said in Latin, which, for reasons I don't understand, had fascinated me from a very early age." She quoted, "'Introibo ad altare Dei, ad Deum qui laetificat juventutem meam.'"

"Which means?"

"'I will go to the altar of God, to God, the joy of my youth.'"

Todd looked enchanted. "Say it again," he requested, so she did, and then was amazed when he repeated it correctly. "I'll have to remember that," he said. "Maybe I can work it into my book. Now you've sparked a new

137

interest—I need to study Latin myself." Thinking about this, he gave a short laugh. "I do know Pig Latin."

Mary frowned, trying to remember Pig Latin, a childhood game. "How does it go? Something about moving the syllables."

He nodded. "Yes, you take the first letter or syllable of a word, move it to the end of the word and then add 'ay.'"

"Example?"

"Om-may eaks-spay atin-Lay."

"'Mom speaks Latin'," she translated. "I've got it now. Well, back to your question about my apostasy. As I said, I loved the rituals of the Church, and the nuns were, for the most part, great teachers, kind and patient."

"For the most part?"

"There was a Superior when I was in the eighth grade; she was our teacher in addition to being the principal of the school. Big woman, not at all kind and patient. She wore a huge oversized rosary that dangled from her belt, and, shockingly, she was known to swat students with it when they misbehaved.

"For what reason I don't know, she particularly didn't like students talking in the lunch line. Mother Superior would make us solemnly swear not to do that, and then when—being young children—we inevitably *did* talk in the lunch line, she would swoop down on us, rosary swinging, resembling a giant angry bat, and yelling, 'HYPOCRITES!' I was fifteen before I figured out that 'hypocrite' didn't mean 'lunch line talker.'"

Todd laughed. "But surely being swatted with a rosary didn't cause you to abandon Catholicism."

"Oh, no. As I said, she was the exception, not the rule. However, as much as I enjoyed the rituals, when I began to explore the *dogma* I became—well—first confused, then unhappy, and then a disbeliever. Take the virgin birth, for example. It just didn't seem likely, much less possible."

"Actually," Todd commented. "It's most probably a mistranslation of the original Hebrew,"

"Huh?"

"I don't remember the details—a simple Google search would supply them—but the original Old Testament prophecy in Hebrew was that an *adolescent female* would conceive and bear a child. The Greek translator changed this, probably by accident, into a *virgin* would conceive and bear a child, and that gave rise to the popular misconception (no pun intended)."

"The things you know!" his mother said with a shake of her head. "In any event, I went to a *public* high school and that triggered a religious requirement that children doing so attend special catechism classes once a week. We met at St. Ellen's Church in the basement every Wednesday night for an hour. I hated going, but once I was there I did find it fun to explore the tenets of Catholicism with the priest, Father Joseph, who taught the course."

"I would *love* to debate theology with a Catholic priest," Todd said, much enthusiasm in his voice.

"Well," Mary explained, "there were two difficulties. The first was that the purpose of the class was to teach us the basics of our religion, not to debate them. Statements like 'Who made us? God made us,' were taken as givens, not as starting points for argument."

"Unacceptable," Todd said, rolling the prohibition over in his mind.

"The second problem was that Catholic priests generally divide into two categories: smart as whips or dumb as bricks. Father Joseph, alas, was in the latter group, and he was very easily confused by any sort of challenge to his basic assumptions. When I started to ask questions and get deeper into what he was really saying, he would lose it and cut me off with 'Don't worry about it—it's one of the mysteries of the Catholic religion.' Finally, after one too many repetitions of this dodge, I told him that there were a lot of *mysteries* in this religion."

"How did he react to that?"

"He called my parents and told them that they shouldn't send me to any more of his classes, that I was 'disruptive' because I 'asked too many questions.' My parents were dismayed—they were quite devout—but they'd seen this coming. It may surprise you to know that when I was little, I was sort of a female version of you, making my own path through life. I was delighted not to have to go back to that basement."

"So that's when you left the church?"

"No, but about this same time I stopped going to confession, and that meant I couldn't make my Easter Duty. I was soul-searching, and this resulted in the startling conclusion that I had no soul at all. Of course, that also meant that the Catholic Church and I had to part company."

"Why did you stop going to confession?"

"I always thought the idea was bizarre, even as a very little girl. You went into a scary dark confined space, knelt down, and whispered your sins to a man you couldn't see, who either sounded bored or far too interested."

"What sort of 'sins' does a little girl have anyway?" Todd asked.

"Exactly! My real problem was with a young priest named Father Andrew. I must have been a great sexual temptation to him when I was fourteen and just beginning to develop physically. All of a sudden he was *everywhere*. Coming up to me after mass, all smiles and questions about my life, studying my breasts while almost licking his lips, inviting me to join in church auxiliary projects, wanting to know if I needed private counseling. One awful time he was the priest in the confessional when I went in, and he proceeded to ask me detailed questions about my 'impure' thoughts and actions. This went on and on until I fled the confessional booth. I never went back."

"Impure thoughts?"

"Did I want to have sex with the boys I saw? Did I masturbate? Had I ever allowed a man to touch me in inappropriate places? As he asked these questions, his voice got huskier and huskier. I got out of there without waiting for my penance . I was scared . . . and angry too."

There was a knock at the door of their motel room, and they both jumped, turning to look at the door. Todd was sitting closest to it, and he rose and called out softly, "Yes?"

"Todd," said the voice on the other side, "it's Stubby. Open the door."

Todd smiled broadly and did so.

CHAPTER NINE

TALES FROM THE CRIB

Wendy, sitting in the passenger seat of Dan and Nan's van, had been steadily crying for the last half hour, and this greatly bothered Dan, who was driving. A crying female of any age always broke him in half, and this Wendy was a child of eight, making her tears all the more pitiful. Dan had endured far too many tears in the past week.

"Don't worry, honey," he said, patting her gently on the knee. "We're not going to hurt you."

Wendy looked at him carefully, trying to control her tears. *"Are you going to hurt my brother?"* she blurted out in a loud, high pitched voice.

Stubby, Mary, Todd and Nan, all seated in the back of the van, looked around at each other. The first three were manacled and fettered.

Dan glanced back at Stubby. "No. No one's going to hurt him neither," he replied.

"What about Todd and Mrs. Whitestone?" Wendy asked, her voice clearer.

Dan drove on, not replying, but Nan spoke up in the awkward silence that followed.

"Pull over here and we'll let them out," she instructed, motioning toward the side of the highway. It was nearing nine in the evening, and they were far out in the country, well away from traveled byways. No lights were visible from the road or the land on either side.

"Have we gone far enough, you think?" Dan questioned.

"Pull over," Nan commanded, and he did it. "Cover the child," Nan ordered him, so Dan got out of the vehicle, walked around to the passenger side, and helped Wendy from her seat, telling her quietly to come with him. Reluctantly, she climbed to the ground, taking his hand to help herself down. They stood there in the ambient light from the van, waiting. Trying not to let Wendy see him, Dan pulled his gun from the holster on his hip and held it lightly at his side. Nan turned to Stubby.

"I'm going to take off your restraints," she told him, "and let you to join your sister. Then we're going to drive off and leave you here."

Stubby looked around wildly. *"Here?"* he asked. "We're in the middle of nowhere!"

"Yes," she replied. "Good luck with that. But you don't want to go where we're going, do you?" She looked steadily into his eyes, hers clouded and dull. Stubby glanced at his sister, helpless by the side of the van, holding the hand of that maniac. Dan was huge, over six and a half feet tall, bushy black whiskers, overweight, a bear of a man. Wendy almost disappeared standing next to him. It made Stubby furious that his sister was anywhere near this asshole.

"No," Stubby said, and then he looked at both of the Whitestones, lighting on Todd. "Sorry, man," he told him. "I've got to think of Wendy first."

"Of course," said Mary replied, speaking for both of them.

Stubby continued, his words tumbling out, repeating what he had already said twice during this journey, "I *had* to do what they told me—they had guns! They kept saying they'd shoot Wendy if I tried anything, and I thought they might do it. *I'm so, so sorry!* I failed you, bro!" He choked on these last words.

"Shut up," Nan said. She bent over by his seat and smoothly unlocked the fetters, then she looked up at him. "Before I uncuff you," she continued, all business, "remember that my husband has a gun on your sister. If you cause any ruckus, she gets it first, then you. Understand?"

"Yes."

She almost smiled as she told him, "You were right in thinking we'd really do it." She paused. "Or, at least, I would," she said, somewhat grimmer, giving Dan a fierce glance. He met her gaze steadily.

Todd spoke up, calm and collected, sounding almost cheerful. "Stubby, we don't blame you, Mom and I. I was a fool to put you in this danger, and I'm the one who should be apologizing to you. Get out and talk care of Wendy. Don't worry about us."

"I'm so, so sorry," Stubby repeated, close to breaking down but holding it together for the sake of his sister. Nan unlocked the cuffs, using the same key she'd used for the leg shackles, and then motioned him out of the van, drawing her own gun as she herself backed out. Stubby followed her, and quickly took Wendy's hand, almost yanking her away from Dan. Brother and sister backed up a step and stopped.

"Get back in the driver's seat," Nan told Dan, her gun centered on the two youngsters. As Dan did this, she turned to them. "Start walking in the direction we just came from. There was a gas station we passed a mile or so back there." She pointed. "There'll be folks around somewhere. Flag down a car or something. Go!"

Stubby nodded, unhappy, and ushered Wendy off in the direction Nan indicated.

"Bye!" Wendy called to Mary and Todd, who were watching from their seats in the van.

Stubby couldn't speak. Phlegm filled his throat and tears his eyes. He

142

steeled himself to keep walking, afraid to speak to Wendy, afraid he would break down completely and collapse in front of her. He didn't look around as the van pulled off. On the trip from Columbus to Dayton Stubby had tried to think of all the things the police would want to know. He memorized what Dan and Nan looked like (she was a stringy, straw-haired woman—in her early thirties, he guessed), the van was an old beat-up Chevy (he had no idea what year), the Ohio license plates were splattered with mud so that the first couple of letters were unreadable, and Stubby guessed that this'd been done deliberately. He managed to memorize the last three letters: 4WB, but he knew that wouldn't narrow it down much.

Wendy twisted to look off at the departing van.

"What's going to happen to them," she asked her brother.

There was silence in the van for a few minutes after it started up again. Nan had resumed her seat in the back. Todd and Mary alternated between helpless gazes at each other and suspicious looks at Nan, who, for the most part, seemed indifferent to them, lost in some other world. Finally Mary spoke.

"What *are* you going to do with us?"

Dan looked in the rear view mirror at his wife. "Honey?" he said, "Ain't it time to tell them things?"

Coming back from her mental wanderings, Nan raised her head slowly, looked at Dan thoughtfully for a few seconds, and then nodded.

"We have a story to tell you," she said to Todd and Mary. "It'll take awhile, but we've got plenty of time before we get to where we're going."

"And where is that?" Todd asked, ready to start triangulating mentally.

"Our farm near Gallipolis," Nan responded.

Todd and Mary exchanged looks again. It was not comforting that these crazies were so forthcoming with important information like this.

"How long until we get there?" Todd persisted.

"Soon enough," Nan repeated. "Do you want to hear this story or not? The ending of it's about you," she looked at Todd, "and even you," she looked at Mary.

"Tell us," Mary said, giving Todd a stare that meant *shut up*. He dutifully complied.

Nan paused as if unsure where to begin. "Okay," she finally said, "let's start with some personal things—our background and such. Dan and I both come from very devout people, and that means religious parents, religious grandparents, great grandparents, and so forth, as far back as we can

143

know. Mostly Baptists, but some other denominations thrown in here and there. Methodists, Lutherans. No Catholics, of course."

"Or Jews or Mormons?" Todd asked. His mother glared at him

"No Jews or Mormons," Nan agreed, as if this were a perfectly normal question for anyone to have asked. "Don't cotton to those kind at all. Christians only, God-fearing and reverent. I was baptized in the Ohio river when I was about four." For some reason this seemed a source of pride to her.

"Me too," said Dan, adding, "but not the Ohio. It's too far away from where I was born, and I was six, not four. I was baptized in a lake, at the same time as three other members of my family: an aunt and two of my brothers."

"I always had a great love for Jesus, and He loved me back. I saw evidence of Him everywhere I went, in everything I touched. I never had no thoughts that there weren't no God."

Mother and son exchanged looks, but Nan went on without seeming to tie this thought to Todd or their present situation. "I'm partial to revival meetings. All that shouting and happy laughter, and folks sharing their glory in the greatness of God. It's something!" A form of joy entered Nan's voice, and she was more animated than she'd been all evening.

Wanting to encourage this spark of humanity, Mary decided to feign interest in the unfolding story. "Did the two of you meet at a revival?" she ventured.

Dan laughed. "No. We met at a gun show!"

"When we were in our teens," Nan added, nodding. "Ever been to a gun show?" Both Mary and Todd shook their heads. "Very macho gathering, lots of Soldier-of-Fortune wannabes strutting around like they knew what they was doing, mostly middle-aged guys with far too much of that middle hanging over their belts. I was there helping my father sell gun accessories, which is still a sideline of his. Dan come up to our booth—actually just a large folding table but we called it a booth—and I could tell right away he was interested in more than ammo clips and laser sights."

"In that crowd," Dan added, "Nan was a rock star! I saw a large group of men gathered around this one booth, and I wondered what the attraction was, so I waded in and there she was: a gun guy's wet dream!"

"Dan!" Nan said, not really scolding him.

"Perky teenager, all decked out in camouflage shorts, tight t-shirt, boonie hat, and shiny combat boots. Men were pawing the ground."

Now Nan laughed. She suddenly seemed a different, a happier person. "We were pushing magazine clips for M-16s, cause Dad had picked up a lot of them (I don't know where), and I figured it wouldn't hurt if I flirted with the boys some as I told them all about our special sale on these clips. We sold out almost right away. Dad was very happy."

"I bought four, and I didn't even own a M-16 in them days!"

"It didn't take us long till we got serious about each other," Nan said. "We had a lot in common."

"We always loved guns," Dan explained. "We have almost sixty of them at our home, and we belong to two local gun groups. Real gun nuts!" Todd and Mary exchanged another look.

"And the N.R.A., of course," Nan said.

"I'm always saying that I love three things in life: God, guns, and Nan!" He laughed, and the laugh itself seemed part of his regular patter on this subject.

"Just three?" Nan said, suddenly quieter again. "Weren't there more things you loved?"

Silence. Mary and Todd had no idea what was going on, but it didn't seem like a good idea to ask questions. A full, long minute passed before Nan continued her narrative.

"You'd never knowed it now, but Dan was a good-looking sucker when he was younger."

"Now, now, woman! I still am if the light's behind me and the sun's going down." Dan laughed again with enthusiasm at this—apparently it was another of his set zingers. "And Nan—she was the prettiest girl in town. The boys used to follow her like dogs! I was so amazed when she chose me as her own. We was married ten years ago. Nan was 19 and I was 23, going on 24. Small wedding on Nan's folks' farm, but, believe me, a good time was had by all. Right away we moved to a different farm that both of our families pitched in to buy for us. It still don't make much money, but we manage to get by with the Good Lord's help. Dairy cows."

"Do you have any children?" Mary asked, hoping to keep the conversation going in this friendly fashion.

It was the wrong thing to say. Both Dan and Nan dried up immediately and didn't reply. Two minutes—a long time for silence in a car full of people—passed before Nan answered Mary's question.

"We always wanted children," she said in a soft voice, barely audible. "But though we prayed and prayed, we didn't have any. It near broke our hearts."

Dan spoke up. "We didn't know what was wrong, and the doctors didn't neither. We went to a fertility clinic, and they gave us some advice and some pills to take, but ain't nothing come from that neither. Then, after we been married nigh on to three years, Nan got pregnant! We was very happy about that, but the Lord didn't want us to have that baby."

"What happened?" Mary asked after Dan quit talking and Nan said nothing to fill the void.

"I miscarried," Nan finally replied.

"I'm very sorry," Mary said, meaning it.

"Then two years later I miscarried again," Nan said in the same low voice.

Silence.

"And two years after that, a third time."

Silence.

Dan spoke up. "Of course, it was all very hard on us both, and particularly Nan. She was just *meant* to be a mother, and we both knowed it. So she started saying crazy things, and I was sick out of my mind with worry."

"That's when I first told Dan I didn't think there were no God."

"Crazy things."

"No God who was really running things could be so cruel to someone who loved Him as much as I did. That depressed me even more. A world without God—just cruelty and more cruelty, and bad things happening to good people. I thought about killing myself a lot."

"I was working hard to keep her going," Dan said. "I told her that God never gave you burdens that you couldn't bear."

"What did she say to that?" Todd asked, genuinely curious.

"She told me that if I ever said something that stupid again she would blow my head off. But I pleaded with her, and, gradually, she got better. Our minister come over a lot, and he told her that prayer, even to a God that she didn't think existed, would eventually bring her back into the fold. She weren't not sure about that, but she gave it a try, anyhow. So we prayed and prayed, and went to church, and, by golly, it did work! Nan believed again, and apologized to Jesus over and over for doubting His goodness."

"We didn't give up on having a baby neither," Nan said. "By this time we'd bought a computer and one of our nephews hooked it up to the phone and showed us how to use it. We went online and read things about problems people have having children. And we talked to some more doctors, and did this and that, hoping for a successful pregnancy."

The silence went on longer this time, until finally Mary asked the inevitable question, already fearful of the answer. "Then what happened?"

Dan answered. "Nan did get pregnant again. We was very worried that it'd have the same terrible ending. But about a year and a half ago, Nan gave birth to our son, Seth."

Nan brightened for a moment. "What a good baby he was, too! Slept through the night after only the first two weeks—and learned to smile before

146

babies were even supposed to be able to. We was thrilled, and we thanked God every night for hearing our prayers and answering them too."

Silence.

Finally Nan continued. "On September 10 of last year, when I went to get Seth out of his crib after his afternoon nap, he was gone."

Silence. Confused, Mary finally said, "Gone? Not in the crib?"

Dan answered. "Gone—dead. That Sudden Infant Death Syndrome thing."

"Seth looked so peaceful in his little bed that I just couldn't believe anything was wrong when I picked him up," Nan said. "But there was sure something wrong, cause he didn't move or nothing. Then I thought he was just sick, and tried to wake him, and then I tried to see if he was breathing, and couldn't find no breath. That's when I panicked, and starting yelling for Dan, and I even tried shaking Seth to see if it would bring him back to me. Shaking that poor little body . . ."

"I found her sitting on the floor, holding the baby close to her chest, screaming and crying, both together."

"That's horrible," Todd said, speaking for the first time in a long while. Mary couldn't talk.

There was another pause before Dan said, "It was the worst time in our lives up till that point. The doctors couldn't say what had gone wrong for poor little Seth. Just kept saying SIDS was it."

"We blamed ourselves," Nan added. "Thought we were bad parents, didn't do things right, must have offended God, or . . . or—we didn't know what. The doctors said that it was just something that happened, this SIDS thing. Nobody knew why"

"There was some talk about parents should not be putting the baby down on his stomach to sleep, but that couldn't be right cause Seth always slept on his back."

Nan took up this thread. "We was always checking on the internet and such for what was said about SIDS, and they kept changing their advice! For awhile they said to put the baby on his side to sleep, but then later they said that was bad too. The baby might roll onto his stomach and die from that. And there were all these rules about keeping loose blankets and stuffed animals out of the crib, and making real sure the baby could breathe. But that weren't the problem with Seth, we was sure. Nothing in the crib could have harmed him that day, nothing!"

"Plus we didn't let him sleep with us in the big bed, see?" Dan asserted. "They say that's dangerous too, but we never even tried that once. I'm a big man, and common sense tells you not to put little things like that where I might roll on them. Shoot, I worry about squashing Nan in my sleep some night. She's ain't so large herself."

"These things are tragic," Mary said, "but they happen without anyone being at fault. It doesn't necessarily have to have a reason."

Nan's voice was bitter as she said, "Oh, I know that now! It just happens for no reasons at all. Yes, Ma'am, I've learned that lesson the hard, hard way! Did you ever lose a child?"

The question made Mary's skin crawl. "No, I haven't," she said, afraid where this would go.

"I've lost *five*." Nan's statement just hung there in the air as Todd and Mary considered what it meant.

"Five?" Todd finally asked.

"Two months after Seth died, I got pregnant again," Nan said. "We was glad, of course, but scared of miscarrying yet again, and scared of SIDS, and scared of all the ways our baby could get hurt or die. Babies is so fragile."

"We tried to stay happy," Dan explained, "and lots of the time we *was* happy, but sorrow was still living right in the house with us. Nan starting having her doubts again—going on about there being no God, refusing to go to church. But the idea of a baby helped, and I told her that she didn't want to bring up a child that weren't baptized or righteous in God's sight. What kind of mother would do that?"

Another awkward pause. Nan finally broke this one.

"Right after Seth died, we'd got rid of the baby things—car seats, and crib, and clothes, and toys, the whole kit and kabootle. Too many bad memories, and we thought that we weren't gonna have no children anyways after that. But then, wouldn't you know, it happened. So we had to go out and buy new for all those things, and it sure was expensive. We couldn't afford to get things as nice as the things we'd got rid of.

"Plus, it scared us to buy baby things. As if that might jinx it, or invite the devil in, or somehow *challenge* God. We'd come to worry it was not His will that we be parents, but on the other hand, why would He let me get pregnant if we couldn't have a normal baby to raise up to be a normal adult?"

"Maybe we was being tested," Dan speculated. "like Abraham who God told to sacrifice his son Isaac on Mount Moriah, but then God stopped the sacrifice at the last minute, so Isaac didn't have to die and Abraham could let him get off the sacrificial altar, not hurt at all. Just a test, you see?"

"Child abuse," muttered Todd, but low enough that only his mother heard him. She glared at him in the dark, but it was hard to tell if he'd seen her.

"But Isaac in the Bible wasn't a baby when he was almost killed," Nan said. "He was a grown man. And we wasn't asked by God to do nothing

148

first. Seth just died without no warning." She sounded like she was about to cry, but then rallied to continue in a more or less normal voice. "So our new baby was born on June 2nd just this year, and we named him Mordecai."

"Mort, for short," Dan added.

"He was a big baby, healthy and happy, just sort of a larger version of Seth," Nan continued. "And we took extra good care of him. For the first couple of weeks one of us was watching him all during the time he was sleeping, checking to make sure he was okay. And he was."

"That was this summer, but things then started happening. Bad things," Dan said.

Neither of them spoke after this, and the pause went on until Mary, unable to stand the silence, finally asked, "What things?" She didn't really want to know—she'd heard enough. All she wanted to do was to grab Todd and get out of the car and away from these damaged people. Any more stories of their unhappy lives would tear her apart. Looking through the dark at Todd, Mary was all too aware that this tale was going to reach a point that explained why they were sitting in the van, kidnapped, shackled, held at gunpoint. And she would learn what would happen next. And that scared her the most.

"The bad things," Nan said, "hit us *bang, bang, bang*—one after another! The first was my father. July 25th he was admitted to a hospital with what he thought was heartburn or maybe an ulcer, but it turned out to be stomach cancer, fourth stage, and it was all over the middle of his body. The doctors did an operation—what was it called, Dan?"

"Gastrectomy was what they said. They cut out his entire stomach."

"The doctors told him that he might live as long as two years after the operation, but he didn't. He died on the first day of September, two weeks ago. He barely lived a month."

"I'm so sorry," Mary said, aware that she had said these same words only minutes before.

"Oh, lady," Nan said with a wry laugh, "it gets worse, much worse! My mother, who was healthy as a horse and only 57 this past March, shot herself in the head the next day. Couldn't live without him, her suicide note said. We gave them a joint funeral." She turned to Dan. "Want to say anything more about God not giving you more burdens you can't bear?" He didn't answer, so she went on. "I loved my folks. Okay, they wasn't perfect, but who has perfect parents? That funeral was *hard*. I kept falling to the ground, crying, couldn't stand up at all. Dan was holding the baby, so he couldn't help me much. But, after that, what kept me going was little Mort, cause he was all about life and the future and good things in the world."

This parade of catastrophes overwhelmed Mary. It was too much. It couldn't be true. Surely life wasn't ever this cruel to anyone.

A great sob suddenly burst from Nan, startling both Todd and Mary, but, tellingly, not Dan. She began to wail without restraint or any attempt to hold back her grief. The sound, horribly, filled the van and rendered conversation impossible.

As if by rote, Dan made comforting noises and said things like "Now, honey" and "Just let it out" and, to Mary's consternation, "it will be all over soon." Mary tried to see Todd's expression in the dark, but couldn't tell how he was taking all of this. He'd been surprisingly silent, not his normal reaction to conversation going on all around him.

Finally Nan's bereavement subsided, and Dan, his face resolutely forward, concentrating on the road as he drove, revealed the climax of this personal nightmare.

"This past Friday, at 6:30 p.m., Nan found Mordecai dead in his crib."

Nan gulped down her agony enough to spit out, "They say it runs in families."

Franklin had supper with Corbin Milk late on Thursday evening, as a way of saying thank you for Milk's kindness and courage in retrieving Franklin's things from the front stoop of his house and making sure the front door was closed and locked (it had been). The two of them went to an Italian restaurant on the north side of town, and Franklin wore his disguise. He was tired of it already and hoping that interest in him would soon be dying down as the media, always hungry for topics, moved on to other stories.

"How's it all going to end?" Franklin mused as they tucked into the antipasto. "Any thoughts?"

Milk looked bemused. "Not a clue," he said after a moment. "At least for the next six months or more it will be dangerous for you to be seen and recognized, or for people to know where you live. Keep that spirit gum handy."

"That's bleak, Corbin. You don't know how much I hate the spirit gum. It itches."

"Bleak, yes. Wish I could predict something better, but can't. You did ask."

"Shit!" Franklin muttered.

"Your wife and boy all right?" Milk asked.

"Yes. They're in a motel in Dayton, and other than being bored silly, they're fine. I talked to them this afternoon."

"I trust that they're being very careful."

150

"Yes. They're hiding Todd in the bathroom when the pizza boy comes, not letting strangers in, wearing the disguises you suggested when they go out, etc. Both of them are very savvy."

"I'd like to meet them sometime, especially Todd. He's an amazing kid."

"He's all that. Todd has astounded his mother and me since he was a toddler."

"Oh? What did he do then?"

"Just after he turned two, one evening after he had worn us both out and we were just sitting, trying to catch our breath, he toddled over and turned on the tv by himself. A cooking show came on, and he was very pleased with himself. He sat there watching it happily."

Milk laughed, a hearty bass rumble. "And can Todd cook?"

Franklin thought about it. "I don't know. Maybe I'm afraid to know. Surely there are limits to how much one person can learn to do, especially in so short a period of time. He's only sixteen." He brightened. "But Todd's headed for college next year." Pause. "Or he was."

The waiter brought them their main courses, and they fell to eating in silence. Then After a bit, Franklin spoke again. "I know it sounds crazy, but if I'm going to be stranded away from home for the duration, I really need to get back in there and retrieve a number of fairly large important things."

Milk looked up, interested. "Such as what?"

"First of all, my files, which include a number of legal matters I was working on that weren't pressing, so I just tinkered with them in my spare time at home. But they can't be ignored for very long. Even if I can't handle them anymore, they need to be returned to the firm. And then there are financial records, and mail with bills and things that I didn't have time to scoop up and take with me. In addition to all that, I'd love to have various books—some for pleasure, some for self improvement, some for work. My exercise equipment, free weights and such. I miss my portable writing desk, which I seem to live behind when I'm working at home, sitting in my easy chair. There's a boom box that'd be nice to listen to, as well as favorite CDs. Other things too. More clothes—winter is coming on. Think there's any safe way to go back in and get all of this out?"

Milk considered it. "Let me cogitate for a day or so and see what I can come up with. I suppose it's necessary for you to be there in the flesh when these things are selected and taken out." Franklin nodded. "Hmm. Maybe we could put you into a very different disguise. There'd have to be a very good cover for your visit—a reason why strangers might be going in and out of the house. Something no one would suspect really involved Franklin Whitestone returning—even very temporarily—to his home. I'll think on it."

Just then, as Milk was adding pepper to his Tortellini Alfredo, he suddenly sneezed.   Franklin came very close to saying, "Turtles bless you," but scotched that for two reasons: first, even a blessing invoking the mythical turtle stack seemed to violate his principles, and, second, there was a perfectly good substitute available in "gesundheit" (German for "good health"). So Franklin said that and let it go.

"Mort was gone exactly one year to the *day*, almost to the *hour*, that Seth had died—like a cruel, cruel joke," Nan said. "But this time I no longer believed that the joke was caused by God. God *was* the joke! He either caused all this, or he permitted it, and that made him not worth worshiping. I was finished with God. Maybe there was now a devil in his place, a devil who done all this to me. Maybe God is the same as the devil."

"Now, Nan," Dan said, "don't blaspheme. God works in mysterious ways. Please don't give up on Him. He loves us."

"Shit," Nan replied. "I couldn't say a prayer now if I tried hard. My lips don't know how to form the words." She turned in her seat to look at Mary. "Last Friday, after . . . all I could do was go to bed, let Dan handle things—calling 911, talking to the police, arranging burial, same miserable crap we'd been through before. I was done with it, done with death . . . done with life."

Dan spoke. "When she finally came out of bed on late Sunday afternoon, she just sat in front of the tv and let it babble on and on, not caring what she watched. I couldn't get her to eat. She wasn't even crying any more. She just sat."

"I was cried out. All these holes in my life—the dead children, the dead parents, the dead God. And, you know, in some ways I missed him most of all. Before all this, I'd thought he'd been with me day and night, and now there weren't nothing there, nothing at all. Blank. No hope—no comfort—no heaven—no hell, just misery, and misery, and more misery. Nobody's life in the whole wide world was worth living. Every time Dan tried to bring up God, I just screamed. Would have hit him if I could. Would have shot him if'n I'd had a gun in my hand."

Dan took over the story. "And then on Sunday evening, I turned on the Jimmy Ball Show. Nan and I have always been big fans of Hubie Lulland, and the promos said he was on that night. I figured that something funny might take Nan's mind off things."

Knowing what came next made Mary squirm in her seat. Please, please, please, she thought, *just shut up.*

But Dan continued. "And Hubie *was* funny, like always, but then the

152

second guest came on. We'd been shocked like everybody else by the bombs on Saturday, but we didn't pay much mind to all that suffering like most regular folks did. We was in mourning ourselves. But we'd seen Franklin Whitestone's video where he saved all those people, and we thought he was a hero like everybody else thought too. They showed that video again on the Jimmy Ball show, and then he and Jimmy talked some, and then came those phone calls, and, well, you know what he said, how he mocked Our Lord! It made me as angry as I've ever been in my whole life! I hollered at the tv, using swear words, and I ain't a man to do that."

"Dan swore he'd like to put a bullet through that man's brain and let him see God for hisself. I thought that was a great idea."

"Why?" Todd said, speaking up of a sudden. "Dad was just saying what you were already thinking."

"But it's an *evil* message to spread," Nan said. "I don't think there's no God, but I know how important it is that *other* people believe in him. You take God away and everything goes out the window! People'll just fall apart, and go crazy. What would stop them from all kinds of badness: rape, murder, incest, looting, torturing folks just for the pleasure of it? God, even if he's not really there, puts the brakes on all that. It's evil, *evil* to take him out of the picture!"

Dan was indignant for a different reason. "YOUR DAD'S DOING THE WORK OF THE DEVIL! He *is* a devil!!! Shooting him way too good for him! They should drive a stake through his heart, burn the body, and scattered his ashes on a dung heap!"

Nan gave a small nod, running one hand through her hair. "So Dan and me, we agreed to take him out. We hardly had to talk about it at all. We were both in the right mood . . .like-minded."

Take him out, Mary thought. Just like that. Vigilantes working their own crude justice. On Sunday, as she'd seen that awful tv show and witnessed her ex-husband's spin, crash, and burn in front of the entire country, she'd worried that people like Nan and Dan were watching. It was what she'd feared most. Now here they were—stepping out of her nightmare.

"We tracked your Dad down, too," Nan said to Todd. "Took a shot at him last night, but this asshole, "she indicated Dan, "managed to miss."

"WHAT?" Todd and Mary said this in unison.

"Yes, *missed* him! A stationary target!"

"I told you, woman, that he weren't stationary! He was moving as I shot!"

"What happened to Dad?" Todd asked, floored by the news.

Dan shrugged. "We don't know. We'd blown our chance at getting him. He ran off into the night like a scared rabbit."

153

"When was this?" Mary wanted to know.

"Last night," Dan told her. "What Nan just told you."

"Franklin never said a word to me about it! We talked earlier this evening and he was all smiles and encouragement!"

"Well," Dan replied, "I'd be smiling too if a bullet meant to pierce my skull didn't do me no harm."

"So," said Nan, "we decided to move on to another target, one easier to get at." She turned to Todd. "You."

"Saw my website, did you?" Todd said, defiant, almost proud.

"Like father, like son," Nan intoned. "Only you, by golly, you went your Dad one better. You laid it all out so that even an idiot could see that it was true—there weren't no God. That's the worst thing ever happened in all of history! *How dare you do that? HOW DARE YOU!*" She was yelling at Todd, who remained stone faced.

"*IT WAS THE WORK OF THE DEVIL!*" Dan bellowed from the front seat, turning to look back, almost driving off the road. The van swerved wildly before he wrestled it back into its lane. All his passengers, including Nan, were alarmed at this. The night was not supposed to end in a car wreck. Something else was planned.

"*The devil!*" Dan continued, now only slightly lower in volume. "It was all lies! Your Master, Satan, put those lies in your mouth and told you to spread them around like that! Satan is the father of lies! And Satan has taken up residence inside you, boy! And we're gonna do battle with him tomorrow! Exorcize him good!"

Mary could stand it no longer. "JUST TELL ME!" she burst out. "Are you planning to kill us?"

Nan gave a little snort of disgust. "No, lady, not you. We're going to let you go free. It's that devil, your big mouth son. He's the one we're eliminating. Just him."

"Let me go?" Mary didn't understand. Why on earth would they do that? If she were free she would certainly make it her mission in life to see that they were tracked down and sentenced to death and fried in the electric chair. It didn't make any sense to set her free.

Nan explained. "At 6:30 tomorrow evening, Friday, exactly one week after Mordecai died, we're going to put a bullet through your brain, Todd Whitestone. Your mother'll get to watch you die. That's her punishment for raising you up to wreak such havoc. Then right after the exorcism is over, we're gonna shoot ourselves."

She paused. There was a shocked silence before Nan continued.

"Then all will be quiet again."

"Amen," Dan said.

154

CHAPTER TEN

LATIN

Stubby, holding his sister by the hand, tried hard to find the gas station the spooky woman had promised was about a mile back, but although they walked for what seemed to be more than an hour, all they saw around them was woods. No cars passed, no lights from farmhouses beamed, it was just dark and cold. Stubby had no idea what time it was. His captors had taken his cell from him, and, for all he knew, it was still in the van.

Not so little at age eight that she couldn't figure out that the Whitestones were in major trouble, Wendy was not holding up well. She cried more or less constantly, sometimes so hard that she had trouble walking. Stubby finally had to carry her, which meant he couldn't make good time or cover much ground, and eventually he stopped and told her that they'd rest here for the night.

Wendy looked at the trees all around her. They were silent and dark, faintly rustling and making scary unfamiliar noises. "Oh, not here, Stubby! *Please* not here! *Let's go home!*"

He hugged her to him and helped her sit on the berm in the tall grass growing there. "I want to go home too, Wen," he said, "but it's far, far away right now and we have to wait until daylight comes to get help. Please do what I say. I'll keep you safe, I promise."

She didn't like it, but stopped protesting, and just snuggled closer to him for warmth.

"Are Todd and his mother going to be all right?" Wendy asked, but he suspected she already knew the answer.

Stubby shrugged. Every minute ticking by meant that the van was farther from them, making it more likely that whatever that bonkers couple was planning would succeed. He didn't know how to answer Wendy, and sudden, mysterious pains in his stomach were giving him trouble. He was afraid he'd soon have the dry heaves if he let himself think about the Whitestones and what he'd done to them.

He abruptly turned and began pounding the ground with his fist. *Once, twice, a third time.* The pain this caused his hand didn't stop him from beating the grass senseless. Wendy's eyes got wider and she moved beyond mere tears into outright bawling. Contrite for having scared her, Stubby pulled her tight again against his side.

"Kitten, kitten," he said in as soothing a voice as he could, "I won't lie to you. Yes, things are bad right now. But when it gets light, cars will start

155

coming along and we'll flag one down and tell the driver we need help."

"And Todd and his mother too—they need help," Wendy insisted.

"And Todd and his mother too," Stubby agreed. "Then we'll talk to the police and they'll find that van and rescue the Whitestones. But right now we've got to make the best of the situation we're in, and, even though it will be very hard, we've got to try and sleep here next to the road."

She shook her head vigorously. "No, no, Stubby, I *can't* sleep here! There's no bed and no pillow, and I'm cold." He didn't say anything, so she added another complaint. "And hungry."

It was true they hadn't eaten since earlier this afternoon. Now that he thought about it, Stubby realized that in spite of his upset stomach, he was hungry too. Great. Another misery to add to a growing list.

He laid her down on the grass and curled his body around her as best he could to warm her and get some warmth in return. "I know it's hard," he told her, "but just close your eyes and try and sleep."

She sniffled for two minutes or so, and then, to Stubby's amazement, she began to breathe regularly. She'd fallen asleep! And Stubby, who would have bet big bucks it wouldn't happen, fell asleep himself shortly thereafter.

Jake Richardson awoke Friday morning when a strange movement in his bed jerked him out of the dream he was having about using Suzy May to battle a bunch of lions in some sort of coliseum. With him at the controls, Suzy May made short work of the beasts, tossing the snarling lions around like stuffed animals. With that exciting image in his mind, it took Jake almost five seconds to realize that he was lying in his bed, a naked woman by his side. It was another five before he could review yesterday and come up with her name. She was Celia Hawkins, the great, Bible-quoting lady who had tracked him down at work and jump-started his sex life. Hallelujah! Praise God!

He looked at her lying next to him. Okay, admit she wasn't a beauty. She was far too skinny to be his ideal woman, but she had been a lioness herself when it came to sex, climbing all over him, making little growls of lust for his body. Jake had loved it. Celia herself seemed pretty pleased at his sexual performance, rusty though he was. Passion had driven him, and, he reasoned, when passion like hers met passion like his, it was bound to make everybody happy.

Jake was amazed to realize that he'd had *nothing* to drink last night! He couldn't remember the last time that was true. Now that he considered it, the absence of alcohol might have improved all that romancing he'd performed so very well. He was almost positive he'd cum three times—

156

wow!—just like he used to do when he was nineteen!

Jake put his arm around Celia and pulled her to him. She purred, half asleep, half awake, and snuggled back against him, spoon fashion. That made him excited all over again, and he doubted that either one of them was going back to sleep. He cupped her breast in his hand and began playing with her nipple. She stirred.

"Oh, Jake," she moaned, "that's heavenly!"

"Okay!" he replied, climbing on top of her. "Let's explore heaven!"

Snoring slightly, Todd was asleep in a metal folding chair, his upper body sprawled across the small wooden table next to him. Mary was seated in an identical chair on the other side of the same table, but she hadn't slept at all Thursday night. Ever since Nan and Dan had recounted their terrible trials and then pulled the van into the yard of their farmhouse, Mary had been thinking. Thinking hard.

Todd moved in his sleep, almost knocking the lamp from the middle of the table to the floor, but Mary reflexively reached up her handcuffed hands and caught it just as it was going over. She righted it on the table, not caring that the lamp's bright red shade was now comically askew. There was nothing funny about the situation. It somehow annoyed her that Todd could sleep at all.

The room they were in was surreal. It had clearly been the nursery for those poor babies who had not survived their infancy, and Mary worried that she and her son were imprisoned here for reasons prophetically symbolic. There had already been two deaths in this room. How many more were it see?

On all four walls, above the light grey wainscoting, happy cartoon tigers danced and played on colorful wallpaper, and it was this alone which identified this room as the former nursery. Otherwise it was almost completely empty. There was a brick red carpet, recently vacuumed, the two chairs on which Mary and Todd were sitting, and that small table between their chairs. The table not only had the lamp with the red shade, but also sported another indication that an infant had once inhabited this room: a baby monitor. Mary presumed it had been placed on the table so that their conversations could be overheard. Both the lamp and monitor were plugged into the wall under the table. The only other pieces of furniture were two metal chairs placed across the room, presumably for Dan and Nan.

And that was it. The room's sparse furnishings spoke hauntingly of emptiness, of loss.

When Nan and Dan had led them into the house late last night, still shackled hand and foot, and covered by revolvers, the Whitestones had first been shown to a bathroom and, one after the other, allowed to use it, and then ushered into this room. Here their leg shackles, connected by a long chain, were locked onto large eye-bolts screwed into the carpeting at the base of the chairs positioned on either side of the small table. Without a key to unlock themselves from the eye-bolts, they weren't going anywhere. Once alone, they'd tried unscrewing the eye-bolts, but they couldn't get them to move. Grudgingly, Mary admitted to herself that she was impressed; their captors had obviously given some thought as to how to keep them from escaping. The handcuffs they were wearing had a ten inch chain between the two cuffs, and this permitted the wearer some free movement, necessary for use of the bathroom, and, shortly after they were incarcerated in the nursery, for eating a meal of soup and baloney sandwiches. Hungry in spite of the terror she felt, Mary had managed to get the soup down, but then her stomach revolted at the idea of the sandwich. It was too prosaic a food to eat before an execution, and she left it untasted. Todd, predictably, had eaten the meal happily. You would've thought he was an invited guest, glad to be here, pleased by the food.

"See if you cain't sleep," Dan had advised them before he and Nan departed for the night. "Ain't nothing gonna happen to either of you until tomorrow at 6:30 in the evening when . . . ," but he left this ugly thought hanging.

Finally alone, the Whitestones had talked for nearly an hour about their situation and the danger Todd was in. Neither could think of anything that might extricate them from this peril, and it was depressing to keep coming to that same conclusion. Finally, after some discussion about leaving the lamp on or off, they settled on the latter. In the dark, they'd both laid their arms and heads on the table, like first graders at nap time, and tried to sleep. Todd, always a snorer, had begun making his usual nightly noises shortly thereafter, but Mary had trouble even closing her eyes, much less actually nodding off.

Apparently Nan and Dan hadn't thought it was necessary for a baby to be exposed to sunlight. There was no window in the room and it was inky black. Long hours passed before Mary heard her captors moving around the house and from this could guess it was morning—the morning of Friday, September 17th. Mary feared that date would become an annual nightmare.

A sleepless night of trying out first this scenario and then another, had produced nothing with the slightest chance of success. Worn out by this futility, Mary stared now in the direction of Todd's slumbering form, and blinked back tears. Crying wouldn't help her. Tears wasted energy.

What to do? What to try? What might actually work? Could she

158

appeal to Nan and Dan's humanity? No, she decided. Dan maybe, but not Nan. Nan's humanity, assuming she'd ever had any, had been stripped away, leaving behind a woman who was merely a bitter shell of a person, alive and dead at the same time.

Dan was still a functioning human being, possibly insane and dangerous for that reason, but the man was enslaved by Nan's desires, and it seemed unlikely he could be talked into bucking her orders. Unlikely? Impossible, Mary concluded, aware that this was not the first time she'd circled this mental loop.

In some ways, Dan wasn't merely Nan's puppet—in some way he was even more crazed than his bizarre wife. He appeared to truly believe that Todd was a devil and that it was Dan's mission to take him out. Ironically, Nan and Dan wanted Todd dead for opposing reasons. Nan, for her part, no longer believed in Dan's God, but saw Todd as infecting the world with a message of helpless surrender to the meaninglessness of it all. She believed in a *belief* in God.

Was there any way to use this dichotomy against them? So far nothing had occurred to Mary, but it was the one wedge that she could think of, and she kept turning it over in her mind, looking at it from this way and that.

Now, she thought, if I were the heroine in a tv show or movies, I'd come up with some clever plan that would end with us fleeing, perhaps with Nan and Dan left behind, unconscious (dead?) on the farm house floor. To her surprise, Mary realized that she wouldn't feel the slightest compunction about killing them, one after another, if that was the only way to keep her child from being murdered.

But what clever thing would a fictional character trapped in this situation think to do? Something improbable? Something wild?

And then, like magic, an idea occurred to her and she began to work out the details.

After asking two of the passengers getting off the American Airlines flight from Los Angeles just after 10 o'clock in the morning at Port Columbus if they were Jonathan Harker, Franklin finally connected with the man he was seeking. Looking back on it, Franklin realized that he should have spotted Harker right off. His appearance boldly advertised him as a L.A. wheeler and dealer. He was impeccably dressed in black turtleneck sweater and handsome cashmere blazer, tanned, good-looking in a Hollywood movie star sort of way, with a confident swagger to his walk.

"Mr. Harker?" Franklin said to him, and when the other nodded, slightly confused, Franklin added, in a softer voice, "I'm Franklin

159

Whitestone."

"Good heavens!" Harker replied, also keeping his voice low, "you look nothing like Franklin Whitestone."

That pleased Franklin. "I'm in disguise," he confessed, fingering his mustache, feeling strangely proud. "Come this way. Do you have checked luggage?"

"No, just this," Harker replied, pointing to the compact suitcase he was pulling. "I'm traveling light, just in and out, and then right back. What time is it here?"

"10:12," Franklin said, looking at his watch.

Harker looked puzzled. "I thought it would be 9:12 on Central Time."

"It would be," Franklin agreed, "but Ohio is on Eastern Time."

"Really?"

"So is Indiana, which is even farther west than Ohio."

"Is it?" Harker said, sounding as if he hadn't a clue where Indiana was, and didn't care to know. "Actually," he continued, "I was very surprised when I saw your city of Columbus from the air. It's much bigger than I thought it would be."

"1.4 million people in the metropolitan area. State capital, Ohio State University (the largest college in the U.S.), the fifteenth largest city in the country."

"Goodness! A well kept secret."

"Easy place to live," Franklin added. He was getting a better look at Harker as they walked through the terminal. The man was somewhere in his 30s, a conclusion belied by the startlingly silver hair at Harker's temples, which contrasted nicely with the dark black waves that made up the rest of his coiffure. Probably dyed, Franklin reasoned, though he was puzzled as to why anyone would want to dye his hair grey. Harker's mannerisms were smooth, and almost effeminate, but, from the careful looks he gave to every pretty woman they passed, it was very clear that he was not gay. Harker must be what they called a *metrosexual*, Franklin decided.

"I thought we'd go to one of the nicer restaurants in town to have our meeting," Franklin informed Harker as they reached the rental car and climbed in. "There's one in the Hyatt downtown that serves a good breakfast and is open all day. Great food."

"Splendid," Harker replied. "I've brought the contracts with me for you to look over and sign—that is, of course, assuming that your training as a lawyer doesn't have you running from the room in horror after reading the steady barrage of boilerplate clauses our lawyers have cleverly inserted into them."

"Give me the short version," Franklin suggested.

160

"Well, the bottom line, Mr. Whitestone, is that currently you are infamous, a bad thing, but if you sign on with the Martin Turnbill agency, we will turn that around and make you famous, a good thing, and, perhaps more importantly, you'll be rich. I mentioned some of the possibilities in our phone conversation, but I have a brochure we give all our clients that spells out in detail the various advantages we offer. For example, there's that protection service you and I spoke of, which, day and night, will keep you and your family safe from the loonies."

"That will be a relief. Hate the loonies."

Harker looked concerned. "How bad had it gotten?" he asked.

Franklin shrugged. "I was shot at two days ago."

"Whoa! That's major! Was it a close call?"

"Yes—the first bullet missed me by inches and plowed into a door jamb next to my head."

"The first bullet?"

"I'm not sure how close the second bullet came. I didn't wait around for measurements."

"Terrible, terrible," the agency man sympathized. "But all that will be behind you if we can reach agreement today. I can have the security in place by Monday afternoon, and you and your family can get back to a more regular existence. How are they, by the way?"

Actually, Franklin was worried about that very issue. He'd called both Todd and Mary's cells this morning and neither had answered. What did that mean? Should he hop in the car and drive to Dayton? Call the police? He calmed himself by deciding that the most likely explanation was that they were having breakfast in some area where the cells had no service, or something similar. That didn't sit easily with him, and he'd already made up his mind to drive to Dayton if he wasn't able to contact them by the time he took Harker back to the airport.

Harker smiled. "I should tell you that as excited as we are at Martin Turnbill to be given the chance to represent you, we'd be double our joyful at the chance to represent your incredible son!"

This came as no surprise to Franklin, and he had no intention of letting it happen.

"Incredible is the word," he agreed, turning the car onto the interstate.

Harker almost hugged himself as he writhed in the passenger's seat, contemplating the possibilities. "What a draw! He could have his own tv show! *TODD WHITESTONE EXPLAINS IT ALL FOR YOU!* It would be a huge hit."

Franklin smiled. "Just another step on his way to world conquest." He almost wasn't joking.

"Having second thoughts?" Dan said to Nan as they ate their breakfast at the kitchen table.

"Not a one. You?" Nan replied.

"Nope. Which one of us is going to pull the trigger?"

Nan looked at him with a steady gaze as if daring him to challenge her. "That's mine, all mine," she told him. "You know that." With a little nod, he agreed.

"Is there more orange juice?" Dan asked her.

The baby monitor sitting on the little table next to the lamp bothered Mary a good deal. It meant she couldn't talk openly with Todd, and by now she had a lot to say to him. She couldn't risk guessing whether or not Dan and Nan were actually listening in. Even whispering wouldn't work since mother and son were on opposite sides of the table, and the monitor was between them. Maybe she could muffle the device in some way—but that would send a message that she had something to hide, which would defeat her plan. Another thought: perhaps she could quickly explain her idea to Todd when Nan and Dan either entered or left the room, before they were in position to overhear hurried whispers between their captives. But then, perhaps there was some sort of recording device taping everything for playback later. Shit.

Mary's plan needed Todd's cooperation too. If he didn't do things exactly right this wasn't going to fly. She needed to let him know what role she wanted him to play, after which she had no doubt he would do it perfection. How to do this?

While she was thinking about it all, the door opened and Nan and Dan appeared, the latter carrying a breakfast tray, which Nan then unloaded onto the table. There was a lot of food: bacon, eggs, toast, coffee, juice. "Hungry?" she asked.

"Yup," replied Todd, beginning to eat immediately. Mary was suspicious of his cheerfulness. Wasn't he worried about the dire straits he was in? Or—now *here* was an interesting thought—did he have his own subterfuge cooking?

Deciding that the success of her plan required her to appear comfortable with the situation, Mary smiled at her captors and, after unfolding the paper napkin and putting it on her lap (a step Todd had skipped), she said, "Me too. Looks good," and began to eat. To her surprise she discovered she really was hungry, and the food was excellent. Apparently

162

Nan (Dan?) could cook.

The meal over, their captors told Mary and Todd that they would be escorted one by one to the bathroom, and Dan left first with Todd. This was what Mary had been waiting for.

"I need to talk to the two of you alone," she said to Nan.

"Sister, you can beg and plead all you like, but it ain't gonna change what will happen at 6:30 this evening."

"You don't understand," Mary replied. "I don't want to change it."

Nan looked at her. "You don't?"

"That's what we need to talk about. It would be best if Dan is there too. Please—it's important."

Nan thought about it. After a bit, she said, "All right, we'll do it when we take you to the bathroom." She looked suspiciously at Mary. "You can't be so dumb as to believe you can make a break for it. We're both armed," she indicated the gun in the holster that hung from her hip, "and even though we don't want to harm you, we wouldn't hesitate to shoot you."

Mary looked as solemn as she could. "I know that."

Dan and Todd returned, and the boy was again secured to the bolt on the floor, at which point Nan unlocked Mary and, motioning to Dan, led the three of them from the room. Nan stood guard while Mary used the bathroom, and when she came out, Nan took her by the arm and said, "This way. We'll talk in the front room."

She led Mary into a paneled room containing a good sized tv and a desk with a computer on it, but what immediately attracted attention was a large safe in the far corner. It resembled the ones train robbers were always blowing up in old westerns. Dan quickly opened the safe's door to reveal more guns than Mary thought would have fit inside.

"Let's give her a tour of our collection," he said to Nan with enthusiasm. Obviously, he loved to show it off.

"Why in the world would we do that?" she replied.

"Make her watch while we're selecting the exorcism weapon—give her something to think about the rest of the day."

That gave Nan pause, and then she nodded. "All right," she said, with a tight-lipped smile.

Pulling a huge, and, to Mary, terrifying rifle from the safe, Dan held it up for her to see. This monstrosity looked just like the bullet-spraying weapon terrorists used when attacking U.S. troops in Iraq.

"Ah, take a gander at this beauty!" Dan said. "It's the pride of our collection, an AK-47. It's sometimes called a Kalashnikov, which is a Russian name, but this one ain't Russian—we can't seem to get one of those. Ours was made in China."

Mary, waging an internal battle between pretended admiration and actual horror, said nothing.

Dan took another rifle from the safe and held it out for her inspection. "This one is our primo hunting rifle: a Weatherby Mark V." This gun was sleeker and Mary judged it a more traditional-looking rifle, but again she had no comment.

Nan joined in the fun. She leaned over and retrieved a slim black rifle. "This here is another favorite—it's so sleek, so 'awesome' as my nephews say—a Beretta Xtrema 12 gauge gas operated shotgun. Isn't it beautiful?" That wasn't the adjective that occurred to Mary.

"Now," Dan said as he extracted yet one more rifle from the safe, "Here's one of the guns we're considering for the exorcism tonight. It's a Beretta 682 Trident Trap Gun, 12 gauge, double-barreled, one of the best guns ever made."

Nan shook her head. "I told you. Its' not right for the exorcism. We need to go with something smaller, easier to use in a room, a revolver." She pulled one out and displayed it for Mary to see. "This is what we'll use," Nan said. "It's a Smith and Wesson model 686 caliber .357 magnum." She turned it over in her hand. To Mary it looked like the revolvers on tv crime shows. The handle was black, and the rest of the gun was a shiny silver.

Nan continued her commentary with, "The Smith .357 magnum is the best combat magnum ever produced. We also have a similar gun, a Smith 629." She took it from the safe, and, as promised, it looked much like the other one. "It's Dirty Harry's .44 magnum. Ever see that movie? Wicked gun, but I don't like it much. Too loud and too much recoil."

Mary couldn't see any difference between the two, but that lead to an important question in her mind. "The first one, the Smith whatever, it doesn't have a big recoil?" she asked.

Dan thought about it before saying, "For a novice it might be scary, but the recoil is manageable." Mary filed that information away.

Nan was done with the gun show. She pointed to a leather recliner and Mary dutifully sat, while they took to a sofa facing it.

"Now talk," Nan commanded.

Mary hung her head for a few seconds and then raised it, looking steadily at the two of them. "I'm Todd's mother, and I can tell you as a fact, that you," indicating Nan, "are wrong about what is going on, and you," indicating Dan, "are right."

"Okay," Nan said. "Explain that. How am I wrong and Dan right?"

"There *is* a God," Mary began, addressing Nan. "You've been sorely tested, just like Job. There's a divine reason for the awful things that happened to you, one tragedy following another. God wouldn't do that to a woman he loves unless the candle was worth the game."

"Huh?" Dan said.

"Shut up and let her natter on," Nan told him. She turned back to Mary. She nodded her head in Dan's direction. "And he's right about what?"

"That there *is* a devil loose in the world, working horrible harm, and planning worse. You two believers have the opportunity to stop him before he gains complete control and chases all of us into hell with him."

"Your own *son*! You think *he's* a devil!" Nan sounded incredulous.

Mary lowered her head again and mumbled, "You may have noticed in the car that all during this situation, Todd and I weren't saying things of encouragement to each other. We didn't talk much at all, right?" Without waiting for their confirmation, she continued, "Part of me reacts with shock and loathing at what you're planning to do tonight. Todd is my son, and I am his mother." Here she looked up, and there were tears in the corners of her eyes. "But another and better part of me—the part that loves God and has since I was a little girl—was *glad*. I've hated Todd for a long time, and have often thought that maybe God wanted me, his mother, to take action myself.

"It isn't easy to say this," she confessed. "I've kept it penned up inside since he was a baby, hoping against hope that it wasn't true, telling myself I was nuts, that it wasn't what I thought." She paused. "But it *was* true, and what's happened in the past week just makes it clearer." Dan and Nan glanced at each other, unsure what to make of these bizarre statements.

Mary went on. "Todd's birth was very painful, almost as if he wanted to hurt me as much as he could as he came into the world. Most babies cuddle happily with their mothers, it's a natural instinct." She looked at Nan. "You know what I mean." Nan nodded.

"Not Todd. He refused to take his mother's milk from the day he was born. His own mother! Instead he would only drink milk that his father warmed up in the kitchen. Strange looking milk—I was never sure where it came from. Franklin said it was made from a Whitestone family recipe. Todd really liked it, and he gulped it down with enthusiasm. He grew quickly."

She looked around the room wistfully. "Todd was a very strange, preternatural child. Super-right, loved his father, but dealt with me only when he had to. I wanted to have Todd baptized right away, but Franklin wouldn't hear of it. Said that we should wait and let the boy choose for himself when he grew up. Said it wasn't right to force religion on children."

"Jesus!" Dan muttered.

"Franklin wouldn't let me take Todd to mass—I was reared a devout Catholic. Outright forbade it. Instead he insisted that the boy be brought up an atheist, like Franklin himself. I tried reading the Bible to Todd when he was still an infant, but, from the way he screamed, you'd have thought I was cutting off his toes! I gave that up right away.

"Odd things, scary things started happening. One day Todd was playing with his toy blocks in front of the tv—I was watching some silly game show—and I noticed that he'd turned three of the blocks on the rug in front of him so that they read '666.'"

"Oh!" Dan exclaimed, shocked. Nan didn't react.

"I knew it was supposedly the sign of the devil, but I just laughed, assuming it was a coincidence that they'd come up that way. I pretended to play with Todd for a second, and while I was doing that I moved the blocks around, turning them every which way, mixing them up. Todd didn't like me doing that, and he reacted violently. He cried hotly and slapped at my arms. When I backed away, it didn't take him ten seconds to snatch the blocks and immediately turn them so that 666 faced up once more."

She stopped and said to them in an urgent voice, "That *terrified* me!"

"I wasn't born yesterday, sister," Nan said with a sneer. "You're making this up."

Mary shook her head. "No. You'll see when we go back in that room that it's true. I can make him reveal his real side. Judge then whether I'm lying or not. But first let me tell it all to you here, where he can't know what we're doing, where he can't interrupt and confuse us with his clever ways.

"The next thing that happened was that the pets died, every one of them, every animal we bought him—a cat, a parakeet, a small Scottish Terrier, a gerbil! They'd be fine when we last saw them, but if we left them alone with Todd we'd find them belly up when we returned. Dead of apparently natural causes the vets said. But I knew it wasn't that. Todd himself didn't seem the least bit upset by the deaths of his not-so-beloved pets.

"The only one that survived to old age was this huge black Doberman Franklin gave Todd on his third birthday. Franklin named the dog 'Iblis' over my objections. I wanted to call him 'Ranger,' but Franklin would have none of it. As a puppy, the dog was cute, and he was always tame and respectful around me, but he adored Todd and Franklin, particularly the boy—those two were inseparable. Iblis guarded him day and night, and made sure nothing bad happened to Todd. At first that seemed good, but as time went on this protective attitude became extreme—Iblis had to go to school with him, stay with him on the play ground, sleep in his bedroom. He whined outside the door when Todd went to the bathroom. That all seemed excessive to me. Franklin pooh-poohed my concerns, and assured me it was all right, I should just relax.

"That dog finally died this past summer at age eleven, and Todd was depressed for a week, which wasn't like him at all. I confess I was glad to see the dog go. Iblis had gotten more protective as he aged, and even Todd thought so. He was always having to tie the dog up so he could go out and lead a more normal life. Whenever Iblis was separated from Todd that dog howled like a banshee.

"'Iblis,' what does it mean?" Nan asked. "You know, don't you?"

"Yes. Do you?" Mary asked her. Nan shook her head. "Well, you're right—I do know. I looked it up. It is the Muslim name for the devil."

"Muslim!" Dan blurted, disgusted.

"Did you see the movie *The Omen*?" Nan said suddenly to Mary.

Mary had really hoped they didn't know about this film from which she was cribbing much of her story. "Oh, yes!" she said as if excited by the reference. "It was fiction, of course, but for me, it was like a documentary! I couldn't stand where the plot was going, and left the theater after I watched the first half hour or so. I was sure something bad was going to happen to the mother."

"She was on this balcony . . . ," Dan began, but Nan shushed him.

"Tell us more," Nan said to Mary.

"I was scared a lot. Todd was almost superhuman, and he accomplished everything he set his mind to, some of them almost impossible things. He was at the top of his class in grades, a star athlete," (this was untrue) "prom king," (another lie) "and the president of so many student clubs and organizations that I lost count. He could be affectionate to me, but Todd could also be quite cruel. One day I realized my favorite rosary was missing. It was very special, as Todd knew, because it had been given to me by my grandmother. She'd brought it to this country all the way from Poland. After searching the house from top to bottom, I asked Franklin and Todd if they had seen it, and they exchanged what I thought of as a significant glance before saying no.

"When I was taking out the trash that week, the bag broke, and all those rosary beads bounced down the driveway and into the street. I was devastated."

Dan looked worriedly in the direction of the nursery. "Superhuman? Could he be in there now pulling up his eye bolt from the floor and freeing hisself from the chains?" His hand went to his side to touch the gun in his holster.

"No, no!" Mary said quickly. "He has no powers . . . yet. But as he gets older, he's more cunning, is capable of more evil. You saw his website, didn't you?"

They both nodded.

"Then you know how clever he can be. I truly believe it's the devil's plan to use him as an instrument for world conquest. Those things he posted

167

on the internet—those awful lies—they went all over the world spreading a message of hate, and they were very, very persuasive. Millions of people must have begun to doubt their faith, to turn their heads away from God. And you know where that leads."

"TO PERDITION!" Dan exclaimed, rising to his feet. "I KNEW IT," he said to Nan. "DIDN'T I TELL YOU?"

"Sit down, Dan," Nan told him. She didn't look at all convinced, but neither did she seem to be scoffing at Mary anymore. Mary hoped Nan was willing to speculate whether what she was hearing was the truth. Much depended on that.

"Why would God make me go through such awful torments if this was all true?" Nan asked Mary.

"Why, to make you arrive at the state you've reached—so angry, so depressed, so put upon that you would seek out this devil, capture him, bring him back here and rid the world of his evil! How many other women—even those with a strong faith—would have the courage, the drive, the desire to do what you two are going to do tonight? God had to get you *ready*, motivate you, make you hate sin that much."

"Why couldn't God just take Todd out Hisself?" she asked. "God's all powerful."

Mary shrugged. "I don't know. God has his reasons, or maybe there are rules—rules we don't understand—about the battle between good and evil and who can do what. All I know is that you two have been perfectly tuned by the hand of God so that you are filled with the Lord's work and will do what he desires."

She paused. "And *I* want to help you—God willing!—I do!" She touched her hand to her chest, as if hesitating to go on. "There's one more thing that you should know, one more thing that makes it important something be done now, before it's too late.

"Franklin and Todd have been talking mysteriously about some ceremony that Todd will have to participate in when he turns eighteen—two years from now. Whenever I ask them what this is all about, they just laugh and say they're joking, that eighteen is just the age when he'll become an adult, and be able to vote and all. But you know what I think it is?"

"HE'S GOING TO BE INDUCTED INTO SATAN'S INNER CIRCLE!" Dan thundered.

Nan made a soothing gesture with her hand—calm down, calm down, it said. She turned back to Mary. "You said you could *prove* all of this when we go back into that room. Is that right? You can?"

"Oh, yes," Mary said with an assurance she wished she felt. "Take me back in there, let me talk to him in your presence, let him know that we all

168

know who he really is, and you'll see his true colors come out."

"That's exciting!" Dan said, eager for the experience.

"Let's go," Nan said, and they headed back to the nursery.

Franklin's morning meeting with Jonathan Harker was a roaring success. The man clearly knew what he was doing, and was so good at making people feel comfortable that Franklin found it easy in the end to sign the proffered contract. Franklin Whitestone was now the newest client of the Martin Turnbill agency, Los Angeles.

Harker assured Franklin that the firm's security team would fly to Columbus on Monday to set up protective services, but he also urged Franklin in the meantime to seriously consider a move to another location (he suggest L.A., of course), at least for a short period of time until things settled a bit. He also promised to spend the weekend drawing up a list of ways that they could start the publicity process rolling, and promised to email his proposals to Franklin.

On the way back to the airport, Harker brought up his the first thing on his list.

"What would you think," he asked, "about appearing on the Jimmy Ball Show again? And by 'again' I mean this coming Sunday night, two days from now."

Franklin didn't have to mull that one over. He replied, "I think I'd rather pull my toenails out one by one with a pair of pliers. Why in the world would I go back to the scene of the crime?"

"A couple of reasons. The first is that it would give you a chance to tell the world what you really meant that night, and, to the extent you feel it justified, offer an apology. If you do it smoothly enough, it could throw oil on troubled waters and buy some relief for you and your family from some of these vicious and ugly attacks."

"Hmm," Franklin said, considering this.

"From the point of view of the Martin Turnbill agency, it would be a major coup. It immediately would become one of the most watched shows in the history of television, and that would light a bonfire under the image of the new Franklin Whitestone. From there on, the honey jar's on your plate: paid speeches, a book deal, a tv movie, the list is endless. As I've been telling you, Franklin, there is a waterfall of money about to cascade onto your head—money that should make your life and that of your son quite comfortable. But—and this is important—you have to be willing to do your share of the heavy lifting. We'll create the opportunities, but you must deliver the goods."

"Hmm. But surely Jimmy Ball already has guests booked for

Sunday."

"Oh, don't worry about that," Harker replied, dismissing it with a wave of his hand. "Jimmy Ball would slit their throats in the green room if that was the only way he could clear a place for you on the show. He knows what a boffo tv event this would be."

"Actually," Franklin said, thinking back, "he said something very much like that last week."

"So? Will you authorize me to explore this with his people?"

Franklin debated it. Oh, why not? he thought. Harker is promising me a whole new world, and it's time to start taking the tour, do some of that heavy lifting.

"Yes, okay" he said at last. "Do it—set it up. I'll start thinking right away what I want to say."

"Good decision!" his new agent rejoiced as they pulled onto the access road leading to the airport. "I'm very pleased we've come to an agreement. It should be a bonanza for all involved!"

"One off-the-subject question, if you don't mind," Franklin told him. "There is something about your name that is very familiar, but I don't know why. Any clues as to why I would think that?"

Harker laughed. "Jonathan Harker was the protagonist in the original *Dracula* novel. I guess my parents had a strange sense of humor—or maybe they didn't know the book—when they named me 'Jonathan.'"

"Haven't they told you the reason?"

"Nope. I was adopted when I was very young, and never knew them."

"What you're telling me," Franklin said, adopting a sinister low tone, "is that I'm being represented by a *vampire*? That's not very comforting."

"*No, no,*" the agent protested as they pulled up in the drop-off area of Port Columbus, "Jonathan Harker was the *hero*, not the vampire! I'm the good guy."

"I'm relieved to hear it."

"Oh, but wouldn't I just like to have Dracula as a client though!" Harker chortled, as he climbed from the car and retrieved his bag from the back seat. "He'd be worth millions, maybe billions!"

"Guess that's right," Franklin agreed. "I'd watch the Jimmy Ball show the night Dracula was the guest celebrity."

"See what I mean?"

They laughed, shook hands again, and parted. Content, Franklin punched on the radio as he drove off.

He was still on the airport's access road when the hourly news came on. The lead story was that Todd Whitestone and his mother had been kidnapped in Dayton last night and were being held in a place unknown.

He almost drove off the road.

Todd, alternating between being terrified and bored, looked up as his mother as Nan and Dan reentered the room. His mother sat down on her chair, but, interestingly, they didn't lock her chain to the floor bolt. What did that mean?

Nan and Dan dragged the two chairs that were against the far wall closer to their captives, and sat down looking expectant. Something was clearly up.

Mary spoke first. "Todd, it's time for you to hear the truth. That post you put on the internet was a mockery of God, and your time has come to pay for it."

Hmm, Todd thought. This is a new direction. He didn't think for one second that she actually believed her last sentence. Best to keep still until he understood the game. Todd said nothing, just looked back at her stonily.

Mary was very pleased when Todd didn't immediately blurt out something that wouldn't go with the scenario she was trying to sell to Nan and Dan. She had to get Todd into the script and saying the right lines, so she hurried on, turning to face her captors.

"Of course, he's not going to just confess, but I have a way to make him show his true colors," she told them.

"What's that?" Nan asked, very suspicious.

"Latin," Mary replied. "I told you I was raised a Catholic, and just once I made the mistake of taking Todd to church with me to attend mass. His father, of course, would've strongly opposed that, but Todd and I were on one of my many trips, and we were in Italy, far, far from Columbus. Todd was about eight, and he went along willingly enough, but I don't think he appreciated what a mass was going to be like.

"This particular mass was said in Latin, and Todd's violent reaction on first hearing it confirmed my growing suspicions that he was not a child of light, but had come to me from a very dark place."

Catching a whiff of where this was going, Todd dropped his voice into a low register and growled, "MOTHER!" in a convincing tone.

She turned and pointed at him and chanted loudly, "Ollow-fay y-may ead-lay!:

Todd promptly decoded that as "follow my lead." Then, as if they'd carefully rehearsed it, Todd recoiled back in his chair and began rocking back and forth as if in pain, nearly knocking the chair and table over.

Mary kept her finger pointed straight at his writhing form as she intoned, "Introibo ad altare Dei, ad Deum qui laetificat juventutem meam!"

171

She figured it would be a good idea to throw in some real Latin, and this phrase was actually taken from the mass.

At this, Todd threw himself forward in the chair, lunging at her, making a hideous hissing sound. All three of the others, most particularly including his mother, were so startled by this attack that they jerked back, out of his reach. Todd had even scared her, but Mary didn't have time to appreciate his performance. "All-fay o-tay loor-fay!" she screamed. She knew Todd might hurt himself if he did fall to the floor as directed, but she didn't care about that. Broken bones they could deal with; his corpse they could not.

Todd went over sideways with a crash, landing heavily on his left shoulder, his body pulled at an odd angle by the chain attached to the floor. Without stopping for a second, he screamed and hissed, his face bright red, writhing horribly.

Dan was on his feet, his wife rising beside him. "HE'S GOING TO PULL OUT THE BOLT!" he yelled over the tumult, drawing his gun and pointing it at the not-quite-human spectacle now pounding both hands and feet loudly against the carpet.

"NO!" Mary demanded, stepping quickly between Dan and the boy. "I already told you!—he doesn't yet have the power to do anything more than normal humans can do—physically, I mean. Save him for tonight just like you planned!"

Dan, trembling, kept the gun pointed at the devil he saw before him. "NAN?" he said, begging for her advice, willing to abide by her decision.

She put a hand on his and made him lower the gun.

"Let him suffer," she said, her voice flat. "I'm glad of it. We know now what he is, and what the Lord wants us to do to him. His mother's right. Save him for the ceremony. That's when we'll send him back to the hell he came from."

Unable to stand, Mary sat down hard on her chair.

CHAPTER ELEVEN

EXORCISM

Catherine Whiteside first learned that Todd and his mother had been kidnapped when her favorite soap opera was interrupted by a news bulletin.

"Sixteen year old Todd Whitestone and his mother Mary Whitestone, ex-wife of Todd's father Franklin, were abducted at gun point last night from this motel on the eastern side of Dayton," the attractive female news anchor read from the teleprompter. The video showed the outside of a typical motel of the type where guests could pull cars right up to the door of their rooms. "Todd Whitestone, who caused a sensation last Tuesday when he posted on his website an attack on the existence of God, had been in hiding with his mother, according to his best friend, Warren Allen, who was with the Whitestones last night and was abducted along with them." The video now shifted to a shot of Stubby Allen, talking to a reporter. Catherine had met Stubby at a number of functions that involved Todd, most recently at Todd's birthday party. She thought him a decent sort, if not overly bright.

"Todd asked me to bring him some things from his house," Stubby was saying, "and so I went there with my sister Wendy and we were captured by this man and woman and made to go with them to Dayton to collect Todd and Mrs. Whitestone."

"Did you get their names? The kidnappers?" the reporter asked.

"No. They called each other 'Dan' and 'Nan' and words like 'honey,' so I guessed they were married. They seemed really angry with Todd."

The reporter, an articulate black man in his 30s, posed a series of questions to Stubby and elicited the information that the van was a Chevy of unknown year, and that after driving for awhile, the kidnapper's van had stopped on a dark country road and left Stubby and his sister there. Stubby had no idea what the kidnappers planned to do with Todd and his mother. The camera then shifted back to the anchor, who informed her audience that a massive manhunt was now in progress to find this Dan and Nan.

More upset than she'd been in decades, Catherine picked up her phone and called Franklin. He answered almost immediately, seeing her name on caller-ID.

"Do you know anything more than what's on tv?" she asked him.

"No," he replied. "I just learned about it myself from the radio. I called the Dayton police to get what I could from them. They didn't want to say much on the phone, but I agreed to drive to Dayton immediately and do what I can to help. I'm on Interstate 70 now."

Catherine nodded her head at this. "Good," she said. "You need to get into the thick of the investigation. It'll keep you from going crazy with worry."

"I'm already crazy with worry," he assured her.

"Well, stop that!" she commanded. "This is no time for you to fall apart. Todd and Mary need you, and they need you clear-headed and concentrating on all the things that might lead to the discovery of where they are. Is there any indication why they were kidnapped?"

"You mean other than Todd pissing off the entire world?"

"Yes," she replied, matter of fact. That was what she meant.

"No, but it's bound to be that. Todd made a lot of people angry, and some percentage of those will be crazies who decide to punish him in the name of God."

"One doubts that God, even if he did exist, would be pleased by kidnapping."

"Mom," Franklin insisted, "I can't talk anymore now. I'm having trouble driving as it is, and I got to pay attention to the road."

"All right, but let me hear from you as soon as you learn things. Do you promise to call me?"

"Yes," he replied, and they both said goodbye. Franklin knew that he'd better do it too, even though calling his mother could normally be put off until the next eclipse of the moon.   Catherine sat still in her lounger, holding the phone and thinking whether there was something she could do to help. Her tv soap opera was exploring a story line in which a wronged woman posed as her own twin sister in order to punish her cross-dressing husband, but Catherine lost interest and snapped it off.

1   Very disturbed by the same tv interview with Stubby Allen, Celia Hawkins phoned Jake Richardson, who was at work, getting him on his cell, and asking if he'd heard the news. When he said no, she described what was going on, and he was much surprised.

"What kind of people would kidnap a boy and his mother?" he asked. "That's nutzo. I mean, as I said, I'd like to talk to Franklin Whitestone and see if I could persuade him to accept Jesus Christ as his savior, but that'd just be talking. You can't force Jesus down someone's throat. This is bad, Celia. This is very bad."

"Oh, Jake," Celia said, "I fear for their lives. Maybe we could both say prayers for them."

"Yes, yes," Jake replied with enthusiasm. "We should do it tonight— get together and pray."

174

And, when they got together at her house later in the day, they did manage to work in a few prayers for poor Todd and Mary Whitestone before moving on to other things.

Kelly was coming out of an Appointments Committee meeting at the Ohio State law school when one of the secretaries gave her the news, adding in a guarded tone, "Don't you know Todd?" Kelly noticed that, significantly, the secretary did not ask if she knew Mary.

The news almost felled Kelly in the hallway, and she walked unsteadily back to her office. Todd and Mary—prisoners somewhere, fighting for their lives! It didn't seem real or possible that it was actually happening.

But, on considering it further, Kelly decided that it wasn't that farfetched. On Wednesday night, true to her renewed devotion to her faith, she'd attended a Bible study class at the Baptist Church just down the block from her home. No one there had any knowledge of her connection with the notorious Whitestones, father and son, and the group's comments about them had greatly troubled Kelly. In addition to the predictable forecasts that they were heading straight to hell for their very public sins, there were some apparently religious people who made it clear that they would like to hurry the process alone.

"Someone ought to make an example of them. Show them the fury of the righteous when aroused by vile transgressors," one said.

"Jesus commanded death for non-believers!" asserted a matronly woman of fifty.

"He did not!" exclaimed Kelly, shocked by the idea.

"Luke 19:27," the woman replied, and she recited it from memory. "'But those mine enemies, which would not that I should reign over them, bring hither, and slay them before me.'"

Another, a palsied older man, added, "Jesus said it more than once. 'Think not that I am come to send peace on earth: I came not to send peace, but a sword.' Matthew 10:34. Look it up."

Shaken, Kelly did examine these two verses when she got home that night, and was distressed to find that they had been accurately quoted. How could that be? Both seemed terribly wrong, out of balance with Christ's usual message of love, peace, and tolerance. Could they have both been mistranslations? Interpolations? Would Jesus really say such militant things?

The next day, Thursday, she'd had an even more disturbing thought, one that had come to her in what she was now calling "Todd moments," moments she hated but couldn't seem to avoid.

175

What would Franklin or Todd say about these biblical passages? She could imagine only too well how it would go: the Bible was written by men, many different men, and of course they mixed in views that did not always mesh so well together. With no God to keep them "on message," the result was a hodgepodge, some of which played better than others. Kelly tried to wipe this heresy from her mind, but she was a trained analytical thinker, and it kept coming back like an unwanted melody endlessly recycling on an internal jukebox.

Now, on Friday, having just heard the shocking news about Todd and Mary, Kelly knew that she might as well give up on the possibility of sleep. Her brain would roil all night contemplating what it would be like to be kidnapped and be at the mercy of possible killers. She resolved to pray, asking God's help in restoring these two trapped people to their home again. After an internal struggle, she also decided she would give Franklin a call as soon as she got home from the law school.

When Franklin arrived at the Dayton police station, he identified himself, and was promptly ushered into the presence of the police team working on the case. The officer in charge, to whom he was introduced, was Lt. Robert Startup, a grave and handsome man in his 40s, who shook Franklin's hand and invited him to a meeting in his office for a detailed exploration of all that was going on. As it happened, that took some time. Not only did Startup and his assistants have a great many questions, but they were constantly interrupted by phone calls and people knocking on the door with important information or queries, and this sometimes led the lieutenant and others exiting suddenly.

Franklin had spent almost an hour explaining and answering their questions, when he finally got around to narrating the events of Wednesday midnight when he'd been shot at. That interested the police very much, and he had to go over it, detail by detail, as they probed to learn everything they could about the incident.

"There is a good chance," Lt. Startup told Franklin, "that the same people who shot at you are connected in some way with the disappearance of your son and ex-wife."

Franklin didn't see how that necessarily followed, but then he wasn't a trained criminal investigator, so he kept his opinion to himself. He also downplayed the fact that he was a lawyer, knowing from previous experience that the police had no great respect for members of the bar. Franklin did mention that he specialized in commercial law, and that his practice had nothing to do with criminal matters. They didn't seem to care much about this one way or another.

When the police were done with him, they showed Franklin to a waiting room and asked him to stick around in case there were developments that either he should know or that he might shed some light on.

When he entered the room, he was surprised to find Stubby Allen there, sitting with a little girl that he supposed was Stubby's sister. They both looked like they'd been cast as consumptive orphans is some low budget school play.

Stubby was equally surprised to see him, and seemingly dismayed at having to face him.

"Stubby!" Franklin said on realizing who the boy was, and walked quickly over to where he was sitting.

Stubby jumped to his feet. "Oh, Mr. Whitestone," he pleaded, "please forgive me. You know I'd never do anything that would hurt Todd and his mother if I could help it!" As soon as he said it, Stubby mentally kicked himself. This statement would shake up Wendy, who he'd managed to get stabilized into a more or less normal frame of mind after the police had spent some time gently asking her questions about what she remembered.

"Of course, I know that," Franklin told him. "No one is blaming you."

"*I'm* blaming me," Stubby said, bitter at his own carelessness. "I led those creeps right to them."

Franklin started to ask Stubby questions about his ordeal, but thought better of it when he noticed the little girl staring at them with trembling lower lip. So, instead, he leaned down and addressed her directly. "Hello," he said in as friendly a tone as he could manage. "My name is Franklin. What's yours?"

"Wendy," she replied, barely audible.

"I know you've had a rough night last night, Wendy," Franklin continued. "But you should be proud that you were strong and helped your brother find the police."

Wendy didn't reply, but this seemed the right thing to say. She no longer looked like she was about to cry.

Franklin turned back to Stubby. "Why are you still here?" he asked.

Stubby shrugged. "I'm wondering the same thing. The police called my parents, and I talked to them. They said they were on their way to get us, but it's been three hours and they still haven't showed. Maybe they're lost."

"Did you get anything to eat?"

"Oh, yes," Stubby said. "They fed us here at the station just a little while ago, and the police who first got to us early this morning took us to Bob Evans for breakfast."

"I had pancakes with syrup!" Wendy volunteered. That was never allowed at home—their father was a dentist and had strict rules about sugar—and she was pleased by the forbidden pleasure.

"You were dumped along the road last night, isn't that right?"

Stubby nodded, looking worriedly at how this question would affect his sister, but she didn't seem to care. Franklin continued, "Did you walk all night? Get some sleep?"

Again watching Wendy carefully, Stubby explained, "We managed some sleep by the side of the road."

"I slept in the grass!" Wendy reported, still in awe of the fact.

"Let me do some checking around," Franklin said to Stubby, "and see if I can find out anything about where your parents are."

The boy looked relieved. "Thanks, Mr. Whitestone. I really appreciate your help. I guess the police have been too busy to care much about how we'll get back to Columbus."

"Don't worry. I'll see to that, if I have to drive you myself."

As he went back toward the door, Stubby touched his arm and stopped him.

"Mr. Whitestone," he said, "I'm also very interested in hearing the *other* developments. You know what I mean?"

Franklin nodded, and glanced at Wendy who was pulling up her socks, paying no attention to them.

"Have there been any developments?" Stubby looked very worried about this.

"Not so far," Franklin said. "But if I hear anything and you're still around, I'll make sure you know."

Stubby nodded. "Again, thanks.. I've been praying it will all turn out right."

Franklin didn't know what to say to that, so he just nodded, and went out the door to talk to the police about Stubby's delayed parents.

Dan and Nan talked it over, and then, apologetically told Mary that they'd have to again chain her to the floor while they ran errands.

"We hate to do it, Ma'am," Dan told her.

"But we don't completely trust you . . .," said Nan, finishing his thought, trailing off.

Mary assured them that she understood completely, and sat back down in her chair so Dan could reattach the chain to the eye bolt lock. She was still wearing the leg shackles, but they had taken off the handcuffs 45 minutes earlier, when the three sat and talked through the details of the exorcism. Of course, Mary was sorry that she was now unable to move around freely, but pleased that there were no longer any restrictions on the movement of her arms. That should prove useful.

Mary's idea for escaping from this house of horror had a number of alternative ways to go, but the decision to keep her fastened to floor eliminated two of them.

At one point in their discussion of the "exorcism," Mary had openly questioned their use of the word. It occurred to her that if she could sell her own version of the ceremony to them, that would be the easiest way out of this mess.

"A true exorcism drives the devil out of someone, but it leaves that person alive, open to the glory of God. Why not try that? We could perform the rite ourselves."

"Well," Dan had replied, "we don't know none of the words or what to do."

Mary had been enthusiastic in her answer to that. "We could pull all we'd need to know off the internet. It wouldn't take ten minutes! And— think of this—all the words would be in Latin! Oh, how that devil encased inside him would howl, be frantic to escape!"

Nan had just shaken her head. "No," she ruled. "We shoot him. It's too dangerous to leave him alive, pretending to be rid of the devil, working mischief. You were right when you said it was God's plan that we free the world of him and his evil message."

"Then it's not really an 'exorcism,'" Mary had pointed out.

"All right. Just say 'execution' if you think that's better. Call it what you will, it happens at 6:30."

And that was that.

On to Plan B, Mary thought as Dan and Nan left the room. She glanced distastefully at her leg restraints.

Todd suddenly spoke up, loud and aggressive. "How can you do this to me?" he questioned. "I'm your son! You *can't* help them kill me! What kind of mother are you?"

Mary was very pleased he could do this so convincingly, play his part so well. He was right on the money with this outraged condemnation of her. As Todd had concluded, Dan and Nan would immediately go to the receiving station and listen carefully to what mother and son said to each other when left alone.

"I'm a mother who loves her God more than some supposed duty to nurture a devil and allow him to pollute the world."

Todd exploded with rage. "CURSE YOU! CURSE YOU!" he screamed. "LET ME OUT OF THESE CHAINS AND I'LL STRANGLE YOU!"

"*Pro bono sic semper tyranis coitus interruptus!*" Mary screamed back, stringing together all the Latin phrases that occurred to her.

Todd almost lost it. He started to laugh, caught himself, and then decided to go with it. He turned his laugh into a maniacal hysteria that any self-respecting demon would be proud of. "Your Latin doesn't faze me anymore, woman," he sneered. "I'm getting use to it!"

"You don't get to listen to much more of it," she told him. "The evening draws nigh." Hmm. Nigh? Where had that come from?

Todd had run out of invective, and he was tired of playing the archfiend, so he opted for silence. Quietly, he looked at her, asking questions with his eyes. What are you planning? How can I help?

What to reply, she wondered, and how to do it?. She chose to wink at him, and nod encouragingly as she gave him a thumbs up.

Clueless as to where his mother was going with all this, Todd sat in anxious anticipation of whatever was coming. She wasn't just playing it by ear, he knew. Mary Whitestone had always been a planner, sure of what she wanted and clever at getting it. She had fought her way out of a house of poverty, attained an education three levels above that received by any other member of her family (she had an M.A. in English), and was a successful writer with devoted readers all over the world. So what next?

What actually did come next occurred half an hour later when Nan and Dan returned to the room to explain their plans to Mary.

"We're right on schedule," Dan said, looking at his watch. "It's two thirty, so we have plenty of time to set up things for this evening. Nan's gonna run some errands first."

"I have some letters to mail to our families," Nan explained. "We wrote them over the last couple of days, figuring that letters would be a lot more personal than suicide notes."

Mary was very glad to get Nan out of the house so that her foes were divided, but a simple run to the mailbox wasn't enough time for all she had in mind during Nan's absence. She had to stretch those errands out.

"Are you sure you have everything?" she asked Nan, using this question to buy time to think.

"Oh, yes," the latter replied. "We've been planning this for days, going over and over it, step by step. We told you most of it earlier."

"Do you have enough candles?"

"Candles?"

180

"They would be a fine touch. About twenty candles placed around the room would add a religious tone to the proceeding that would please God a great deal."

Nan looked skeptical. "Candles?" she repeated. "What would we put them on? I don't have that many candlesticks."

"Put them on ordinary plates. Just use the hot wax to stand them up."

Dan chimed in. "I like the idea, Nan. Makes it more official," he said.

His wife mulled it over and then shrugged. "Okay," she agreed. "Might as well do the thing up brown. I'll stop at Wal-Mart and get candles."

"And wine," Mary added. "You do have enough wine?"

"Wine!" Dan said, mystified. "We ain't drinkers!" He sounded offended by the implication.

Mary raised one finger, like a school marm. "Ah, but Dan, this is a *religious* occasion, and wine is perfectly appropriate."

"That's a Catholic thing," Nan scoffed.

"On, no," Mary assured her. "It's part of many sacred rituals. Jesus drank wine at special events: the marriage at Cana, the Last Supper. This is to be your last supper, right?"

They thought about that. Dan and Nan had tasted wine only a couple of times in their lives, and hadn't liked it all that much, but it did seem like the thing to do on the final night they would be together in the physical world.

Nan decided. "Okay. I'll also get wine. I guess Wal-Mart will have that too. What kind of wine?"

"Something red," Mary suggested.

"Goes with blood," Dan contributed, proud of this analogy.

Todd almost laughed again, but turned it into a mini-growl. They glanced at him and then went back to making their preparations. There were some new ideas batted around for additions to the planned supper, and the decision to add wine freed them up to opt for a more elaborate meal than they had ever before fixed at home.

"Doesn't much matter what it costs," Dan observed with a grim smile.

Nan left to put on her coat, and then stuck her head back into the room.

"You're in charge," she told Dan, "and I expect you to be *real careful*. If that demon gets loose it'll mean more than just the three of us getting hurt. Remember how big a deal this is, and what we are chosen by God to do."

Dan promised to take extra care, and Nan went.

With her out of the room, Dan moved to question Todd more closely. He dragged a chair over near the table, sat and looked the boy in the eye.

"I don't care much for no devils," he said, "but tell the truth while you still have time, and who knows what we might work out. We're on to you, boy, and you know that, right? What was you planning, and what would you do if you was free?"

Todd considered the question and how to structure his answer. Finally he said, "Please believe me! You've got it all wrong, Mister. So does my mother. I'm *not* a devil—I don't even think that devils really exist! I'm just an ordinary sixteen year old boy, and it would be a crime to kill me. You'd be murderers!"

Mary jumped into this one. "I knew it!" she said, as if in triumph. "That's what he *always* does when cornered. Turns all nice and sweet—what a good boy, wouldn't harm a fly." She turned to Todd and snarled, "Want to hear some more Latin."

He glared at her, his eyes mere slits, his lip curled. "Fuck you!" he said.

Dan slapped him so hard that the boy's chair rocked. "Devil or not, you ain't supposed to talk to your mother that way!" He drew back his hand, but Mary, close enough to do so, grabbed his upper arm and pulled it back.

"Let it go, let it go," she urged. "He'll get what's coming to him soon enough." Silently, she was very proud of the way Todd played this scene, accepting pain as a byproduct of deception.

Time to move to another topic. Mary turned to Dan. "I have something I want to ask you. Which of the guns did you and your wife finally decide to use?

"For the exorcism? The Smith and Wesson 686," he replied.

"That's one of the handguns, isn't it? Not one of the rifles."

"Right."

"Will a gun that small do the trick? Won't it require multiple shots?"

Dan shook his head. "Oh, no, Ma'am," he told her. "That gun has a 96% one-shot stop. There was a crook, drilled by a Texas Ranger with that gun, who actually had his heart blowed into eight pieces!'

"Wow!" Mary said, the impressed amateur.

"He didn't make it," Dan joked.

Todd, not at all acting, looked very uncomfortable at this information.

"Could I please see the gun? Examine it carefully?" Mary asked Dan, and then seeing the expression of doubt clouding his face, added, "I don't mean *loaded*. Take the bullets out. I just want to hold the gun, that very important gun, and think about the part it will play tonight in working the will of God."

Dan thought it over. Why not? he decided. "Be right back," he told her, and left the room.

182

Mary winked at Todd again, hoping to reassure him. He peered intently at her, not even close to guessing what she had in mind, and wondering whether he should be prepared to help in some way. What could she possibly do with an unloaded gun?

Dan returned with the shiny revolver. Its cylinder was open, and Dan was removing the bullets as he came. He pulled his chair in front of Mary's, and, after a small hesitation, he handed her the gun.

"It's beautiful," she said in admiration, turning the weapon over in her hands and looking at it from various angles. "How much does it weigh?

"Don't rightly know," Dan replied. "Close to three pounds I would guess."

"Is this a new gun?"

"Oh, lordy, no. We've had it for years. Shot it a lot. Targets and such."

"What's this on the handle?" she asked, holding the gun by its barrel, peering closely at the butt of the gun which she lifted up near her eyes. "DAN, THERE'S SOMETHING IN WRITING ON HERE! IT HAS A LATIN PHRASE WRITTEN ON IT. *'Ull-pay ug-play ow-nay,'*" she read, pronouncing each word carefully.

"IT DON'T!" Dan said in wonder, feeling sure this was a sign from God. He leaned forward to see what she was pointing to, and the lights went out.

In the blackness that engulfed them, Mary put all the fury she'd built up in the last 24 hours into the blows she rained on Dan. She repeatedly smacked him hard across the face with the butt of the gun. The first blow hit his left eye and broke his nose, and as he fell she managed to hit him again, and then a third time. He started to go over backwards, but she needed to keep him within her reach, so she grabbed him with her free hand and got part of his shirt. She pulled Dan toward her, and his head fell against her knees. Easy target there, she thought as whammed the butt twice more into his head, and then let him go. Dan slumped to the floor. The only sound he'd made the whole time she was striking him was one little "uh" noise at the first blow.

Silence.

Mary held the gun up, at the ready, prepared to do more if necessary, but Dan was a dead weight resting against her feet. He wasn't moving.

"Put the plug back in," she told Todd, and, after he fumbled with the task for what seemed to Mary far too long, the lamp came back on, blinding them both.

Dan was lying at Mary's feet, as if cuddled up for an inappropriate nap. Blood covered his face and upper body, and was pouring out of his various head wounds. It was later determined that he'd lost his left eye when she first hit him, and that subsequent blows had done an extraordinary amount of damage. He eventually survived this attack, but thereafter vision in his right eye was never any better than 60%, and he spoke with great difficulty, struggling to form the words, his mind that of a child.

Todd, who'd only guessed what was going on when the room went dark, looked at the carnage his mother had caused, and his jaw dropped open.

"AWESOME!" he said in stupefied admiration. "I never saw that coming!"

Mary looked at Dan. "Neither did he," she said, setting the gun gently on the table.

"*Mom! You were incredible!*" Todd enthused.

She smiled at him, shaken and invigorated, both at once. "You were incredible too, son. Every cue I gave, you handled as if we'd rehearsed it. When I told you to pull the plug, you immediately jerked it out of the wall. Good job, Todd. I'm very proud."

He beamed back, filled with love and renewed appreciation for his fantastic mother. "Now what?" he asked, looking around.

"We have to act fast, though it will probably be awhile before that spooky woman returns with wine and candles. First of all, find the keys." Somewhat gingerly she began to touch Dan's body.

"They're on a key chain on his left side, hanging from a belt loop," Todd told her.

"I know that, but I can't seem . . . oh, here they are." She unclipped the keys and stared at the collection she held in her hand, trying to figure out which keys were the ones she wanted.

"The skeleton key," Todd told her. "It unlocks all the things we have on, though there's a different one for the lock to the eyebolt. But," he pointed out, "if you get us out of these," he rattled his chains, "just leave the leg chains bolted down. That won't matter."

In under a minute they were both standing, and the hug they gave each other went on for a long time. Reactions to what they had just gone through began to set in. Todd trembled, his knees unexpectedly buckling, and he more or less fell onto his chair.

"I . . . I didn't realize how much tension I was carrying," he said in a halting voice. "I need a little quiet time to pull myself together."

"So . . . you're human after all," his mother joked.

"Very." He looked at Dan. "Shouldn't we tie him up or something?"

Mary considered the issue. "Yes," she said, "but that's not the first thing. It doesn't look as if he's going to be active anytime soon. He may even be dead." She stepped back to avoid the spreading pool of Dan's blood. "The first thing we have to do is load this gun and get ready for Nan. Help me find the bullets."

"He has a gun in his holster," Todd pointed out. "It's probably already loaded."

"Hmm. But is it as good a weapon for really hurting someone if we have to use it? That woman is a force all her own. Dangerous as a cobra."

"You mean: does the holster gun have a '96% one-shot stop'?" Todd quoted.

"The things these people say!" Mary clucked, still searching Dan's pockets for the bullets. "They treat their guns like children, and they are oh-so-proud of them. Ah! The bullets!" With some difficulty she and Todd rolled Dan on his side, and she extracted them from his shirt pocket. She held them in her hand and studied them. Then she picked up the Smith and Wesson from the table.

"Do you have any idea how to load this thing?" she asked Todd, holding it out to him.

"Hmm. Let me have a look," he replied, taking both the gun and bullets from her.

This was the sort of task he was good at—figuring things out. It didn't prove to be difficult. In less than a minute Todd snapped it all back together.

"Loaded," he announced.

"Is there some sort of safety that's on?"

Todd examined the gun carefully. "No safety. It's ready to go."

"Good," his mother replied, holding out her hand for the gun.

Todd was reluctant to let it go. "Mom," he protested. "I should be the one to cover Nan."

"*NO!*" Mary said, vetoing the idea. "There could easily be criminal charges from this," she indicated Dan on the floor, "and from whatever happens when she comes through that door. I'm already implicated, but you're not, and I don't want you to be. Todd Whitestone is a name that's already hated enough."

He thought about that. It made sense, but he didn't like it.

"I could get out the other gun, the one in Dan's holster."

"Yes," she agreed, "get it. But all I want you to do with it is to put it out of his reach if he happens to come to. *Look at me, Todd,*" she commanded as he went to one knee to retrieve the holster gun.

He glanced up, her tone making him attentive.

"For *hours* I have planned this out, and I've planned it well. I'm not sure what exactly is going to happen when that woman returns, but I'm very sure that you aren't going to be involved. I'm your mother, and right now you owe me a lot. True?'

"True. A lot."

"Then trust me to get this right. I'll handle Nan. I particularly don't want *you* firing any guns. Are we clear on this? Do you promise me?"

"What if *she* shoots *you*? Can I shoot her then?"

Mary thought for a moment. "All right. Then and only then."

"You got it, Mom. I promise."

It was another half hour before they heard the van pull up outside and the sound of Nan coming into the house. By agreement, Todd stood behind the door as it opened, Dan's holster gun in his hand. Mary, having watched enough police in movies and on tv, stood five feet from the door, her legs wide, both hands on the Smith and Wesson. She extended it straight out in front of her. She told herself to brace for any recoil that might occur if she were forced to fire. Mary was afraid of that recoil, and wanted to make sure it wouldn't throw her out of her shooter's stance. Both their lives depended on her getting this right.

Todd was wide-eyed as he crouched down next to the door.

Mary's heart was pounding so hard she was afraid it might throw off her aim and cause her to miss if she *had* to shoot, which was not her plan. Her plan was to yell "FREEZE!" at Nan, just like the cops did, and then have Todd disarm her.

But it didn't happen like that at all.

Nan opened the door, one plastic grocery bag in each hand, and before she could say a word or react in any way, Mary shot her. That bullet struck Nan in the chest, throwing her back against the door jamb, but it wasn't the only one that hit her. Successfully battling the recoil, Mary emptied the gun into Nan's twitching body, and then, with the gun actually smoking, Mary collapsed on the floor right where she stood.

Todd was speechless for a few seconds. His ears were ringing. Then he rushed to his mother, falling to the floor beside her, pulling her up so that she wouldn't fall over on her back.

"Oh, wow! Mom," he said, very concerned. "Did a bullet ricochet and hit you?"

"No, no, I'm fine," Mary replied, leaning against him, spent. "But Nan . . . is she dead?"

Todd peered at the heap that once been Nan. He nodded, certain. "Looks like all six bullets exceeded the 96% one-shot stop estimate," he told her.

CHAPTER TWELVE

AFTERMATH

That Friday afternoon, pacing nervously around the waiting room at the Dayton police station, Franklin was startled when Lt. Startup abruptly stuck his head in the door shortly after 3 p.m.

"Good news!" he said with a grin on his normally sober face. "They've been found and both your son and ex-wife are okay."

"*YEOW!*" Franklin exclaimed, leaping from his chair. He'd been waiting a long time, and had devolved into an emotional mess. "Where are they? What happened?"

"The Gallia County Sheriff's Department is holding them, and I don't have any other information beyond the fact that apparently they're unhurt. The officer who called wanted that much to get out as soon as possible, and promised to supply details shortly. He said his people are interviewing the Whitestones right now."

"Please let me know as soon as you know what that all means," Franklin begged.

"Sure thing," the lieutenant replied, withdrawing his head and going.

In what was one of the happiest moments in his life, Franklin danced wildly around the room. He felt tension draining from him in a rush, and then, worried he was getting too lightheaded, he sat down on one of the vinyl covered chairs, splayed in all directions like a dropped marionette.

Todd and Mary are safe! he thought. *Safe!*

Franklin had tried to keep his hopes up, but deep down inside he'd been sure that news would mean he should come claim their bodies. Now, like a storm followed immediately by sunshine, the situation had reversed itself, and everything in life seemed sunny as well.

Should he call people (say, his mother, his siblings, the Allens) with the good news, or wait until he could tell them more? Thinking this over, he decided that if he called with only partial information, he'd have to make second calls later. That sounded like a lot of unnecessary work, so he opted to wait.

This decided, he didn't have anything to do. Tired of inactivity and knowing he couldn't just sit, Franklin resumed pacing, but in a completely different mood than his earlier walking frenzy. He turned over the happy news in his mind, constantly reassuring himself that it was real. But then he wondered about Todd and Mary's current state. Were they okay mentally? Where were they? What in the world had they been through?

It wasn't long before Lt. Startup was back, notebook in hand, that same grin on his face. He motioned Franklin into one of the chairs, and sat in another himself.

"You're not going to believe this," he said, "but apparently your ex-wife and son overpowered the kidnappers and then called the police."

"Mary and Todd?" That seemed more than unlikely. "How?"

The lieutenant's grin got bigger. "According to the Gallia authorities, Mary Whitestone herself took them both out. One she shot six times with a revolver, a woman named Annette Black, and immediately before that she bludgeoned the woman's husband, Daniel Black, into unconsciousness with the butt of the same revolver. The woman is dead and the husband is in the county hospital in critical condition. Neither Todd nor Mary Whitestone was hurt at all."

Franklin sat, so stunned he was a statue. The lieutenant continued with the story.

"Mary Whitestone will be held for more questioning. Apparently she and your son were kidnapped Thursday night from that motel room here in Dayton, and driven to Gallia County where the Blacks have a farm. They were told by the Blacks that your son Todd was to be executed this evening. Before of that could happen, your ex-wife somehow got hold of a Smith and Wesson revolver—we're not sure how—and first beat up the husband, and then pumped six shots into the wife, killing her instantly. It looks like all six bullets hit their target. Your ex-wife is quite the marksman."

Franklin was shaking his head back and forth rapidly. No. This couldn't be true. All during their marriage, Mary Whitestone wouldn't even use the fly swatter—she literally wouldn't kill a fly. So the thought of her taking a gun and then . . . .

"There's a complication," Startup continued. "While the Black woman was wearing a holster with a Colt .45 in it, she didn't have that weapon drawn, and, it appears, was actually holding two plastic grocery bags, one in each hand, when your ex-wife gunned her down."

Franklin frowned. Criminal law was not his forte, but he knew enough that this development was troubling. Shooting someone who was not actually attacking you didn't sound like self defense. It sounded like homicide. Was Mary about to be arrested? Tried? Imprisoned?

None of that sounded likely, but these bald facts were damning.

He decided to ask Startup what he thought. "Is she in jeopardy? Suspicion of murder or anything like that?

Startup shrugged. "Not clear," he said. "But we know that the Whitestones had been cuffed and shackled, held at gun point, made to view a gun collection from which the son's execution weapon was to be selected, and generally terrorized for more or less 24 hours by their potential killers. Mary Whitestone's quick thinking and determined actions turned things around. The killers became the victims, and the victims walked away unscathed. Sounds like a bad movie."

"It does. But what's your professional guess as to what will happen to her?"

"I wouldn't worry much about it. She'll have to go through a lot of hassles—an inquest, lawyers arguing, maybe being brought up before a judge, and all that, but I believe the chances of charges actually being filed are nil. Prosecutors are very jealous of their win-loss ratio, and, in this case, there is isn't a jury in Ohio that would convict her of anything. In the end, I predict she'll be let go with nothing more than a stern warning to avoid gunning down any more fellow citizens."

Relieved, Franklin laughed. He'd been thinking the same thing.

On Friday morning, Jonathan Harker phoned Catherine Whitestone, and explained that he was now the media consultant who was representing her son, Franklin. He began their conversation by thanking her for making the original suggestion that Franklin get in touch with a PR firm, leading to the Martin Turnbill agency's acquisition of a new client.

"You're very welcome, Mr. Harker," Catherine replied. "I thought it would be a good idea, and I'm pleased it's come to fruition."

"Jonathan, please. And you were right. However, Mrs. Whitestone . . .," he continued.

She interrupted. "Catherine." Normally she didn't allow such an intimacy anywhere nearly this fast, but Harker seemed very charming, and Catherine Whitestone had always had good instincts when it came to her first impressions.

"Catherine," he corrected, pleased. "I asked and received your son's permission to call you. The real reason I'm doing so is to explore the possibility that you personally would allow the Martin Turnbill agency to represent you."

That was a surprise, and she was rarely surprised. "Me?"

"Oh, Catherine, I've been quizzing you son. *What a story you have to tell!* And, here at the agency, we can help you tell it right, in a way that the world will take notice. Is it true that you raised all four of your children to be atheists?"

"Why, yes. Of course I did."

"But, Catherine, you have to know that very few freethinking mothers do that, or at least would then be willing to talk about it."

189

"Oh? So they lie to their children?" She knew what he meant, of course, but thought it might be interesting to make him string it out.

"Yes, they do, or, if not, they teach their children to hide their nonbelief. Otherwise the children would be socially handicapped in our very religious world."

"I see." She didn't sound much interested.

"And surely your children did have problems dealing with others on this issue."

Catherine thought back. How much to tell him?

"You're right, of course. Inevitably they did. Let me see—I'll take them in order. The oldest, Jefferson, was suspended four times for altercations at his elementary school, and then had to switch high schools after his sophomore year. This last occurred because a teacher actually spit at him. Being well trained, he spit right back."

"Hmm." Harker was making notes. Great stuff! he thought.

"Franklin's difficulties you already know. But he's always been so low key before that his statements on that awful television show surprised us all. Franklin was never an activist.

"Abigail too didn't have much in the way of difficulties on this score. She was far too busy with activities, things she did so well that others looked up to her. Abby was the captain of I don't know how many teams, in all kinds of sports: baseball, basketball, volleyball, and a couple of other balls I don't quite remember.

"The youngest, Martha, takes after me. She's a talker and not to be trifled with. Martha tends to wear people down, and they soon learn the folly of pressuring her on any topic. Also, alas, just like her mother, she has a temper—well, truth be told, they all do—but, unlike me, Martha rarely makes her point in any physically unpleasant way."

That was a curious statement. "Unlike you? You've attacked people physically?"

"We'll have to talk about that later," Catherine said, thinking back to a brick and that childhood bully.

Glancing down at the notes he'd written before calling, Harker said, "Moving on. Is it true that you were raised in a circus?"

Catherine gave a little laugh.

"Oh, yes! Born and bred in the big top. My parents were trained from childhood as jugglers, and very good jugglers they became—widely known and envied in the juggling world. Mom was a tiny thing, but Dad was a great big bear of a man. That gave them a striking visual contact, which was useful in the act. They'd take the center ring and do all kinds of spectacular tricks with balls of various sizes, Indian clubs, bowling pins, etc. They could stand

190

fifteen feet apart and do an eight club pass, which any juggler will tell you is a lot. From the time I was little I'd sit there in the audience and watch the clubs flying back and forth at a dizzying speed. Then Mom and Dad put those down and did the same thing all over again, but this time with flaming torches. Dad could actually juggle three regulation size bowling balls. They were very good—1948 charter members of the International Jugglers' Association."

"Did you get into the act yourself?"

"Certainly. Most circus children did what they could to help out. So, yes, I can juggle, and if we meet I'll show you some tricks, but I must confess that I was never more than middling good at it. Mostly I did chores around the big top, or was an extra for the blow off or the spectacle, riding an elephant, waving at the crowd—that sort of thing. Like many girls, I had a special love for the horses, and for a short period when I was still very little, I was given a turn in the center ring, cracking a whip while the liberty horses ran a circle around me."

"Liberty horses?"

"Horses with no riders on them."

"And you really know how to crack a whip?"

"I never lie. For that particular turn, we used the helicopter crack. You swing the whip in a big circle over your head, then suddenly reverse it, producing the crack. Did you know that the crack itself comes from the whip's tip breaking the sound barrier?"

"No. How very interesting!"

"I can also do what is called a 'ringmaster's crack.' In this one the whip goes from resting on the ground in back of you, is pulled over your head and then snapped forward, with the crack coming from a flick of the wrist. It's harder than the helicopter crack, but, actually, it was the first one I learned. And it was taught to me by a real ringmaster. He made me practice for weeks until I could do it without thinking."

"And just how old were you when you were standing in a circus ring cracking these whips at your liberty horses?"

"Hmm. Ten, maybe."

"But, Catherine, weren't you supposed to be in school at that age?"

"I suppose so, but you have to understand that we were on the road most of the time, or resting at our winter quarters in Florida when not. It was hard to get much formal education. Fortunately I was an autodidact, and a good one at that."

"Autodidact?"

"Someone who teaches herself. I just devoured books and explored all sorts of things when we traveled. I questioned everyone I met to find out the

191

interesting things they knew. I ended up with a great deal of useful knowledge about a large number of topics. By the time I got to college, I was well ahead of most students around me. My grandson Todd inherited those very genes."

"Ah," Harker said, switching happily to this topic, "let's talk about your grandson and you."

"Oh, well, now Todd's a special case."

Their conversation continued like this for over an hour. Harker was charmed. So was Catherine. Thus began years of a friendship that lasted until she outlived him.

About 3:45 that Friday afternoon, Franklin talked the Gallia County Sheriff Department into putting his ex-wife on the phone.

"Hello, Franklin," Mary said, happy as a songbird. "You okay?"

"Me! It's you that we're all worried about. I've been bouncing off walls thinking about the two of you. And now I learn that you're the fastest gun in Ohio. Who would have thunk you had that in you?"

Mary paused, sobering up. "Oh, Franklin. It was awful! That horrible couple—the same thugs who shot at you—were going to execute Todd at 6:30 this evening. They threatened to force me to watch."

"And then kill you?"

"No. They were going to let me go."

"Huh? That would just lead to the police tracking them down."

"That wouldn't be hard. They were planning a suicide pact at the scene."

"Oh." He paused and thought about that. "Okay. But why do you think they're the same ones who shot at me?"

"They talked about it. More than once. Nan was still angry at Dan for missing you. You're lucky she hadn't been the one with the rifle."

Actually this was good news on top of good news. It meant that the people who'd shot at him were no longer lurking about.

"Do you know why they were shooting at me and trying to execute Todd? Was it the one/two punch of the Jimmy Ball Show and out son's webcast?"

"Yup. Drove them right over the edge, and they were already crowding that edge pretty hard even before you two came along. Life had been very cruel to them, and they reacted badly in turn. I truly felt sorry for them."

"This is before you gunned them down."

Now she paused. "Yes, before that," she said.

192

"The police tell me that you put six bullets into the wife."

"Well, I guess that's true too. It amazed me. I'd never fired a gun before in my life, but apparently I didn't miss a single shot. Granted I was right on top of her, and she was about to kill Todd. I was motivated."

"The police claim that she wasn't holding a gun when you shot her."

"What can I say to that, Franklin? I didn't plan to shoot her at all. My intent was to take her prisoner, and have Todd tie her up while I held the gun on her. But I guess I got excited, or panicked, or something. I don't remember *deciding* to shoot her. It just sort of happened."

Insufficient control of the turtle-decision-making process, Franklin thought, but let that go. The Great Turtle insight would have to await a lighter moment.

Now Mary had another question. "You're the lawyer. Tell me, counselor. Am I in trouble? Should I clam up? Do I need more competent legal counsel than a commercial law lawyer calling me long distance?"

"It's like this," he replied. "You're going to be trapped for days in a bureaucratic labyrinth, and it will seem so endless and frustrating you might wish you had your gun back to hasten things along, but my professional opinion is that—in the end—you'll be fine. I've called around and I think I've found you a lawyer. You should hear from him tonight, but I'm not sure what his name is. He's being recommended by a friend in Athens, Ohio. So if the police tell you that your lawyer's arrived, just nod and go talk to him . . . or her, whichever. But, Mary, getting a lawyer is just a precaution. When you attacked those awful people, you were acting under pressure of maternal urges probably going back millennia to Lucy of Africa. Your only child was in danger and you ended the threat. Everyone on the planet, except perhaps Dan and Nan's children, will understand that."

"They didn't have any children," she replied in a low voice.

Unable to find Franklin (his voice mail was "full" according to a recording), Kelly cast about, trying to think how to contact him. There was his mother, of course, but Kelly, like most people, preferred to steer clear of Catherine Whitestone. The woman had a way of taking over your life, even if you were more or less a complete stranger.

Finally Kelly chose to call Martha Waxman, Franklin's youngest sister, who lived in Cincinnati. They'd been friends ever since three years ago when they'd met at a birthday party Catherine had thrown for Franklin at her lovely home. About thirty people, friends and family, were in attendance.

Towards the end of the party, Kelly, wanting to escape all these people she didn't know, had wandered, drink in hand, out to the beautiful garden in the back yard. Martha was standing on the other side of a yew tree, and Kelly was surprised to see she was smoking.

"I didn't know you smoked," Kelly commented, and Martha jumped at the sound of her voice. She spun around and then looked down guiltily at the cigarette.

"No one does—not even my husband. It's a secret vice. Please don't tell. Mom would kill me if she found out."

Kelly smiled. "It's just between us girls," she promised.

"Filthy habit. I'm going to quit soon," Martha assured her. "I'm down to five or six a day, and it's been nerve wracking hiding it from it everyone. I feel like a spy in my own home."

Just then Catherine appeared at the back door, saw them, and came briskly down the cobbled path to join them. She said, "There you are, Martha!"

Without pausing to think about it, Kelly grabbed the cigarette out of Martha's hand, dipped it in her drink, and stuck the soggy mess in her pocket. Taking Martha by the hand, she pulled her away from the lingering smoke smell and walked to meet Catherine.

"What were you two doing?" the latter asked, curious and suspicious at the same time.

"Becoming good friends," Martha had replied, meaning it.

Now, on Friday afternoon, when Kelly phoned, Martha answered, and Kelly said hello and that she hoped she wasn't catching Martha at a bad time.

"Of course not," she replied. "How are you, Kelly?"

"Miserable," was the answer, delivered in a tone that confirmed it.

"Oh, honey, I'm sorry. What is going on?"

So Kelly told her all about the disastrous trip to New York City and the quarrel that followed. She concluded her tale by saying, "And now I'm regretting everything. Oh, Martha, Franklin is my love!"

"How can I help?"

"Ah, well, really that's the thing. I have two odd questions to put to you, one prosaic and one existential."

"Wow! Bring them on!"

"The first is that I can't seem to locate Franklin. His voice mail is full and he's not answering emails, and I know he's not at his home."

"You're right. He's not. He was shot at the last time he tried to make a quick trip there."

"SHOT AT? *That* wasn't in the news! How do you know? Was he hurt?"

"He's fine. They missed. I know this because Franklin told his new

194

public relations agent, who then called my mother to sign her up as a client, and during their two hour conversation, Franklin's near miss got mentioned."

"I guess I'm way behind. Franklin has a public relations agent?"

"Mom too. Same agency. There's a lot going on. You do know about Todd and Mary?"

"Oh, yes. Every sentient being in the country has heard their horrible story by now. They're fine too, right?"

"I haven't talked to them, but, yes, that's what I hear. The people who kidnapped them are in a bad way. I always knew Mary was not someone to be trifled with."

"That's a scary thing to contemplate if you're the woman dating her ex-husband."

They both laughed.

"What I most want to talk to you about, Martha, is something else. I'm having what my minister would call a 'crisis of faith.' Ever since last Sunday when Franklin first made his stupid statements on the Jimmy Ball Show, and Todd posted that bizarre webcast, I've gone back and forth between being a devout member of my church, and someone who wonders if there is a God at all. Because of this I'm having a lot of trouble sleeping—it's tearing me in two. Franklin is my man all right, but a large part of me hates him for what he's said, what he's done, how he's hurt me. I'm not usually a crier, but I'm crying a lot these days. I don't know what to do, and I need to talk to somebody about it. I've always respected you, and I wonder what advice you have for me. Got anything to help me regain my equilibrium?" Her voice caught. "Oh, hell, I'm about to cry right now."

"Whoa! Whoa!" Martha said. "That's a lot to answer, but you need to take it one step at a time. How about having lunch with me tomorrow and we'll talk about all this then?"

"Lunch? We're a hundred miles apart!"

"Yes. I know a great restaurant about halfway between Cincy and Columbus, a reasonable drive for each of us. We can meet, talk, eat, solve the problems of the world."

Kelly thought about it for only a brief moment. "Oh, yes, Martha! That's just what I need! And having something that concrete in the works will make it easier to sleep tonight."

So they arranged the details, and said goodbye.

In one of those strange coincidences that shouldn't happen, but do, not five minutes after Martha finished talking to Kelly, her phone rang and it was her brother, Franklin.

"Hello, Marty," he said. "I suppose you've heard the good news about Todd and Mary. I'm in my car on the way to southeastern Ohio to be with them, but I wanted to check in with you and ask you to pass along to the rest of the family the fact that all three of us are all right, and that things are looking brighter by the hour."

By "pass along to the rest of the family" Martha knew he really meant "call Mom so I won't have to," but that was a small thing to help out a brother who was busy scaling a mountain of troubles.

"Of course, Franklin. I'm so pleased about everything. But I hear that you yourself were shot at. Is that right?"

He paused. How in the world would she know about the shooting? He asked her.

"Well," she replied, "I should tell you that there's a lot going on with the rest of the family as a whole, and we're all exchanging information like gossips over the backyard fence."

"A lot going on? What have I missed?"

"Let's see. Jefferson has found a good paying job and is getting married, Abbie has come out of the closet and she and Beth joined a church, Mom has signed with the Martin Turnbill agency—there is talk of an appearance on the Jimmy Ball show—and I've just arranged to have lunch tomorrow with Kelly Keyfold to discuss both her romance with you and her wavering faith in God."

Franklin pulled the phone away from his ear and stared at it as if it were malfunctioning. Finally, bedazzled, he put the cell back up to its usual place, and spoke cautiously to his sister.

"You're not making any of this up, are you?"

"Not a word," she replied, quite cheery. Whitestones lived for moments like this.

"Leaping turtles!" he said.

"What?"

"A paraphrase of the ever-quotable Little Orphan Annie. Here's more astounding news you can pass on to the whole family: I'm now religious myself. Tell them that I've converted to the Cult of the Great Turtle." So he explained to her how this nonsense went, and they spent the next five minutes exchanging turtle jokes.

Celia Hawkins had become very concerned by the fact that Jake Richardson never invited her to his house. Both of their trysts so far had taken place at her house in Worthington, and never having seen his own home had begun to raise alarms in her mind. What if he were secretly married and didn't want her to learn about his wife? Or had been lying to her about having a house at all? Or was, say, living with his mother? Or his male lover?

On Friday evening right before Jake arrived for supper, Celia resolved to press him on the subject, and see if she couldn't obtain an invitation to his place and soon. But when he rang her doorbell, and she opened the door to see him, all clean-shaven and in what appeared to be new clothes—*God, he looked more handsome every time she saw him!*—she elected to postpone the discussion until later. First, and before any words were said, he took her in his arms and kissed her gently on the lips. Jake was a great kisser, which had surprised her—he looked like such a ruffian. He always started with a kiss so light she could barely feel it, and then worked up through the ranks until the finale involved every moveable part of their bodies and a quick orbit around the moon.

But, of course, they couldn't start that space trip right here in the entryway. Neighbors might be watching (perhaps already scandalized by Jake's overnight visits). She smiled at him, took his arm, and moved him into the house.

"What a looker!" Jake lied, putting his arm around her Olive Oyl slim frame. "'Thy two breasts,'" he recited as he fondled them, "'are like two young roes that feed among the lilies.'"

Celia and Jake, happier than either had been before in their lives, had taken to quoting the Song of Solomon when things got romantic. Last night, stroking his penis, she had whispered, "'This thy stature is like to a palm tree, and my breasts to clusters of grapes. I said, I will go up to the palm tree, I will take hold of the boughs thereof.'" He had cum almost immediately, exploding in excitement over this mingling of the holy and profane.

Now, hand in hand, a girl and her beau, they went directly to the dining room, where Celia had carefully set out their supper. On Jake's first time here she'd cautiously asked him if he ever drank alcohol, but he'd looked so shocked at the suggestion that she had not brought up the idea of pre-supper libations again. It sort of disappointed her that he was a teetotaler, for Celia sometimes did like drinking something light before dining (say a beer), and she didn't think of this craving as in any way irreligious. Goodness, even Jesus had a suppertime drink or two! Oh, well. Another verse from the Song of Solomon, which she'd been re-reading right before Jake rang the doorbell, seemed to answer this objection: "Let him kiss me with the kisses of his mouth, for thy love is better than wine."

As she served him salad, spaghetti and meatballs, with oven-fresh rolls, she asked him if he'd heard the news about the daring escape of Todd Whitestone and his mother from their kidnapers.

"Amazing, right enough!" he enthused, pouring far too much dressing on his salad, and immediately biting into a roll without either tearing it in two

197

or buttering it. "That Whitestone woman should be made a swat team leader or something. For sure, we'd all be a lot safer."

"Did you ever meet either of them?" she asked.

"Nope," he replied. "I haven't even met Franklin excepting just to wave at him from Susy May that day I rescued him. But, Celia, I'm dying to get to know him, be his friend, bring him to the embrace of Jesus. Can't find him, and I've looked. All last week."

"He's probably on his way to Gallipolis right this minute to be with his loved ones."

Jake jerked his head up at that. He didn't reply, but his brow furled. Celia switched the topic.

"Tell me about your house, Jake," she said. "Exactly where is it? How big? How long have you owned it? Things like that. I'd love to see it!"

To her surprise, Jake abruptly stood. Had her questions somehow offended him?

"Celia, I've got to go," he said with determination. "Sorry, gal, but it's important!"

"But . . . but, I've made supper!" she said, waving her hand over the uneaten contents of the table, upset.

"Thanks, darling, but this just came up and I really can't stop to explain. I'll have supper with you some other time, cook it myself at my place. I promise. Tomorrow maybe." But he immediately reconsidered that as he moved rapidly to the door. "Well, no, probably not tomorrow neither. Sunday or Monday, Good Lord willing. Trust me. It'll happen, I promise, promise."

"But . . .," she began—speaking too late, for he was grabbing his coat off the hook by the front door.

"See you soon, honey lamb," he said. And with a quick kiss to her cheek, he was gone.

Left alone with all that still-cooling food, Celia said a word out loud she almost never used. Then she said it again.

Todd found himself looking at his parents with new eyes.

The three of them were sitting at breakfast on Saturday morning in an establishment called "The Good Egg," right across the street from the Holiday Inn where they'd spent last night. Yesterday morning Franklin Whitestone had shown up at the police station to spirit them away for a much needed respite from the craziness that had constituted their lives for the past couple of days. The police had released them into his custody with the understanding that they would not leave the county.

Todd realized with no particular regret that there was no going back to way things had once been. Not ever. "Normal" was history. All three of them were famous now, and only his mother was currently in the public's good graces.

As she picked at and sampled the breakfast items she'd selected from the Good Egg's scrumptious buffet, Mary chatted cautiously with her ex-husband about this and that. Would this new protection service really keep them safe? Was it wise to move, even temporarily, to Los Angeles, and, if so, how did that affect Todd's last year of high school? Was M.I.T. now out of the picture? How could they retrieve their personal belongings from their house?

As he listened to all this, Todd noticed that her questions had to do with ensuring his own welfare, one way or another. Had she always been this solicitous? The way she'd dispatched Dan and Nan with the Smith and Wesson, using first one end of the gun and then the other, had forcibly impressed upon him how strong her maternal instinct was, and what a formidable person she became when her son was threatened. He'd never thought much about the matter before, but now he was swimming in a newly discovered love and admiration for SuperMom.

Dad too was impressive. He'd the courage to say what he really thought when asked about God on national tv, and this morning he was all Mr. Organization. Since Dad had first shown up at the police station last night, the man had been busy making phone calls, settling their plans, calming them down, all bounce and confidence.

The first call he made had been to SteadyLife, the L.A. protective company that Jonathan Harker's agency used. As quickly as possible, Franklin wanted to set up the firewall that would protect them from more attacks. That had resulted in the startling advice that the three of them should get on a plane and fly to California, and there take temporary shelter in a guarded safe house, before moving to an equally well protected new residence in a suburb of L.A. Franklin himself had demurred, saying he needed to stay in Columbus at least until Tuesday. He had a meeting on Monday with his law firm to determine if he still had a job, and various other details of his life had to be resolved before moving. But Franklin made some calls and arranged that Todd and his mother had reserved plane tickets from Cincinnati to the west coast. The flight would leave at 3 p.m. this afternoon, always assuming the county police could be talked into letting them go.

Then Dad had made a flurry of other calls. One of them had been to the intriguing Corbin Milk, the mysterious man who'd advised them all on disguises, evasion techniques, and even how to lose a tail. Todd would very much like to ask Mr. Milk a host of questions about his past and other

199

pertinent matters (Dad said he'd once been a C.I.A. agent!). Next was Dad's new agent, Jonathan Harker, who was pleased to confirm that Dad was booked for the Jimmy Ball Show tomorrow night. Todd instantly asked permission to join that adventure, and had been told no by adamant parents. A final call was to the irresponsible local lawyer who had failed to show up the day before at police headquarters, and who now endured a scathing earful from an irate Franklin Whitestone, who fired the miscreant on the spot.

Both parents were all action, and both were in large part working primarily just to protect him. Were all parents this driven? Would he too be like that when he had his own kids? Fascinated, Todd decided it was time to do some reading on this new topic. As both a biological and anthropological phenomenon, there was obviously much more to parenting than he'd previously appreciated.

"Franklin, was it smart to make plane reservations when we don't even know if we're allowed to leave the State?" Mary Whitestone asked.

"Yes. Oh, sure, perhaps they'll go to waste—that's a possibility, of course. But I'd rather have unused tickets waiting for you at the Cincinnati airport than have no way to get you out of here quickly if and when the police say you're free to go."

"But it's *expensive* to buy tickets to the west coast for two people and then not use them. The airline won't give you your money back if we're detained."

"I don't care. Harker has convinced me that money is about to be no problem. For that matter," he said to Mary with a wink and a quick glance at their son, "we can make a fortune offering Todd to the highest bidder. List him for sale on eBay. Get filthy rich."

Todd spoke up. "Are the police really likely to let Mom go? She's still a 'person of interest' in a criminal investigation."

"I'm not just a suspect," she told him. "I confessed. I'm it—the guilty party. We both confirmed everything that happened in that farm house. The only issue is whether they'll arrest me or not."

Franklin wiped his mouth with his napkin, and placed it on his plate. "Finish up," he commanded, "and let's go find out."

So they drove the rental car to the Gallia Sheriff's headquarters, and were floored to find the place surrounded by media trucks, three deep in some places. Before they attracted attention from the mob storming the station, Franklin made a quick turn and sped back the way they'd just come. When they were safely out of sight, Franklin pulled the car into a small shopping center and parked.

He pulled out his cell and called the number of the chief investigator for the county, the woman who had given him permission to take Mary and

Todd to a hotel for the night, and told her of his plans to send his loved ones temporarily to California for their own safety, and asking her what she thought about that, and would she approve?

"*I'm going crazy here*," she replied, stress highlighting every syllable. "I've never seen such chaos in a police matter!" She paused. "They want to feed off your family like you were a steak dinner. Worse than that, I've had two phone calls threatening your lives. One of them was from someone I know personally! Said that if I just turned my back for a minute or two the problem of the demonic Whitestones could be resolved." She paused again. "Okay, okay. I'll let them go, but only if I have your solemn word, Counselor Whitestone, that they'll return when requested, and that I won't have to go through some messy extradition procedure."

"We all promise that," Franklin assured her, and, after an exchange of contact details, the call ended. There was a loud knock on the driver's side window as Franklin was putting down his phone, and they all jumped. A tall, wiry man was standing next to the car, a big smile on his face.

Very suspicious, Franklin lowered his window only a couple of inches.

"What?" he said, sure that a member of the press had recognized them and somehow followed them here.

"Mr. Whitestone," said the man. "My name is Jake Richardson, and I've been trying to talk to you for a week. I'm the guy who was operating the Big Claw that tore out the stadium wall and allowed you to escape from that terrorist attack. Got a minute or two for me?"

Ah, Franklin thought, this is the troublemaker my mother warned me about. Were they in danger from this man?

What to do? He decided on boldness.

"Step back, Mr. Richardson," he said. "I'll get out of the car."

"No, Franklin!" Mary urged, panicked. Todd thought it was a bad idea too, and said so.

"Just be a minute," Franklin replied, and stepped out, shutting the door behind him. Then he noticed that the man was carrying a book—a black book, almost certainly a Bible. Here we go again, Franklin thought.

The man smiled even more broadly. "Thank you, good sir," he said, shaking Franklin's hand enthusiastically.

"What do you want with me?" Franklin shivered slightly in the chill of the morning. (It *was* the cold causing him to shiver, right?)

"Well, sir, I heard what you said about God and all, on that Jimmy Ball Show last Sunday night, and I thought you should know that it weren't right to blaspheme like that."

Franklin had not put on his disguise this morning when he got up,

201

figuring that it was important the police recognize him and know he was who he said he was, but the result of that decision was he'd now attracted this loony and endangered his family. Was there to be no end to this kind of attention? He pictured the three of them constantly on the run, pursued by a Bible-bearing version of the Night of the Living Dead.

"You could be right, Mr. Richardson," Franklin said, "but it's a bad time to talk about it. I have to get my family to a safe place. Give me your number and I'll call you."

Richardson was having none of that. "You'll take this take along, I hope. Here," he held out the black book. "I bought this special for you. It's the word of God and you need to start reading it now. Your soul is in terrible jeopardy, Mr. Whitestone."

"No thank you. I'm not supposed to accept gifts. The police told me that." Would this lie discourage the creep? Probably not, but he had to say something. He was not going to take the Bible. Doing that would allow Richardson to allege he was successfully converting the famous atheist, Franklin Whitestone.

"Please don't turn away from Jesus!" Richardson begged, the Bible still extended.

Angry now, Franklin opened the car door. "Somehow you don't look like Jesus." He climbed back in.

Richardson put both of his hands on the top of the door, holding it open. "Now, wait, wait!" he urged.

"Take your hands off the door," Franklin commanded, "or I'll slam it shut and drive off with your fingers hanging from it." Then before Richardson could react, he pushed the door forcefully into the man, knocking him back a step, and quickly shutting the door when Richardson let go to regain his balance. Franklin immediately locked the car's doors, and started the engine.

Furious, Richardson pounded twice on the driver's window before the car sped off across the parking lot and turned onto the street. By the time he got back into his truck and followed, they were gone.

CHAPTER THIRTEEN

JAKE MAKES PLANS

Martha Waxman and Kelly Keyfold embraced in the restaurant's parking lot when they met for lunch on Saturday afternoon.

"I'm so pleased you're willing to accommodate me like this," Kelly said.

"Nonsense," Martha replied. "We all need have someone to throw us a lifeline now and then," and they entered the restaurant. A sign posted just inside the door instructed them to seat themselves, so they did. While looking over the menus, Martha and Kelly made small talk, and both ordered salads when the waitress came to take their order.

"I told Franklin you called," Martha said as the waitress departed. "He was much surprised, and, you may want to know, pleased."

Kelly gave her a small smile. "We're a long way from agreement," she said, "and we parted badly. Since then, I've cried at the slightest thing. You see . . . that man . . . your brother . . . " She paused, tears starting in her eyes as she remembered her last glimpse of him as she shut the car door and fled into her house. She couldn't finish.

"Franklin misses you. He said so when we talked yesterday. When I told him we were meeting for lunch today, he was very interested in that." She paused and looked anxiously at Kelly before continuing. "I also mentioned to him that we were going to talk about your religious beliefs. Was that all right?"

Kelly shrugged. "It's true. He'd have to be an idiot to think that topic wouldn't come up."

"All right. Just what is this 'crisis of faith' you mentioned?"

So Kelly launched into a soliloquy about her early upbringing in the Baptist Church, her subsequent lapse from regular observances, and her renewed commitment to God on hearing Franklin's shocking statements on the Jimmy Ball Show. Then she related to Martha an account of their subsequent quarrel in the limousine, and the damage it did to their relationship.

"That's when the crying jag started in earnest. But another, and very important reaction was the fervor with which I returned to the church. Three times in the last week, plus Bible study groups twice."

"Bible study," Martha said, with no particular intonation.

"Then on Tuesday came Todd"s bombshell. Suddenly it was everywhere you turned. I read what he posted and couldn't believe it. My first reaction was anger, then, after thinking about it steadily for over a day, I read it again, trying hard to do so with an open mind. That was what precipitated my current angst."

"Why?"

"Because it caused me to think about a possibility I had never before seriously entertained."

"That there might not be a God."

"That there might not be a God," Kelly agreed, nodding. "Franklin also had stung me on Sunday with an accusation of being lax as lawyer, law professor, and careful human because I accepted my religious beliefs without evidence, without rigorous examination. That hurt."

"So you've been doing that."

"Yes. And then, damn it, I couldn't stop myself from reading Todd's webpost over and over again. It became a kind of mania. I didn't agree with it, of course. Instead I battled Todd's arguments, pooh-poohing them, dissecting each idea point by point, but never entirely did this to my complete satisfaction. Most of the basic assumptions of my religion, I found, require a certain amount of bald acceptance, not capable of being reached by proof or investigation."

"Not just *your* religion, I'm afraid. All of them."

"The Bible study groups didn't help at all. There was very little discussion of how to use Christianity as a force for good in the world. The participants mostly alternated between reverent readings of texts that were either obvious or impenetrable or ludicrous, and then the   discussion would veer off topic, wandering into rants about all sorts of unrelated issues."

"Such as?"

"Franklin and Todd were a favorite."

"Oh, I'll bet."

"The parishioners were particularly vicious when it came to them. If Franklin and Todd had suddenly come walking through the door they might not have made it out again. I'm not exaggerating."

"Marked men."

"But it wasn't just that. I was shouted down whenever I tried to introduce rationality into the debate. Homosexuality, for example. I'd point out that the scientific evidence now shows overwhelmingly that people are born gay, that it's not chosen, and I would be met with citations to biblical passages and lectures on sin. No one even cared about what the truth was. They wouldn't hear it, wouldn't listen. Their hatred was cemented into place by their religious beliefs. It astounded me. One woman told me that she 'didn't do science.' She didn't believe in it."

Martha grinned. "What was your reply to that?"

Kelly grinned back. "I asked her if she 'did' gravity."

Their salads arrived, and, when the waitress had left, they began to eat.

"So," Kelly said, as she speared a fork into an artichoke heart, "I don't know what to think, what to believe. Have you read the book 'Reading Lolita in Tehran'?"

"No," Martha replied. "I've been meaning to."

"Fascinating, terrifying. Tells what happens to women when religion conquers a country and dictates how everyone must behave. But at one point the author says that her worst fear would be losing her faith, because then no one would be her friend. And she adds it would be like dying, and having to start new again in a world without guarantees. That's how I feel too."

"It is scary."

"It's beyond scary. If there's no God and we're just the dominant species on a rock flying through space, then we're on our own. Lonely. Without guidance. At the edge of an enormous cosmos and clueless. It's depressing."

"Of course it's scary," Martha agreed. "We spend much time figuring out how it all works, and so we invest huge amounts of faith in our ultimate conclusions. We hate to see that challenged, and resist mightily having to start the whole process over. So how are you handling it?"

"I called you," Kelly replied. "How do you handle it?"

"Well," Martha said, "it was never that scary for me. In the Whitestone household we all grew up knowing that we were on that rock flying through space, with no divine navigator. There was no crisis of faith. Instead our focus was on what we could do to live productive lives. It worked fine for us."

"And did no one in the family ever flirt with believing in God?"

Martha looked at her strangely. "You don't know?" she said.

"Know what?"

"Franklin had a period—his early college days—when he shocked us all by announcing that he was exploring which religion to join, and was thinking about switching his major to theology."

"FRANKLIN!" Diners all over the restaurant looked in their direction.

"It didn't last long, and it upset the rest of us, particularly my parents, greatly. But the lamb didn't stray from the Whitestone fold very long. His was just an act of rebellion, the sort of thing that most teenagers go through before settling on their adult identity. In the end, he took a degree in Poly Sci. You'll have to ask him about it someday."

"I most certainly will. He never said a word to me!"

"He buried the whole incident long ago. We never speak of it, and, of course, it would cause him huge embarrassment now if it were discovered. As far as the rest of us go—and I can't speak definitively for Jefferson and Abby, but I'd be surprised if they disagreed—I don't think any of the rest of us seriously 'flirted' with a belief in God. Certainly my parents didn't. On his deathbed, in the ICU, my father amazed the staff by refusing to allow a minister to comfort him. Dad got to yelling something about mixing 'voo-doo' with medicine. In fact, he was ranting about that the very hour he died."

"I'm pretty sure I could never go that far, never be that sure that God didn't exist. On the other hand, I can't seem to find a version of God that seems real or even possible. I don't know what I think." She looked miserable. "Martha, I'm a mess. Help me!"

"I don't have a magic answer, and you knew I wouldn't. But I can tell you this. You're working too hard on the whole problem."

"What do you mean?'

"It's perfectly all right to just throw up your hands and say you don't know whether there's a God or not."

"An agnostic?"

"Even that's too big a word. It's a label, and most people resent being labeled. It's always been my guess that there are an enormous number of people who seriously doubt God exists—at least the overpowering God of the Bible—but who don't care much about the issue either. They just avoid talking about it, nodding their heads reverently when God comes up, staying away from the trouble that comes from expressing doubt, going along to get along. If a pollster asks them if they believe in God, they say yes. If asked whether they go to church, they reply that they don't attend as much as they should."

"That sounds true," Kelly replied. "And a lot of people in church aren't there because of personal beliefs. Society pressures them into pews."

"My point is that you don't have to reach a resolution. You can do what most people do: live in doubt, try your best to live as good a life as you can. Nothing more is required. That's a lot."

Kelly thought about it. Of course, it was a solution—give up thinking about it—but the lawyer in her wasn't happy at all.

"Telling yourself not to think about something almost ensures that then it's all you do think about," Kelly said, "but I might as well give it a try. Thanks for the advice." She looked around for the waitress. "Since I'm becoming such a sinner, might as well go all the way. Let's have a rich dessert and switch the topic to something lighter."

"Good idea! Diet be gone! You want to hear about my mother's planned book deal?"

Kelly laughed. "You're kidding!"

"No I'm not! She has an agent and all."

"An agent! What's this book going to be about?"

"Her amazing life, of course. It really would make for fascinating reading—I can't wait to get my hands on a copy. Mom's not like anyone else. Did you know she was raised in a circus?"

Kelly nodded. "Franklin mentioned it. Wasn't there also something about being arrested?"

"Yes. During the Vietnam war she was nabbed when police raided a garage where a group of dedicated hippies were making bombs. She spent a year in jail, and is still proud of it. Have you seen her tattoo?"

"Tattoo? No. Tattoo?" Kelly's head was spinning. "What's this book going to be called?"

"Mom hasn't decided, but her current favorite is 'Pushing on the Pull Door.'"

At four o'clock that Saturday afternoon, Celia Hawkins paused before she rang the doorbell at Jake Richardson's home on the east side of Columbus. The place, small and crammed uncomfortably amongst similar houses, had been surprisingly easy to find. Through the wonders of Google, she'd discovered the address both on a deed in the Franklin County Recorder's Office and Jake's divorce papers, which were also a matter of public record. Too late, she realized that before all her e-detective work she could have simply checked the phone book; he was listed there too.

Her finger not quite touching the doorbell, Celia stood like a statue for a moment. She was very tempted to withdraw the finger and sneak back to her car, and, now that she thought about it more clearly, that did seem the smartest course. Celia was nervous about what she'd find here, and how Jake might react to an impromptu visit. Would he be upset? Angry? Welcoming? Aroused?

This is a very bad idea, she told herself, and she decided to turn and go, when—from what impulse she did not know—she suddenly rang the doorbell. It peeled a loud DING-DONG, which made her jump as if she hadn't known how doorbells worked.

For almost a full minute nothing happened, and Celia began a new internal debate between re-pushing the bell and a quick departure, but the door abruptly opened and Jake stood there blinking vacantly at her.

"What do you want?" he asked, looking at her as if he had no idea who she was—as if she were a solicitor.

"Jake, it's me, Celia! Surprise!" She said this with as much enthusiasm as she could muster, but she knew to her toes that she'd made a big mistake. He was a mess. Shirt out, unshaven, bleary eyed (*was he drunk?*), gravel voiced.

"Celia?" At least he'd recognized her. "Ah, well, I can't talk now. Bad things going on and I have to make plans."

"I see. Well, I'm sorry to have bothered you. Call me when you're available." She turned immediately to leave. But before she could take a step, Jake reached out and grabbed her arm.

"Wait! Wait!" he said in a warmer tone. "You just surprised me, that's all, baby doll." That was a name he had never called her before, and she didn't like it. He smiled unevenly. "I weren't expecting the bell to ring." He looked over his shoulder into his living room. "Uh," he stammered, "come in for a few minutes if'n you can stand the mess. I guess I didn't clean up yet this morning."

By now Celia was most certain she didn't want to see the inside of his house. Jake's beer breath overwhelmed her, and his slovenly appearance was repulsive. He appeared to be wearing the same clothes he'd had on last night at dinner. He'd obviously slept in them, and they were now ready for washing, fumigation, or even Goodwill. What had she been thinking to come here uninvited?

"No, I can't. I'll just go and talk to you later."

Jake's grip on her arm tightened. "Don't go," he said. It was an order, not a request, and he pulled her inside. She almost tripped from the unexpected move, and more or less stumbled into the living room.

Celia looked around in horror. The only word was "pigsty!" Garbage was piled haphazardly on top of other garbage, clothes thrown about, unwashed dishes surviving from different meals were stacked here and there, beer bottles and pop cans littered the floor in an almost perfect circle around a leather recliner that looked like its days of actually reclining were over. The air was putridly offensive with its toxic mix of uneaten food, beer, dried sweat, and other unidentified but alarming odors (that couldn't be urine she smelled, could it?).

"Sorry it looks so bad in here," he apologized, not sounding sorry at all. He retained his iron grip on her right upper arm. Then he leaned toward her, far too close to her face, leering, alcohol blurring his words markedly as he added, "But the *bedroom* is lots better. Well . . . except for the bed. It ain't made, but, hell, we'd just mess it up anyway!"

Now she went from offended to alarmed. "Let me go, Jake! I want out of here!" She yanked her arm from his grasp and backed away.

208

"Goodbye!" she said in the no-nonsense tone of voice she had inherited from her mother.

"Now, wait, honey," he said, reaching for her arm again. "Don't you ruin this great visit. I'm real, real glad you come to see me."

"*Goodbye*," she repeated in an even sterner tone, dodging his grasp and reaching for the door knob.

At this he lunged again, and she deftly feinted around his arm, taking him by the wrist and yanking him hard towards the floor. This caused him to fall forward, and as he went down she gave him a swift knee to the jaw. There was a sharp crack, and an agonized yelp as he rolled across the floor away from her, holding his head and using a word good Christians shouldn't know.

Celia jerked open the door and exited quickly, slamming the door behind her.

In their prior two meetings, apparently Celia hadn't gotten around to mentioning to Jake that she conducted a self-defense class every Tuesday evening at the YWCA.

He knew now.

Sitting on the American Airlines flight parting the clouds on its way across Nebraska, Mary Whitestone reflected on the fragility of life. A week ago her familiar existence seemed set in cement: making sure Todd was all right, meeting deadlines for the travel column and her new book, doing all the routine chores that keep a household and professional life going, having fun with friends, and even the occasional romantic encounter. Now everything had blown up in a mad whirl of confusion, very like the contents of a shaken toy glass globe which sends snowflakes dancing.

Making sure that Todd was all right. Now there was a task.

She looked at him, sound asleep with his head against the window, a contented traveler who you'd think had no troubles darkening his young existence. The truth was, she reflected, that he was widely despised, fleeing for his life to an unknown future, guarded by a worried mother who'd already been forced to kill one human being and maim another to keep him safe. Once again she was annoyed by how easily he slept while she was an emotional mess.

Unknown future. The one bright spot in all this was that Mary's job was not tied to any one spot, so she could easily move to L.A. without missing a professional beat. In fact, LAX would be an easier jumping off point for her many travels, since it connected to a great many more destinations than did Port Columbus. On the other hand, in the five or six visits where she'd spent any time in Los Angeles, she'd found the city too big to appreciate—strangers crowded on top of other strangers, a highway system where road rage was a contact sport.

So she'd be fine, but Todd? Would he be fine too?

She smiled. To ask the question was to answer it. In spite of the current madness, no one who had watched him through the years as he'd accomplished one incredible thing after another, would hesitate to buy the stock were he to incorporate himself and make a public offering.

Todd opened one eye and peered sleepily at her, and then he closed it and shifted slightly, as if to return to sleep. But his new position against the window was apparently uncomfortable, for he sat up shortly and yawned.

"How long have I been out?" he asked.

"About three states worth," she replied. "You missed the beverage service, such as it was."

"I have a bottled water in my bag," he said, leaning forward to dig for it on the floor of the cabin under the seat in front of him. "I even have two. Want one?"

"No, thank you," Mary answered, as he emerged, water in hand.

"I also have candy bars too. Hungry?"

"Not for candy bars. Got a creme brûlée in there?"

"Nope."

"Then I think I'll have bourbon," Mary said, pushing the button to call the flight attendant.

"Make it two," Todd requested, ever the sophisticated traveler.

"Stick to bottled water," his mother commanded.

The attendant came and took Mary's request, and returned a minute later with her drink in a small plastic container.

"Ah!" Mary said after taking a sip. "You'll be pleased to know that I'm about to be in a much better mood than I was when we started this journey. I read somewhere that alcohol is more potent at high altitudes."

Todd brightened. "That's true, and the reason is that there's reduced air pressure up here, plus the fact your hemoglobin now has trouble absorbing oxygen. One drink has two to three times the effect it would have at sea level."

Mary grinned. "Then get ready to watch your mother party," she said, and seeing that he wasn't done with his lecture on this topic, she put up a hand. "Tell me no more. Let me experience the effect in happy ignorance. I still haven't recovered from your graphic description of the state of the earth that awaits those who survive until 2075. You long ago convinced your father and me that there is much wisdom in the adage that children should be seen and not heard, particularly our child."

"Was I a handful as a small boy?"

"And every day since," she informed him. "Not that either of your parents would have it any other way. It's been a fascinating journey, and well worth the effort of trying to keep ahead of you. But 'handful' isn't a big enough word."

Todd looked thoughtful, and didn't give his usual quip in reply.

Mary was concerned. "Did I offend you?" she asked. "I was clowning. You're the best son that any parents could have, and we're very proud of you."

"It's not that," he replied. "But I have wondered, off and on, if having to deal with me was the cause of the breakup of your marriage."

That question brought her to full attention. She didn't speak immediately.

Finally she decided it was time to give him more information about that marital catastrophe, while carefully editing the story by a number of key expurgations.

She had a healthy gulp of her bourbon, counting on the multiplier effect Todd had described, and began. "To the contrary, Todd, you're the reason we stayed married as long as we did. We had a number of things go wrong, but you weren't among them. You, fascinating child, were the one constant joy in our marriage."

"What did go wrong then?"

"It's not the sort of thing you can discuss with your son," she confessed. "There were many factors. Franklin and I started out very much in love, and then it just slipped away. We are very different people really, and should never have married. Mostly we like different things and have little in common. There's a long list. I love travel; Franklin hates it. He lives for sports, and I can't stand all that organized brutality. I was always dragging him to the theater, and the ballet, and to concerts, where he would promptly nod off. On the other hand, he plumped for us to go on vacations to Las Vegas, where he hit the gaming tables with enthusiasm, while I sat in the hotel room with a good book, wishing I were elsewhere.

"We began to quarrel a lot, and we both proved so good at it that we made it a regular part of our routine, as if it were an entertainment. Franklin started to eat too much; I became fonder of bourbon." She held up her drink as if it were an exhibit. "Most of the time we avoided each other. Eventually we weren't sleeping together or even speaking much except when you were around. Then, for your sake, we'd don the happy couple facade."

"I see," Todd said, trying to think back whether he had noticed the tension she described. Nothing came to mind. "So one day you both just decided enough was enough, and called it quits?"

Mary took a small sip of her drink before she replied.

"No, it wasn't quite like that. It wasn't that innocent," she said finally. "I was the catalyst for the final meltdown."

"You?" he asked, astounded.

"Me," she affirmed, nodding. "I had an affair."

"*What?*" Like most children, Todd had difficulty picturing his mother as a sexual being, and this news floored him.

"Yes, and I don't want to talk about it anymore. We divorced; we both moved on. Your father met Ms. Keyfold, and they appear to be happy. Let's switch topics." She paused. "Do you like her?"

Todd shrugged. "I barely know her, but she seems nice enough. Smart. She explained copyright law to me in some detail when I had questions about how to protect my writings. I was grateful for that."

They were both silent for awhile, processing all of this.

Finally Todd looked at his mother, and gave her a small smile. "Okay," he said, "let me cheer you up." He turned to face her directly. "You, Mom, are awesome, and this conversation proves it! How many mothers would have been so forthcoming with their sons? Thanks for giving me a better picture of what happened. Being willing to tell me all that, just adds to your list of admirable attributes. After your fast work in that farmhouse yesterday, you have to be the leading contender for Mother of the Year."

She smiled back. "I doubt that the Mother of the Year is known for her facility with a Smith and Wesson 686." They both laughed, and she cupped his chin as she said, "You were pretty darn wonderful yesterday yourself. You can take that demon act and put it right on tv. Draw a big audience."

"I don't want to go on tv tonight; I want to go on tv *tomorrow* night with Dad. The Jimmy Ball Show really, really needs me."

"Parental veto," she ruled, "with both parents voting the same way—I can speak for your father on this one. You're in enough trouble with the viewing audience as it is."

"I guess," Todd said, not happy. Then his tone changed as he added in a soft voice, "I have to tell you, Mom. I'm frightened."

Mary's heart filled with concern. So, he was a child after all, scared and needing his mother! Had he ever before in his life admitted to being frightened?

"Don't worry, Toddie," she said, reverting to his childhood name and putting her hand on top of his. "You're moving into a very structured and safe world. You'll be all right."

Todd shook his head. "You misunderstand. It's not me I'm frightened about."

"What then?"

"It's Dad. All my instincts tell me he's in great danger."

Two different alarm bells went off in Mary's mind. The first sounded because Todd was almost never wrong when making such pronouncements. The second because she's been thinking the same thing.

On Sunday morning, Franklin Whitestone made two phone calls, one after another, trying to get his life back into some sort of order. He planned to leave town on Wednesday and join Mary and Todd in L.A., but until then there were matters demanding his attention.

The first was retrieving certain important belongings from his house, and, since Corbin Milk had told him he'd think about how to do that, Franklin called him first.

A male voice he didn't recognize answered Milk's cell phone. His voice was pleasant, but higher in pitch than Milk's soothing bass.

"Hello. This is Franklin Whitestone. Is this Corbin Milk's number?"

"Yes. He's standing at the top of a ladder as we speak, and he asked me to answer his cell. He's been expecting to hear from you. One moment."

There was muted conversation in the background, and, after a few seconds, Milk was on the line. "Good morning," he said.

"Good morning," Franklin returned. "Any ideas about how we can get into my place without wackos attacking?"

"Yes, as it happens, I've thought up with a plan that should work with a minimum of risk. Two friends of mine, a gay couple, have a small painting business, and I've arranged to borrow both their truck and two of their painter's outfits. Both the truck and the outfits have large logos on them proclaiming they are the property of a company called 'Paint the Town,' the actual name of the business."

"Great name."

"My thought is that we'd get you into your disguise, and we'd both don this gay apparel and drive the truck over to your house. We boldly park it in the driveway, enter the house, move the truck into the garage, load it up, and get out of there. How's that sound?"

"Should work fine. When are you thinking?"

"Monday afternoon? Meet me at Masquerade around two p.m. and I'll have the truck and uniforms waiting."

"Will these togs be big enough to fit us?"

"Yes. Howard and I both work out at a gym downtown, and we're about the same size. His partner, Larry . . . well, he's oversized too, but it's mostly in the waist."

213

"Then I get dibs on Larry's uniform. Won't your friends be needing all these things?"

"Nope. They're in Key West for the week."

"I see. Well, two o'clock tomorrow should be fine. I have a meeting at my law firm in the morning, but that starts at ten, and should be over pretty quickly."

"Quickly? Are you being fired?" They'd talked about this possibility at supper two nights ago.

"Not certain. I have a high powered lawyer that they're afraid of, so I have great hopes she'll work something out."

"Good luck with that."

"Thanks. And Corbin, thank you for everything. Do you want a new job? I'm moving to the west coast later in the week, and my agent tells me I'm about to have the kind of money that allows me to hire a manager/bodyguard/whatever you call it."

"Factotum."

"What?"

"Jack of all trades. Interesting offer. I don't think so, but we'll talk about it tomorrow. I see from the constant tv promos that you're the guest of honor this evening on the Jimmy Ball Show. Gutsy move."

"In the middle of the hole and still digging."

Franklin's second call was to Kelly. His hands were none too steady as he punched up her number, and he wasn't even sure what he was going to say. However, he needn't have worried, since all he reached was her answering machine. Franklin left a brief message that he'd called and would appreciate hearing from her. It was with some relief that he hung up. It occurred to him that a slow approach beginning with a game of telephone tag might break the ice enough that the actual conversation, when it finally occurred, would be less awkward. He certainly hoped that was true.

The stupid doctor who'd put a large bandage on Jake Richardson's nose, telling him it was broken and giving him a list of stupid care instructions, had the balls to charge him $150 for a visit that didn't take more than half an hour. The goddamned nose was swollen and pulsating painfully, and it'd kept him up most of the night. Cursing both the doctor and that bitch Celia Hawkins, Jake had rolled around in his bed mumbling obscenities until he finally got up at three a.m., and switched on the tv to take his mind off of

214

his misery. He'd briefly considered prayer as a means of relief, but decided he was in too much pain to concentrate.

Now, at noon on Sunday, he was having a well-deserved beer and feeling slightly better. The doctor had given him some pills for the pain, and they hadn't helped much last night, but now they seemed to be kicking in. Shaking his finger at Jake as if he were a school child, the fucking doctor had told him not to combine alcohol with the medicine, but to hell with that. One beer wouldn't hurt. Jake was tough and his system could take it.

Whitestone's coming return to the Jimmy Ball Show was all over the tv, and not only in commercial advertisements, but featured on actual news casts. That had given Jake an idea. He could go out to the Port Columbus parking garage and carefully watch the arrivals and departures—maybe find Whitestone that way. Park just inside the entrance to the short term parking area and keep tabs on who came by. He'd only have to watch from about two o'clock in the afternoon, when Whitestone was likely to be leaving for New York, until, say, five, when he'd be in the air, and then, if Jake hadn't run across him in that period, man the same stakeout from eleven at night until one in the morning.

Their fucked up encounter in the parking lot of the Gallipolis shopping center the day before had convinced Jake that Whitestone wasn't likely to respond kindly to whatever Jake said. Hell, the man wouldn't even take a Bible as a gift, and that was an important first step in the conversion process that Jake had mapped out for Whitestone. So words alone were not enough. That was a damned shame, but true. However, Reverend Stephens, Jake's favorite preacher when he was a boy, had always said that if one door closed, open another. Jake owned a gun, and that should make Whitestone willing to go through whatever door Jake chose.

His plans were taking concrete shape. He'd thought a lot about the arguments he would need to convince Whitestone to listen to what he was saying. Jake had prayed a lot about this, and had even asked advice from Celia before she turned mean and attacked him when he tripped. She recommended a slow approach, one step at a time, with each step moving Whitestone closer to an acceptance of the Lord.

Jake had already decided where to take Whitestone once he'd been hustled into a car. Good place. Even comfortable. Whitestone would like it.

CHAPTER FOURTEEN

THE JIMMY BALL SHOW

His usual disguise with the mustache and cheek fillers in place, Franklin drove his rental car to Port Columbus and parked in the lot reserved for private aircraft. As he had the previous Sunday when he'd made this same journey, Franklin brought no luggage with him, carrying everything he needed in his leather briefcase. He checked in at the front reception desk, and then took a seat in the small waiting area, his mind racing, impatient for the signal to board the small jet that would again take him to New York City and the looming Jimmy Ball Show.

I wish I could remember why I agreed to do this, he mused. The waiting area had magazines available to help pass the time, and in his briefcase Franklin had a perfectly good half-read book of his own, but he was too wound up to sit passively as if nothing of import was going on. Instead he was a 21st century Daniel, who, having once escaped from the lions' den, very severely mauled, was now stupidly going back for a second visit. This time he would face an even larger pride, one already drooling and anxious to pounce.

Of course Franklin had thought hard about what he was trying to accomplish on this do-over: what he had to say, and, perhaps more urgently, what he damned well better not say. No more casual statements about an "imaginary friend" and religion as a "superstition." Like most people who've stupidly opened their mouths at the wrong moment and immediately regretted it, Franklin had constantly rethought what he *should* have said versus the terrible reality of what he'd *actually* said. Happily, unlike most people, he was in the enviable position of having a second chance to get it right.

His emphasis would be on closing up the wounds he had so carelessly sliced open in "Jimmy Ball I," and offering a peace pipe to the world in the soberer climate of "Jimmy Ball II." With that goal firmly in mind, but with the details of how to do it still eluding him, Franklin boarded the plane when invited to do so by the same efficient attendant who'd been on duty last Sunday.

Once they were airborne, the attendant, a tiny woman with a soothing voice, asked him if he would like something to drink.

He went with Coke.

Kelly listened to her answering machine message from Franklin twice, even though the message was unremarkable and not, in and of itself, worthy of repetition. It merely said that he'd called and would like to speak with her, leaving his new cell phone number. But even that sparse information caused Kelly's heart to pound. When she finally did erase the message, she was smiling.

After rehearsing out loud what she was going to say, Kelly called him back, reaching his answering machine.

"Hello, Franklin," she began, avoiding the more familiar "Frankie." "It's Kelly, returning your call. Hi. I suppose you're on your way to New York, and I wish you well at straightening all this out when you arrive. Give me a call when you're free to talk." She delivered this brief monologue without hesitation or stumbling, and was pleased with herself as she hung up.

She pondered Franklin's strange situation. What would it be like for him tonight, retracing the steps that had led him to be the notorious subject of a vicious hate campaign? And how *brave* it was of him to be willing to try. Kelly pondered what she would say in his place, but came up only with unsatisfactory platitudes, none of which sounded right.

She could only pray he would be better at this than she was.

On what was Saturday evening Ohio time, but only late afternoon in Los Angeles, Mary and Todd were met as they came off the plane at LAX by Jonathan Harker, who introduced himself and told them he would be their escort to the gated community where they'd be living for the foreseeable future. Both Mary and Todd were impressed with how soothing and friendly Harker was, and the three were soon seated in a limousine, falling into a relaxed conversation that included quite a bit of laughter. He told them that he was only the first of a number of Martin Turnbill employees they'd encounter in L.A., starting tomorrow with the head honcho of the protection service (named, they learned, "SteadyLife").

When they finally arrived there, mother and son were also very impressed with what Todd promptly started calling the "Compound." First of all, to their surprise, it was located in Beverly Hills, which, as it happened, actually did have hills, and steep ones at that. A tall stone fence topped with metallic wires (electrified?) surrounded the place, which was entered through a gate next to a small guardhouse, staffed by a large man wearing a pistol. He was friendly, obviously expecting them, but his broad shoulders and no nonsense manner made it clear he was on top of his job. From the entrance, the winding road climbed a hill covered with exotic plants, the most spectacular of which had clusters of three white flowers surrounded by bracts of bright pink, magenta, purple, red, orange, white, or yellow. When they asked about these, Harker identified them as bougainvilleas. These flowery showoffs were everywhere, making for a spectacular explosion of color all around.

The limousine deposited them at a small cottage, attractive without being overdone, with a red clay roof and a sand-colored stucco exterior. Entering, they found a very modern, exceedingly comfortable interior, tastefully appointed with elegant furniture and wall dressings, and filled with conveniences of all sorts, including a game room with a pool table, a dart board, and two computers. On seeing the latter Todd's eyes glazed over, and, like a hypnotized simpleton, he marched over and attached himself to one of the computer, making happy little gurgles deep in his throat. He was not seen again for hours, until, at last, his mother pried his hands from the keyboard and made him come to supper. The latter was delivered to their door by a woman in a white apron who had apparently cooked it herself, and it was, of course, delicious.

On Sunday afternoon, Mary and Todd, having spent the day exploring the pool, the tennis courts, and the bike path, settled themselves in front of the big screen tv in the living room and prepared to watch the Jimmy Ball Show. Normally the show was tape delayed for the west coast, originating as it did at 8:00 p.m. EDT in New York, which, of course, would be 5:00 p.m. in California. However, for this very special occasion focusing on the notoriously controversial Franklin Whitestone, the show, with its live call-in feature, was being broadcast to all parts of the United States simultaneously.

"I would give anything to be there with Dad!" Todd enthused, not for the first time.

"That's an U.N.C.," she informed him. These strange initials (pronounced "unk") were Whitestone family shorthand for "Under No Circumstances." She continued. "It's my plan to keep you out of the public eye until you turn forty. Then you're on your own."

"Wow! Only twenty-four years to go, and I'll be free of tutelage!" He looked around the handsome room with its plush white carpeting, wood paneling, and dark green drapes that closed when you flicked a wall switch. "We'll know this snazzy place really well by then."

"And be sick to death of each other," she added. "You'll be planning matricide and me—well, whatever the 'cide' is for a strangling a forty-year old son."

Just then the tv picture changed to the bright, familiar logo of the Jimmy Ball Show, while Ball's regular announcer pompously intoned over the show's briskly-played theme song, that this was "A **SPECIAL EDITION** OF THE **JIMMY BALL SHOW**: *ATHEISM VERSUS BELIEVERS*, with Jimmy's featured guest, **FRANKLIN WHITESTONE!**"

Mother and son broke off their idle banter and turned serious faces to the huge television screen mounted flat on the wall next to the entertainment center.

"Maybe we should hold hands," Mary mumbled, only half kidding.

Disappointed at not finding Whitestone at the airport, but hopeful that he'd have better luck when the man came back later that night, Jake Richardson went home to watch the Jimmy Ball Show himself. Fortunately he didn't live far from the airport, so it was an easy trip from his parking garage stakeout.

Earlier this morning, in one of those fits of energy that overtook him from time to time, he'd made a stab at cleaning up the kitchen and living room, and that had taken hours. The living room in particular had been a jungle, and while it was not yet in apple pie order, it also was no longer necessary to hack your way through with guide and machete.

Now he settled down in his old recliner with a beer and a bowl of popcorn he'd nuked in his ancient microwave, and prepared to watch Whitestone blaspheme again against His God on the Jimmy Ball Show.

As Jake waited for the show to start, he once more contemplated how he was going to get Whitestone from the airport to the hideaway he'd prepared for him. The man wouldn't, of course, come along willingly—Jake saw that—and there was no way to keep a gun on him while Jake drove his truck. What to do? Knock the guy out? Tie him up in some way? Get someone to come along and help abduct Whitestone, and then hold the gun on him? He'd have to think of something and soon.

Jake had worried about the same issue all during the last week, and then on Friday had heard on the news that the couple who had taken Mary and Todd Whitestone to their farm had used shackles to hobble them. That sounded cool to Jake—mysterious and manly. But where in holy hell could he find shackles like that?

Jake had a four year old computer, but he really didn't use it for much except exploring the porn sites of the world, which provided him harmless entertainment. As long as there was no actual sex involved, Jake reasoned that God wouldn't care what fantasies he had sitting there, typing with one finger. Jake had talked to quite a few women online, trying to set up meetings, but for some reason none of them were interested.

It occurred to Jake that these same sites could help him locate shackles, so he'd put time into exploring that idea. Finally, in a chat room named "Beginner Dungeon," he had posted his question to the whole room, and three different people sent him IMs about websites that sold leather goods and s/m equipment. Looking into that led to a very interesting hour in which Jake had to keep reminding himself to blink. Whoa! The things people thought up! Jake was strangely thrilled, and that bothered him a little. He wasn't a violent man. Finally, he'd ordered some cheap ankle and wrist restraints on Friday night from one of these sites, requesting expedited shipping, but it looked like the package wouldn't be delivered until Tuesday, though perhaps it would come in tomorrow, Monday, if he was lucky. In the meantime, if he snagged Whitestone at the airport, he'd have to improvise.

The Jimmy Ball show came on and Jake steeled himself against the heresies about to invade his home. Maybe it would be best to have his Bible on his lap while watching, but it was in the bedroom, and the show was starting. He decided that if things got bad, and he needed the moral certainty it offered, he'd fetch the Bible during a commercial break. And put it on the end table by the recliner. Next to his gun.

Kelly's phone rang a little after seven that evening, and it was Franklin calling from New York City. "Where are you?" she asked.

"In the limousine on my way to the television studio. I thought maybe you could buck me up. I'm in a bad way."

"Bad way? Because?"

"Nerves. I keep thinking that coming here was a major mistake. Maybe I can get it right this time, but also maybe not. The show is going to begin with a debate between atheists and devout Christians, and that could poison the air before I say anything."

"Oh, my. That might really be a problem. A debate like that isn't likely to be a calm, considered affair. They'll be hurling insults at each other inside five minutes."

"It'll warm things up fast," Franklin agreed. "I'm just hoping the set isn't on fire by the time I have to sit on it."

She hesitated slightly before saying, "I want you to know that I think you're very brave, Franklin. It is a rare person who would dare to go back like this. I'm very worried about you. Your safety and all."

"No alcohol this time," he assured her. "Going cold turkey for this one."

"Good. What line are you planning on taking?"

"Conciliation. Pour oil on troubled waters."

"Excellent plan. I'm rooting for you."

There was a slight pause before that personal statement gave Franklin the courage to say, "I'd like to get together with you when I return. Would that be all right? Just to talk?"

"Yes. I'd like that. Call me tomorrow."

"Perhaps a late supper tomorrow evening? I have a chore to perform at my old house and then I'll be free."

"Splendid."

"I'll pick you up at, say, 7:30."

She agreed to that, and they discussed where to go for a few minutes more, settling on The Windbreaker, a favorite restaurant near her home, and then they said goodbye.

"Break a leg," she told him, but after she hung up she found herself considering how much of the tv audience would be glad to help Franklin snap a bone or two.

Deep in thought, Kelly began wandering pointlessly around her kitchen, bedroom, and living room. I'm a nervous jumble, and shouldn't watch this show alone, Kelly thought. I should have someone with me, someone to bounce ideas off and who would provide perspective.

But even if it hadn't been too late to do so, she didn't know whom she would have called. Her law school friends were mostly liberal types, and Kelly would be hurt if they said hateful things about religion, as some might. The people she knew from church would create the opposite problem, undoubtedly consigning Franklin to a fiery end even before he opened his mouth.

So, completely alone except for her dog, Ralph, a mid-sized black mutt of no identifiable ancestry, she turned on the television, afraid of what she'd hear, and unclear what her reaction would be to whatever was said.

Ralph whined, pleading to be allowed to climb up into her chair, and after a moment's hesitation, she nodded and patted her lap. He joined her before she could blink, and, turning around once, settled down. She petted him absently, as the theme music came on the air. At least Ralph wouldn't have a religious viewpoint to share.

When he first entered the green room at the NYC studio, Franklin was introduced by Mr. Malone, the production assistant, to the four other people who would also be guests tonight, the panelists for the atheism/belief debate that would make up the first half of the Jimmy Ball Show. They were a diverse group.

The two non-believers were Dr. Richard Samuel, a professor of philosophy from Australia, who had written a number of best-selling books refuting the very idea of God, and Andrew O'Brien, a leading secular humanist in the United States. Dr. Samuel was a distinguished looking man of about 60, with a neatly trimmed goatee and rimless glasses, which gave him an appropriate professorial look. O'Brien had fiery red hair, beginning to thin significantly, and was a man in his 40s. He'd given up exercising some years ago, and, judging by the roundness of his torso, needed to get back to it soon.

Facing them on the up-coming panel were the Reverend Melinda Frost, a woman also of about 40, who ran an evangelical training school in Atlanta, and Dr. Ronald Wainwright, a professor of theology at a university in Canada. The Reverend Frost, like O'Brien, was overweight, but she carried it better than he did. She had whitish spiky hair (which seemed to Franklin a very modern choice for an evangelist), and was quick to laugh and make jokes about herself and her first visit to the Big Apple. The theology professor was also cast against type: he was of indeterminate age, but, judging by his imposing bulk and large broken nose, it appeared that he'd once been a professional boxer.

The four were friendly enough when introduced to Franklin, and they made small talk about how nervous they all were. Melinda Frost asked Franklin if he had any advice, and he promptly responded, "Avoid alcohol." She assured him that she was not a drinker, but O'Brien, who was agitated and perhaps too excited, chimed in with a comic suggestion that they all might be better off skipping the show and repairing to a nearby pub. No one bothered to reply to that.

At 7:45 p.m., Malone came to get the panelists and escort them to the studio, and Franklin was left alone. The large tv screen hanging from the ceiling opposite the door was tuned to the Jimmy Ball Show, and Franklin, with some trepidation, sat down facing it to view this first segment. Obviously, whatever the panelists did would influence what followed. The call-in audience would probably refer to it when he was in the hot seat, so— good or bad—he needed to watch it all.

The show began and the announcer introduced Jimmy Ball, who smiled happily at the camera and bobbed his bald head slightly as a way of greeting his unseen audience, hands raised, palms out. He looked very pleased with himself for having arranged this video coup. He clearly believed that this show would be a highlight of his long career, and, as it happened, he was right. Nothing Ball ever did thereafter topped this. On his deathbed he would look back on it with a big smile on his face.

Ball was seated in the middle of five chairs, all facing the camera, with Richard Samuel and Andrew O'Brien on his right, and Melinda Frost and Ronald Wainwright on the left. There was no desk or table for them to lean on, as was usual for guests. The panelists sat rather stiffly, hands folded in their laps, except for Andrew O'Brien, who had his legs crossed, one ankle atop the other knee, looking far more relaxed than he had moments ago in the green room. Franklin wondered if O'Brien was this good at covering up his real feelings, or if, perhaps, he had mysteriously found some liquid way to brace himself against the terrors of television. Perhaps he'd run into Hubbie Lulland in the hallway.

"GOOD EVENING, AMERICA," Ball said with enthusiasm, "and also those of you watching from Canada, Mexico, and other venues. As you know, last week, Franklin Whitestone, a lawyer from Columbus, Ohio, was one of my guests, and his appearance has set off arguments all across the world about atheism and its relationship with religion." The camera zoomed in for a closeup on Ball. "Mr. Whitestone had been invited to appear on that particular program because of his heroic actions earlier that same Sunday when he helped rescue a large number of people from the collapse of a stadium during a college football game. But it was his remarks afterwards that lit up our phones. Here are some highlights from that show."

As Franklin squirmed in the green room, the screen switched to a montage of snippets from last week: a bit of the famous tape showing Franklin holding the girder, a few jovial words exchanged between host and guest, and then, in its entirety, the phone call from the woman in Utah, and Franklin's disastrous "imaginary friend" rant.

The camera returned to a live shot of Ball, and he said, "We'll have Franklin Whitestone himself on in the second part of this show, but first we have a distinguished panel who are going to discuss this contentious issue: what is the place of atheism in a religious world?" The camera pulled back to include all five of them, and Ball introduced the guests one by one, with the camera honing in on each as Ball mentioned names and accomplishments.

Ball then turned to Dr. Samuel on his far right, and asked, "Dr. Samuel, you have written a number of books on atheism. What is your response to all the criticism that Franklin Whitestone has endured during the past week?"

"Well," the professor replied in his Australian accent, "he could certainly have phrased things more diplomatically, but what he said is basically what a lot of people feel. It's wrong to count on a mythical supernatural being to solve concrete problems."

"And," O'Brien added, interrupting, "the older you get the more ridiculous a belief in God seems. It would be funny if it weren't so dangerous."

"Dangerous?" Ball asked.

"All those wars, all this terrorism, all this discrimination against those who believe something other than what you believe and are condemned for it, that's what is dangerous."

"No. What's dangerous," Melinda Frost corrected, "is depriving the world of a belief in God when that belief is vitally necessary for survival! *Atheists* are dangerous! They have nothing to believe in!"

"Nonsense!" O'Brien countered, his voice rising. "Atheists make decisions based on rational factors. They aren't torching their fellow man because he doesn't revere a certain ancient book."

"If Osama bin Laden had only atheists to work with, the World Trade Center would still be standing," Dr. Samuel commented.

Professor Ronald Wainwright jumped in. "What you're ignoring," he said, calm and authoritative, "is how *necessary* religion is for us all to function. Just imagine what sort of chaos would ensue if God were subtracted from the picture, and sufferers had no hope of a better life than the constant misery many must endure every day."

"Yes!" the Reverend Frost said louder than needed. "We all need God in order to survive, to care for each other, to give us hope!"

"'Religion is the opium of the people,'" Samuel quoted.

Professor Wainwright jumped on that thought. "Karl Marx is the author of that bit of heresy!"

"Marx!" Frost exclaimed, and she turned to Samuel sneering. "Communist!"

"So you're a patriotic American are you?" O'Brien asked her with a sneer of his own.

Frost was indignant. "Yes, of course, I am!"

"Then let me ask you a question. If you had to choose between what your Bible says and what the United States Constitution says, which would you choose?"

The reverend paused, uncertain where this was going. "What do you mean?"

"Freedom of religion, for example. Making sure the ten commandments are not posted on the walls in the schools. Not allowing intelligent design in the classroom. Treating all religions equally."

"Those things are very bad," she told him, no longer in doubt. "The Bible clearly says so. There is only one true religion and that is Christianity, and our schools have fallen to their current terrible state because that has been forgotten."

O'Brien laughed. "I think that makes my point," he said. "If your group takes over, out goes the Constitution!"

Frost had a response for that. "And if your group takes over religious people will be herded into corners and shot!"

The discussion, already descending, went downhill faster from this point, volume and tempers rising. Both professors tried to keep things on an intellectual plane, but their debating partners had no patience for that. At one point O'Brien and Frost abandoned any pretense of civility, and began exchanging epithets, like "BIGOT!" "BLASPHEMER!" "RELIGIOUS ROBOT!" "TOOL OF SATAN!" Suddenly the two combatants rose from their chairs, starting for each other. No telling what would have happened except for the courage showed by Jimmy Ball himself, who immediately jumped between them, arms spread wide, palms planted on the chest of each. Both of the professors grabbed at them too, and for a moment they were all five frozen in this bizarre tableau. It became a famous photo of the event.

"CALM DOWN! CALM DOWN!" Ball shouted, sounding none too calm himself. With a look of distress on his face, the embattled host risked a panicked glance up at the booth where his director was stationed, as if calling for the network's waiting troops to storm the stage and restore order. As a matter of course, his microphone was set louder than any of the guests, so he was most certainly heard as he yelled, "YOU'RE ON TELEVISION, FOR CHRIST'S SAKE!" at Frost and O'Brien. This strange ejaculation seemed to do the trick. Both of them looked in confusion at the tv cameras, realized with a start where they were, and sat back down, much embarrassed.

Mollified and relieved that the Jimmy Ball Show had not turned into World Wide Wrestling, Jimmy Ball, somewhat shaken, glanced around to make sure that all guests were firmly seated, and, having confirmed this restoration of decorum, said directly into the camera, "We'll be right back with our featured guest."

In the green room, his mouth frozen open in horror, Franklin Whitestone stared at the screen. He thought briefly about opening the door and making a run for it. Otherwise, not only was Daniel walking into the lions' den, but someone had just flogged them into a frenzy. The door opened and Malone stuck his head into the room. "Come with me, Mr. Whitestone," he said, calm as a funeral director. "You're on."

"Well," Todd said brightly, "I think that went well, don't you? I wonder if after tonight we'll ever see old Dad again. Do you think they'll ship the body back to us if they find enough pieces?"

Mary sat with her head in her hands, stunned, miserable. She was speechless.

But Todd wasn't done with his always snappy commentary. "Maybe I

225

should fire up my computer and create another webcast to deflect attention from dear old Dad. What do you think, Mom? I could break the news that there's no Santa Claus either."

She looked up at him, her eyes devoid of emotion. "I think you shouldn't be joking," she said. "Franklin is in terrible, *terrible* trouble."

Kelly thought so too. In her living room she was walking frantically back and forth, hugging her arms to her body, saying the word "fuck" over and over, louder each time, until she was screaming it.

Her dog, Ralph, threw back his head and helped things out by howling.

During the commercial break the set had been transformed from the panel discussion setup, back to its normal configuration: a desk with Ball sitting on one side and that evening's guest on the other, with a pitcher of water and tumblers between them. As Jimmy Ball introduced him, Franklin, given his cue by Malone's tap on the shoulder, walked onto the set and, for the second time in a week, shook hands with the host.

All joviality, Ball almost winked as he said, "Things have really changed for you since you last sat in that chair. Isn't that right?"

Franklin ruefully nodded. "Ye—just as you predicted the minute we were off the air—and, Jimmy, that came true in spades. I've lost friends, am having professional troubles, my family nearly escaped death, and I myself have been forced into hiding. It hasn't been fun."

Ball looked very sympathetic. "Franklin, if you could go back to last week, would you change any of the things you said?" he asked.

"Of course, I would," Franklin replied. "And let me talk directly to your audience about that." He turned and looked into the camera nearest him, and, cued by the alert director, that camera moved in for a close up.

"I want to apologize to all of those I offended last Sunday when I was on this show and said things I now deeply regret. Let me tell you how I came to be so imprudent." And then Franklin related the story of how one glass of wine at supper had turning into two, along with the subsequent sips he had taken from the flask Hubie Lulland had so kindly left for him in the green room.

"I'm not much of a drinker," Franklin confessed to the listeners, "and having that much alcohol to 'calm my nerves' was a very bad idea. It loosened my tongue, as they say, and the unfortunate remarks that came out of my mouth were the unhappy result.

"While it's true that I am unbeliever myself, I certainly respect the rights of others to believe whatever they wish. Our country was founded on the concept of freedom of religion, and, as a lawyer and a good U.S. citizen, I would give my life to protect that important right. If anything I said can be construed to the contrary, I assure you that was not my intention. Like most of you, I am surrounded by religious people, but I don't judge them by that criterion. Instead I ask myself whether they are good people or bad people— moral, friendly, hard working, etc.

"Finally, I would ask all of you out there to judge atheists by that same standard. Not what they believe or don't believe, but whether they are worthwhile human beings. Moreover, it's a measuring stick that I hope you'll apply to me. I've lived my life, as most of you have, trying my best to do what is right—for my family, my neighbors, my community, and my country. My clients and associates would tell you I am honest and trustworthy, and so far I've avoided any troubles with the law, except for an argument with the IRS over my tax deductions back in 1999—a matter that has been settled somewhat grumpily by both parties." He smiled. "I'm kind to children and dogs, (with the exception of that German Sheppard down the block that barks all night and disturbs the entire neighborhood.)." He turned back to Jimmy Ball. "That's all I have to say."

His host looked thoughtful. "Impressive," he commented, "but tell me this. If you don't take your moral compass from religion where does it come from?"

"Actually, the Bible."

"Oh?"

"I am a firm believer in the Golden Rule. 'Do unto others as you would have them do unto you.'" Franklin smiled again as he told his host, "Don't look so surprised, Jimmy. The Bible is filled with wisdom and concepts that no rational person would dispute. For millennia the Bible has been a bulwark for the protection of the weak and the helpless, and its genius lies in its encouragement of good behavior in all people. Like many ancient books, the Bible has much of value to say about how we should lead our lives."

"Have you actually read it?" Ball asked.

"Oh, yes," Franklin replied. "In my youth I went through a period where I explored all the major religions on the globe, one by one, seeing what they had to say, accepting more than I rejected. I've read the Bible from cover to cover."

"But you still don't believe in God."

"I do not."

"There's no 'imaginary friend' looking out for you?"

227

"Now, Jimmy," Franklin reproved him, "please don't get me into more trouble than I'm already in. I'm working hard here to square things with the good folks out there whom I offended by stupid comments like the one you just mentioned."

"All right," Jimmy Ball said, facing the camera again, "when we return, we'll take some phone calls and see what you listeners want to ask Franklin Whitestone." He stayed frozen for a second, looking steadily at the camera until the red light blinked off, and then he returned his attention to Franklin. "That was good—what you just told them," he said.

Franklin shrugged his shoulders. "I'm trying to avoid being shot at again."

"You were SHOT AT? I thought it was your son and ex-wife who were the ones in danger."

"They were," he replied. "But last Wednesday evening two shots were fired at me when I tried to retrieve some items from my home. The police are fairly sure that the same couple who terrorized my family are also the ones who did it. Ballistics will soon confirm that or not."

"Terrifying! But—hey—I don't want to ask you anymore about the shooting now. Wait until we get on the air. This is too good for private conversation."

'Good?' Franklin thought, but let it go.

"Two minutes!" the stage manager informed them.

"Have you heard from Hubie Lulland lately?" Franklin asked Ball.

He laughed. "Oh, yes. Hubbie called me and begged to be put on with you tonight. Said you were his new best friend, claiming last week was the biggest publicity boost his career ever had. That dreadful movie of his is selling out—obviously a sign that the end of the world is fast upon us."

They exchanged a few more remarks before Ball was given the signal to get ready, and then the red camera light blinked back on.

Ball told his audience, "We'll get to your phone calls in a moment, but first, I have just learned during the break that Franklin Whitestone was shot at last Wednesday. Is that true?"

"Ah, yes," Franklin replied, and he related for the audience a brief version of what had happened.

"Wow! That had to be scary," Ball commented, with feeling.

"Not as frightening as the horrible ordeal my son and ex-wife had to endure. All three of us are hoping that life will soon return to normal."

"I hope so too. Okay! Let's take those calls," Ball said. He listened through his earpiece for a second. "This is Alan in Boston. Hello? You're on the air."

"Hello," Alan replied after a slight pause, his voice filling the studio.

"I just want to ask Mr. Whitestone if his son Todd is all right. A lot of people were quite angry at him too."

"Yes," Franklin told him, "Todd is fine. Both he and his mother have been moved to a safe place for their protection. And for all you folks out there who are still upset with Todd, please remember he's a sixteen year old boy, whose primary motivation was to help me out by taking some of the heat on himself. Unfortunately that worked only too well. But you might ask yourself if you, at sixteen, ever made mistakes that you really, really regretted."

"Does he really, really regret it?" Alan asked.

"He'd better," Franklin replied, causing Ball to laugh. "Just kidding. Of course he does. I spoke with him today, and he's anxious to get back to his high school and prepare for college next year."

"Thanks for calling, Alan," Jimmy Ball said. "Now to Rhonda in Birmingham."

"Have you tried praying to God to forgive you? That might help," a woman's voice said.

"Let me ask you," Franklin replied, "have you ever considered the possibility that there might not be a God?"

"Of course not. Jesus Christ is the Lord Our Savior, and I would risk my immortal soul if I questioned His existence. You'd better think long and hard about that, Mr. Whitestone."

"Let me ask you this. Do you believe that Jesus ascended bodily into heaven?"

"Yes, I do."

"Millions of Muslims believe that Mohammed rode to heaven on his horse. Are they wrong?"

"Yes, they are. That couldn't have happened."

Franklin raised his hand in a gesture of peace. "They'd say the same thing about your belief. That's what makes dialogue about religion so difficult. You believe one unlikely thing, and another religion believes a different unlikely thing. Each will say that it is right, and the other is wrong. Neither seems to consider a third explanation: they both are wrong."

Franklin tilted his head. "I myself take nothing on faith alone. You do. But, Rhonda, I'll give you this. If you're right, you're right. If your guess as to how the universe works is superior to mine, then so be it. Congratulations on picking the winner."

She didn't like that at all. "But your immortal soul is in danger! Aren't you worried about that?"

"No."

"What if you die and you get to heaven and St. Peter asks you how

229

well you served your God?"

"That would be an interesting conversation," Franklin admitted. "But let me ask you this. If you were God and had created the earth, would you then sentence good people to eternal damnation just because they didn't believe in you?"

"Yes." Rhonda was firm.

"Rhonda, if you were God, why would you *want* to be worshiped?"

"Why? Because I'm *God,* that's why!"

"Are you a mother, Rhonda?"

"Yes."

"All right, tell me this. Should your own children be condemned to hell forever if they don't worship you when they grow up?"

"Yes! Honor your father and your mother is one of the ten commandments."

Franklin gave a small shrug, and looked at Jimmy Ball as if to say "Can't we move along?"

Taking the hint immediately, Ball said, "Thank you for calling, Rhonda. Now on to Raul in Dallas."

"Hello, Jimmy. I love your show."

"Thanks."

"I want to ask Whitestone why he and the other atheists have declared war on Christianity, and are working so hard to keep it out of the government and the schools and such?"

Ball gave an inquiring glance at Franklin.

"I think you have things backward," Franklin said. "Christians are already well represented at all levels of our government from the President down. Our current difficulty is keeping them from so overwhelming the system that freedom of religion ceases to exist. Certainly *atheists* aren't in power. Not a single member of Congress is an atheist, and that's also true in state government. You couldn't be elected to any office in the United States, federal or state, if you were outed as an atheist."

Ball spoke up. "I saw a poll not long ago that over ninety percent of the people questioned said they could vote for a woman, black, or Jew as President, and seventy-some odd would vote for a homosexual, but only 38% would back an atheist."

"Here's a sobering thought," Franklin commented. "We're the most discriminated against minority in the country, and nobody cares about eliminating that discrimination. It's perfectly all right to condemn atheists because of their religious beliefs. We wouldn't tolerate such a bias against other groups. It's for this reason that most people who wonder whether there's really a God or not, keep their mouths firmly shut, don't mention their

230

doubts, and stay deep in the closet."

"But life would be a disaster if atheists ran things!" Raul asserted, distressed. "Atheists have no incentive to be good because they don't think they'll be punished in the hereafter if they're not."

"Just the opposite. Atheists are concerned about making the *present* world as perfect as it can be, and that's precisely because they think the present is all there is. Christians can get their judgment mixed up with their faith. Ronald Reagan had a Secretary of the Interior who was sure that Christ was about to return to the earth, so he didn't care much about the environment. He did almost nothing to protect it—for example, giving companies exploiting the wilderness free reign. And, remember, *this jerk was Secretary of the Interior*! Wouldn't you agree that an atheist would be a much better choice for the job?"

"You're going to go to hell, Whitestone!"

"So I'm told."

CHAPTER FIFTEEN

BREAKING AND ENTERING

As he turned off the tv, Jake Richardson admitted that Whitestone was a clever man. He made mocking God sound like something you could just do and get away with it—as if God wouldn't care if you took His name in vain (hadn't Whitestone ever read the ten commandments?). Jake wondered how many dopes would fall for this line? Any? Many? Hell, with an audience that big, there probably were lots of people who'd turn away from God just because Whitestone told them it was okay. People who didn't much like going to church. People who were only pretending to be good Christians. Jake knew a lot of these, and he thought they were scum.

Well, it was time to get back in the truck and hunt Whitestone down and show him the how the righteous behaved. The next time that man appeared on the Jimmy Ball Show he'd sing a different tune.

A hymn.

Knowing that even though it was eleven at night his time, it was still early evening in California, Franklin, with the flight attendant's permission, called Todd and Mary while still in the air on his way back to Port Columbus. They answered on the first ring.

"Hello?" It was Mary's voice.

"Mary, it's Franklin. Just checking in."

"Oh, Franklin! Todd and I were both so impressed how you handled things on the show!" Todd could be heard in the background loudly saying, "*Dad! Let me talk to Dad,*" before she shushed him.

"I was trying to word everything to see if we couldn't reverse some of the animosity directed at us. Well, not you, but Todd and me."

"People do like hearing wrongdoers apologize. It really should help ease the pressure."

"Stay safe in the meantime. Okay?"

"Of course. Tomorrow we meet with the head of security and learn all the new tricks we must master to avoid the public gaze, while leading as normal a life as possible. I'll give you a call when we get some idea how it all works. Want to talk to your son? He's jumping up and down next to me like a seven year old." That got her a dirty look from Todd, but he immediately quieted down and looked mature.

"Put him on."

Todd took the phone, his natural exuberance returning. "You were awesome, Dad! Nice save after that debate brawl! Gave you cred and props."

"Thanks . . . I think."

"When you first started talking I was worried," Todd said.

"Worried?"

"Well, for a moment there, I thought you might be trying to fake a public conversion just to make things easier for me. But, thank God, that didn't happen!"

"'Thank God'?" Franklin asked, mocking him.

"Oops."

"Common mistake among atheists. Let me reveal to you, my son, the ways of the Great Turtle."

The next morning, Franklin put on his mustache, inserted the cheek fillers, donned his "Go Bucks!" cap and drove his rental car downtown to the office building housing the law firm of Factor, Marroni, & Ray. He was pleased to see that there were no reporters outside as he pulled into the building's own parking lot (though he could not, of course, risk parking in his usual reserved spot). His attorney, Carol Lebeau, had agreed to meet him in the first floor lobby, next to the statue of a horse that stood near the elevator banks, and she was indeed there waiting for him as he emerged from the parking garage. He was smugly pleased to realize that she didn't recognize him as he walked up to her.

"Buy you a drink, pretty lady?" he asked with a leer.

Both surprised and indignant, she turned to rip him to pieces, but the light dawned just in time, and she smiled broadly.

"It's you!" she said. "Who would have guessed it? It's incredible how very different you look!"

They shook hands as Franklin replied, "I thought I'd take it all off in the elevator going up the 32nd floor, and return to my usual dignified appearance."

"Good plan."

"I'm not used to the role of client. Any advice for me?"

She nodded. "Yes. Keep your mouth shut and let me do all the talking. That will be hard, but I expect you to do it. Are we clear on this, *client*?" She emphasized the last word.

"Yes, counselor."

From the reception desk in the waiting area of Factor, Marroni, & Ray, they were shown into the primary meeting room, with its elegant and

233

elaborate paneling, and large mahogany desk, where five of the senior partners were already gathered. Howard Ray came in immediately after Lebeau and Franklin entered, and everyone shook hands. Franklin thought it was odd that Paul Factor, the senior named partner, wasn't present. Perhaps he'd succumbed to terminal curmudgeoness at some point in the past week. Everyone in the firm would like that.

Carol Lebeau took charge immediately. It was her philosophy that in any given legal dispute one key person was running things; she always worked to make sure that person was her. "We are most interested in hearing when Factor, Marroni, & Ray plans to allow my client to resume his usual practice, which, I assure you, he is most anxious to do."

The partners all looked at each other in a "you go first" manner, and Howard Ray, the managing partner, who had been thumbing through a manila file he had brought with him, extracted a sheet of paper, and slid it across the table to her.

"Here is the termination agreement we've drafted," Ray told Lebeau. "I think you'll find it fair."

She didn't bother to look at it. "Termination?" she questioned. "Franklin is not interested in terminating his participation in the partnership. Why would he do that?"

Ray, who thought of himself as the alpha dog, was all confidence and congeniality as he replied, "Oh, come now, Carol. Let's not pretend that what's happened, hasn't happened. Franklin brought a cloudburst of trouble through our doors, and it's not going away any time soon. More or less unanimously, our clients don't want him here. Some of the staff and even a number of the lawyers have been much offended by what he has been saying publicly. The press, tv, and the internet are vilifying his name. Factor, Marroni, & Ray would be perfectly within the law in terminating him without any compensation at all, so I suggest you take a good look at the generous severance package we're offering."

Franklin started to open his mouth, but Lebeau put a hand on top of his and spoke before he could.

"My client is being let go because you don't agree with his religious beliefs?"

Ray was having none of that. "Oh, no, no, no. The problem arises from the bad publicity caused by his reckless statements on national tv, which were then amplified by that ridiculous webcast his son posted on the internet."

"Statements and webcast both being solely about the Whitestone religious views, which, I gather, you disagree with, not to mention the shaky ground you'd be on for firing him because of something his son said."

"It's *conduct*, not speech that's the problem," Ray countered. "Franklin keeps going on television and making things worse—inviting even more attention to his unconventional views."

"Unconventional *religious* views," she reminded them, trying to keep the focus on the inadvisability of firing Franklin for reasons that would flagrantly violate the civil rights laws. "Let me ask you a question, Howard. Do you think that Franklin's views, as you understand them, are in any way immoral?"

Randal Jackson, one of the other partners spoke up. "Nietzsche said that 'If God does not exist, everything is permitted.'"

"Actually," Lebeau replied, "it was Dostoevsky. And he put those words in the mouth of a fictional character, one who was simply wrong. If and when we all end up in court," and she looked around at them ominously as she said this, "you're going to have to show that atheists are more immoral than the rest of the population, and the statistics won't bear that conclusion. You'll look ridiculous. Particularly to a jury which has been purged of fanatical religious types and sworn to play fair with my client."

Ray frowned. He remembered now just how much he hated this woman. Bothered, he contemplated how distasteful it would be to take the witness stand and have her cross examine him for an hour or so in open court.

"We are *not* going to keep Franklin on as a partner," he said, with a finality in his voice and manner.

"Then we'll file the lawsuit by the end of the week," Lebeau countered, making as if to rise.

Ray was indignant. "You haven't even looked at our proposed settlement!" he sputtered. "Surely you owe that to your client."

Carol Lebeau exchanged a look with Franklin, and she picked it up and, without reading it, put it in her briefcase.

"We'll examine it and get back to you. However, I can tell you without having to peruse it carefully, that if the offer is anything under $3,000,000, further discussions are a waste of time."

That caused quite a buzz. "THREE MILLION DOLLARS!" Ray thundered. "That's ridiculous!!!"

Lebeau stood, and, hurriedly, and after she tapped him lightly on the shoulder, Franklin rose with her. "We'll have to see if a jury doesn't think that your violation of the civil rights laws, and the destruction of the legal career of one of your best lawyers, isn't worth that or even more. That figure doesn't, of course, include court costs, punitive damages, nor my attorney's fee, etc. Judging by your apparent insistence on a prolonged lawsuit, that fee will be quite substantial. Good morning to you all."

Franklin, stunned, followed her from the conference room, leaving behind, he was sure, six distressed lawyers who were about to begin a heated discussion that could go on for hours—perhaps days.

When the two of them were alone in the elevator on their way to the lobby, Franklin finally spoke. "THREE MILLION DOLLARS!" he exclaimed, in an almost a perfect echo of the way Ray had said it.

Lebeau smiled. "That *was* fun, wasn't it? It's going to make them most interested in treating you much more generously when they make their next offer."

"Might a jury really award me that much?"

"Perhaps. I wouldn't have said it if I didn't believe it was a possibility. That would be unethical."

Franklin looked at her in wonder. "You're my hero," he said with quiet admiration. "I'd be terrified of you if I were Factor, Marroni, & Ray!"

She smiled at him. "As well they should be. I'll let you know when I hear from them. My guess is that it'll be soon."

They shook hands and parted, and Franklin drove back to his bed and breakfast in a great mood. Contemplating his tv appearance last night combined with the way Lebeau had just slapped his former partners around, he concluded that things really were looking bright. It was about time.

Promptly at two p.m., Franklin showed up at the Masquerade costume store which Corbin Milk owned, and found the big man already dressed in a cream-colored painter's outfit that was baggy even on Milk's large frame.

"Di Vinci probably wore one of those," Franklin commented, "though his fit better."

"I don't think he painted many houses," Milk replied. "A wall or two and that was it." Indicating some folded clothes on a counter, he added, "I have an identical one for you. See how it fits."

"I'm sure it will be just lovely."

Soon Franklin was suited up identically to Milk, and the two of them walked out to the "Paint the Town" van that was parked just outside the store.

"Do we also have paint cans and brushes and such?" Franklin asked.

"Of course we do. In the back. When we go up to the front door, we should be carrying all of that, plus a large drop cloth, etc. We must look like we're all business, very professional. Not particularly interesting, or worth anyone's attention."

Milk got in the driver's side of the van, and Franklin went around and climbed in next to him. As they started out of the parking lot, Franklin spoke, "Do you mind if I ask you a personal question?"

"Is this more about my checkered past?" Over supper a few nights ago, Corbin Milk had told Franklin some things about his brief career as a C.I.A. employee; he had joined the bureau right out of college and worked there for two years before being let go. It had been quite a story, including fascinating details about how the C.I.A. made major use of homosexual operatives, and the bizarre story of his firing.

"No. I just wanted to ask about the man who answered your cell phone when I last called."

Milk smiled. "George Yancy, my life partner. We've been together for six years. You'll have to meet him."

"Is he a big guy like you?"

"No," Milk replied, laughing. "He's pretty small. I could pick him up and throw him across my shoulder." He thought about that. "In fact, I have."

"What does he do?"

"I.T. director for an insurance company. You'll have to meet him. He is very interested in meeting you."

"Why?"

"Well, he's quite religious, and he wants to see if he can't convince you of the error of your wicked ways."

"Oh. Well, I'm certainly looking forward to that, but he'll have to take a number and wait his turn. You're not religious, are you?"

"Nope. Card-carrying atheist, just like the infamous Whitestones."

"And how do the two of you reconcile this startling difference?"

"We don't talk about it. There were some bad days early on when we made the mistake of thinking it was important that we agree. We finally realized that it wasn't. Things have worked out well since then, though we both have to be careful to avoid remarks that could rekindle the early brouhahas."

"Such as?"

"Hmm. My last misstep, about a year ago, was saying that I thought astrology was even stupider than believing we all get to have a conversation with St. Peter when we die."

"Does George believe in astrology?" Franklin shared Milk's disdain for this nonsense.

"In the end, we agreed not to talk about astrology either."

"I see," Franklin said. Then, mischievously, he added, "By the way, what's your sign?"

"'Slippery When Wet,'" Milk replied immediately.

Franklin laughed. "It doesn't sound like the two of you have much in common."

"That would be wrong. He's very smart, personable, caring, and he loves me a lot. I didn't have the easiest time of it—growing up—and so it's

237

wonderful to come home every night to someone whose main concern is making you happy."

Franklin nodded. "That is important."

"Plus," Milk added, one eyebrow raised, "there's all this hot sex too."

"Also important," Franklin agreed. That made him think about his planned supper this evening with Kelly. He broke out in a big smile which had nothing to do with the banter with Milk.

It'd been a good moment for Jake Richardson when he found Franklin Whitestone's liquor cabinet in the den of the lawyer's house. That had been an hour ago, and now he was in fine shape, having sampled the single malt scotch, the Bombay Gin, plus some kind of fancy beer from the refrigerator. Hell, he decided, looking around the place, he didn't care if Whitestone ever came home. Jake could just move in to stay.

The idea to break in Whitestone's house had come to him last night during his second futile stakeout at Port Columbus. Whitestone, he reasoned, was bound to return to his own house sooner or later, and so, if Jake was patient, Whitestone would come to him. What could be easier? All he had to do was figure a way in, and that too had proved simple.

In the year he'd spent in prison, (for manslaughter when he got drunk and crossed over the center line of a highway and took out two stupid teenagers who hadn't been paying enough attention), he'd learned something about breaking and entering from Lite Light, his cell mate, who was a professional burglar. L.L. (as he was called) had done pretty well for himself by confiscating other people's property, until one sorry night when he encountered a Doberman in the dark, immediately suffering serious injury (he'd lost his right ear). The dog, ear in mouth, was called off by the owner of the house, gun in hand.

L.L. explained to Jake a lot about of the tricks of the burglar's trade, and though Jake had no intention of putting them to use (he was afraid of the dark), he'd paid attention out of boredom. One interesting tip L.L. gave him was that almost all homeowners hide a key on the premises somewhere on the outside of the house, normally near the front door. It was simply a matter of finding it. Sometimes the key was sitting on top of a ledge, or under a flower pot or a paving stone, or—the hiding place of the truly uninspired, L.L. said—under the welcome mat.

In the case of the Franklin Whitestone residence, it had taken Jake almost five minutes to find the outside key (a dangerous length of time in which to search, according to L.L., because the neighbors soon became suspicious of strangers poking around the front porch). Whitestone's key was inside the false bottom of a fake rock, set on the ground, in the corner where the side of the porch met the front of the house. One minute after that, Jake was inside. Two minutes later he took the fancy beer from the refrigerator, and four minutes after that he found the liquor cabinet. Now he was a happy man.

He considered how to pass the time until Whitestone returned. He had all day to lie around if he wanted to—he'd phoned in sick at work. Should he risk turning on the tv? He loved ESPN, and they were always showing reruns of classic sporting events, which Jake loved. Sports, primarily basketball and football, (but really, hell, almost all sports) were his life. He'd played basketball in high school (until he dropped out), and still enjoyed a pick-up game now and then at the court outside the community center a mile from where he lived. Of course, these days he was nowhere as near as good he'd been when he was in his twenties, but even so, at 38, he still wasn't really bad, just maybe slower. If he turned the tv on low he could watch while keeping an ear cocked for any sounds of Whitestone coming home.

Jake looked at his watch. It was almost 2:30 p.m. He decided to see what was on after he fixed himself another drink. Maybe vodka this time.

At that same moment, Kelly was in her office at Ohio State, dealing with a Contracts student who was scared by the words "promissory estoppel." Contracts was a first year course, and such students were great fun to teach. They came in clueless, and hungry for legal knowledge, but also frequently frightened by strange new concepts, and prone to panic. Kelly was fond of saying that teaching first year students was like training a flock of birds: you had to be careful because if you made a sudden movement, they'd all fly. By Christmas break, however, the Contracts students would have settled down and started to become lawyers (which in some ways was a shame—they often lost much of their individuality in the process). This particular student in her office, a doleful young woman with her hair cut very short, had heard the mysterious words, "promissory estoppel," and, not understanding what was meant, had panicked. Kelly spent five minutes calming her down.

"We haven't covered promissory estoppel yet," she explained. "It will be a major topic in the course starting next week. So don't worry if you're confused now. All will become clear, I promise."

"But what does it mean?" the student insisted.

So Kelly gave her a précis, describing the basics of the doctrine, somewhat annoyed that the student was making her teach this concept early. Grateful, the student thanked her and left the office.

Good, Kelly thought. That was her last appointment and now she could get out of here and go home.

And plan for her dinner tonight with Franklin! In every free moment she'd had since yesterday's phone conversation with him, Kelly had thought of little else. The return of Franklin Whitestone as a major player in her life filled her with joy. She'd missed him far more than she had admitted to herself, and, embarrassingly, she turned into a lovesick schoolgirl at the thought of him.

There were still problems of course. He was an atheist and she was . . . well, she wasn't sure anymore what she was. She still believed in God, but she'd become suspicious of religion's claim to provide all the answers (or even to ask the right questions). Kelly would have to work all that out over time, and she was counting on Franklin to give her the space she needed in which to do it.

Then there was the coming Thanksgiving visit of her family. Whenever her thoughts moved to that topic, her heart speeded up and an adrenaline rush made her palms moist. Though they hadn't discussed the matter, surely by now someone in the family would have connected the "Franklin" she was living with for the last few years with the infamous "Franklin Whitestone" of Jimmy Ball Show fame. Over and above the trouble caused by her having yet another relationship with a white man, the fact that her intended was a notorious atheist might lead to her father carefully positioning a coffee table immediately behind Franklin during their very first meeting.

But that confrontation, no matter what the result, was in the future, and Kelly refused to let it dampen her mood. Today she felt wonderful. It was going to be a great night.

Corbin Milk backed the painters' van into the driveway at Franklin's house, and shut off the engine when the vehicle was nearly touching the garage door. The plan was to enter the house, go to the garage, raise the door, back the van into the garage, close the door, and then load up.

Before he climbed out of the driver's seat, Milk said to Franklin, "You get the drop cloth and the ladder from the back, and I'll take the paint cans and brushes. Try and look like our being here is no big deal—a routine paint job. Ready?"

"Ready," Franklin replied, not nervous at all. It was a beautiful sunny day, perfect fall weather, and recently everything had been going splendidly.

In a mock commando's voice, Milk growled, *"Okay, we're going in!"* and opened the door on his side of the van.

Franklin did the same, and they went around to the back of the van, unloaded the assigned painting supplies, and carried them to the front door. While Milk nonchalantly scanned the neighborhood for signs of trouble, Franklin unlocked the door, and they toted their supplies inside. Franklin shut the door behind them, and they grinned at each other. So far, so good.

"All right," Milk said, still the leader of this expedition, "let's get the van into the garage. Which way?"

Franklin pointed toward the kitchen, so they went through there, opened the door to the garage, and both entered, closing the kitchen door behind them. It was a matter of only two minutes before they had opened the garage door, backed the van in, and closed the door again.

"Piece of cake," Franklin said, as they returned to the kitchen.

"What now?" Milk asked.

"Let's start with the den," Franklin said. "That's also my office, and it's where most of my files and records are kept." He started off in that direction, but Milk put out a hand to stop him.

"Let me go first," he said in a low voice. "We need to be careful until we're sure there's no one in the house."

Thinking that Milk was being over dramatic, but also reminding himself that the man was an expert on these sorts of things, Franklin nodded, and, pointing in the direction of the den, he followed the big man out of the kitchen.

As they entered the den, a voice from their right, on the other side of the partially open door, said, "Hold it right there!"—just like a bad cop show—and the man Franklin recognized as Jake Richardson, stepped from behind the door with a pistol in his hand, casually aiming it at them.

His face stoic, Milk said to the man, "Who are you?"

"Fuck that, asshole," Richardson replied. "Who are you?"

"Painters," Milk said. "We're here to paint the den." He gestured, taking in the whole room.

Richardson was confused by that. The den was covered from floor to ceiling with wood paneling. "What's to paint?" he asked, his words slurred. He looked around.

That slight bit of inattention to them, coupled with the obvious fact he was drunk, was enough to spur Milk into action. His hand darted out to grab the gun. It went off.

Milk slammed backwards into Franklin, who collided hard with the door jamb. They both went down. Richardson, furious, fired another round into Milk, who was rolling away, trying to rise. Milk slumped down and, after that, didn't move. A pool of blood spread quickly under him, creating a large dark red circle in all directions. Franklin was alarmed by how fast the

241

pool formed. Was Corbin dead?

Richardson turned the gun on Franklin, who was struggling to get up, partially trapped by Milk's legs. Clearly Richardson's plan was to shoot Franklin next, but suddenly he stopped—turning something over in his befuddled brain, trying to make sense of what he saw.

"Your mustache's coming off!" he said in amazement.

Franklin reached up to feel it. One side of the mustache was fine, but as he touched the other, which was hanging down, barely attached, it fell to the floor. Franklin looked up at Richardson—unable to think, in shock.

"*WHITESTONE!*" Richardson exclaimed, a hideous grin breaking out across his emaciated face. "DAMN THE DEVIL AND HALLELUJAH! GOTCHA! GOTCHA! GOTCHA! YOU SON OF A *BITCH*!" His chortle turned into a belly laugh, as if this were the funniest thing that had ever happened to him. Franklin, still pinned on the floor, didn't move. Couldn't move. Stiff as a figure in a diorama.

Richardson laughed so hard it made him cry, and he wiped away the tears with the hand not holding the gun, making a little "whew" sound as he did. "In disguise, Frankie? Well, it ain't fooled old Jake Richardson one bit, did it? I knowed it was you, you dog-humping bastard. Get up. Slowly." He gestured with the gun.

But Franklin was frozen in his diorama.

"GET UP OR I'LL SHOOT YOU TOO!" Richardson bellowed, and he reached down with his free hand and grabbed Franklin's shoulder, tugging hard.

With effort (he had to yank his leg out from under Milk's), Franklin stood up, shaken, scared. His mind had ceased to work.

"Sit there!" Richardson commanded, pointing the chair at Franklin's desk. Mutely, Franklin sat—collapsed—onto it. His right hand was dripping blood that he knew wasn't his.

Holding the gun at arm's length, pointed at Franklin, Richardson bent down slightly to peer at Milk, who still was not moving. That spectacular pool of blood that was still expanding.

"Dead," he declared, with no particular emotion. "Who the hell was he?"

Franklin didn't reply, and, in fact, couldn't have. There was only a buzz of confusion in his head. Corbin Milk dead? He understood the concept, but had trouble deciding what it meant. Milk dead. Franklin Whitestone dead too? No, that wasn't right. He wasn't even hurt.

"I've been looking for you for a long time, Frankie, boy," Richardson said, almost giddy. "Should have pulled a gun on you and your family last Saturday in that parking lot, but I didn't have it with me. Just had the Bible

242

that you wouldn't take, stupid asshole!" He fanned the gun close to Franklin's face, as if to pistol-whip him, but whether it was only meant to scare him (Franklin jerked backwards, reflexively) or was an alcohol-induced miss, was hard to tell.

However, the movement of his head was an actual physical reaction to the situation, Franklin's first. His initial shock still paralyzed him, but he was beginning to think more rationally about his plight. Okay, okay, Corbin was down, maybe dead, but Franklin couldn't help him now. He needed to concentrate of what he should do, could do. Rush Richardson? No. That was what had gotten Corbin shot, and he quickly vetoed it. Yell? Hadn't the neighbors heard the two shots? Was help on the way?

"Look, Frankie, boy," Richardson cackled, "I've got *duct tape* for you. Bought a ton of it as a hardware store on my way over here." He held up a large grey round object. Franklin had no idea what this meant. "Take it!" Richardson commanded, and, moving slowly, Franklin did so. He looked at the role of tape blankly, as if he'd never seen one before.

"Well, *go on*," his captor demanded, sounding annoyed, "unwind some of it, about a foot. Do it or I'll shoot you dead."

Complying, Franklin pulled at the end of the tape, prying a bit of it loose from the rest of the roll, and, jerked. The roll made a loud "thrrrrupp" noise as the strip separated. Franklin stared down at his hands. About two feet of tape was spread out between them.

That seemed to satisfy Richardson, and he made a circular motion with the gun as he said, "Now wrap the end around your wrist two or three time." Franklin went to tear off the tape he had exposed, but Richardson stopped him. "No, don't tear it off. Leave it connected. Wrap it connected." He made the same circular motion with the pistol.

Awkwardly, Franklin held the end of the tape in one hand and then wound the roll around the other hand twice. This accomplished, he looked up at Richardson.

"Stand up," the latter said, gesturing with the gun.

Franklin stood.

"Give me the roll." Franklin handed it over, and Richardson pulled out a longer section, with the tape making the same protesting noise as it separated. To do this maneuver, Richardson
needed both hands, so he stuck the gun in his armpit, and then pulled out a few feet of tape from the roll. It was a stupid act of carelessness on his part, but he'd had quite a bit to drink. Too late, Franklin realized that he could've rushed Richardson while he was distracted.

Richardson pointed the gun at Franklin again. "Turn completely around," he commanded, and Franklin turned obediently. As he did so, the tape wound around his body until it came back to the tape on his wrist, and Richardson patted it all together, sticking to itself. Then, after some unwieldy maneuvers that involved switching the gun from one hand to the other, Richardson exposed more of the tape and made Franklin turn again, until he was encircled by another loop of duct tape.

This was repeated until much of the large roll encased Franklin's body, arms at his side, pinned from wrists to shoulders. Richardson pulled it tight, and Franklin knew his chance for rushing the man was long gone. Richardson had trussed him up good, and in fact it was overkill—half the amount of tape would've done as good a job.

"Come with me," Richardson said, pushing Franklin ahead of him out the door of the den and towards the kitchen. Once there, Richardson looked into the garage, saw the van positioned so that its rear doors opened next to the steps leading down from the kitchen. He murmured, "Ding dang perfect!"

"Get going," Richardson commanded Franklin, nudging him into the garage with the gun. "Climb in the back of the van."

"How can I? My arms are tied." Franklin was angry now, defiant.

"Do it or I'll just knock you over until you fall in."

Franklin looked unhappily at the van. Clumsily he leaned into the back, and turned onto one side, pushing himself up and in with the one leg that remained on the floor. Then he rolled on his back, which hurt his left hand as it caught under him, and used his right knee against the side of the van to a maneuver his body further inside. Bracing another knee against the door gave him enough leverage to slide his body along the metal floor, finishing closer to the back of the driver's seat.

"Good," Richardson said, quite pleased. He put the gun down on the garage floor, tore off some duct tape, and wrapped it tightly around Franklin's ankles. Then he stepped back to admire his work. Franklin lay supine on the floor of the van, knees bent, staring up at the van ceiling.

"Not going nowhere," Richardson bragged. He walked around and climbed into the front seat of the van, and then tore off a piece of tape that was less than a foot long. Leaning over his seat into the back of the van, he grabbed Franklin's hair and lifted. Franklin started to protest that it hurt, but before he could do more than say "ow," Richardson slapped the tape across his mouth and then sealed it to Franklin's cheeks.

"That'll keep you from attracting attention while we're driving," Richardson explained.

Franklin pulled in a large gulp of air through his nose. It was all right. He could breath.

Richardson slapped another strip of duct tape over Franklin's eyes.

"Lights out, Frankie," he said. Returning to the back of the van, he took a rope the painters had conveniently hung on a bracket secured to the van's interior, and used it to encircle Franklin's legs more securely. He then tied Franklin's body to both sides of the van, making it impossible for him to shift his position.

Well, he didn't kill me, Franklin thought, trying to find hope in all this. Where was he being taken, and why? Would he be traceable? His thoughts returned to Milk. The terrifying pool of blood that had encircled the big man's utterly still body probably meant . . . what? Before Franklin could finish that miserable thought, Richardson spoke as he closed the doors at the back of the van.

"You wait right here, Frankie. Don't go nowhere now." This witticism made Richardson cackle. Franklin was trussed up tighter than a turkey.

"I'll be right back," Richardson promised him, sticking his head into the van on the passenger's side. "Just got to load up all your liquor, and then, you and me, my man, we're gonna *party*!"

CHAPTER SIXTEEN

DUCT TAPE

Neighbors had heard the shots, and two of these called 911. But on their way to the Whitestone house, the police were delayed by a traffic accident on Martin Road and this prevented them from getting there immediately. One cop car, coming the other way, from Riverside Drive, actually passed the "Paint the Town" van going in the opposite direction, but didn't know of the vehicle's involvement in the shooting. Within one minute of this police car's arrival at the scene, four others pulled up with the EMT ambulance just behind.

The garage was standing open, and the police entered that way, cautiously exploring the kitchen, main hallway, and then coming across the den, where they found Corbin Milk lying in a lagoon of his own blood. The police called for the paramedics immediately, and the latter stepped hurriedly through the red mess to examine the victim.

"That guy on the floor—he's a painter," one cop said to another as they watched the medics work. "Look at his uniform. Covered with paint smears."

"Hey," said the young police officer who had been the first on the scene, "I passed a painter's van as I rounded the corner."

A third officer headed for the door, saying, "The neighbors yelled something about a paint van as we got out of our unit."

Very quickly, a manhunt was underway for the same van that a very drunk Jake Richardson was driving down Riverside Drive, not two miles away. If he hadn't turned left into a side street, so he could pull over and be sick by the side of the road, they would have caught him, since by then they had blanketed Riverside Drive with police vehicles. As it happened, Jake perfectly threaded his way through the police search, blind luck rewarding each of his intoxicated choices, until he was southwest of the city, heading for the place that he'd carefully prepared for the upcoming religious conversion of Franklin Whitestone.

At 7:35 p.m. that evening, Kelly noticed that Franklin was running late, and began what her college roommate Cathy had called the "four steps of being stood-up." These four steps were: Realization, Appreciation, Anger, and Dread.

Realization she had just experienced; Franklin was late. That, in and of itself, meant nothing. Franklin was usually a punctual person, but it was easily possible that he was caught up in the travails of life (traffic problems, sudden illness, phone call before when leaving home, etc.) and would be here shortly. She didn't think much about it, and went on doing minor chores preparatory to going out for the evening (making sure Ralph, the dog, had water, closing the drapes, seeing to clean towels in the half bath by the front door), even humming to herself.

The second stage, Appreciation, came at 7:50 p.m. Now it was clear Franklin was seriously late, and she began to worry about him. Why hadn't he called? He would know that she'd be looking at her watch, confused by his silence in the face of his non-arrival. A typical reaction during the appreciation stage was annoyance. Not calling when running late was rude. Franklin had better have a really good excuse. She dialed his cell, but only got his voice message.

At 8 p.m., just ten minutes later, she advanced to stage three: Anger. Did he think so little of her that he would let her stew and worry about his nonappearance? Might he have stupidly forgotten their date in the press of some new exciting adventure in his colorful life? How could he do this to her? By now, Kelly was pacing, going back and forth from the living room to the hallway near the front door, making a little growling noise deep down in her throat.

Dread, the final stage, replaced anger slowly over the course of the next fifteen minutes. Common sense told her that if he were not coming he'd have called. Franklin was nothing at all like the various jerks that had done this to her in the past. During the last few years he had more than demonstrated his love for her, and he'd worked very hard at keeping her happy. Since he neither came nor called, there was a sinister explanation. Was he hurt? Did one of his enemies do something terrible to him?

Who could she call to find out? Kelly couldn't think of anyone who would know more than she did about his whereabouts. Franklin had mentioned a chore he had to perform before coming to pick her up, but she didn't know what it was, or how to find out. Something about his house. Should she go over there?

By 8:30, she began to cry.

She didn't find out what had really happened until she turned on the 11:00 news.

George Yancy, Corbin Milk's partner, proved to be the one who led the police to a correct reconstruction of the crimes of Jake Richardson.

Milk had been rushed to Riverside Hospital and was immediately taken into surgery to see if they could keep him alive in spite of major insults to his pelvis area and lung, resulting in both external and internal bleeding. After delivering Milk to the hospitals' emergency entrance, one of the EMT paramedics remarked to a nurse, that "it didn't look too good for this one."

Under the painter's coveralls, Milk had been wearing his usual jeans, and his driver's license was in his wallet. That led to police officers, one male and one female, knocking on the door of the small house that Milk and George Yancy shared in German Village, in the central part of town. It was just after 5 p.m. when Yancy, a small man with a mustache and a goatee, opened the door to find uniformed officers on the stoop. They introduced themselves and asked if Corbin Milk lived here. Yancy replied that, yes, he did, and they told him they needed to talk. He stood back and motioned for them to enter, led them to the living room, and, with a furrowed brow, asked them what was wrong.

Five minutes later, George Yancy had his head between his knees, gasping in deep, very audible breaths, worried that he was about to pass out. Corbin was at Riverside in surgery, critical condition, shot twice! It couldn't be true. Ah, shit, he thought, of course it could! For years, this was just what he'd feared would happen. Corbin—that idiot!—had a passion for getting into dangerous situations, and it was only been a matter of time until one of them went seriously wrong.

The police wanted to know what Corbin had been doing this afternoon.

After thinking it through for a few seconds, Yancy replied, "He was with Franklin Whitestone."

"WHAT?" both cops said at once. They knew all about the infamous Mr. Whitestone.

Yancy nodded, slowly, trying to remember exactly what Corbin had told him. "They were going to put on disguises—Corbin *lives* for the chance to put on disguises—and visit Whitestone's house to pick up some things he'd left there. I'm pretty sure they borrowed a truck and togs from two of our friends who own a business called 'Paint the Town.' They were going disguised as painters, do you see?"

The policemen nodded. That fit with what they knew about the crime scene and Milk's clothing.

The female officer asked Yancy, "Do you think Whitestone might have shot Mr. Milk?"

Yancy shook his head. "No. They were thick as thieves, good buddies. But Corbin was very worried that someone would someday get to Whitestone and do him major harm. It looks like that's come true." His face clouded over, and he had trouble going on, but then he rallied and asked,

"Have you talked to Whitestone?"

"No. We didn't know until we spoke to you that he was involved. Do you know where he was living away from his home?"

Yancy nodded. He told them about the Rise and Shine bed and breakfast, which, as it happened, was also run by a gay couple he and Corbin knew well.

They thanked him, and left to explore the B & B. George Yancy put on his coat and went out the door, on his way to the first of many visits to Riverside Hospital.

"I'm going to hold the gun on you all the time you're using the john," Jake Richardson said to Franklin Whitestone. "Make a break for it, and you're dead. Understand?"

Franklin, very unhappy, nodded. His wrists were duct taped together in front of him, and he was standing at the entrance to a small bathroom just off the somewhat larger office room into which Richardson had brought him.

"Need to use it now?" Richardson asked him.

Franklin shook his head.

"Okay, then just sit there over there. Nice and comfortable." He indicated a swivel desk chair on rollers, padded back and seat, standing next to a large wooden table. The office was almost barren of furniture. In addition to the chair and table, the only other items in the room were an identical chair pulled up next to a tiny desk. Two light fixtures with bare bulbs in them, one in the office and the other in the bathroom, were attached to the ceilings. That was it. The office—Franklin estimated it at 10 x 20"—had two windows with pull-down Venetian blinds, and, judging by the patina of dust, appeared to have been deserted for some time. He had no idea where they were.

It was now three hours after he'd seen Corbin shot. Franklin he knew he was still in shock, and, to make things worse, this barren room was also late-September chilly, leading him to shiver. It was getting dark outside.

Seeing his discomfort, Richardson told him, "I'm going to bring a space heater in here tomorrow, and for tonight I've got a pillow and some blankets for you. This place is the main office at a construction site we was working on this past August, when the owners ran out of money, and things got shut down. The electricity still works, though that will probably go off at the end of the month. But, what the heck, you and me, we should be out of here long before that, right?"

It was September 20th. What, Franklin asked himself, did "be out of here" mean? Would this madman let him go by then? Kill him? What exactly

249

was the point of all this? Still, though these questions and a dozen others swirled around in his head, Franklin kept his mouth shut. Richardson was as unstable as water, and Franklin didn't want to say anything that might rile him.

"Sit down," Richardson repeated, pointing at the chair, and Franklin did as he was told. Richardson rolled the other chair over and sat, and then tore off two large strips of duct tape from the roll he'd brought with him. He used these to secure Franklin's elbows to the arms of the chair. Then Richardson looked at him silently for a few moments, face to face, staring deep into his captive's eyes.

He spoke softly. "Franklin, my friend—and you *are* my friend, though I know I'll have to prove that to you—I really don't want you to worry too much about all this. Nothing, and I mean, *nothing*, is gonna happen to you. I brung you here for your own good, and for no other purpose than to do the Lord's work, so just relax and get used to our temporary home." He looked around the room, and then continued. "Now, buddy, here's my plan. I'm gonna leave you here while I get rid of that van, and then go get my truck, which I left near where you live. But I don't want you wandering off while I'm away, so I'm gonna make sure you can't do that. That means more duct tape for you and also some rope, I guess."

He stood and wound the duct tape roll around Franklin's chest and the back of the chair, once again overdoing it. Then he took a rope of about eight feet in length, and tied it to the base of the chair, securing the chair to the large table so that it couldn't roll anywhere.

Finally, Richardson stepped back to admire his work, and then nodded slowly.

"Now pay attention," he commanded. "We ain't close to no people way out here, and probably no one's gonna come by accidental like, just looking around this abandoned site. Why should they? So it likely wouldn't do you any good to start hollering while I'm gone getting my truck. But, I'll be a couple of hours, I figure, and I don't want to risk it, so I'm gonna have to gag you again." And with this, he tore off another small strip of duct tape, and put it over Franklin's mouth. Just minutes before, Richardson had ripped off the first strip when he brought Franklin into this office, and Franklin's mouth was already red and sore from that. The new strip was even more uncomfortable than the first because it was larger, causing more of his face to itch and sweat.

"You be a good boy, and I'll be back soon. Then we're gonna talk, you and me. Gonna talk a lot over the next day or two." He looked around the room, checking to see if he'd forgotten anything, and then he patted Franklin lightly on the head, as if he were a small child in need of reassurance. He

250

went out the office door.

Once Franklin heard the van pull away, he began thrusting back and forth, testing his bonds to see if escape was possible. At most he could make the chair roll a few inches, but he accomplished nothing. Three minutes of this futile thrashing had only the effect of wearing him out, so he quit rocking and just sat there, dripping with sweat.

Franklin came to the unhappy conclusion that Richardson was right—fuck!—he wasn't going anywhere. He was trapped in this stupid chair, strapped down by yards and yards of duct tape covering much of his body, including his mouth.

A line from MacBeth came to him. "They have tied me to a stake; I cannot fly, but, bear-like, I must fight the course."

But he didn't feel like MacBeth. He felt like a mummy.

The two police officers who had visited George Yancy were soon inside Franklin's room at the B & B. He was not there, nor was there anything that would hint at where he'd been taken by his abductor. They called this in to headquarters, and the information was relayed to Lieutenant Leon Burnside, the man in charge of an investigation that was already a cause célèbre—which, in French, actually means a famous legal case. It was certainly all of that. At Columbus Police Headquarters a large number of personnel were working on it with studied attention. But the news that Franklin Whitestone was somehow involved in a shooting at his own home reached the local media within minutes after the police learned of it, and from there it went nationwide instantly.

Lt. Burnside was a man in his early 50s, with craggy wide face and black hair fast going grey that was styled in a buzz cut that somehow looked good on him. Everything about the lieutenant was oversized: his build, his gut, his raucous laugh when amused, and the dramatic touches he brought to whatever he did. Burnside was from South Carolina, and the smooth lilt of that state still rolled around his mouth when he spoke. He was popular both with those who took his orders and those who gave orders to him.

Now Burnside was directing traffic in the central conference room, coordinating the search for Whitestone and the man who had shot Milk. Burnside knew that the first hours of an investigation were the most important, and offered the best chance for producing results before the trail went cold and phones stopped ringing. He'd ordered officers to knock on doors in the Whitestone neighborhood, then put out an APB for the painters' van, contacted all of the Whitestone's relatives, etc. From long experience, the lieutenant also knew how useful the media could be in helping the police track down a perp on the run, so he'd called for a meeting with the press, and they were assembled in the police headquarters auditorium, which is where he headed now.

As Burnside entered the room it was only half full of reporters and their crews, but was filling rapidly as others came pouring through the doors. His appearance caused the buzz to increase by a factor of four. He strode straight to the forest of microphones, and faced the cameras, naturally at ease in the center of all this attention.

"Ladies and gentlemen," he began in his big voice, silencing them all instantly, "the rumor you've heard is true. Franklin Whitestone was abducted this afternoon from his house on the northwest side of the city by a person or persons unknown, and for reasons we have yet to ascertain. Mr. Whitestone had gone to his house with a friend named Corbin Milk, both of them disguised as painters so that they could get into the house without attracting undue attention. The purpose of the visit was to retrieve various items that Mr. Whitestone had left behind when all the controversy about his views forced him into hiding.

"Apparently when Whitestone and Milk entered the house, the perpetrator or perpetrators were already there. Mr. Milk was shot in the chest and pelvis, and is currently in critical condition at Riverside Hospital. The perpetrators took Mr. Whitestone with them when they escaped in the painters' truck that had been parked in the garage by Whitestone and Milk when they first arrived.

"So far we have no idea why Mr. Whitestone was taken."

"But we have a pretty good guess!" some wag yelled from the crowd, and Burnside frowned in the direction from which this had come.

"If you have any information that would help us, I certainly want to hear it immediately. One man has been shot and another is missing. Tell us what you know." He paused dramatically and stood waiting for a reply. There was only silence.

Finally he resumed. "I thought as much. No more joking. I need your help. Please spread this story as fast as you can and ask anyone with information to contact us immediately and tell us what they know. I'll take questions."

They all shouted at once, but he pointed at one reporter after another and answered their questions. "Is Milk dying?" "Was Whitestone shot?" "Were any messages left at the crime scene?" "Has the painters' van been sighted?" "Where did Whitestone get the van?" and so on. For most of these he had no helpful replies.

An officer walked up behind the lieutenant and tugged as his arm. Burnside turned, an eyebrow raised. "What?" he asked.

"We think we know who kidnapped Whitestone," the officer said.

Burnside ended the press conference immediately with a peremptory wave at the reporters, and followed the officer from the room.

Catherine Whitestone had just taken one bite of the pizza she'd ordered, when she learned that her son had been kidnapped and was missing. She was sitting in front of the tv, which she had just turned on, planning to watch the latest episode of "Survivor," and was beginning to chew when the program was interrupted with the breaking news.

For a full minute she sat there in shock. Ever since the abduction of Todd and Mary, she'd been worried that something like this (or worse) would happen. On Sunday night she'd learned, to her annoyance, that Franklin hadn't bothered to ten her he'd been shot at! She had to learn that from the Jimmy Ball Show! Of course, she knew why he hadn't told her—it's not the sort of thing you worry a mother with, but still. Catherine wasn't an ordinary mother, and who knows what she might've thought up to protect him better? Wasn't he supposed to be under the umbrella of some expert service that would keep him from harm? That Harker man had mentioned something like that.

On hearing of her son's abduction, Catherine's thoughts flashed back to the bizarre visit she'd had from the man named Jake Richardson, and immediately she knew it was important that she alert the police to the possibility that he was the very man they were seeking. She was reaching for the phone to call the authorities, when it rang. It was her daughter Martha.

"Mom, have you heard the news?" Martha asked, both cautious and concerned.

"No time to talk now, honey," Catherine replied. "I think I know who has Franklin, and I need to call the police. I'll call you back." She hung up and quickly dialed police headquarters.

Identifying herself as Franklin's mother got her their attention, and she was soon relating her story of the Richardson visit. She explained to the police officer that Richardson was the operator of the crane that had pulled down the wall of Ohio Stadium, freeing her son and the others trapped in there, and that he'd twice given tv interviews to Harold Wang of Channel 7. Those videos, she speculated, should still be around somewhere, and they would give the police a really good idea of what Richardson looked and sounded like.

"Of course," Catherine admitted, "I don't know that he's guilty of anything, and, if not, I owe him an apology. But my instincts tell me that he's the one who has Franklin."

253

The officer said that they would check out this lead right away. As he was hanging up, he asked one final question.

"You wouldn't know how to reach Richardson, would you, Ma'am?"

"Yes, I do," she replied, remembering. "He gave me his address and phone number when he was here. I wrote it down in the notebook I keep next to the phone. Are you ready to copy?"

After she'd recited this information to the officer, she hung the phone, but then quickly dialed Martha's number and related what had just happened. They talked for half an hour.

Catherine's pizza never did get eaten. About midnight she put it down the disposal.

After first wiping the "Paint the Town" van as best he could to get rid of fingerprints, Jake drove it to one of the city's dumps and left it. It later turned out that he'd done a bad job of concealing his identify, missing a large number of telltale prints. These would be introduced at his subsequent trial to prove he'd been in the van.

Jake then walked a half mile to a city bus stop. Not long thereafter a bus pulled up and took him to the center of Columbus, where he caught the express bus to Dublin. He'd left his truck two blocks away from Whitestone's house, and within the hour he was in it and driving back to his own house, where he arrived just before 8:00 p.m. Jake was pleased to find a package on his front stoop, which, on being opened, proved to contain the shackles and restraints he'd ordered off the internet. Hot damn! he thought. This would make handling Whitestone a walk in the park.

Jake was worn out, and he briefly considered staying home for the night, and dealing with Whitestone in the morning. He could kick back, relax, watch "Survivor," which was just coming on as he considered his options.

But then he remembered the large stash of Whitestone's fine liquor that was now sitting in a cardboard box in a corner of the office at the abandoned construction site, and decided he'd best spend the night with Whitestone. And the liquor.

So he filled the truck with more blankets, pillows, the promised space heater, a portable tv, and some eating utensils. Canned goods that had been sitting in his kitchen cupboard for some time were added to the mix, as well as an opener and a portable cooking stove he'd used only once before, on a camping trip six years ago.

Jake looked around, knowing he wasn't remembering all the things he'd later want, but too tired to think about it anymore. He needed to get out of here—have a drink or two, get some sleep. He'd come back tomorrow and pick up whatever else he'd forgotten.

The truck's radio came on as soon as Jake started the vehicle's engine, and it was playing golden oldie rock music as he drove away. But before he reached the end of his street, the program was interrupted by a special bulletin talking about the disappearance today of Franklin Whitestone. Jake paid careful attention, particularly when the announcer astounded him by saying, "Police believe they have a lead as to the identity of Franklin Whitestone's abductor, and hope to be able to name him shortly."

Huh? That didn't sound right. How could they know about Jake so quickly? He hadn't left a trail they could trace in just a couple of hours. Or had he? Okay, there were probably fingerprints in the Whitestone house, but it would surely take days to match them with the ones on file somewhere with Jake's name attached to them. It just *couldn't* be him they were talking about on the radio. Couldn't be. Must be a mistake pointing to somebody else. Good.

He had just reaching this reassuring conclusion as he turned onto 5th Avenue and headed towards the freeway when he was passed by two squad cars, their lights flashing and sirens blaring, heading back in the direction he'd just come.

"Holy fuck!" he said aloud. The cops were sure a lot better at this than he'd thought they'd be.

Norman Hapwell, the head of security for SteadyLife, the protection service used by the Martin Turnbill agency to keep its clients safe from unwanted attention, called Mary Whitestone on Monday afternoon with the news that Franklin Whitestone had been abducted from his home, and that Corbin Milk had been critically wounded in the same incident.

The news shocked her to the point where she couldn't respond at all, but sat staring with the phone held up to her ear. She and Todd had just met with Hapwell the day before, and been very impressed by the operation he ran and the advice he had given them on how to survive as celebrities in a world filled with stalkers and paparazzi. He'd laid it all out and made it sound so simple. Now he was telling her that her ex-husband had been snatched by the same sort of crazy zealot he was supposed to be keeping at bay.

"Mrs. Whitestone?" Hapwell queried when she didn't respond right away to his news.

Mutely, Mary handed the phone to Todd, who was sitting on the couch next to her, worried by her odd expression.

"What is it?" Todd said into the phone. Hapwell repeated the same

255

bad news. Todd, normally the steadiest of individuals, was instantly furious. "I thought your people were protecting him! Protecting us all! And now your so-called protection leaks like sieve—your client has been *kidnapped*!"

In a somewhat huffy tone of voice, Hapwell replied, "Mr. Whitestone declined our protection until this coming Wednesday, when he was to fly out to California and join you in our protected community. His safety had not yet become our concern when this unfortunate incident occurred. We're very sorry for what happened, but it is wrong to put any of the blame on SteadyLife."

"Probably so," Todd agreed, angry in spite of this explanation, "but you're all I have to yell at, so *take it!*" He slammed down the phone.

Mary looked at him glassy-eyed. She still didn't speak.

Todd did. "He said they weren't due to start protecting Dad until he got out here on Wednesday. *Shit!*"

Now Todd looked at her closely and became worried by her lack of reaction. "Mom?" he said. "Talk to me."

She turned her gaze to him. "What should we do, Toddie?" she asked, in a reversal of their normal roles.

He didn't reply right away, thinking it over, both impressed and disturbed that she had asked him. Finally, he said, "I don't know, Mom. I can argue both sides of it. You and I understand what it's like to be in the clutches of these fanatics, and we certainly don't want to leave the safe haven we've found and risk that again. On the other hand, it seems wrong to just sit here and do nothing. Isn't there some middle ground?"

"Middle ground?" she mused. "I don't know how there could be."

"If we went back, even for a little while, until Dad's situation is clearer, what steps could we take to make sure we'd be okay?

Mary was returning to life. "Well, no one knows where we are, and no one saw us in the disguises Mr. Milk suggested we use. We could probably fly back to Columbus undetected, particularly if we took other precautions."

"Such as?"

"Say, not only dyeing our hair and wearing contacts that change our eye color, but also travelling as if we weren't together—two people who just happened to be on the same flight. We don't sit with each other, or even talk. We wear clothes that don't make us look like Mary and Todd Whitestone."

"Hmm. What would we do when we get there? Where would we stay?"

Pause while they thought about that.

Todd spoke first. "I have an idea."

"Yes?"

"Grandma Whitestone."

Mary rolled her eyes. "Oh, Todd, I don't know. That woman and I have such a history, and it hasn't always been pie and ice cream. We haven't spoken for years, and we were never great friends, even in the early days."

"Then you suggest something, Mom. Staying in a Columbus hotel seems like a really bad idea."

Another pause.

"The thing is," Mary said, "I just can't sit her in this safe environment while your father is in the clutches of his own 'Nan and Dan.' I think we *have* to go back until this is resolved, and then, when he's rescued, the three of us could get out of there and return here."

"I agree."

"Give me the phone," his mother said to Todd, sighing. "I'll call Catherine."

Miserable—even more miserable than he'd been a week ago when he'd been trapped in the rubble of Ohio Stadium—Franklin Whitestone sat for hours duct taped to this stupid chair and passed from one extreme emotion to another. He was terrified. He was angry. He felt sick. He was cold. He was bored. He was concerned for poor Corbin Milk. He needed to take a piss. His back hurt from sitting in the same position. He wondered where the police were, and on and on. Having cycled through these stages, he'd pause, and then, after a moment, cycle through them again, resolving nothing. Miserable.

Most of all, when taking a break from the above anxieties, he would worry about Richardson and what was likely to happen when the madman returned.

It now seemed clear that Richardson didn't plan on harming Franklin—at least not right away. The man had said he wanted to convert Franklin, turn him into a God-fearing Christian, and that was the same goal he'd announced on Saturday morning when he tapped on the rental car window in the Gallipois parking lot. He must mean it.

So what should Franklin do about that? What would keep him alive until the police finally got here?

He thought about Mary's clever work in fooling her captors. It had been her finest moment, and he was proud of her. Could he do something similar? If she were sitting her strapped to this chair, what would she be thinking, planning?

Franklin's gut reaction to Richardson's forced religious conversion was to tell the man to drop dead, but that wasn't wise. No. Smarter to keep him calm, happy with Franklin, perhaps even—here again Mary was his model—trusting him.

The way to do that was obvious: pretend to give in, change his mind, embrace Richardson's idea of God. If the jerk really believed it was happening, he'd lap it up like honey. Hell, they might end up in church together.

Yes, that was the smart thing, Franklin concluded. But how to do it? He couldn't just announce that Richardson had won, claim to have seen the light, and then have the man unwind him from the duct tape, yelling "Hallelujah!" Richardson was not bright, but neither was he that dim. It had to seem true.

So Franklin sat and thought hard about how to stage his incipient abandonment of atheism and his surrender to Richardson's proselytizing.

He heard a car pull up outside and a car door slam. He took a deep breath.

Show time.

CHAPTER SEVENTEEN

THE CONVERSION OF FRANKLIN WHITESTONE

When Jake Richardson returned to the construction site office Monday evening, Whitestone was still sitting where he'd left him, and Jake was pleased with his security arrangements. They would be even better once Jake replaced the duct tape with shackles. Conversation would be less forced, more like friends talking.

When Jake peeled off Whitestone's gag, the man winced in pain but surprised him by saying nothing. When Jake asked how he was doing, Whitestone merely said he needed to go to the bathroom. Jake nodded and told him to hold his horses, they would get to that in a minute.   On his way to the construction site, Jake had stopped at a Krogers three miles away and bought a huge store of food and other things they'd need. The police were looking for him so he figured that he wouldn't dare risk such a trip after tonight. But this evening no one had paid any attention to him at the grocery store, and, since it was far from the place he'd stashed Whitestone, he didn't care if someone remembered his presence, or even if he showed up on a security camera. Fuck 'em.

After carrying in the things from the truck, Jake took time practicing locking and unlocking the new shackles, making sure he knew how they worked. Wouldn't want them coming off and have Whitestone making a run for it. Then Jake untied the rope holding the chair in place, unwrapped the tape from around Whitestone's legs, and put the ankle shackles (having a foot and a half of chain from one to the other) in their place.

This accomplished, Jake began unwrapping the tape from around Whitestone's body, and as he did so he told his captive what was going to happen next.

"When I get this tape off," he explained, "you'll be free to stand up. I'll have the gun on you, so don't try anything funny. You know I'll use it." Whitestone reluctantly nodded. "Good," Jake said. "You'll be able to walk in those things as long as you don't take big steps, so go use the bathroom. Don't close the door. When you come out, sit back down, put your hands out, and I'll put these things on you." He held up the wrist restraints, which were similar to the others, but smaller. "Try anything and I'll make you regret it. Is that clear enough?" Whitestone nodded again.

The restroom visit went off without complications, and Whitestone returned to the chair. Jake put the wrist restraints on him, with this hands pinned in front of his body (Jake figured it would be too hard on poor

Whitestone to make him sleep with his hands behind his back). He fastened the long chain that ran between the leg and wrist restraints and locked it into place on each. Whitestone couldn't remove it without the key.

Next, Jake made up two adjoining beds on the floor, using the blankets, sheets, and pillows he'd brought from home, and then had Whitestone lie down on one of them.

"I've been thinking about it," he told his captive. "Don't want you wandering off during the night, so we're gonna use ropes to make sure that won't happen. One will be tied around your waist and knotted in the back, and then I'll tie the other end to the table. I'm gonna sleep on top of the rope that goes from you to the table. That way if you start trying to move around it'll wake me up. I figure you'd have a peck of trouble getting the rope loose if it was tied to your backside. And if you try to get up to reach the rope at the table end, that'll wake me up too, see? Clever, right?"

Whitestone said nothing, but he appeared to Jake to be impressed with these plans. So, very carefully, watching Whitestone for any sudden movements, Jake tied the rope as he'd said. He told Whitestone to lie down, but decided to wait awhile before he himself lay down on the similar bedding he had placed between Whitestone and the table to which he attached Whitestone's rope. Jake needed to relax some. It'd been one bitch of a day.

"Want something to drink?" Jake asked Whitestone, as he rummaged around in the large cardboard box filled to the top with the liquor he had taken from Whitestone's den.

"No," Whitestone said. The man wasn't saying much.

"Suit yourself, Frankie." Jake opted for the vodka. There weren't no ice and vodka went down the best without trimmings.

Next Jake plugged in the small tv he'd brought along, and played with its antenna until he brought in a pretty good picture on Channel 7. And—by golly—there was Harold Wang hisself—Jake's old friend from the stadium disaster—talking about the latest developments in the "ongoing saga of Franklin Whitestone."

"Saga," Jake repeated, trying out the word. He liked that, being part of a saga. Didn't they write songs about folks in a saga? That was worth thinking about. The Ballad of Jake Richardson.

"Police are now hunting for John Harold Richardson," Wang was saying on the tv, "a construction worker who was instrumental in pulling down the wall that freed people trapped inside Ohio Stadium on September 11th. Mr. Richardson told a number of witnesses that he was very anxious to talk to Franklin Whitestone, apparently wanting to discuss Whitestone's unorthodox views on religion. The following tape is from two interviews this reporter had with Richardson during the ordeal at the stadium."

The videos, cut up some, were played, one after another, and Jake, vodka in hand, his feet up on the table, was pleased to watch them again. In both he mentioned his devotion to God, and, as he heard himself say this, he nodded happily. Actually, he was very impressed that the police and the press had figured it all out so fast. Amazing—ding, dang, amazing! How'd they do that?

"No one can say whether Mr. Richardson is involved in the Whitestone disappearance or not, but police do think it suspicious that he seems to have abandoned his own home, and cannot be found. There is a massive search underway for both Richardson and Whitestone."

"What you think, Frankie?" Richardson chortled. "We're famous, you and me. Famous. 'Richardson and Whitestone.' It's like . . . like . . . Lewis and Clark, or something."

Whitestone didn't reply, but to hell with that sourpuss, Jake thought. He took another drink out of his tumbler filled with vodka, and leaned down close to the man on the floor.

"Bet you didn't know my middle name was 'Harold,'" he said with a grin.

It was after midnight when Lt. Leon Burnside let himself in the front door of his home in Italian Village, a little community not far from The Ohio State University. He was surprised to find that his wife Dolly was still up. That was very odd. She was a teacher at a nearby elementary school, and she had to rise early Tuesday morning.

"Waiting for me?" he asked, as he entered the living room. She rose from her chair in front of the television. On the screen, David Letterman was introducing his next guest.

"Yes," she replied, giving her husband a kiss. "Didn't seem sleepy, and thought you might want some company when you came home. Want some decaf?"

He gave her a guilty smile. "How about some hot chocolate instead?" he asked.

"Now, Burns," she replied, using her nickname for him. "You know it'll be bad for you. Chocolate has caffeine, and you need your sleep. Not only that, the doctor says you've got to watch your weight, and no kidding."

Burnside wrapped his arms around her. Her build matched his own: bigger than life, a lot to hold on to when things got exciting in bed, a great woman. "Now, my sweet, sweet darling," he said, chiding her, "you know one little hot chocolate won't hurt me, and I truly need something to make me relax. Been a long, complicated day. Man needs a treat after a long, complicated day. It's not as if I'm going to do anything really bad, like knock back a whole bag of potato chips, or the like. I promise you, just one cup of hot chocolate, and then off to bed. You know me, once I hit the pillow—like a bear in hibernation, caffeine be damned."

And, as he knew she would—this was a familiar routine, after all—she gave in and he followed her into the kitchen.

As she mixed the chocolate with milk and put the mug in the microwave, Dolly asked him, "Is this Richardson truly the man who kidnapped Franklin Whitestone?"

"No doubt about it. We've got any number of witnesses who say that for the last week Richardson talked about little else than turning Whitestone away from his wicked path and setting him right with God. We heard it from Whitestone's mother, Richardson's co-workers, and even a woman Richardson had been dating lately. All said the same thing."

"Whitestone's mother knew Richardson?"

"He visited her home last week, asking where Whitestone could be found. Even gave her his address and phone number." He smiled. "That turned out to be useful."

"Are you going to catch this Richardson?"

He nodded. "Oh, yes, my darling, we are. We almost had him tonight at his home—missed him by minutes. Hell, we almost got him at the scene of the crime. The man has the luck of the devil on his side. No idea how he got away.

"But his picture is all over television and the internet now, and everybody in creation is on the lookout for him. A reward's been offered, and whoever turns him in will be famous. History books will be written about this whole mess. Plus we know what this man's truck looks like and have its plate number. All the police and sheriff cars in the State of Ohio are keeping a careful watch for it. He's toast."

"And here's your hot chocolate," his wife said, taking it from the microwave and putting it on the counter.

"You are so kind, my darling darling."

Her eyes twinkled as she said to him, "You'll be in those history books too, Burns. Maybe you should have a reward of your own. Would you like me to put just a little brandy in your mug to help you sleep?" It was a familiar question at this stage of the ritual, and he'd been waiting for it.

"You know I would, Dolly, my love. Thank you so very much for the suggestion."

At 10:30 p.m. that same evening, Kelly phoned Franklin's sister

Martha, and, when Martha answered the phone, she identified herself and said, "I'm sorry to call you so late, but I need another dose of advice. Do you have time for me?"

"Of course," Martha replied. "I won't be going to bed anytime soon. I just finished serial conversations with my mother, my brother, Jefferson, and my older sister. None of us has any idea what to do, but let's see if I can at least help you in some way. What is it??"

Kelly thought about how to put it. Finally, she just blurted it out. "Should I cancel my classes for tomorrow?"

Martha considered it. "I need more information. How are you holding up?"

For an answer, Kelly burst into tears, and it took her awhile to regain enough control to be able to talk, with Martha murmuring things like "calm down, dear" until Kelly did so.

"Forgive me, Martha. Franklin and I were supposed to have dinner tonight, and I was looking forward to it like it was my first date ever. Then when I learned what had happened, I just fell apart. It's so unfair, so *cruel* that Franklin is in the hands of another maniac!" She stifled sob. "He could be dead by now! So—to answer your question—I'm a pathetic mess, and I'm dumping it all on you. Help!"

"None of us is doing particularly well with this. Well—maybe Mom. She's always good in a crisis. Level headed, thinking fast. Todd and Mary are flying back from California to stay with her."

"Really?"

"Yes, and you mustn't spread that around.. I'm annoyed with myself—I really shouldn't have told you. Todd and Mary could still be targets too and no one must know where they are."

"I promise to keep it to myself."

"Back to your question about your classes. Have you ever taught while suffering from deep personal distress?"

Kelly gave a little snort of amusement. "Oh, yes! All this past week. Last Monday was almost as bad as I'm afraid tomorrow will be. I was a wreck."

"Did your classes suffer as a result?"

Kelly didn't even pause before answering that one. "No," she said. "I told myself the students had paid their money and expected to be taught law no matter what my personal life was like. In a way, being able to escape to the classroom was cathartic."

"If you cancel classes will you have to make them up?"

"Yes."

"Will that cause a lot of scheduling problems? Decreased attendance?

Less understanding of the material."

"Okay, okay. You've convinced me. No cancellations. I knew it would help to call you. Thanks, Martha. I owe you a lot."

"You're welcome. Are you praying for Franklin?"

Kelly paused before answering. "Yes. Would he mind, do you think?"

"Prayer never hurt anyone," Martha replied.

"Do you think there's any chance he is praying himself?"

Martha laughed. "No I don't," she said.

But she was wrong.

In the middle of the night, Franklin wasn't sleeping. He was trying to remember the Lord's Prayer so he could use it to convince Richardson that he was serious about wanting to have a religious experience. He mumbled the words to himself, but couldn't seem to get it right. He kept hanging up at "give us this day our daily bread," not sure what followed. Another difficulty was that during his brief flirtation with religion, he'd learned the Catholic version, and he knew that it varied in some key ways from whatever it was the Protestants said. They even added a new sentence at the end. How did that go? He searched his memory, but came up blank.

Enough moonlight came through the window that Franklin could make out much of the room. Richardson, asleep on the floor next to Franklin, was snoring with the enthusiasm of a lumberjack. The man was still lying squarely on top of the rope that went from the back of Franklin's belt to the table. Franklin had tried to reach the knot behind him, but his manacled hands wouldn't allow that—the chain between his wrists was too short. And with Richardson in the way, there was no way to get to the table without waking him.

Or was there? How soundly was the asshole sleeping? Richardson had drunk an incredible amount of liquor. Perhaps he was out for the count, and, if Franklin took it slow, his unconscious body could be rolled off the rope.

Franklin decided to try. He scooted over next to Richardson, and gently shook him. If he woke up, Franklin would simply say that the man's snoring was keeping him awake. It was even true.

Nothing. Franklin got on his hands and knees and moved lower on his bedding, the rope tugging at Richardson's inert body. It wasn't going to slide from under the man without some major movement to give it both slack and room. Franklin pushed Richardson over onto his side, and moved the rope down a little, then rolled him back. He clambered over the man and rolled him the other way, freeing the rope for a descent of a few more inches. This might work. Franklin's heart rate increased to the point where he worried Richardson might hear it and wake up.

He was just scooting back over to the side he had started on, getting ready for round two, when Richardson's elbow caught him squarely in the chest, knocking the wind from him. He fell back heavily onto his own bedding.

"*What the fuck are you doing, Whitestone?*" Richardson's bleary voice demanded.

"Trying to wake you or turn you over," Franklin replied. Your snoring is driving me nuts. I can't sleep."

Richardson turned to face him. "*Stay in your bed*," he said, meaning it. "I can make it even harder for you if I want to. You wouldn't like that."

Franklin repressed the fury he felt. "What should I do about your snoring?" he asked frustrated on many levels. "It sounds like a plane taking off."

"Learn to like it," Richardson snarled, and lay back down, pulling the rope up under his waist once again. He resumed snoring so quickly that Franklin wondered if he were kidding.

Richardson was still snoring when Franklin, who had finally fallen asleep only three hours ago, awoke on Tuesday morning. The space heater had warmed up the room nicely, and he wasn't cold, but he was stiff from sleeping on the floor, protected from its hardness by only a thin comforter. Bright sunshine filled the barren office. He sat up and looked around. A large pile of items that Richardson had brought in from the truck stood against the wall next to the only outside door. Might it contain something that could help Franklin get out of this mess?

In the new hope that came with morning, and the possibility that Richardson would stay asleep long enough for him to accomplish something, Franklin again considered escape. It occurred to him that if he could get out of his pants he might be able to slip off the rope that circled his waist. But then he thought better of this. The chain that went from the wrist restraints to the ones on his ankles would trap his pants between them.

Could he throw his arms over Richardson's neck, and strangle him with the wrist chain? The problem was that even if Richardson were to cooperate and hold still while Franklin garrotted him, the chain was too short to be a serious threat to Richardson's air supply. Reluctantly, Franklin discarded the idea. Have to think of something else. The possibility of using the chains themselves as a weapon was worth some thought. It intrigued him, and he turned the idea over in his mind. How about using his leg chains to strangle Richardson?

The man stopped snoring, turned over, then, after a pause, turned back. He yawned.

"Morning, Frankie," he said, pleasant and pleased. "Sleep well?"

Franklin decided it was time to cooperate fully. Go along, get along, get out alive.

"Not bad. You really do snore."

Richardson laughed. "Just what my ex-wife was always bitching about. A giant reason for the divorce. Can't do nothing about it. Sorry. Need to go to the john?"

Franklin said he did, and Richardson slowly rose, untied his captive, walked him to the bathroom, and then watched while Franklin took care of his needs. This done, Richardson asked if Franklin was hungry, and on getting an affirmative, they feasted on four Pop Tarts that Richardson warmed up in the toaster he'd brought from home. They ate sitting on either side of the big table.

"May I brush my teeth?" Franklin asked when they were done with this wholesome and too filling breakfast.

"No toothbrush. Didn't even think to bring my own from home neither." Looking at Richardson's yellow and badly stained teeth, Franklin wondered whether the man actually owned a toothbrush.

"Could you please get me one, and some toothpaste when you next make a run to the store?"

Richardson regarded him carefully. For some reason that Franklin didn't understand, he seemed to find the question suspicious.

Finally, Richardson just said, "Maybe." He rose from the table, went over to the pile of objects next to the door, rummaged around, and returned with a small black Bible. He sat and opened it.

"All right, Mr. Franklin Whitestone," he said in a half-joking, half-serious manner. "It's time to start talking about religion. I know you say you don't believe in no God, and I can't tell you how much that saddens me, causes me pain. And I'm not the only one. Thousands—hell, probably millions—of people became sad with me when they heard you say such nonsense."

Franklin lowered his head and looked contrite. "I didn't mean to make people feel bad. It's just what I think. I'm sorry if I caused offense. That was never my intention."

Richardson held up the Bible. "Did you ever read this book."

As a matter of fact, the answer was yes. In his early college years, Franklin had read it from cover to cover, being amazed at the things it said, and the myriad of subjects it covered. The Bible was obviously an ancient book, much treasured through millennia, the work of many hands. It mixed wisdom with fascinating tales, with pointless stories, with passages that sounded like a true historical record, with tedious recitations of irrelevancies, with great insights into the human condition, and with fantastical fables that only the unquestioning could believe. But saying all this to Richardson would be a mistake.

"Never have," he confessed.

Richardson brightened considerably at hearing this. "Oh, Frankie," he said with enthusiasm. "You have been missing the greatest story ever told, and the greatest book ever written!"

"Have you read all if it?" He wasn't sure the man could read anything.

"Every word. Memorized lots of it too."

"I've heard it has some beautiful passages."

"It does! It does!"

"Read me your favorite."

"Okay." Richardson thumbed through the well worn book and then opened it at the spot he had been looking for, his eyes shining with excitement.

"It's called the Sermon on the Mount. Jesus gathered his people around him on this very high mountain and told them all the important things he knew." He began to read the Beatitudes, many of which Franklin too could recite. Franklin was impressed that Richardson thought the Sermon on the Mount was the most beautiful part of the Bible, because he agreed with that assessment. It contained the core of Christian philosophy, and if Christians would only follow it to the letter, things would go a lot smoother for the human race.

After the Beatitudes, Richardson paused to say, "Isn't that gorgeous?" Franklin nodded, smiling. Encouraged, his teacher/captor went on reading the other famous lines: "salt of the earth," "resist not evil," "turn the other cheek," "light of the world," and "judge not, lest ye be judged." The Golden Rule was in there too, and finally the Lord's Prayer. Franklin was pleased to hear Richardson read it. This refreshed his faulty memory of its phraseology. It occurred to him that the last time he'd heard it said aloud was deep in the rubble of Ohio Stadium.

Finally, Richardson was done, and he looked up at Franklin expectantly, his eyes brimming with tears.

"Ain't that grand?" he asked in triumph.

"It is one of the most beautiful things I've ever heard," Franklin said with sincerity. It was true.

"Can't you feel Jesus's words just pulling at you? Saying you should come to him?"

Franklin paused. He shouldn't make this look too easy.

"But isn't the Bible also filled with things that are not beautiful? A flooding of the world that killed babies along with adults, a destruction of a city because God didn't understand homosexuality, an annihilation of innocent tribes whose only fault was annoying some passing Hebrews?"

Richardson shook his head in sorrow. "Oh, Frankie, Frankie. That's a piss-poor way of looking at it! My old pastor, the Reverend Stevens, used to say that one of the greatest sins is for a mere man like you or me to try and judge God. *God!* God don't have to please you! You have to please God! No man can understand why God does things. God has his own reasons, and He acts in mysterious ways His wonders to achieve."

"I suppose," Franklin said, not supposing this at all.

"Let me read you some more," Richardson said with enthusiasm, searching through his Bible for the desired text. "This is from Revelations."

Franklin tried to look interested, but as the lesson progressed and Richardson read more and more passages, laboriously and with ludicrous mispronunciations, it became harder to act the part of a dedicated student. There were two hours of tedium before Richardson finally put down the book.

"Am I getting through to you, Franklin?" he asked with great concern, very interested in the answer.

Franklin raised his manacled hands and rubbed his face, as if considering this deeply. He gave a dramatic sigh. "I don't know, Jake. You've confused me. I'll have to think about it all."

"Good! Good!" Richardson rose from the table. "Then let's take a break and watch some television, and then—you know what I'm gonna do next?"

"What?" Franklin asked, suddenly alert and dreading the answer.

Richardson smiled. "I'll read you some more!"

"Oh." Pause. Franklin smiled. "That'd be nice," he lied.

Norman Hapwell, the head of security for SteadyLife, had proven very useful to Todd and Mary in helping them arrange their trip back to Columbus. He contacted authorities at TSB and LAX and explained that the famous Whitestones were trying to return to Ohio without attracting undue attention, and then worked out the details so that they would have minimum troubles in checking in and getting through security. Of course, they had to travel under their own names, but there were ways of keeping most airline employees from knowing what was going on, and Hapwell made sure they were all utilized. As planned, Todd and Mary did not sit together, or acknowledge each other in any way until they were both loaded into Catherine Whitestone's car in the passenger pickup area.

"Hello, Grandma," Todd said, kissing her.

"Hello to you both," Catherine replied as she pulled away from the curb and into the lane that led to the exit from Port Columbus. "Much trouble getting here?"

"No," Mary replied from the backseat. "Surprisingly, things went smoothly. Is there any word yet on Franklin?"

"No. The police are still looking for him. I've been talking to the head of the investigation, a lieutenant named Burnside, and he seems certain that there will be a breakthrough soon. He says that there just aren't that many places that Richardson could use to hide for very long.

"How is Corbin Milk doing?" Mary asked.

"Still alive. He's been through surgery and is listed in critical condition. He's at Riverside. I have the phone number of Mr. Yancy, his partner, if you'd like to call him."

"How did you get that?" Todd asked, impressed as always by his grandmother's resourcefulness.

She smiled. "I have my ways. What are your plans while you are here?"

Mary sighed. "It's all rather vague. We didn't want to stay in LA when this was going on, so we moved closer to the action. We're sorry to impose on you."

"You're not. I *love* having you as my guests. Stay as long as you like."

"Thank you," Mary replied, while thinking that she would prefer that Franklin be found in the next few minutes so that the three of them could be winging their way back to California by nightfall. Her very first encounter with Catherine Whitestone had been problematical. She and Franklin had just begun to date seriously, and he'd taken her dinner at his parents' house. Her future-mother-in-law took her aside to give her a lecture on birth control, and things had gone downhill from there. Mary had no desire to stay any longer in Catherine's house than required. She consoled herself with the thought that at least it was good for Todd to spend time with his grandmother, though that too was not without its dangers. The two of them always got along a bit too well, and if Mary didn't watch them carefully, Catherine would be suggesting some new scheme to Todd that might get them all in more trouble. Even now they were sitting in the front seat laughing about something she'd missed.

Mary joined the conversation, determined to keep up.

Jake was very pleased with the progress that Whitestone had made during this long day. They'd had three sessions of Bible reading and discussion, and there was a wonder in Whitestone's voice that Jake had heard often in the past when those who'd fallen by the wayside were drawn at last to the message of Jesus Christ.

After 90 minutes, the third session ended with St. Paul's glorious lecture on the necessity of love in 1 Corinthians 13, and Jake could tell that Whitestone was moved by the famous epistle.

"'The greatest of these is love,'" Whitestone repeated as Jake finished reciting the passage. "I think that's right," he said with awe, "love is the greatest virtue of all. Hearing it that way fills *me* with love, even for you, Jake. Even for a man who forced me here against my will, but did so only because he was determined to show me to the greatest of all loves."

Jake nearly hugged him, but stopped for two reasons. One, if Whitestone was faking, it might be a good opportunity for him to try and jump Jake, and, two, it was too homo a thing to do. Instead, he closed up the Bible on the table before him, and told Whitestone, "I think we can quit right there for awhile, with that message just hanging in the air and making both of us feel blessed. How about we relax a little? Maybe have some of your fine liquor. Want a drink?" He rose and went to his stash by the door.

Whitestone laughed. "Why not?" he said. "After all I've been through, a drink would taste great!"

"Name your poison. We don't have any ice."

"Scotch. Neat."

"Neat?"

"Just scotch in a glass, and thank you kindly. Also, how about you turn on the tv and we see what the rest of humanity is doing?"

Jake snapped it on, and then fixed their drinks. Four women on some talk show began babbling about family life.

After a bit, Whitestone spoke. "You have a family, Jake?" he asked, friendly as a puppy.

Jake thought about how to answer that. "Just Jesus and the angels in heaven," he replied. "My parents are dead—at least Daddy is. Don't know what happened to my mother. I have a brother somewhere, but haven't seen him in years."

Whitestone took another sip of his drink, which relaxed him. He sat back in his chair with a satisfied sigh.

"My Daddy's dead too," he said. "But my mother—you met her, right?—is still alive, and I have three siblings."

270

"Siblings?"

"One brother and two sisters. One older brother and two younger sisters."

"They religious folk?"

"They didn't use to be, but as we've aged, each one of them has begun to think new thoughts about God. My sister Abigail has just joined a church, and goes every Sunday with her spouse."

"When I met your mother, I didn't get the idea she was religious," Jake said.

"She's embarrassed by it," Whitestone confided. "My father was dead set against religion, and he made my mother leave the church and forced her to bring up the children as non-believers. But once he died, she's slowly changed—began to read the Bible again. Surprised us all."

"And what about you, Mr. Famous Atheist? You beginning to feel the pull of God?"

Before Whitestone could answer, the local news came on, and the lead story was the so-called "Whitestone Abduction." A big, burly police lieutenant was interviewed by Harold Wang, and he said that the police were still looking for leads as to the whereabouts of Whitestone and the man who appeared to be his captor, John Richardson. He promised to keep Wang in the know if anything developed. After the interview, Wang solemnly intoned that the whole world was hoping that Whitestone was all right, and then he turned the program back over to the anchors in the studio. They kept talking about the story while showing a video of the outside of Whitestone's condominium. The female anchor sounded quite jolly as she reported that Corbin Milk was still listed in critical condition at Riverside Hospital, but now thought likely to make it.

"Good," Jake said, finishing off his tumbler of vodka, and rising to make himself another one. "I didn't mean that man no harm. He attacked me, and what was I supposed to do? Who was he anyhow? Big fucker."

"Just a friend who was helping get things out of the house. I'm glad to hear he's going to be all right."

"Another scotch?"

"No. Still have this one. Don't have the tolerance for it that you do."

"Don't much like scotch. Too sour for me. Actually, I like beer best, but no way to keep it cold out here, and, besides, it's good to take a break and try some of this stuff you had at your house. Always did like vodka."

Whitestone smiled and allowed as how he liked vodka too.

Drink secured, Jake sat down again at the table opposite Whitestone.

"Tell me true, Franklin. Is God beginning to revive your soul? Don't lie to me now. I wouldn't like that a bit."

271

For a long moment Whitestone said nothing, just stared down at the tumbler of scotch sitting on the table between his manacled hands. Then he raised his eyes and looked at Jake, looked deep into his eyes. Spoke with conviction.

"Those passages you read—particularly the Sermon on the Mount and the last one, what St. Paul said about love—it's hard to hear those without thinking there must be something divine and wonderful behind their composition. Men don't write like that. Not even the greats, like Shakespeare and Milton."

Jake was thrilled. He slammed his hand down on the table, making Whitestone jump. "That's right! That's right! They don't! The hand of *God* wrote those words—whispered them right into the ears of His followers, who just turned around and put them in the Holy Bible. And now —think about this—for the first time, you're hearing what He has to say, what He had to say *particularly* just for you, Franklin Whitestone! Just for you! Think about that! *Think about that!* Isn't it *mind blowing?*"

Whitestone shook his head in wonder. "I don't know what to say, Jake. I feel this warm glow all through my body, and it isn't the scotch causing it. It's a glow that's been growing inside me all day, and . . . well . . . it makes me feel happy in spite of my bizarre surroundings." He looked around the room, as if seeing God there too.

Jake reached across the table and took tight hold of Whitestone's hand.

"Look at me," he commanded, very serious. "If you mean what you say, I've got a deal to make you. If you'll just say that you believe in God— nothing more—that will be enough. I'll let you go and praise the Lord for the work I did here."

"You'd let me go?" Whitestone sounded like he didn't believe it.

"Frankie, I *never* meant to hurt you. I always just wanted to bring you to the Lord, and knew that'd be enough for me. All that stupid stuff you said on tv, that wild talk hurt me, and it hurt all those who heard it. Caused people to turn from God. So, it's important that you change your mind. Important!"

"I hurt people?

"Damned right! Major hurt!"

Whitestone looked down again. "I feel so bad."

"Look at me!" Jake commanded again. Whitestone dutifully looked up, his face awash with distress and confusion. "If you say what I asked— that you believe in God—we're done! I'm outa here! Of course, I'll have to have a head start, but I'll hop in my truck and hightail it to Mexico or somewheres like that, and then, as I leave, I'll call 911 for you on my cell. You'll be free. And you can tell the world about the transforming power of the Almighty! What do you say?"

Whitestone thought for a second, and then sat up straighter.

"I believe in God," he said, innocent as a child.

Jake leaned across the table and grabbed the man by the shoulders, shaking him in delight. "*Hallelujah!*" he yelled. And then he yelled it again, and rose from his chair, making whooping sounds as he danced an Irish jig around the small room. "*I did it! I did it!*" *he* repeated, whirling in a circle, mad with joy.

"Time for another drink!" Jake told Whitestone.

"Want to set me free first?" Whitestone asked. "Surely I'm no danger to you now. After all, Jake, you're my hero."

Jake smiled.

"Oh, we're not completely done yet, Frankie, my boy. There's one more small step before it's completely over and we're out of here."

Whitestone looked confused. "One more step? What step?"

"Don't you worry none, Frankie. This step'll only take a couple of minutes. Let me get my drink and I'll tell you all about it."

The whole day had been like one long visit to an incompetent dentist, and Franklin was more than ready to escape from the dental chair and go home.

He didn't think of himself as an actor, but he'd been proud of the thespian skills he'd displayed today for an audience of one: John Harold Richardson, master teacher and religious nut. Of course, Franklin, the lawyer, was trained as an advocate, and he had developed impressive talents for talking an adversary into accepting his position. Put all that together, and Franklin was pleased with himself and with how things were going. He would sleep in a real bed tonight.

Now that Richardson was convinced of Franklin's conversion, all that remained was this "one more step," and, whatever it was, once accomplished, Franklin would awaken from this nightmare. So. What did the man want him to swear to? Pray to? Sing about?

Bring it on.

Richardson, drink in hand, sat down again at the table. He pulled out his wallet and extracted a business card. Then he retrieved his cell phone from his jacket by the door, and walked back to the table, standing next to Franklin. Richardson laboriously dialed the number on the card. Holding up one finger in Franklin's direction, the universal gesture these days for "wait a minute," he spoke into the phone.

"I'd like to talk to Harold Wang," he said. He waited until the person

273

on the other end of the phone said something, and then he replied, "Oh, I think he'll talk to me. Tell him Jake Richardson has a major scoop for him. He'll remember me from our past interviews. Hell, he gave me his card."

Franklin's mouth opened to speak, object. But he had no idea what he'd say, so it closed it again. A certainty came over him as to what was about to follow, and he desperately needed more time to decide how to deal with it.

"Harold, old buddy!" Jake said in a delighted tone, only slightly too drunk to sound completely sober. "This is Jake Richardson, and I can't talk long. Don't want nobody tracing this call. Do you have some way to record what we're saying?" Pause. "Good. Turn it on." He gave Franklin a wink.

"Gonna go public, Frankie," he said in a stage whisper. "Get ready."

Franklin felt like a bucket of ice cold water had been dumped on him. Everything changed in an instant. This was no longer just a con job on some simpleton; that simpleton was outsmarting him. He was about to be asked to announce to the entire country that Franklin Whitestone now believed in God.

What should he do? Could he just say it and count on people not believing it? Retract it as soon as he was free? Yes, he thought. Yes. That's what he'd do.

"You ready now, Harold?" Jake asked. "Wonderful! Hello, America! This is Jake Richardson, and I have Franklin Whitestone right here with me. We've spent the day talking about God, and I know you'll think I'm kidding, but Franklin has seen the light! It's really him you're gonna hear next, and he has something important to say to you all." He put the phone up to Franklin's ear. "Go ahead and tell them," he said, not at all concerned. "You're on, my friend."

And Franklin meant to say it. He really did. But on some very basic level—four or five turtles down—he knew it was impossible.

Alexander Whitestone, the father he dearly loved, had always told him that a man needs to decide what he stands for in life, and, having made that decision, use the answer to guide all his further actions.

Franklin had only a nanosecond for this to go through his mind, but it caused him to balk, no matter the penalty. It was one thing to lie to a lowlife like Richardson. It was another to humiliate himself in this most public of ways.

Franklin Whitestone stood for something better than that.

"*Tell him*," Jake urged in a whisper, a look of concern now wrinkling his brow, something dangerous beginning to stir inside him.

Stall for time, Franklin thought. Give them an opportunity to trace the call.

"Hello, Mr. Wang," he said. "This is Franklin Whitestone, how are you this evening?"

"I'm fine," Wang replied, impatient with the question. "Where are you, Franklin?"

"I'm not sure. I think . . ." Before he could finish that thought, say something about an abandoned construction site, Richardson snatched the phone away and punched the Off button.

He turned and looked down at the man sitting shackled hand and foot before him.

Without saying a word, he backhanded Franklin as hard as he could, and then pushed over the chair so that Franklin slammed painfully to the floor. In a frenzy of action, insane with anger, Richardson started kicking every part of Franklin's body he could reach. His leg pulled back as far as it would go, Richardson landed the kicks with all the force he could put into them. Franklin tried to dodge the blows, vainly raising his shackles as if they might somehow serve as a shield. When his right leg tired, Richardson switched to the left. Franklin was kicked in the face, the chest, the ribs, the back, the hand, the knee, the neck. The blows made a "whoomff" noise each time they hit, one whoomff hard upon another. Franklin himself emitted only grunting noises, nothing more. The attack tore open the victim's skin in bleeding rows. The blood stained Franklin's body, the floor around the table, parts of the wall, and Richardson's legs and boots.

The kicking didn't stop until Franklin passed out and Richardson, breathing hard, finally noticed that the man wasn't reacting. Then he kicked him once more, hard.

He stood looking down at the body.

"Asshole," Richardson said in a very quiet voice.

CHAPTER EIGHTEEN

ESCAPE

On Wednesday morning, Mary Whitestone was sitting at the dining room table in the home of her former mother-in-law, very unhappy. Since Richardson's aborted call to the tv station, nothing more had been learned of Franklin's fate, and it was difficult not to worry constantly, like someone trapped in an exit-less maze. How horrible it was just to wait—wanting but unable to do anything, not knowing what to say when people called, pretending confidence when Todd was watching, finding sleep impossible, battling a sense of hopelessness and depression that all but overwhelmed her.

What made it all the more difficult was that Todd and his grandmother seemed to be handling the pressure so much better than she was. Their conversation about their missing father/son was filled with optimism, and they both had a no-nonsense attitude that left them free to move on to other things. Right now they were in the living room, whooping it up over a game of canasta. Canasta! Hadn't that died out years ago? How in the world did Todd know the rules? From what she could tell from the raucous commentary, he even appeared to be winning.

Mary decided to call Lt. Burnside and see if any progress had been made on the manhunt, which now had spread across the country, and most particularly to the states surrounding Ohio. He had interrogated Todd and her at length yesterday, focusing on the brief encounter they'd had with Jake Richardson in that parking lot in southern Ohio. She couldn't imagine they'd told him anything that helped, but what did she know about police investigations and what would be important to an expert? She'd last spoken to Lt. Burnside the evening before when they'd discussed the Richardson phone call. That call could not be traced, he told her, though the police were analyzing it for background noise and other clues. It distressed her to realize that he no longer sounded as upbeat as he had earlier in the day.

She dialed the number he'd given her—his cell—and he answered at once.

"Hello, Ms. Whitestone," he said, seeing her number on caller ID. "I was about to phone you."

"Yes?" she said, both dread and hope rising in her.

"Now, I don't want you to make too much of this, but a truck has been spotted abandoned by the side of the road near Cincinnati, and we're looking into whether it belongs to Richardson. We found it about daybreak. Unfortunately, it has no license plates, and that's delayed identification."

"If it *is* Richardson's truck, what would that mean?"

"We don't know that either. Obviously, he and your ex-husband wouldn't get very far on foot. They might have holed up somewhere near there, in which case we ought to find them soon. Or, more likely I'm afraid, they may have found some other way of getting around. High-jacking a car, for instance, or getting an accomplice to pick them up."

"I see."

"In any event, it's a new development, and I wanted to share it with you. I'll let you know if and when the situation becomes clearer."

"Thank you, Lieutenant," she said, feeling herself falling back into her previous torpor.

"Hang in there," he advised, and hung up.

Mary sat staring at the wall for a few minutes, knowing and not caring that this inactivity wasn't going to help. Of course, she should get up and do something. Watch tv maybe, or read a book. Both seemed to require more concentration than she could likely muster. It then occurred to her that she had a column to write for the magazine, but she dismissed this too. It would have to wait. Any column she wrote in the mood would just have to be rewritten.

The phone rang, and she answered it. "Hello?" she said.

"Is Mary Whitestone there?" asked the male voice on the other end.

"Speaking. Who is this?"

"My name is George Yancy. I'm Corbin Milk's partner."

"Oh, yes, Mr. Yancy. I was planning on giving you a call later on today."

"It's like this, Ms. Whitestone," he began, but she interrupted with "Call me Mary," and so he continued with, "Mary. I'm George. At Riverside Hospital, Corbin has been moved from the intensive care ward to a private room."

"I'm so please to hear that," she said.

"Me too. He's surprisingly alert. Sitting up and talking."

"What does he have to say about the attack?"

"Alas, he had no memory of it. He remembers pulling the painters' van into the garage, but after that it's a blank. Whatever happened must have occurred so fast it never made it to his long term memory, or even, for that matter, into short term memory. The police have just left here, and they obviously were hoping for more."

"A shame. Maybe it will come back to him."

"Maybe," Yancy agreed. "But here's the thing. Corbin has learned you're in town, and he wants to talk to you and your son. He says he has only spoken to you on the phone and would like to get to know you in person.

Might you come to the hospital this afternoon? Visiting hours start at 2 p.m., and his doctor told me he could have outside visitors for no more than twenty minutes."

"We'll certainly be there. May I also bring Franklin's mother?" Catherine would insist on this, Mary knew.

"Two visitors at a time is all they allow. Even I won't be able to be in the room when you two are there. Perhaps she can visit later in the evening if Corbin feels up to it. I don't want too much excitement for him, though."

"Perhaps," Mary said, thinking that a visit from Catherine might not be the best medicine for anyone trying to keep on an even keel while healing, or, come to think of it, even for someone perfectly well. "In any event, George, I'm so happy you called. Todd and I will be there promptly at two."

They said their goodbyes, and Mary hung up.

But her spirits were lifted a little. Having something to do this afternoon made her feel better, more like a functioning person. Hearing laughter from the living room, Mary went to tell Todd and Catherine the news.

As usual, Jake's head was pounding when he awoke Wednesday morning, and his back was stiff from sleeping on the hard floor. His legs ached, and it took him a minute to figure out why. Both legs had had quite a workout. With a groan, he raised himself up on his elbows and considered his surroundings.

Whitestone was still lying on the bare floor next to the upturned chair, and Jake wondered if he was alive or not. If Whitestone had died, how bad would things be for Jake? Would they call it murder? That didn't sound right. Whitestone's death would be Whitestone's fault. He'd made Jake to lose his temper and strike him when he tried to make a fool of Jake in front of that stupid Harold Wang. Manslaughter maybe. And kidnapping. And shooting that other guy.

Jake decided not to think about it anymore. He rose slowly from his bed on the floor, and walked unsteadily to the table, where he sat down with a little grunt. If his head would stop hurting so much it would be easier to think. There was no aspirin. He hadn't thought to bring any, which was stupid, because he always went through a lot of aspirin.

Could he risk a quick trip in the truck? Get aspirin, and coffee. Coffee sounded important. Buy Whitestone his stupid toothbrush. Maybe doughnuts.

No, Jake decided. Too dangerous. Must be cops everywhere keeping a lookout for the truck and for him. His photo was all over tv. Have to make do with what was in the room. He rose and shuffled his way into the bathroom. After taking a whiz, he splashed ice cold water on his face in the bathroom sink, and then cupped his hands and drank a big gulp. He looked at himself in the mirror. Bloodshot eyes. Needing a shave. Hair sticking up in all directions. Hell, he ought to call Celia and see if she wanted some romance! That made him smile, and, as soon as he did, his reflection told him that under everything he was still a good guy.

Whitestone might yet be saved. Just because he wasn't willing to talk about God on national tv didn't mean that he remained a nonbeliever. Jake had seen the man's sincerity yesterday as he listened to the words of the Bible, and began to glow with the wonder of its meaning. The man was not hopeless. In this situation, Jesus wouldn't give up, so Jake couldn't either. Jake looked at the man on the floor. Sleeping? Unconscious? Dead?

Maybe he *had* overreacted.

Jake left the bathroom and went over to the supplies next by the door. Something to eat maybe. He found a banana and a Diet Pepsi, carried them over to the table, and managed to get both down without upchucking. He was pleased with that. Made him feel better. After awhile it would also probably help to have a hair or two of the dog that'd bit him, but of course it was too early for that now.

Again Jake considered the motionless form of Franklin Whitestone. How had the man gotten so much blood all over this body? Think back. Well, he'd kicked Whitestone in the head, and head wounds, Jake knew from prison fights, were always bloody. It didn't mean much in and of itself. Still it was likely to be a good idea to clean the guy up some, and maybe even say he was sorry for losing his temper. He should get Whitestone some breakfast, and then resume the Bible lessons. He rose, went to the bathroom, ran the water in the sink until it heated up, wet a washcloth, and then went over and knelt down next to Whitestone's body.

The man was lying face down, his nose squished against the floor, and Jake mercifully turned him over on his back, being careful not to let him bang his head too much as it flopped back down. Whitestone made a little protesting noise at this. Good. He was alive.

Gently, Jake began to wipe Franklin's face, sponging the worst of the blood off. The man had welts and bruises all over, and his left eye, all puffed up, was three different colors, swollen tight. Had Jake caused all these bruises or did Whitestone already have some of them when he came in here two days ago? Jake tried to remember. Probably, he decided, the bruises and welts were all new. From last night. When Whitestone provoked him.

It was two hours before Whitestone spoke. Jake wasn't even aware that he was awake until he heard the man croak out the word "water." It tugged at Jake's heartstrings—he wasn't a vindictive man. He jumped up

279

from his seat in front of the tv he'd been watching, and filled a tumbler with water. Bringing it back, he knelt down on the floor, and lifted Whitestone's head, guiding the water down his throat. Whitestone gagged twice, but kept it all down. Grabbing a pillow from the nearby bedding, Jake put it under Whitestone's head as he lowered it once more.

"What happened?" Whitestone whispered after a bit. He appeared not to know where he was.

"You fell," Jake told him. "Just rest and get better, and we'll talk some more later."

Catherine Whitestone was very upset when she learned that she couldn't visit with Corbin Milk at the same time as Mary and Todd. She even suggested that she and Mary should go, leaving Todd behind. "He's just a boy," she explained. "I'm not sure that the hospital even allows children in the intensive care unit."

"It's a private room, not the ICU," Mary corrected, suppressing the urge to yell at the old bat, "and Todd is not a child anymore, if he ever was."

Todd grinned. "What does that mean?"

"But . . . ," Catherine began, but Mary cut her off.

"No more, Catherine," she barked, a level one step below yelling. "If you want to talk to Mr. Milk yourself, go this evening. I'm sure he'll benefit from your company."

Mary could tell that the sarcasm had been rightly decoded, but, to Catherine's credit, she gave up, and was even gracious in helping them get out the door.

On the way to the hospital, with Mary driving Catherine's car, Todd suddenly asked his mother, "Do you still love Dad?"

She thought about what to say. The answer, of course, was "no," but it was a qualified "no." How best to summarize all the emotions that had piled up in the last two decades of constant interaction with Franklin Whitestone? When they first met, they'd progressed quickly from dating, to living together, to marriage, and then to parenting. Along the way had been love, fierce and fine, the joyous union of male and female, tender and passionate. Like many romantic fools, they'd come to the utterly selfish conclusion that no other couple in the history of human kind had ever felt as deeply, cared as much, as they did. They actually said this to each other, knowing full well how silly it was, and that it couldn't be true. This idyllic period lasted about five years, and then, like night falling, came the troubles, and love proved not enough to unweave the tangles. There was no obvious cause. He did this, she did that, and they stopped being a couple, became just two people who were legally married, but no longer wed in either their hearts or in their bed. She began to realize that she couldn't keep living with Franklin, that their marriage had to end. He had known it too. Without undue rancor, they parted. Mary had no desire to rekindle their relationship, and wouldn't do it even if Franklin were to come out of this whole and beg her. Still . . .

"Yes," she said to Todd, and let it go at that.

By early afternoon, Franklin had regained enough humanity that he could force himself to a sitting position on the floor, leaning against a leg of the table. He couldn't manage getting into the chair alone, and was damned if he'd ask the psycho for help with anything. His skull creaked alarmingly when he moved his head, and that scared him. One eye was swollen shut and felt like a spike had been driven through it directly into his brain. Franklin's tongue informed him that he was missing teeth and that still others were hanging, having only the vaguest connection with the rest of his mouth. As his tongue painfully made these explorations, he was rewarded with the taste of blood from the reopening one or another of his internal mouth wounds.

The same was true of the rest of his body. One of his arms, the left one, appeared broken. It hung at an odd angle. Strangely it only hurt him when he tried to move it, lapsing into tranquility if he wisely left it alone. Broken ribs too, apparently. Breathing was painful, particularly if he inhaled suddenly or deeply, which happened whenever he moved and some other part of his body came alive with its own contribution to his misery. He had yet to stand, which would doubtless reveal bad news about his lower limbs.

Must have really pissed him off, Franklin thought.

The events of the previous evening slowly returned to him one by one, until he had a pretty good picture of the whole debacle. He alternated between a remembered terror of the ferocity of the attack, and a strange pride that he'd been willing to endure all this to maintain the standard that his father had set for him.

What next?

Franklin regarded Richardson, who was sitting on the other side of the table, watching tv. Franklin, sitting on the floor, could see only the man's lower half, and was surprised that he hadn't attracted the Richardson's attention when he sat up with such effort. If Richardson noticed him now, what would happen? Another beating? Franklin didn't think of himself as a brave man, and the mere possibility of Richardson kicking him again caused an involuntary whimper.

Richardson stuck his head down, peering under the table. Must have

281

heard the whimper.

"How you doing, buddy?" he asked in a gentle tone. "Ready for some food?" He rose and came around to stand next to Franklin. "Need to use the john?"

So they were buddies again, were they? So be it. It was better than the alternative.

"Help me up," Franklin croaked, but too low for Richardson to hear. The man said, "What?" and Franklin repeated the request.

Richardson looked doubtful. "Think you can stand? Maybe you'd better lie down some more. Rest."

"Up," Franklin insisted, trying to use the table leg and the legs of the overturned chair on the floor next to him to rise. Richardson, seeing that he was serious about the attempt, sprang to help, and slowly, with huge gasps of pain, Franklin made it to his feet. He leaned against both Richardson and the table. Richardson looked concerned, one arm tightly wound around Franklin's shoulder, the other circling his waist. "You better sit," he advised. Balancing Franklin against the table, he leaned down, righted the chair, and lowered Franklin into it. The shackles and chains made this all the more difficult, but it was finally accomplished. To his great relief, Franklin settled.

He was very pleased to discover that none of the bones in his legs appeared to be broken, though the suckers were screaming at him with a volume of pain matching any in the rest of his poor body. But Franklin was encouraged. He knew that if he had to he could walk, escape, maybe even run. Hope fluttered by and he seized upon it.

He sat there, with Richardson saying nothing, until Franklin's head stopped swimming and he was sure he wasn't going to pass out. He looked at Richardson. "Water," he rasped.

"You got it!" Richardson said almost jovially. "Want some scotch with it?"

Franklin shook his head. No scotch.

"Dad says you were in the C.I.A. and got fired for being gay," Todd said to Corbin Milk not long after he and his mother had entered the hospital room at Riverside, and seated themselves. George Yancy, a small and wiry young man with strange mysterious eyes, had met them in the lobby and walked them to Milk's room. There were introductions all around and then Yancy left them there to talk.

Todd was very impressed with Corbin Milk. Even with bandages encircling his torso and head, he looked overpowering—a big man, very muscled, quite alert in a situation where most people would seem distant and frail.

"Not exactly," Milk replied to Todd's question.

"Todd," his mother said, "you don't know Mr. Milk well enough to ask a question like that."

"It's all right," Milk said. "Better to talk about that than my injuries or . . ." He let that thought trail off. They all three knew where it went, and were as anxious as Milk to discuss anything else.

"The truth is that the C.I.A. always knew I was gay, and that was fine with them. The agency uses its gay personnel in very interesting ways when it sends them abroad. I can't go into it much, other than to say that gays have always been good at working below the radar, and at meeting each other for romantic encounters. It doesn't matter that they don't speak the same language, are not from friendly nations, have never formally met, nor that they have no plans to ever see each other again.

"How can I put this? There are some men who are very attracted to bodybuilders. That proved quite useful to the agency, and so I had an . . . adventurous career. I'd write a book about it all if I could figure a way to get it published."

"So what happened?" Todd asked.

"A man high up in the agency became infatuated with me, and when I refused him, out I went. I obviously wasn't fired because I was gay. The truth was the opposite: I wasn't gay enough to suit him. I tried various other jobs, but my former boss did what he needed to do to wreck them too. Nasty man. He had—*has*—too much power, and too little in the way of integrity."

Mary had a question of her own. "Wouldn't that be sexual harassment? Isn't that illegal?"

Milk smiled. "You'd think so, wouldn't you? And, in theory, the C.I.A. is subject to the same laws that govern us all. But in this case, for reasons I can't go into, a lawsuit wouldn't have succeeded." You could see him replay something in his mind, and then reject talking about it. "So," he concluded, "that's how I ended up owning a costume shop in Columbus, Ohio."

Todd was outraged. "That's awful. I hate that this guy got away with it."

Milk regarded them for a few seconds, as if deciding whether to say more. Then he smiled. "Oh, I didn't mean that he got away with it."

"What did you do?" Todd asked, very curious.

Milk shrugged. "Long story. Some other time. So now I'm a Buckeye, and it's a pretty good life. The store makes enough money to pay the bills. I met the love of my life in this city. All in all, I'm happy." He looked down at his bandages. "Perhaps 'happy' isn't the right word for my current state," he amended, and they all smiled.

"Is it true you don't remember the shooting?" Mary asked.

"True. Complete blank."

"But the doctors think you'll make a complete recovery? Physically?"

"That's what they tell me. I was in great shape before the shooting, and that must have helped, but still I'm dumfounded. I was shot twice, including once in the head, and nothing particularly vital was hit, except my spleen, and apparently I can live fairly well without it. The doctors say I should take it easy for awhile, no workouts. I don't like that so much. Exercising has been a passion of mine since I was a skinny gay little boy who didn't much like the names the other kids pinned on him, and decided to do something about it."

Corbin Milk looked at Todd and Mary carefully. Brave people, both of them. You could see worry lines on their faces, but they were slogging on, doing what they could to keep it altogether.

"I don't think it's a good idea for the two of you to be back in Columbus," he told them. "You must know you're risking serious danger by being here."

Mary nodded. "We talked about it, and you're right. We shouldn't have returned. It was irresponsible of me, but, well, we found it impossible to stay in California. However, Todd and I agreed earlier today that if Franklin isn't found by tomorrow at noon, we'll get on a plane and go back to L.A."

Todd looked annoyed. "Mom," he said, "*I* didn't agree to that."

"Yes, you did," she replied in her "mom-has-ruled" voice, daring him to contradict her.

Instead, Todd turned back to Milk. "You're a professional. How much danger do you think my father is in?"

Milk looked up at the ceiling and didn't reply immediately. Finally he shrugged. "I wish I knew," he said. "I lie here and try and imagine what he's going through, and I draw a blank. But there's hope. Franklin's a clever man, just like the two of you were clever, and he may find a way to escape, just as you did. Or—and this is even likelier—the police may rescue him at any moment. We'll have to wait and see. Cross our fingers."

"If you had been taken hostage with him would you be useful to my father?" Todd asked.

"Yes," Milk said. "I would." He didn't elaborate.

Franklin managed to eat another banana and to drink a bottle of flavored water that Richardson brought him. He was pleased he could keep it down, and he felt himself gaining strength from the fuel it provided. Trying

284

to find a comfortable position, he carefully adjusted his back against the chair, and then leaned heavily on the table, almost sprawling across it. His useless left arm he set down gingerly in his lap, and as soon as he quit moving it, its stabbing pain stopped. It would be of no help if he needed to attack Richardson. Or to fend off a renewed attack by the man.

Richardson was in the liquor box again, and it seemed like he was drinking both more and earlier each day. Physically, he looked almost as bad as Franklin felt, and Richardson's breath would send a horse to its knees.

Now the man stood, turned off the tv, and moved back to the table. He had the Bible in his hand.

Franklin's mind rebelled. No more readings. No more dogma. No more. He didn't care if Richardson beat him for it. He was through with pretending, and, along with that, he was done listening to Richardson mangle the passages he read so poorly. No more.

"Let's try some of Genesis," the idiot said, opening the Bible.

"I can't," Franklin managed.

"Can't what? What do you mean 'can't'?"

Franklin let his head sag sadly. "I've been embarrassed to tell you, Jake, but now it's time to let you know the truth."

"What truth?"

"The reason I've been so intractable is that I'm already committed to another religion, and you won't be able to talk me out of it."

"Intra–what? Another religion? Which religion?" Richardson was truly flummoxed.

Franklin raised his head, and with his good right eye, looked steadily at the man across the table.

"I am a disciple of the Great Turtle," he said without a trace of humor in his voice.

Richardson's eyes widened. "The Great Turtle? What is that? I never heard of such a thing."

"It is a very ancient religion," Franklin explained. "Common in some parts of the world—South America, New Zealand, Finland. I encountered it in my trips into the Land of Whimsey."

"Don't know that either."

"It's in northern Asia. Devotees believe that the world rests on the back of a giant turtle, and that the turtle broadcasts wisdom to its followers 'above the shell,' as we say."

Richardson looked disgusted. "The world don't sit on the back of no turtle!"

"Yes. It does. You can see it from space."

"No you can't!"

"Have you ever been in space?"

"No. But it just *can't* be. I know I never seen no fucking turtle pictures. You're making this crap up!"

Franklin splayed open the fingers of his good hand in the Vulcan salute. "I swear to you on the honor of the first twelve lesser turtles that I'm not. *You* can't see the Great Turtle because you don't believe in him. He's like Tinkerbell—invisible to the uninitiated."

"Like who?"

"Your education has been sadly neglected, Jake. I'll have to tell you the parable of Tinkerbell later on—she's one of the lesser turtles. But first, let me recite for you the sacred paean to the G. T. 'Oh, Slow One, please turn tortoise, and show us you carapace . . . "

"*Stop it! Stop it!*" Richardson screamed, and Franklin knew he had gone too far. Time to backtrack.

"Okay, Jake. No harm meant. I guess it's wrong for me to proselytize, but you let me know if you want to hear more. There's a hymn too. I could sing it if you're curious." He cleared his throat as if in preparation, but then shook his head. "For now, could I get a drink, please?" he asked.

Richardson stopped, confused, but attracted by the question. He'd just been thinking the same thing. Time for that dog hair. "A drink? More water?"

"No," Franklin replied. "We've got brandy right? Always good for the wounded—helps with healing. Doesn't require ice either. Neat. Why don't you join me?"

"Never had no brandy."

"Excellent stuff. You owe it to yourself to sample some. Sip it slowly and see if it doesn't take you to a good place. The bottle that's over there in that box is a splendid example of its kind. Just what we both need. Try and find it."

A bit unsteady from the drinks he had already consumed, Richardson climbed to his feet and lumbered over to the liquor box. Laboriously, he pulled out a couple of bottles, squinting at their labels, before he came to the oddly shaped brandy bottle and held it up for closer inspection.

"That's it!" Franklin said on seeing the shape. "Pour some in our glasses."

Richardson looked around for a container to hold Franklin's brandy, and finally picked up Franklin's old tumbler from where it had fallen on the floor. He returned to the table, sat opposite Franklin once again, and clumsily poured out two healthy servings of the dark liquid. He handed one to Franklin, who raised his glass in a toast.

"To new friends," Franklin said, wishing he had one.

As Lt. Leon Burnside was walking from his car to the back entrance of police headquarters, a wispy thin woman in her 40s reached out a hand to him and said, "Lt. Burnside?" He nodded. "I am Lenora Palmetto, and I may have some information about the Whitestone abduction."

That got his attention. "What is it?" he asked.

"I hope this doesn't sound too silly to you, but last night I had a dream about Franklin Whitestone, and I saw his situation rather clearly. I think I can help you find him."

Burnside's attention immediately began to wander. Ever since a popular fictional tv show featured a psychic who gave very accurate predictions to the police, copycats had abounded, and he was forever having to shoo them off. These cracked eggs called themselves "mediums," but to the lieutenant they seemed more like "soft-boileds."

"I appreciate your offer of help, ma'am," he said, trying to get past her, "but we're very busy with other leads."

She stepped in front of him as he turned to go, raising both hands this time. "No, please," she pleaded, "hear me out. Mr. Whitestone is being held in an abandoned building—maybe a farm house. Not much furniture, small room. He has been trying to escape and is badly hurt. He has a broken arm."

It was all Burnside could do to keep from rolling his eyes, but he figured the fastest way to get back to his office was to humor her. "Did Richardson break Whitestone's arm?" he asked.

She shook her head. "No," she replied, "Mr. Richardson himself is being held captive, and made to do things like that phone call last night to the tv reporter."

"I see. Who is the kidnapper then?"

"Four Muslim terrorists—the same group that set off the bombs in the stadiums. Mr. Whitestone was their original target, but Mr. Richardson got taken along because he happened to be there when the terrorists showed up the Whitestone house. They're the ones who shot poor Mr. Milk, not Mr. Richardson."

"Thank you for your input, Ms. Palmetto. Do you have a number we can call you at if we need to follow up on this?" Eagerly she gave it to him, and he dutifully wrote it down in his notebook. Then he shook her hand and fled.

Sitting at the large table, carefully feeding himself potato chips from a cannister, Franklin was trying to decide between three choices: the door, the gun, or the chain. Snoring with enthusiasm, Richardson was asleep at the same table, sprawled across it in a drunken coma. The time for Franklin's escape attempt had come. Ah yes, but what form should it take?

First choice: the rush for the door. If Franklin were careful and quiet he should be able to shuffle over, open it and go out, and then see if he could either get far enough away or hide somewhere Richardson couldn't find him. The difficulty with this choice was that all too many things could go wrong and fast. Richardson might awake before he could vanish. Or, Franklin's strength could fail him even if he could get to the door and outside, leaving him fallen and trying pitifully to crawl to safety. Finally, even if he could manage the physical challenges, there might be nowhere to go. All these considerations made the door choice seem a poor one.

Then there was the gun. It had to be somewhere in the room. If Franklin could find it he could . . . well, he wasn't sure what he would do with it. Hold it on Richardson, perhaps, threatening him with it—okay, sure, he could certainly do that. But the man was a trigger-tempered psychotic, and holding a gun on him might be like waving a red cape at an injured, angry bull. Thus the moral dilemma came down to whether or not Franklin could just shoot Richardson *now* while he slept. It would certainly be the smart thing to do, and probably have no resulting legal repercussions even if technically murder/manslaughter (once again Mary had paved the way here), but the harder question was whether Franklin could actually pull the trigger on a sleeping man. He didn't think so, but maybe, just maybe, he could talk himself into it. Other problems also complicated the gun choice. Could he find it? Only one of his eyes was working, and it was frequently clouded by tears and sweat and other fluids he didn't want to think about. The gun wasn't laying around in plain view, and might even be on Richardson's person, which would eliminate it as an option. Was it loaded? Was there a safety, and, if so, could he, vision compromised, figure out in time how to turn it off? If he did shoot, how could he be sure the shot would take Richardson down and keep him down? Franklin had never fired a gun in his life. All of this made the selection of the gun iffy.

That left the long chain. It ran from the short chain between his wrist manacles down to the short chain between the ankle fetters. The more he thought about it, the more Franklin could see ways to use it as a weapon. If he could somehow bring his arms and legs close enough together, he might then loop it around Richardson's throat, perhaps tonight when Richardson slept on the floor. Or, failing that, he might figure out how to swing the chain hard enough to turn it into a bludgeon, smack Richardson in the face, take him down. This was the sort of thing that worked in Hollywood, but it sounded forbiddingly awkward and Franklin had little faith in its efficacy as a real life solution here in Columbus.

So Franklin ate potato chips and ran "door, gun, chain" through a mental version of "rock, paper, scissors," dithering over the possibilities but staying seated at the table, frozen in indecision.

Suddenly, as often happens, the Great Turtle made the choice for him. To Franklin's surprise he found himself rising quietly and beginning a labored shuffle toward the door to the outside and freedom. Inevitably, he made some noise as he rose—the chains rattled together no matter how carefully he moved and Franklin emitted a series of muffled groans—but nothing caused Jake Richardson to stir.

With each movement pain engulfed Franklin's entire body. Teeth clenched, he steeled himself to the agony. Assuming he didn't pass out, it simply must be endured. Franklin knew that if he stayed in this room, he would likely die in this room. The survival instinct was strong upon him, and he actually made pretty good time in covering the five feet or so between himself and the door.

Arriving there, he paused to try and control his breathing, which consisted of ragged gulps that were far too loud for comfort, but which now couldn't be effectively silenced. Franklin glanced back at Richardson, but the man hadn't moved at all. Was still snoring. Very, very good.

Using his working hand, Franklin opened the door, and almost had it snatched out of his grasp by a cold gust of wind yanking it outward. He managed to hang on long enough to sidle through. As quietly as he could, he shut the door behind him before he lost control of the damned thing.

Successfully outside, he knew he should walk/scamper/crawl/run as fast as possible and flee this madness, but here his body betrayed him. All he could manage was to stand and gasp for air. Stabbing pain told him that his ribs were angled at odd directions inside his chest, and something was keeping his lungs from filling as they should. The laborious movement across the room and through the door had made his head swim, and all this effort filled his good right eye with tears.

Franklin looked up through the haze of his vision, and saw Richardson's truck parked immediately outside the door. With an effort, he staggered over to it, leaning against the hood and front grill. Was it at all possible he might somehow escape in the truck? Were the keys in it? Could he even drive in his condition?

Blinking furiously to clear his sight, Franklin looked around the abandoned construction project to find better sanctuary. Other than the little building he'd just exited, there wasn't much to see. A tall fence with a sign on it that said "OH-MID-IO, Inc." in big letters ran behind the office structure, but there was nothing on the other side except for isolated piles of construction debris—odd pieces of lumber, pipes, empty cardboard boxes, and trash of all kinds. A tarp covered some larger object in the distance, but Franklin couldn't tell what it was, and it hurt his eye to stare at it for very long, or, for that matter, at anything. Mounds of dirt further off suggested some sort of excavation, perhaps where Richardson and his giant claw had once been digging. What the original purpose of a construction project on this site had been couldn't be determined by casual inspection.

Turning in the other direction, Franklin saw a road leading through some trees and then veering to the right out of sight. That was probably the best escape route, but Franklin was very worried that he couldn't even get from the truck to the first tree without falling, much less from that tree to others and so on into the woods.

Should he give this all up and just go back inside? No. The Great Turtle was very sure about that.

The truck then.

With a steely resolve, Franklin gritted his remaining teeth and more or less rolled his body around to the driver's side of the pickup. There was no key in the ignition, but, to his amazement, Franklin saw the keys laying on the passenger seat. He marveled at this piece of improbable luck.

"Must sacrifice a worm to the Great Turtle as an offering of thanks," he mumbled under his breath as he moved out of the way of the door and pulled it open.

Climbing in was a nightmare. None of the relevant parts of his body appeared either able or willing to get him off the ground, around the steering wheel, and into the driver's seat. The effort to accomplish all of this caused him to yelp in agony. Frustrated, he sprawled across the driver's seat, and using his legs to push and his one good arm holding on to the steering wheel to pull, he tried to drag himself into the front seat, head first.

He did manage to get off the ground before he was roughly stopped by a hand on his belt.

"Going somewhere, asshole?" said a familiar voice behind him.

Before Franklin could even look around, Richardson yanked him from the truck and flung him to the ground. He landed on his back with a massive thud. Fury and bitter disappointment engulfed Franklin. As he fell he managed to scream out, "LET ME GO, YOU LUNATIC!!!"

"LUNATIC?" Richardson bellowed back. "*ASSHOLE, ASSHOLE, ASSHOLE!!!*"

Rocking back and forth, every part of his body exploding with pain, a one-eyed Franklin somehow managed to see Richardson clutch the truck door to steady himself. Very slowly he pulled back his foot and then kicked Franklin hard in the stomach.

Blackness clamped down and he saw nothing more.

CHAPTER NINETEEN

SALVATION

The question that unlocked the secret to the whereabouts of Jake Richardson and Franklin Whitestone came just after five o'clock on Wednesday evening. Lt. Burnside had ordered his force to round up the six people closest to Richardson who worked with him at the construction firm. The six, all men, were taken to the interrogation room and made comfortable. It was made very clear to them that they were not in any way suspects, but were there only to help the police come up with leads in the ongoing investigation.

Lt. Burnside entered the room and was introduced to the men, and then everybody sat. Burnside had at his elbow Sgt. Aaron Tanker, his chief assistant, who was taking notes.

"I'll level with you," the lieutenant said to the men. "We've hit a dead end in the pursuit of John Richardson and his captive, Franklin Whitestone. They seem to have vanished from the face of the earth, but my guess is that they're still on the planet somewhere, probably right here in central Ohio. First let me ask, is there any doubt in your minds that Richardson is capable of shooting one man and abducting another?"

They all shook their heads. One said, "He's capable of a lot worse. If Whitestone is still alive he's in big trouble. Richardson's mean as a snake. Crazy too—no sense at all."

"We hated working with him," another added. "We actually worried he'd get mad over some little damn thing and come after us with Susy May."

Burnside nodded. "All right. Now here's the chief question I have for all of you. Assume you're Richardson and you're planning on kidnapping a man and holing up with him somewhere for awhile. Your hiding spot must be out away from normal traffic, in a location where there are few people around who could come across you and blow the whistle. So, it's got to be someplace isolated." He paused for a few seconds to let them absorb that. "The place you choose must also have protection from the elements—a building of some kind. We know that Richardson took both a space heater and his toaster with him when he fled his house, so the building has to have electricity too." He looked at them one after the other, his expression almost pleading. "Now think. If you had to choose such a place where would you go?"

291

"How about the home of a relative or a friend?" said a heavily bearded man on Burnside's far left.

"No. We tried that. His only living relative is a brother he hasn't seen in decades."

"Richardson didn't have no friends," another of the construction workers volunteered.

Burnside tried another suggestion to prod them along. "How about some place you worked on in the past year or so that isn't quite finished yet?"

A youngster sitting across the table from Burnside who didn't look old enough to leave home, much less work a construction job, spoke up. "You know," he said, "it could be the OH-MID-IO project."

"That's right," another agreed. "It's sitting empty and abandoned while the owners try and scrape up money to finish the damn thing."

"Finish?" said another. "We barely got started and they pulled the plug."

"Someone in the main office told me they've filed bankruptcy. We're not going back there anytime soon."

Burnside was excited. This is what he was looking for. "Is there a building with electricity?"

They all nodded as one. The bearded man explained. "There was a construction shack we threw together so we'd have a place to work out of— kind of the main office for the job. It had electricity, and even a working toilet. The union insists on at least one working toilet on every project."

"Where is this place?" Burnside asked.

"Southwest of here about an hour," the youngster replied. "I could show you."

Burnside nodded at Sgt. Tanker, who scurried from the room to set it up.

"Richardson, I've got you now!" Burnside thought to himself. Aloud he said, "Many thanks, men. I think we just broke this case wide open." He indicated the youngster. "Son, what's your name?"

"Noel, Sir."

"Well, Noel, we're going to take you up on your offer. You're about to take a very fast ride in a police car. Come with me."

About this same time, Kelly put down her newspaper and stared straight ahead, facing but not seeing the tv in front of her. It was off. Without being aware of planning to, she rose and then carefully lowered herself to her knees. She clasped her hands together and closed her eyes.

"Dear Lord, please protect Franklin Whitestone, who is in the hands of his enemies and needs your help. You know him to be a good person, Lord, even if he is a doubter. Your message has always been love, and surely you love all your creations who are themselves loving beings. Franklin loves me, and his son, and life. And, Lord, I love him. Please, please take care of this gentle and kind man."

It would've astounded Franklin to learn how many people all over the country and even outside it were praying for his safe return. Of course, they didn't agree with his religious views, but that didn't stop them from caring about his welfare. Good people all, they asked their God to intervene on his behalf. Franklin had made a favorable impression on his last tv appearance, and while he was still much reviled in certain circles, most devout people did not demand adherence to their own brand of faith. They had forgiven him his original rash comments. And certainly they didn't want his body to be found and his death blamed on a religious fanatic.

When Franklin regained consciousness this second time, it again took him a long while to appreciate his circumstances. Then he remembered the original abduction from his home, followed by the Bible lessons, and, finally, his pitiful escape attempt outside at the truck. As he swam back to life, he came to the startling conclusion that he was very close to dying. A number of his bones appeared to be broken, and some of his ribs were cruelly spearing other organs or rubbing against one another, jolting his body with electric agony at the slightest move. All those kicks—it scared him to think how many there had there been—what important internal works had they wounded or shut down, perhaps irreversibly? Like a dropped watch, his body might stop at any moment.

The pain was so bad that he half wished for that to happen.

His eyes were closed, and he had little desire to open the one he could open, but he did so when he discovered that, mysteriously, he couldn't move any of his limbs. Something was holding him tight. At first he didn't care, but eventually he regained enough sense of place and curiosity to investigate the source of his confinement.

When his right eye pried itself loose from the gunk that was sticking the lids together, he couldn't get much of a fix on what had happened to him. He appeared to be propped up at an angle, lying against some kind of long flat board, which was leaning backwards, attached to the wall above him. His head, facing up, was slanted with the board, resting on it, and his feet were barely touching the floor at the board's base. Franklin couldn't feel his left

293

arm—the one he was pretty sure was broken—at all, not even when he tried, and failed, to move it. Turning to the right, the only side he could see, he discovered that his other arm was once again duct-taped—this time to another board, one placed horizontal to the floor, shoulder high, somehow attached in the back to the other vertical board.

For the longest time he puzzled over this. What was that maniac doing to him now? How could he eat in this position? Defecate? Sleep? But Franklin was a smart man, and the terrible truth finally crawled into his befogged brain.

He was duct-taped to a pathetic imitation of a cross.

A number of emotions crossed his mind, pilling on top of one another, as this startling realization dawned. They were: incredulity, outrage, anger, fear, confusion, and, finally, even a rueful humor at how pathetic a mess he was in and how silly he must look.

What could Richardson hope to accomplish by this nonsense? It was crazy.

Franklin looked around the room for the man, but couldn't find him in the limited range of his faulty vision. He decided to call out.

"Jake?" he said as loudly as he could muster. "Can I get some water, please?"

No answer.

He swallowed. "*Jake!*" he called in a more urgent tone.

Still no answer.

Had Richardson left him here? Run off to escape, abandoning Franklin to his fate? Could that be, and, if so, what did it mean to Franklin himself, trussed up as he was? There were various possibilities. The best was that the police would arrive soon and find him here. Okay, okay, it would be embarrassing to have to be un-duck-taped from Richardson's homemade cross, but Franklin would welcome that embarrassment if it meant he was finally safe. After all, most of the ridicule would fall on Richardson himself, who had somehow thought this foolishness was a good idea.

The worst outcome was that no one would find him in time. His beaten and damaged body might fail, and then his decaying corpse would hang here in this ridiculous posture for who knew how long before someone stumbled across it and alerted the authorities.

He thought long and hard about what that would mean to his loved ones—Todd, and Kelly, and his family. Mary too. That he had died like *this*—in some outrageous caricature of the death of Jesus—would haunt them for the rest of their lives. Todd would never live it down—forever branded as the son of a man who had died in this bizarre and sacrilegious manner.

It would skewer popular opinion about him too. As much as he rued it, Franklin now realized that he had become an historical figure in the story of atheism. What an awkward ending to his supposed biography! It would overpower everything else that had happened, all the things he'd tried to say. In the words of his father, it would queer what Franklin "stood for." People would gossip that he'd gotten what he deserved.

Rage took over. Franklin thrashed violently against the boards, oblivious to the pain, trying desperately to break free, screaming with frustration. The vertical board jiggled some, but by the time he wore himself out and just hung there, he'd accomplished nothing except to increase his already serious injuries and reopen surface wounds that had begun to scab. Every single part of his body seemed to hurt and demand individual attention, but he forced his mind away from the constant agony. He ate his pain, felt it rise back up in his throat, and swallowed it down again.

The outside door opened, and Richardson entered. He was carrying things, but Franklin, with his faulty vision, couldn't make out what. Whatever they were, Richardson put them down on the table, and then came over to where Franklin was tied down—the wall farthest from the door.

Richardson smiled at him, examining him up close, looking him up and down in admiration.

"How you doing up there, Frankie?" he asked with a smirk.

Franklin said nothing. If he spoke he would just anger the man, and that wouldn't be wise.

"I been out foraging," Richardson told him. "Do you like the setup I created for you?"

Franklin couldn't let that go. "No," he said, spitting it out.

"Of course, you don't—big atheist like you! Makes you feel funny, I bet. Remind you of anyone?"

Franklin clamped his mouth tight. His first reaction was sarcasm, and he suppressed first one zinger and then a second.

Richardson didn't like his silence. "*Talk* to me, Frankie. Here's the deal. I want you to feel some of what Jesus Christ hisself felt when they put him up on a cross. Uncomfortable, right?"

No response.

"If I'm ever going to bring you to the Lord, you got to know something about how Jesus suffered. You got to know that it ain't just some silly story they made up a long time ago. It was *real*! I want it real for you too."

Franklin was clueless as to how to deal with this insanity. After a moment, he did summon up a question.

"How long are you going to keep me up here—duct-taped like this—

295

in a mockery of your God?"

"Mockery? Big word, but—surprise!—I know what it means. Hell, Frankie, this ain't no mockery. This is *truth*, and truth leads to *light*, and light leads to *repentance*. I want you to find God. That was the reason I brung you here, and it's still my main goal. I'm praying for you!"

"When do I get to come down?" Franklin asked again, tired of it all. He was suddenly sleepy. What did that mean? Sleepy couldn't be good.

"Why, Frankie, I'll take you down right now! All you have to do is tell that Wang guy that you believe in God, and it's a done deal."

"No," Franklin said without hesitation.

Richardson shrugged. "Figure you'd say that. Stubborn asshole." He put his face close to Franklin's. "That's what you are, you piece of shit. A stubborn asshole." He turned and went to the table, picked something up, and returned to the jury-rigged cross. "Have to up the stakes then. Get your attention. Lookie here what I got."

He held something up for his captive to examine. It took all of Franklin's concentration to focus enough to see anything at all. Some sort of wire, wrapped up in a coil.

"Know what this is, Frankie?"

Franklin was fading, ceasing to care. He said nothing.

"I made it out of barbed wire I found out there on the other side of the fence." He held it closer to Franklin's good eye. "It's a crown of thorns," he said, waving it slightly.

That did it. Franklin snapped. Rage overcame him and—the sleep urge gone—he lunged forward with all his waning strength, trying vainly to pull the board from the wall, straining to get to Richardson. Morality be damned—Franklin was ready to kill this monster.

"*Temper, temper*," Richardson scolded, stepping back. "It's not *that* bad. I'm only gonna set it on your head, not pound it in or nothing. Just a kind of symbol, see?"

"Drop dead," Franklin managed.

"Me? Not me," Richardson commented. "But, who knows? Maybe *you* if you don't start cooperating. You don't want to die, do you, Frankie?" No response, so Richardson pressed it. "Probably a good time to come to God, you know—when you're dying."

"Atheist/foxhole," was the mumbled reply.

"*What did you call me?*" When Franklin didn't answer, Richardson, confused, dropped the question and put out a hand to lift his captive's chin. The gesture was strangely gentle. "Now look here, Frankie," he said, "I'm gonna put this on you, and if you jerk your head around it really will hurt. Your choice."

Carefully, he laid the wire on Franklin's head. It was too big, and immediately slipped down almost covering Franklin's eyes. So Richardson adjusted it. He took it off, and repositioned it so that the bulk of the wire was in the back. The front just touched the top of the bound man's forehead.

Richardson stepped back and examined his work. "Not bad. Doesn't look much like the one Jesus wore, but you get the gist."

Knowing it was futile, Franklin decided to try reason. He had to say something.

"Jake, *please* don't do this."

"Do what?"

"*This.* Hang me up like this. What if I died hanging from this thing?"

"Why, Frankie! If you repent, you'd go to *heaven*! That's what I want! And, well, if you do die, what the hell? Nobody could die a better death than the one that killed Our Lord. You should be proud."

"*PROUD!*" Franklin lost it again. He screamed, "IT ISN'T AN HONOR. IT'S TRITE! IT'S BANAL! IT WOULD BE A *DEMEANING* WAY TO DIE!"

Richardson looked truly hurt, like a little boy who's been called names. "Fuck you!" he mumbled. "I don't know what all those big words mean."

"It means that it's a *bad* idea to do this to me."

"Bad for who? Hell, I mean for you to feel bad!"

"Bad for me, yes, but even worse for you."

"Huh? Why?"

Franklin paused to figure out how to say this. He had to dumb it down to the man's level to get through to him.

"Okay, listen. If the police come through that door now and save me and arrest you, they'll see this setup and the whole world will know what you did."

"So? That's good!"

"No, Jake, that's bad. It'll make you look like a fool. To mock Christ's terrible suffering on the cross by letting an atheist go through what he did is very, very bad. It will seem like you're saying it's the same thing— what happens to me and what happened to Jesus. And they're not the same! You know that! Pretending they're equal is wrong, and sinful, and embarrassing!"

Richardson was infuriated.

"You're saying that Christ's death was *embarrassing*!" He yelled this in Franklin's face, so close that even through his blood-clogged nose Franklin could smell the alcohol on Richardson's fowl breath.

"No, no! I'm saying that treating *me* the same way embarrasses *you* because you're saying that I'm like Christ. You don't think I'm like Christ, do you?"

Richardson turned away and paced back to the door. He paused there and then came back.

"What did those other big words mean?"

Franklin tried to remember what he'd said. "Oh, trite . . . banal. Yes. Well, they mean it doesn't look good, not *real*, like . . . unbelievable. If you put it in a movie, people would think this was all impossible. They'd walk out, shaking their heads." He searched for another word. The one he found was a mistake. "It's corny," he concluded.

"CORNY! THE WAY CHRIST DIED WAS *CORNY*?"

"NO, NO! THE WAY *I'D* DIE WOULD BE CORNY."

"Well, we'll see about that, Mister Asshole! I won't have you talking about Our Lord like this. *I won't have it, see?*" He turned and took something off of the table, and came back again to Franklin. He held his hands up.

"Hammer and nails," he explained. He put them up close to Franklin's face. "I got them out of my truck."

"NO! NO! THAT'S EVEN WORSE!"

"You got that right!"

Franklin howled in frustration.

"Jake," he said urgently. "I don't want you to do it just because it will cause *me* pain and probably kill me. I also don't want you to do it because it'll make *you* look bad. Religious people will think you've done a terrible thing, stringing me up like this and torturing me to death, a nickel and dime version of the way Jesus died. They won't praise you. They'll hate you!"

"Shut your mouth, ass-wipe!" Richardson commanded, not listening any more.

But Franklin kept after him. "The *opposite* will happen from what you want! People—*religious people*—will feel awful about the terrible way I died. I'll be a hero, a martyr who suffered and died in the cause of non-belief! Think of how that sounds! The atheist who died the same way Christ did! You don't want to help out atheism, do you, Jake? If you're going to kill me, just *shoot* me. That would be better for both of us."

Richardson shook his head dismissively. He held the hammer and nails up again.

"Now here's the deal, Whitestone. I'll call the Wang guy and you tell him that you believe in God. Do that and I'll take you right down from here, let you go. Hell, you don't even have to *mean* it. Just say it! That'll set you free and I'll be on the way to Mexico five minutes later. Deal?"

Franklin gave up. You can't reason with a rock. He didn't reply.

"Your call," Richardson told him, experiencing his own sad

resignation to what was coming. He put one nail in his mouth, and positioned the other against the palm of Franklin's numb left hand. "Speak now or forever hold your peace."

Franklin did speak. "Jake, *think!* I've lost a lot of blood. Making more come pouring out of my hands might put me over the edge, kill me! That'd be *murder!* You're a *Christian!* Christians don't kill their fellow human beings!"

Richardson laughed. "But I'm not killing you, Frankie! You're killing yourself!"

He waited, hammer and nails at the ready. Franklin closed his eye and scrunched up his face, anticipating the blow.

It came.

Franklin, who'd thought his left arm impervious to pain, found out how wrong he was. He screamed and jerked his head back, banging the board hard. The barbed wire cut into the rear of his head, triggering yet another scream.

Blood spattered everywhere, but, unfazed, Richardson moved quickly to the other hand. Efficiently, he drove the second nail home, and Franklin went wild from the pain. He thrashed violently against the boards.

Then—all of a sudden—he went limp.

Richardson leaned in close to Franklin's ear. "*REPENT!*" he yelled at top volume, and Franklin jumped again, his ear's pain joining the rest.

Richardson lowered his voice to an urgent whisper. "*Listen, asshole,*" he continued. "I'll make it real, real easy for you. Just tell me now that you do believe in God and I'll pull these nails out and bandage you right up. That's all you have to do, Frankie! Hell, say it even if you don't *mean* it! It's enough I can tell folks your words!" He smiled, nodding to himself. "Okay? Okay? So say it!"

Everything was a blur to Franklin, a phantasmagoria of lights and shapes filtered though his crusted and tear-stained eye. Richardson began a bizarre chant of "*Say it! Say it!*" and some part of Franklin still had enough sanity to consider doing it. Save his own life. Get away from this lunatic. What could be wrong in that? The sane thing to do. He was still sane, wasn't he?

But Franklin—both eyes closed now, his head resting on his chest—said nothing.

Richardson couldn't stand this! With his fist he pounded the board just above Franklin's head, striking it quickly twice, making the whole structure bounce, but Franklin, a rag doll, was past reacting. Richardson stared hard at Franklin's face, close up, trying to read whether he was about to give in.

"Say it!" he repeated, lower this time, snarling the words.

Franklin lifted his head ever so slightly. He tried to open his eye, but couldn't.

"Fuck you," he said, and died.

AUTHOR'S NOTE

I wish to thank the large number of friends who read this novel and offered suggestions. They were very, very helpful. I am particularly grateful to James Griffith, Joel Cohen, and Mabel Sturdivant for their detailed proofreading. From years of publishing my professional books I know that it's impossible to eliminate all errors, but their dedicated input has helped tremendously. I also thank Thomas Jeffire for his insight into the world of evangelicals, and most particularly for helping me create the cover design of the book.

My biggest appreciation is reserved for Ponce Yañez, who shared his extensive knowledge of guns with me, and all but wrote both the "gun show" paragraph and Nan and Dan's effusive description of their weapon collection. He let me examine the actual gun that Mary uses to such effect in the nursery segment, thus reassuring me that it could do the things she planned.

Barbara Shipek, my manager and good friend, did her usual splendid job in moving this project along and in helping me figure out how to publish the book.

Finally, to all readers and any reviewers, an author's request: please don't reveal the ending and what finally happens to Franklin Whitestone when he comes under the control of Jake Richardson.

Should you wish to contact me, I can be reached via email at WhaleyNovel@aol.com.

Douglas Whaley
Columbus, Ohio
September, 2008

1666304

Made in the USA